# THE
# ENDGAME

## MATT AYNES

DANCING ROBOT PRESS

Biblical passages were translated by the author.

Published in Duncanville, Texas, by Dancing Robot
Press LLC (*https://dancingrobotpress.com*).



Library of Congress Control Number: 2025905031

ISBN (paperback): 979-8-9906950-3-0
ISBN (ebook): 979-8-9906950-4-7
ISBN (hardback): 979-8-9906950-5-4

Book Cover and Typesetting by Damonza (*https://damonza.com*)

"And what does God demand of you except
to do what is right, to love mercy, and to
walk with humility before your God?"

*- Micah 6:8*

∾

"In all chaos there is a cosmos, in all disorder a secret order."

*- Carl Jung,*
*from The Collected Works of C.G. Jung*

Chapter One

# The Terrorist

Paul Veliu stepped off the elevator onto the thirty-fifth floor of the Bann Commercial Building. He slipped in the earpiece Youth Corps Intelligence had given him. "I'm near the position," he said, his voice pitched just above a whisper. "Do I have confirmation?"

"You have confirmation," Commander Firlenko replied at once. "Deliver the package and get out of there."

Paul walked straight to the reception desk. The young brunette glanced up from her computer monitor and looked him over with a pair of striking blue eyes. She offered him a warm smile, which he immediately returned.

"May I help you, sir?" she asked with the accent of a native Berliner.

"I have a meeting with Herr Gorstadt," he replied.

"Your name?"

"Jorgen Handelssohn."

"One moment please." She began typing on her keyboard, sneaking another glance at him as she did so. He caught a faint whiff of rose-scented perfume.

"Please go in, Herr Handelssohn," she said. "He cleared his morning schedule for you. Fourth door on the right."

"Thank you."

Paul breathed in the fragrance of roses as he passed her desk. He hurried down the hallway until he came to the door. He raised his hand to knock, then hesitated.

What if the Party's intel was wrong? That girl at the desk wasn't what he'd expected. Could such a cheerful, carefree young woman be so deep in the enemy's plans? The targets here looked exactly like civilians. He missed the battlefield, where uniforms and positions defined the boundaries between friend and foe.

He pursed his lips and steeled himself against the possibilities. A soldier couldn't question the Party, and the Commander was waiting.

He knocked twice, heard Herr Gorstadt's reply, and let himself in.

Viktor Gorstadt was a middle-aged executive with a few flecks of silver in his brownish-blond hair and wide swaths of it in his perfectly trimmed beard.

"Welcome, Herr Handelssohn." Gorstadt leaned forward in his desk chair. "Shut the door, will you? I've already spoken with our board, and our people have confirmed your company's assets. Very impressive."

Our people. Yes, that's how the enemy would talk. The Party was never wrong. This innocent-looking businessman with his tailored suit and impeccable smile was a monster, a terrorist, a demon.

Paul closed the door behind him. "Call me Jorgen."

"Very well, Jorgen. You took a risk cold calling us like that, but it worked. We're going to accept your proposal."

"I'm glad to hear it."

Paul Veliu pulled a handgun with a suppressor from his suit coat and squeezed the trigger. The first bullet struck Gorstadt a few inches above the bridge of the nose. Paul followed it with two more shots in rapid succession, both hitting the left side of Gorstadt's chest. Gorstadt collapsed face-first on his desk. A pool of blood began to form around his head.

At least the man's suffering had been brief. More importantly, by taking out the leadership of a terrorist organization, Paul could save hundreds—maybe thousands—of civilian lives.

He slipped the handgun back into his suit coat. He walked to the desk and set his briefcase on it. A photograph in a carved wooden picture frame rested near the corner of the desk. In the image, Gorstadt had his arm wrapped around a youthful woman with platinum blonde hair and a face that beamed with motherly contentment. Four children flocked around them, three girls and a grinning boy who looked no older than five or six.

A strange paralysis crept over Paul as he examined the faces of Viktor Gorstadt's family.

Something felt wrong. First the girl at the reception desk, and now this.

He stumbled backward, knocking over a chair beside the desk. He swallowed down the bile that had surged into his throat.

"Lieutenant?" the Commander's voice hissed in his ear. "Are you there? What's happening?"

"I'm here. Give me a minute."

Could Intelligence have made such a terrible mistake? He needed something—anything—that would prove Gorstadt's true identity. He rifled through the desk drawers and found nothing unusual. The computer was no better. He took a few minutes prying around, but all he discovered were financial spreadsheets and mundane emails. No locked files, nothing encrypted, none of the code words Intelligence had given him. Then he searched the pockets of the man's suit coat and discovered a folded piece of paper.

Yes, this would be it. A list of Gordstadt's next victims? A ciphered message from his terrorist organization?

He unfolded the paper.

*Ich hab dich lieb, Papa!*

*Johann*

*I love you, Daddy.* The letters were absurdly large. Six stick figures with balloon-like heads were holding hands at the bottom of the page. A father, a mother, three girls, and a little boy.

"Did you kill Gorstadt?" Commander Firlenko asked.

Paul couldn't tear his eyes away from the note. His heart was racing. He was nearly hyperventilating.

"Yes," he replied. "I murdered him."

"What was that?"

"Gorstadt is dead."

"Good. Now arm the device and get out of the building. Your driver is waiting."

Paul pressed the palms of his hands against his forehead.

"My God," he groaned. "What have I done?"

"What the devil's going on, Lieutenant?" the Commander snapped. "Do you need backup?"

"We made a mistake." Paul's voice trembled. "Nothing here links Gorstadt to the terrorists. He has a picture on his desk. Four children and a wife. His boy's name is Johann. Intelligence was wrong, Commander. He's not who we thought."

"Listen carefully, Veliu." The Commander's tone became very calm, very soothing. "You are following the direct orders of Chairman Markhov. The family in that photograph is not real. It's part of Gorstadt's cover. We'll prove everything to you as soon as the mission is over. What you need to know right now is that Gorstadt was a terrorist. His organization has murdered countless innocent civilians in our beloved Khatizan. You are going to put an end to it. Do you understand, Lieutenant?"

Paul's heartbeat slowed as he listened to the Commander's voice.

What better cover for a terrorist than that of a devoted father and husband? Gorstadt could have written the note himself, forging the whimsical contours of a child's handwriting. Or perhaps his family knew nothing of Gorstadt's true nature.

Besides, what terrorist would leave dangerous files lying around on a computer where any janitor could find them? The man probably ran the operation off his phone.

Gorstadt was the enemy. This was war.

That's all there was to it.

"I'm sorry, Commander," he said. "I don't know what came over me."

"No apology needed," the Commander replied. "You haven't been on many field assignments, after all. Now complete your mission."

Paul took a deep breath. He flipped open the latches on the briefcase. Mounted to the inside was a bulky silver cylinder with a scanner attached to it. He swiped his thumb to confirm his identity, heard the expected click as the energy bomb armed itself, then closed the briefcase and slid it under Gorstadt's desk. He left the room, locking the door from the inside and closing it again as soon as he had passed through.

The hallway was empty. He walked back toward the elevator.

"That was a short meeting," the receptionist said as he passed her desk.

"We got straight to the point."

He looked in her eyes. Such beautiful calmness in their expression. Could she be a terrorist? It was unthinkable, unimaginable. No, they must have hired her for that very purpose, to throw any suspicious visitors off the scent.

"Herr Gorstadt wanted me to tell you that he's going to be in a videoconference for the next half hour," he said. "Apparently, the board was interested in doing business with our company."

Her eyes widened. "The board? Whoa, that's big. Congratulations."

"Thank you. And listen…"

He froze.

Fool. What could he say to her? Commander Firlenko heard every word.

He fought down the urge to grab her by the hand and take her with him. The Party had no tolerance for insubordination. If he made one mistake, both he and his parents would pay for it with their lives.

"It was good meeting you," he said at last.

"You, too." Her smile now became an invitation. She brushed some strands of hair over her ear with her fingertips. "I hope you'll be back soon."

"I'd like that."

He walked to the elevator and pushed the down button. He checked his watch. Nine minutes left. Plenty of time if all went well.

"Sir," the receptionist called suddenly. "I think you forgot your briefcase."

He swore under his breath. She would notice that, of course. She liked him, so she noticed every detail. To think that everything could hinge on this coincidence, on the romantic interest of a young woman who happened to smell like a rose garden.

"No worries," he said. "It was meant for Herr Gorstadt. Thanks for checking."

Her cornflower blue eyes watched him in expectation. She wanted him to make the next move, and it would be so easy. Perhaps she could go on a break. Take a walk with him outside.

And when the Central Party got its hands on her, what then? Foreign terrorists and homegrown traitors shared the same fate in the prison factories.

The elevator chimed.

"I hope…" He lowered his gaze. "I hope you have a good morning." He stepped onto the elevator, pushed the button for the first floor, and looked back at the reception desk.

Now there was a trace of sorrow in her eyes. Could there be something more? He knew it was impossible, but he always felt that in that moment she somehow understood everything and forgave everything and simply wanted to ask him one question.

Why?

The elevator reached the first floor. He hustled across the lobby and stepped out into the brisk air of a Berlin morning. A sleek black sedan with darkened windows pulled up to the curb. He opened the passenger door and climbed in.

"Did you complete your objective?" the driver asked in Khatiz. Her voice had all the warmth and softness of a stained guillotine. Youth Corps Intelligence officers made his skin crawl.

"Of course," he replied, matching her brusqueness. "I think there were civilians in those offices. One, at least."

She pulled onto the road and hit the accelerator. "You don't kill civilians?"

"I'm a military officer. I fight to protect civilians."

"And I'd always heard our lieutenants were cutthroats."

"What's your name, soldier?" he asked.

She flashed a tart smile and rested her hand on his leg. "Unavailable."

He shoved her hand away. "I think you misunderstood me."

"I doubt it."

Suddenly she smacked the steering wheel and swore.

"What?" he asked. "What's wrong?"

"Traffic."

"It's Berlin, isn't it? Besides, we're a few hundred meters from the building already. It's a surgical strike on the top floor, just enough to kill the terrorists. A twenty-meter radius at the most."

She stared at him with wide eyes. "They didn't tell you?"

"Didn't tell me what?"

She slammed her foot on the gas, drove the car onto the sidewalk, and sped forward. Berliners on their morning walk dove out of the way with screams and angry shouts. Most of them avoided being hit. Some did not.

"Are you insane?" he yelled. "I thought we were trying not to get caught."

"We're trying not to die," she shouted back.

"Die?" He turned to look out the rear window. Suddenly, it all became clear. "No. Dear God, no. That wasn't my mission."

"And why not?" she hissed. "Do you pity these people? Like you said, this is Berlin. The heart of the beast, and we're driving a dagger into it. You'll be a Youth Corps hero, comrade. Let's hope you live to enjoy the benefits."

She swerved back onto the road and swung onto Bundesstraße 2 at eighty kilometers per hour. They were only on the highway for a few seconds when he heard it. A deep, deafening boom, like the roar of a thousand cannons firing in tandem.

"Close your eyes," the girl yelled. She slammed the brakes. "Don't look behind us."

The impact from the blast struck the car with the force of a hurricane, instantly shattering all the windows. He hurtled forward and was slammed back against his seat by an airbag.

Seconds ticked by, one after another. He opened his eyes, but everything was blurry. He could hear nothing except his own breath and the ringing in his ears.

His vision cleared. He looked at the driver. She was motionless, her head resting against the driver's side airbag, her face and neck covered in blood from pieces of glass shrapnel. He leaned over and checked her pulse.

Nothing.

The B2 had been transformed into a disaster area. The cars that were in motion when the shockwave hit had slammed into each other at full speed. The casualties from traffic accidents alone had to be in the hundreds.

He turned his head and glanced through the opening where the rear window used to be. What he saw—or rather, what he didn't see—was incomprehensible. As he stared at the craterous vacuum that had been an entire block of downtown Berlin, the weight of what he had just done struck him. He leaned over and vomited out the passenger door window.

"Lieutenant Veliu?" The Commander's voice was faint over the ringing in his ears. "Are you still there?"

"I'm alive," he murmured. Miraculous that the earpiece still functioned. "My driver is dead."

"An extraction team is on route. Stay where you are."

"*Ich hab dich lieb, Papa*," Paul murmured, his mind wandering.

"What was that, Lieutenant?"

Paul leaned back against the headrest. The moment he closed his eyes, he saw the lovely contours of the receptionist's face. The questioning gaze would forever linger in those pools of deep blue.

Why?

Over the acrid stench of burning cars and tires, over the screams of the dying and the silence of the dead, over the shrieks of oncoming police sirens and ambulances—through it all, Paul heard once more the gentle melody of her voice, and he breathed in the scent of roses.

# Chapter Two
# Ambush

SILVERY MOONLIGHT GLIMMERED through the dense canopy of branches. A breeze lifted itself, sighed through the newborn leaves, and died away. Charles Ferguson breathed in the moist, earthy aromas of leaf mulch and the decaying stump of a golden birch just outside the campsite. He exhaled slowly.

Paradise on earth.

Almost.

Boris Petrov's rumbling snores cut through the tranquil night with the potency of a gas-powered chainsaw. How Nadia could get any shuteye in the same tent with her father verged on the miraculous. The man sounded like a grizzly bear with a deviated septum.

He squeezed Nadia's hand. "Come on, it's now or never."

She had bundled herself up in a warm knit pullover and matching beanie. Her dark eyes gleamed in the moonlight beneath long lashes. Her cheeks dimpled with her smile, and her hair peeked out from beneath her ski hat in silky raven tresses. She was, in his humble and rigidly impartial opinion, the most beautiful creature ever to grace the North Carolina wilderness.

Come what may, it was time to do something about it.

He'd stowed away his mother's old diamond engagement ring in his pocket, where it had remained undisturbed for the entirety of their two-week camping trip. Boris had made it his personal mission to keep him and Nadia under twenty-four-hour surveillance, which was why they were about to sneak off from the campground like a couple of teenagers.

She glanced back toward her tent. "What if Safiya wakes up?"

"She'll be fine. Your dad's with her."

He tugged her hand gently. She didn't budge.

Amazing how much the kid had changed their lives in the space of a few months.

Safiya was a four-year-old girl they'd rescued from the hellish confines of Level Nine in Magnus Headquarters. Her mother had been killed by Magnus's Control scientists the day before Level Nine had been liberated, leaving an adorable, defenseless toddler all alone in the world.

Nadia had started the process of adopting Safiya in February. Now everything hinged on the decision of a surly immigration judge who had relocated to Chicago from rural Alabama. The odds weren't good.

"Listen, Nadia," he said. "You do realize that if your dad had his way, I wouldn't be here at all? That was the plan. Boris gets a vacation with his girls while I stay at the Home Office eating wobbly jello and counting ceiling tiles."

She arched an eyebrow. "How do you know that?"

"Gavriel told me a few nights ago."

She drew a circle in the dirt with the toe of her shoe. "You two must be getting close."

"Yeah, well, that happens when grown men share a pup tent designed for an eight-year-old. Neither of us can sleep through the nightly Russian bombardment, so we've had time to chat."

Not that he wanted to sleep. He'd been having a recurring nightmare about an island lately. He wished he could forget it, but his freakish mind remembered everything that crossed his sensory aware-ness, right down to the minutest detail.

They heard a soft popping sound from the pup tent. Gavriel was wide awake and blowing bubbles again. He and Boris were trying to ditch the smokes with nicotine gum, which meant their mouths were usually in constant motion. They looked like a pair of militant squirrels. Or Russian baseball players, if such mysterious creatures exist.

Two weeks into his recovery program, Gavriel still went through a pack of nicotine gum every day. On the plus side, his breath smelled like cinnamon sticks from dusk to dawn, which turned out to be a criti-cal factor in the tuna-can confines of their pup tent. The young soldier had struggled to blow bubbles until he started mixing his nicotine gum with regular chewing gum to get the best of both worlds.

Another pop.

"You're right," Nadia said. "Let's get out of here."

He led her up the trail. Just holding her hand and knowing there was no Boris Petrov breathing down their necks was unalloyed bliss. They perched on one of the wooden park benches at a scenic overlook.

By daylight, the spot offered a majestic panorama of rolling moun-tains blanketed in the deep verdure of spring. In the starlit night, he could barely make out the shadowy silhouettes of trees and the daguerreotype contours of the mountain ranges. But the night held a beauty all its own, the pregnant silence of a world awaiting new birth with the coming dawn.

Nadia leaned over and gave him a slow, lingering kiss that made him feel like he'd been plugged into a high-voltage electrical circuit. Then she tickled him and burst out laughing when he tried to get her back. Finally, she snuggled up against him. He could feel her breath rising and falling as he held her in his arms.

He wished there was a guide for this, some clear-cut instructions that would always lead to the perfect marriage proposal. As a scientist, the colorful and mellifluous nebula of human relationships terrified him. You never knew what would happen next.

Life in the laboratory was precise, clean, predictable. Life with Nadia was real, which meant messy, imprecise, and utterly wonderful.

"I want to know everything," he said. "I want to be the world expert on Nadia Petrova."

Her eyes widened in mock surprise. "You don't know everything already?"

"I think I do, then I find out you've got more layers than a five-year-old in a snowball fight. You're amazing."

She rested her head on his chest. "Your heart's beating fast."

"Well, I did just get kissed by a gorgeous woman."

She sat up. "Alright, Casanova, what do you want to know?"

"Uh…" He froze. Panicked, in fact. Was this the part where he proposed? Wasn't it too early? "We, um, we haven't done the deserted island game yet."

Deserted island game? What was he thinking?

He was an idiot. That's all there was to it.

"What's that?" she asked.

He swallowed. "You know, you're stuck on a deserted island and you only get to take three books with you. Which ones would you take?"

"That's too hard," she said.

"Why?"

"I'd take dozens of books. Can I get a bigger suitcase?"

"Stick with three, Petrova. Them's the rules."

She sighed. "Fine. The Bible, Wordsworth's poems, David Copperfield. Happy?"

"Why David Copperfield?"

"Betsey Trotwood," she replied without hesitation. "I had to read the book for English class in high school. When I came to the part about Aunt Betsey and Uncle Dick, I just broke down. Have you read it?"

Deserted island game. Great idea, genius. How the blazes was he supposed to steer this ship from Betsey Trotwood to a marriage proposal?

At least he was learning something about her. That was the point, right?

"Copperfield never came up in molecular biology."

"I suppose he wouldn't," she said. "Long story short, Uncle Dick had a mental disability, but Betsey Trotwood didn't care. She protected him and showed the whole world how important he was."

"That's how you are with your brother." Nadia's brother, Peter, had Down syndrome.

"I hope so," she said. "People can be so cruel when you're the odd one out."

He leaned over and kissed her forehead. "I wish he'd gone camping with us."

"He's not a fan of zippers," she replied. "Especially tent zippers. But what about you?"

"Tent zippers?" He cleared his throat. "I'm not morally opposed."

She giggled. "Not zippers, the game. I want to know what three books the world-renowned Charles Ferguson would take to a deserted island."

He pressed his lips together, pondering. "Alright, here goes. Dawson's Zoology textbook. Second would be that Ansel Adams one that used to sit on your coffee table. Third's an art history book, the biggest one I could find."

"Your books all have pictures," she said. "Why is that?"

"You know how I remember everything?" he asked.

She patted his leg. "It's your superpower."

"I remember books the same way, which means I'd be taking a whole mental library to that island whether I wanted to or not. But pictures are different. I can remember them, too, but there's something about seeing a beautiful thing in person, about having it right in front of you..."

And *that* was how you steered the ship back on course. He let his eyes roam over the contours of her face, then rested his hand on her cheek.

"As long as you're on that island," he said, "I'll be set for life."

She came close so that their lips almost touched. "Good answer, Doctor Ferguson."

She kissed him and rested her head on his shoulder. He ran a hand through her hair and then traced a line with his fingertip along the curve of her neck. They watched as an owl fluttered silently across the star-drenched sky. A vivid orange bloom along the eastern horizon foretold the coming dawn.

He'd done it. He hadn't even stuck to the plan, but here they were. This was the moment.

He slipped his hand into the pocket of his jacket and wrapped his fingers around the soft felt lining of the jewelry box. His heart was pounding so violently that he could feel the pressure in his ears.

"Listen, there's something I've been wanting to ask you."

She sat up and met his gaze. He took her hand in his.

"Nadia, will you—"

"There you are!" Boris Petrov's voice smashed the mood with the subtlety of a sledgehammer. Nadia's six-foot-four, bearlike father clambered up the path and stood towering over them. "Sneaking off with my daughter at four in the morning! You must be planning some funny business, eh, Mr. Charles? Don't forget, no monkeying around until I hear wedding vows."

Charles instantly summoned a mental image of Boris stuck on one of those mythical Inuit icebergs that bore away the annoying elders. Fading off into the mists, never to bother the young folks again.

Nadia scrambled to her feet. "Where's Safiya?"

"Relax," Boris said. "I left her with Gavriel."

"You *what*?" Nadia's hands balled into fists. "Gavriel isn't a babysitter, he's a commando. They don't even speak the same language."

Boris flung his hands in the air. "I'm the sole defender of my one and only daughter's sacred vestal treasury, the lone paternal bulwark standing between her and the miry depths of hedonistic infamy and shame. What do you expect me to do when some hotblooded man runs off with her at four in the morning?"

Charles buried his head in his hands. "We've been dating for almost a year now, Boris. Can't you just give us a little privacy?"

"Privacy?" Boris shouted. "Oh, I know what *that* means, Mr. Charles! If you think I'm about to let my delicate Elysian sunflower get trampled on by every hormone-infused male who thinks she's a looker, you've got another thing coming."

"I don't believe this." Nadia shot her father a glance that could turn a Gorgon to stone, then stormed off down the trail. "And for the record, I'm perfectly capable of taking care of my own *sacred vestal treasury*, thank you very much. I'm going back to the campsite. Charles can come with me."

"I'm sorry to disappoint you, my ethereal seraph," Boris replied in his thickest Russian accent, "but I'm going to have to borrow Mr. Charles."

Nadia whirled on him. "What's that supposed to mean?"

Boris shrugged apologetically. "Just a stroll through the woods together. You know, like that little hike he and I took last year after we had lunch together at the Bamboo Dragon Palace. Wasn't that a wonderful hike, Mr. Charles?"

Charles leapt off the bench. "I'll take a rain check on that one, Boris."

A massive hand clamped down on his shoulder and yanked him backward. "Not so fast, Mr. Charles," Boris said, lowering his voice so Nadia couldn't hear him. "This isn't a request."

"Look," Charles hissed through his teeth, "I like you and all, but in case you forgot, we were almost murdered by a professional assassin during our last hike in the woods."

"I had everything under control." Boris leaned closer and whispered in his ear. "We're going to visit Mr. Flying Hawk."

Charles blinked. "You said he already left Cherokee."

"He's back."

"Are you coming, Charles?" Nadia called.

"Just a minute," he shouted back. He lowered his voice again. "What about Nadia? You're going to make her walk to the campsite all by herself? Your Elysian sunflower and all that?"

"Of course not." Boris raised his voice. "We'll take you back first, Nadyezhda."

"You can't make him go if he doesn't want to," she said when he and Boris had caught up with her. "We're on vacation, remember?"

"It's all right," Charles replied. "I want to go."

"Really?" Her eyes widened. "You want to go on a walk with my father? Alone? In the wilderness?"

He forced a smile. "What's the worst that could happen?"

Golden light from the morning sun carpeted the verdant mountainside, transforming a drab, low-laying cloud into a brilliant nimbus. Charles hunched over with his hands on his knees. Drips of sweat fell from his face like raindrops. The heat was tolerable. The humidity was another story.

"How much…farther…is it?" he gasped, his words syncopated by heaving breaths.

Boris slid a backpack off his shoulder, pulled out a water bottle, and handed it to him. "Twenty minutes."

He guzzled the icy water with rapid gulps, as if he'd been wandering through a bone-dry desert instead of hiking in the muggy Appalachians. "You said that twenty minutes ago."

Boris grunted. "We've only been walking for two hours, Mr. Charles."

The same old story. Mid-fifties Russian super-alpha male hikes mountains for days without breaking a sweat. Youthful biology professor can't go sixty minutes without collapsing into the fetal position.

"We're not walking," he shot back with more whine in his voice than he'd intended. "We're hiking. Two hours on a decent sidewalk and two hours trudging through trackless wilderness are very different things, you know."

Boris folded his arms over his chest. The man was a strong believer in printed tees. For today's hike, he'd donned a dark gray, form-fitting shirt with the words *My Granddaughter Is Better Than Yours* emblazoned on the front in blaring white letters. Those words were now partially obscured by a pair of rocklike forearms. "Thirty years old and you're already a *babushka*. Over this next ridge is a valley, and at the bottom of the valley is a stream. If our source is correct, Mr. Flying Hawk's residence should be close."

"He lives in the woods?"

"Not a bad place to disappear."

"I wonder if he really knows my dad." He handed back the water bottle. Boris took a light swig and tucked it in his backpack.

"Nothing's certain," Boris said. "We know Mr. Flying Hawk has an invisible friend. We also know he contacted that friend the day before your fake funeral, which could explain why he drove up to Virginia to attend."

Charles frowned. "An invisible friend?"

"An email address. My associates hacked into it, but all the messages are nothing more than a series of numbers. We're working on it. My hope is that the invisible friend is your father."

"You're enjoying this, aren't you?"

Boris barked a laugh. "Oh, yes, Mr. Charles. I'm enjoying myself immensely. There's nothing I'd rather do than spend my days hiking with a thirty-year-old male babushka."

"I'm a scientist, not an athlete."

He winced at the sound of his own shrill voice. Blast it, he really would need to toughen up one of these days. As soon as there weren't any maniacal sociopaths threatening to wipe out humanity, he'd sign himself up at one of those thirty-dollar-a-month gyms, roll back his sleeves, and pump iron. He wouldn't stop until he could bench press two hundred pounds. He'd have muscles, real ones like Boris's with visible contours that filled out shirt sleeves. He'd roll back his shoulders and Nadia would fall speechless at the overwhelming display of pectoral prowess. He'd challenge Boris to an arm-wrestling match right in front of her. He'd bask in her proud gaze as he finally put the old tiger in his place.

"Daydreaming, Mr. Charles?"

Charles cleared his throat. "Just thinking about something important."

"Care to enlighten me?"

"Oh, I will. Sooner than you think."

Boris reached into his pocket and pulled out a folded-up piece of notebook paper. "I have something for you."

Charles took the paper, unfolded it, and began to read.

1. *Susan Lockheed – 537-493-2219 – suzielovespancakes@myglobe.net*
2. *Katie Woodrow – 568-441-9298 – katieladywoodrow@mailer.com*
3. *Amy Weisenhauer – 471-388-9113 – crazycatgirl95@softbyte.com*

The list kept going. Twenty-four names, phone numbers, and email addresses. Charles scratched his head.

"What the heck is this?"

Boris wrapped an arm around his shoulders and gave him a squeeze that made his back pop. "Options, Mr. Charles."

"Options?" he squeaked, trying, and failing, to break loose from Boris's vicelike bear hug.

"I realized something," Boris replied. "You've been dating Nadia for almost a year now, and you still haven't proposed to her. How could any warm-blooded male with no tragic deficiencies of a psychological nature spend more than six months in the presence of my daughter without falling at her feet and begging her to join him forever at the sacred shrine of Hymenaeus?

"You're dragging your feet, Mr. Charles. I can only assume you're looking for an out, maybe considering your options." He tapped the piece of notebook paper. "Here are twenty-four of them! Twenty-four reasonably alluring females, all free of criminal records and former mésalliances. Each has confessed under solemn oath to an inscrutable predilection for socially impaired biology professors. In other words, they're perfect matches for you, Mr. Charles."

Charles gritted his teeth and crumpled the sheet of paper in his hand. He knew three things about Boris. One, Boris was insane. Two, Boris knew how to kill people. Three, for some inexplicable reason, Boris did not want him to marry Nadia. The third fact was even stranger since Boris had, until a few weeks ago, been treating him like his future son-in-law.

Enough was enough. Maybe the man could fold him in half like a pretzel without trying, but he wasn't going to stand for any more of this.

"You're mad because I haven't proposed?" he shouted. "How am I supposed to do that when you're breathing down our necks every waking moment of the day and night? I can't even hold her hand without you glaring at me, much less propose to her! And if you really want to know—"

"Actually, Mr. Charles, I don't," Boris interjected. "Now, we'd better get moving if we're going to catch Mr. Flying Hawk."

Boris tromped off down the precipitous slope. Charles stared at him, fists still balled up, his teeth clenched together.

He could kill his future father-in-law.

Actually, he couldn't. If he had a loaded gun in one hand and a samurai sword in the other, the odds of him even scratching Boris Petrov were infinitesimal. The man was a former CIA assassin who looked like he could take down a grizzly with his bare hands.

"The old codger's testing you," he muttered to himself. "Trying to get under your skin. You're better than that."

He stomped after Boris. But with each step, his anger dissipated, lulled into calmness by the lush Appalachian surroundings. The mountain wilderness felt like a primordial Garden of Eden. A whispering breeze sifted over patches of damp moss and liverworts and fluttered the delicate, feathery leaves of a fern. The expectant silence of Nature was broken only by the chirruping of insects and the flapping of wings when a bird startled at the approach of the solitary humans. It felt like he and Boris were the only people left in the world.

They both carried stout walking sticks with handles roughly carved into eagle heads, a splurge that had set them back forty dollars each at a tourist shop in Cherokee. Whenever they stopped, Boris twirled his around and practiced what looked like some arcane form of martial stick-fighting.

Charles, on the other hand, leaned on his walking stick more and more with every passing step. He probably looked like an old man. Or maybe a Russian grandmother.

They crossed the ridge Boris had mentioned, and on the way down the slope they began to hear the gentle gurgling of a stream. Boris lifted a hand and made a soft shushing noise. They crouched down and crept forward. Boris moved with the silent, measured steps of a leopard closing in on its prey. A biologist could do *that,* anyway. He could be silent as a ninja. He could—

His heart leapt into his throat when he heard the stiff crack of a branch beneath his shoe. Boris turned and shot a fierce glare in his direction, then jabbed a thick forefinger against his lips.

"Sorry," Charles mouthed.

Athlete? Nope.

Ninja? Nope.

Babushka? You bet.

The stream at the bottom of the valley was shallow and three feet wide at its narrowest. They leapt across, then turned and followed it southward. Charles took another wrong step and buried half his shoe in the muddy bank. There was a moist, squelchy sound when he pulled it back out. Boris muttered something that sounded very Russian and very coarse.

Then Boris froze and pointed at something ahead of them. Charles peered forward, saw nothing, and held his hands up in question.

"Mr. Flying Hawk's house," Boris whispered. "There."

Charles took a closer look and finally spotted the hints of a dingy, one-story house through a dense band of trees.

"Let's get a closer look," Boris said.

As they drew nearer, he could see that the house's darkened windows were filthy with grime and mold. The pale roof peeked out from beneath thick patches of leaves and fallen branches that were like tufts of hair on a balding head.

"No place like home." Boris slid his handgun from its holster at his side. "Shall we?"

Charles swallowed. The place might as well be a haunted house. It was worse knowing that someone was living inside, allowing all that decay and filth to spread unchecked around them. How could they do that? Didn't everyone have that little inner voice that shrieked at them when the dishes piled up in the sink or crumbs fell off the dining room table?

"Shouldn't we knock first?" he asked.

"If we knock, Mr. Flying Hawk might shoot us."

"And you think he won't shoot us if we break down his front door?"

Boris shrugged. "Maybe I'll have a chance to shoot him, too. But since you're worried, we'll go around to the back."

They snuck through the woods bordering what should have been a yard but was instead an ocean of waist-high grasses and weeds that surged against the house as if they meant to swallow it whole.

"I hope you put on your bug spray, Mr. Charles," Boris said. "This place must be swarming with ticks and chiggers. Maybe a few copperheads, too, if we're lucky."

"Thanks, Boris. I can tell you're doing everything you can to make this whole experience as enjoyable as possible, and I appreciate it.

Really." He knelt and tucked the bottom of his pants legs into his socks. "Are you sure he's here?"

"If not, he'll be here soon."

"I still think we should just knock."

Boris leaned closer. "There's something you should know before we go in. Some people came looking for our friend when he was hiding out here a year ago. The descriptions the locals gave us matched those of four Magnus Foundation hit men who went off the radar around the same time and were never seen again. My guess is our friend here killed them all."

"What?" Charles stumbled backwards. "He killed four professional hit men? All at once?"

Boris clapped a hand over his mouth. "Quiet, Mr. Charles."

"Sorry," he mumbled through Boris's thick fingers. Boris pulled his hand away. "You could have warned me."

"I just did."

"I meant before we went trudging through the wilderness. If I'd known the guy was a cold-blooded killer, I would have stayed back at the campsite with Nadia."

Boris rolled his eyes. "That's why I didn't warn you earlier, babushka. This is our best chance to learn about your father. Are you ready?"

Charles let himself hyperventilate for a few moments before forcing himself to ignore the icy fear coursing through his veins. "Let's go."

They circled to the back of the house. Boris motioned for him to get behind the trunk of an enormous Eastern hemlock, then waded into the weeds and grass.

Charles peeked out from his hiding place and watched as Boris approached the back porch, crept up the stairs, and then, in one sudden motion, kicked in the back door and charged inside with his gun levelled. He vanished into the darkness within.

The seconds dragged on into minutes. Charles checked his watch and tried without success to calm his frayed nerves.

Was Boris still alive? Had he already disappeared forever like those Magnus thugs?

He suddenly remembered his prayer rope, the one Father Anatoly had given him when he visited the monastery the year before. He rested his fingers against the soft, woolen knots. The prayer rope had gone with him into the depths of Magnus Headquarters, staying by his side through the darkest chapter of his life.

He silently recited the Jesus Prayer. At first, he could only manage the words themselves, a bare repetition. Then, slowly, their meaning came alive in his mind. He took a deep breath and felt a growing peace.

He pulled his phone from his pocket. No reception.

It had been at least five minutes. Should he stay and wait? Run back toward the campsite and call for help as soon as his phone got a signal?

He was just about to try the last plan when Boris emerged from the doorway.

"Come on, Mr. Charles. The coast is clear."

He let out a deep sigh. Thank God.

Now he had to deal with the yard. His best theory was that if he sprinted through the vermin-infested grass, they'd have less of a chance to attach themselves to his legs, or sink their fangs into his ankles, or whatever other ghoulish plans they had in store for hapless visitors to the haunted house.

He took a deep breath and held it, as if the air itself would be poisonous. Then he ran full speed into the sea of grass. Giant stalks of weeds brushed against his neck and face and tickled his arms as he sped by.

He bolted up the wooden steps, one of which creaked under the weight of his foot, came to a screaming halt by the doorway, and allowed himself to breathe again.

"Are you okay, Mr. Charles?"

"Huh?" Gasp. "Yeah." Gasp. "Why?"

"You only ran fifty feet, babushka. Not exactly a marathon."

"I held my breath."

Boris muttered another colorful-sounding Russian phrase and tromped off into the house. Charles followed him with cautious steps. He paused on the entryway to let his eyes adjust to the dim lighting within.

"Whoa," he said. "Not what I expected."

No piles of filth littered the floors, no billowing cobwebs dangled from the ceilings. The place was immaculate. There was even a lemony hint of cleaner in the air, which probably had something to do with the reflective sheen on the hardwood floor.

"It's like a form of psychosis, isn't it?" Boris replied. "A filthy outward appearance concealing a perfectly ordered mind. Mr. Flying Hawk grows more interesting by the moment. Come on, I've found something unusual."

He followed Boris into a bedroom whose bare walls were illuminated by yellowish-brown sunlight through a single, filthy window. Filthy on the outside, at least. A twin-sized bed sat in one corner, its sheets and blanket arranged with boot camp precision. On the opposite wall sat a desk and office chair.

"Over there."

Boris pointed at the desk, on top of which rested a ponderous book. Charles's breath caught in his throat when he realized what it was. *A Textbook of Zoology* by Herbert Dawson. He hurriedly flipped through the pages and recognized his own handwriting in the margins. Words he'd written when he was seven years old, right before that fateful road trip with his father.

He tried to speak, but the words stuck in his throat. Holding the book brought everything back. The unbridled joy of a camping trip with his dad turning into the nightmare of becoming a human research experiment.

How did this book end up in John Flying Hawk's bedroom?

"Dad left us the week after we got home from that trip. This was in his truck when he left." He set it back on the desk. "Why did John Flying Hawk leave it here? It's almost like he expects us."

"Sweet Saint Anikitos, you're right!" Boris glanced at the window. "Can you hear that?"

There was an odd rustling noise outside.

"Someone is coming," Boris said. "Or many someones." He pulled out his handgun and edged toward the window. "Stay where you are, Mr. Charles. Let me get a look at them first."

Boris leaned forward to peer through the window. He frowned, then inched nearer, as if trying to get a better view.

"Do you see anything?" Charles asked.

The rustling grew louder.

"I'm not sure what I'm seeing. It's almost like…"

Boris suddenly lunged back, his gun trained on the window.

"What?" Charles shouted. "What is it?"

"I have a question, Mr. Charles," Boris replied in a strained voice. "An entomological one, right up your alley."

"Entomology? Not what I was expecting, but shoot. Not the gun, don't shoot the gun. You know what I mean."

"Roaches, Mr. Charles. Do they travel in swarms? Big swarms, like those ants down in South America?"

Charles frowned. "Nope, no swarms. They're social insects, but the groups aren't very large. We call them herds. Why do you ask?"

The rustling intensified. Then they heard clicking. First a few clicks, then more, then a whole avalanche of them, like tiny hailstones pelting a metal roof. Chittering, rising, mounting, the sound grew louder by the moment.

"We need to get out of here," Boris shouted. "Now."

The dingy light from the window vanished as a writhing, opaque mass swarmed up the panes and covered them from the outside. In the same moment, both doors into the house slammed open.

"Too late," Boris added. "Close the door behind you."

Charles scrambled back and shoved the bedroom door closed. The room was plunged into near darkness. He threw his hands over his ears as Boris fired two rounds at the window. The bullets pierced the glass but had no effect on whatever had covered it.

Boris fired again, and a ricocheting bullet whizzed past Charles's ear. "Are you insane? You almost killed me."

"That might have been an act of mercy, all things considered. See for yourself."

Boris pulled a flashlight from his backpack, clicked it on, and aimed it at the window. An undulating, scrambling mass was pouring into the room through the broken glass.

"Sweet Saint Tryphon," Boris muttered.

Roaches.

Thousands upon thousands of roaches.

And they were bulletproof, apparently. Boris fired every round in his gun to no avail.

There was an abrupt, deafening roar. The bulb in Boris's flashlight exploded, casting the room into pitch blackness.

Charles screamed as a swarm of cold, clicking roaches scrambled up his legs.

## Chapter Three

# Flying Hawk's Mystery

"Y ou need to remember something."

A man's voice. The words were softly spoken in a dialect that was hard to place. Breathy and half-whispered, like wind gliding through the treetops.

Charles groaned and opened his eyes, but he couldn't see anything. He seemed to be lying flat on his back on a concrete floor. He couldn't move his arms or legs. In fact, he couldn't even *feel* his legs. He could barely wiggle his fingers, and his arms might as well have been made of concrete.

One thing was certain. The next time Boris Petrov asked him to take a harmless little hike in the woods, he wouldn't just say no. He would turn the other way and run as fast as his feet would carry him.

"Can you hear me?" the man asked.

"Where…am…I?" Charles found that he could speak, but his words slurred together.

"Just listen. Are you ready?"

"Ready for…what?"

"Sierra Alfa Oscar One Four Three Hotel Delta One Nine Six Seven Eight Seven November Sierra Victor Seven Two Five…"

The bizarre, monotone concatenation of numbers along with letters from NATO's phonetic alphabet went on and on, then stopped abruptly.

"What was that?" Charles asked.

"You may need it someday. I want to help you, but I'm afraid I would kill you instead. I can't always control it." The voice came closer, whispering in his ear. "Do you ever see the Island when you dream? The children…I can't save them. None of us could, but you might be different. They're not safe, not yet. They're bleeding, they're dying. I can't—" The man's voice, which had grown almost feverish with desperation, broke off suddenly. "Goodbye, Charlie."

Charles felt a sudden jab of pain as something pierced the side of his neck. He gasped and tried to pull away, but it was too late. His mind grew hazy and dull as it slipped back into the darkness.

"Wake up, Mr. Charles."

Boris Petrov's voice emanated from somewhere behind him as if it belonged to a disembodied spirit. He opened his eyes but couldn't see anything. He closed them and opened them again.

Still nothing.

He seemed to be tied to a chair this time. He wriggled around, but coarse ropes held him fast. The air was redolent with a sickly sweet, mildewy odor.

"Where are we?" he asked.

"Basement," Boris said. "Or maybe a storm shelter."

"Did he talk to you?"

"Who?" Boris asked.

"I don't know," Charles replied. "John Flying Hawk, I think."

He heard Boris's breath catch. "Sweet Saint Nikon! What did he tell you?"

"I think it was a code. A bunch of letters and numbers. I can repeat it if you want, but it goes on for a while. Then he talked about a dream, something about children and an island."

He shivered. He'd been having his own nightmares about children and an island lately. Was that a coincidence?

"If we ever get out of here," Boris said, "the first thing I want you to do is write it all down, just in case it's important."

Charles swallowed. "I could use some water."

"That makes two of us."

"How long was I out?"

"No idea," Boris replied. "I can't move my hands enough to use the light on my watch, but I've been up for at least an hour."

"I thought those roaches were going to eat us alive." He shivered at the memory of all those tiny legs scampering up his body. "They felt so heavy, like they were dragging me down to the ground."

"Same for me," Boris said. "Then my mind got fuzzy, just like it did at those parties when I was in college."

An interesting possibility. "You think we were hallucinating?"

"Both of us, at the same time? Oh no, the roaches were real, Mr. Charles. I killed one of them. Broke it, rather."

"Broke it? Wait, are you saying—"

"Yes, Mr. Charles. The roaches were machines."

Charles exhaled slowly. "Boris, you know what that means?"

"It means Mr. Flying Hawk has a weapon remarkably like Magnus's Harvesters. He was a Foundation scientist on the run, which is why those hit men were after him."

"At least he let us live."

"He also tied us up and locked us in a basement. Can you reach into my back pocket? I'm tied to a chair right behind you."

"What's in your back pocket?"

"A small flashlight."

Charles's hands strained against the rope as he stretched them back toward Boris's chair.

"Okay, here goes."

He bit his lip and tried not to think about the fact that his fingers were touching Boris Petrov's backside.

"Are you trying to tickle me, Mr. Charles? If you are, it's not working."

"Shut up, Boris."

He finally found the pocket.

"I've got it." He pulled out the compact flashlight. "How do you turn it on?"

"Twist the top."

Easier said than done when your hands were tied together, but he finally managed to get the thing turned on. A cone-shaped beam of pure white light illuminated a small area around them. He slid the flashlight between his fingers to get a better angle with the beam of light.

"Don't drop it, Mr. Charles. Can you see anything?"

"Looks like a basement," he said. "Broken bookshelves, lots of dust and cobwebs. Not much else. I'll point it your way. There, what do you see?"

Boris was silent.

"Boris? Can you see anything on your side?"

"Yes, Mr. Charles. I see four skeletons strapped to chairs. They're sitting back-to-back, just like we are. There's also a rat, a very large one, staring at us."

"That's not good." Charles's heart started pounding. "That's really, really not good."

"Are you going to hyperventilate?"

"Maybe. Probably."

"Are you going to scream?"

"No. Well, not yet."

"That's too bad. You're really good at screaming. You should have heard yourself back there in Mr. Flying Hawk's house. If all else fails, you could be a nameless victim in some B-grade horror flick."

"Thanks, Boris, but I think we've already wandered onto the set."

Charles rocked back and forth against the ropes, his breath coming and going at a sprinter's pace.

"Okay, we don't need to panic," he said aloud. "Just because he left them to die doesn't mean he'll do the same to us."

"I'm not panicking, Mr. Charles."

Of course not. Russian super-alpha males never panicked. "Gavriel knows we're here, right?"

"He knows we were going to Mr. Flying Hawk's house. Whether he can find the basement is another question entirely. I don't remember seeing it, which means the entrance is probably hidden."

"But you have a tracker or something, don't you? Some high-tech gadget that tells him exactly where we are right now?"

"I had a phone. It seems to be missing."

Charles tapped his pants pockets with his elbows.

"Mine's gone, too."

"Are you still wearing your tennis shoes?"

"Yeah, why?"

"Then we'll be fine."

Charles angled the flashlight downward and peered at his shoes. "I don't get it. What's the plan?"

"We wait."

"Because I'm wearing tennis shoes?"

"Yes, because you're wearing tennis shoes."

"You lost me, Boris."

"We put trackers in all your shoes. You're an important man, Mr. Charles."

"Why my shoes?"

"When you were in a coma after we rescued you from Magnus Headquarters, Gavriel thought we should have a surgeon hide a GPS tracker in your gall bladder. I voted for shoes. You take them every-where you go, and kidnappers usually let you keep them."

"Whoa. Um, thanks, Boris." A remarkably unpleasant thought struck him. "If Gavriel shows up, won't he get captured, too?"

"Possibly," Boris replied calmly, "but I think Mr. Flying Hawk's already disappeared again. He'll assume that someone will come for us. For all he knows, it could be a small army."

"So what now?" Charles asked.

"I already told you." Boris began to croon an off-key Russian folk song that was clearly meant to be sung if and only if the singer had consumed an ungodly amount of vodka.

"All right," Charles muttered, "so we wait."

He rolled his neck from side to side to get out the stiffness. Next, he entertained himself by pressing his eyelids together until he could see little balls of light, then opening his eyes again so he could watch the balls dance around in the pitch blackness.

Suddenly Boris stopped singing. "Mr. Charles?"

"Yeah?"

"I have a confession to make. I know your secret. In fact, I probably know more about it than you do."

Charles caught his breath. How could that be possible? Had Father Anatoly told him?

"When we raided Magnus Headquarters," Boris went on, "I found a fireproof file cabinet in Magnus's private quarters. The folders inside were divided into four sections. One section had your name on it. Two others were for John Flying Hawk and someone named Sierra Morgan. The fourth section had no name attached to it. They were the Paragon Project files."

An icy dread crept over Charles. He knew at least one other thing that would be in those files.

"Most of it was just surveillance records," Boris said. "The Foundation kept close tabs on you all those years before they brought you in. John Flying Hawk and Sierra Morgan were the other named

Paragons who survived the experiments. They have similar capabilities to yours, but unfortunately the procedure shattered their sanity. The Foundation murdered their parents and kept them as slaves for all practical purposes, though Mr. Flying Hawk obviously escaped."

"What else?" Charles said, his voice cracking with emotion. "What did it say about me?"

"There were parts I couldn't understand," Boris replied. "Something about a plan of theirs called Project Twilight. There weren't many details, but the name showed up in several places. You seem to be a central part of all their machinations."

"That's it? That's all you found?"

Boris didn't reply.

"Boris, what aren't you telling me?" he cried. "I need to know."

"Nothing we can be certain of," Boris said at last. "Let's focus on the positives. Today we met Mr. Flying Hawk. I admit things might have gone a little better, but we got all the information we needed."

"We did? When?"

Boris cleared his throat. "We know Mr. Flying Hawk was one of the other children Magnus experimented on. He must have spent most of his life as a Magnus scientist, but then he escaped. I imagine those roaches had something to do with it. He knows your father, maybe even stays in contact with him or someone else on inside the Foundation. He gave you a code. Does it have anything to do with those emails? We'll have to see if my friend in the CIA can solve the puzzle. In the meantime—"

They heard a scraping metallic noise followed by the sound of a door swinging on rusty hinges.

"Boss?" Gavriel shouted. "You alive?"

"More or less," Boris yelled back, his voice a little raspy. "You didn't hurt Mr. Flying Hawk, did you?"

"No. Already gone."

Charles blinked as Gavriel's high-powered flashlight burst into life.

Gavriel scrambled halfway down an aluminum ladder, then hopped the rest of the way to the basement floor. "I have good news."

"He made contact again?"

Gavriel blew an enormous gum bubble and popped it. "He sent email. Kenjiro caught it."

"Excellent," Boris said. Kenjiro Nakamura, his operations manager, ran the team's logistics from the Home Office. "But we're a little tied up at the moment. If you don't mind…"

"Oh." There was a glimmer of steel as Gavriel pulled a tactical knife from his belt. A few deft strokes and they were free.

"Any idea where that email went?" Boris stood and rubbed his chafed wrists.

Gavriel glanced at Charles. "Khatizan."

Boris grunted. "I get the feeling you and I will be taking a little vacation, Gavriel. What do you think? Any good tourist spots over there?"

Gavriel grinned. "Maybe prison factory?"

They climbed up through the basement's hidden trapdoor and emerged in the sole bedroom of John Flying Hawk's cottage. The bed had been moved to one side. Exhausted, Charles sat on the bed. It was cozier than it looked.

"So he hid the basement entrance under the bed?" Boris asked.

Gavriel nodded.

"Glad you figured it out. What time is it, anyway?"

"Almost five."

"We were down there longer than I thought." Boris stretched his arms. "You didn't see our cell phones, did you? Not that there's much reception out here, but if we're lucky, Mr. Flying Hawk kept them. They'd be easy to trace."

"Not lucky." Gavriel pointed toward the desk.

Their phones were sitting side by side near the center of the desk. Next to them was Charles's old copy of *A Textbook of Zoology*.

"When you're ready, babushka," Boris said, "we'd better get back to the campground. Our Nadia will be worried sick."

Charles clambered to his feet. "I'm ready."

"Nadia's not worried," Gavriel said smugly. "I tell her it's all part of plan. You and Charles take long hike and don't come back until evening."

Boris clapped Gavriel on the back. "You're my right hand, Gavriel Abramovich. Always thinking on your toes."

Charles grabbed his phone and the textbook and followed Boris and Gavriel out into the wilderness of weeds surrounding the cottage. When they reached the stream, Boris zipped open his backpack and handed out water bottles and quart-sized plastic bags packed to the brim with trail mix.

"It's not stir-fried shrimp," he said apologetically, "but it'll do in a pinch."

Boris stuffed a massive handful of nuts and dried fruit in his mouth. With his cheeks puffed out on both sides, he looked more like a militant squirrel than ever.

Charles heard a dull buzzing sound overhead. He glanced up and saw a small black aircraft flying over them toward the cabin.

"Get down!" Boris shouted.

Gavriel grabbed Charles and shoved him to the ground. A second later, there was a tremendous booming sound behind them. Charles turned his head to look. All that remained of John Flying Hawk's cottage were burning remnants of the outer walls. The rest had been incinerated by a massive detonation.

"Guided missile," Gavriel said calmly. "Tactical drone delivered payload."

Boris rose, dusted off his pants, and helped Charles to his feet.

"Your timing was impeccable, Gavriel. Five minutes later, and Mr. Charles and I would have been buried under that heap of burning rubble. The Foundation must have tracked Mr. Flying Hawk back to his home. This time, they didn't risk any more of their assets. Let's hope, for his sake, the Foundation assumes they have killed their target."

They hiked back at a leisurely pace, Gavriel popping gum bubbles after he finished his trail mix. Charles clutched the zoology textbook tightly to his chest and thought about his father. Could he ever forgive the man? Was it righteous anger he felt or outright hatred?

They'd neared the campsite when Boris's phone erupted into a series of shrill beeps and chirps.

"Finally got a signal." Boris pulled the phone from his pocket and tapped in a passcode. "Sweet Saint Isidore! Eight voicemails and a dozen text messages. No rest for the wicked, eh, Gavriel?"

Gavriel grunted.

"First one's our new director," Boris said. "She's going to kill me." As he listened to the voicemail, his face grew more and more somber.

"What is it?" Charles asked.

Boris lowered the phone. "As soon as we get to the campsite, we're packing up and heading back to the Home Office. Gavriel, call the Chemist and have her bring Raj and the others in immediately."

"Of course, boss. Problem?"

"A terrorist has bombed Berlin," Boris replied grimly. "They're estimating ten thousand casualties, but the real number may be much higher. It was some kind of new energy bomb, like a tactical nuke without the radiation. Nobody's seen anything like it, and everybody's pointing fingers. NATO is holding an emergency meeting as we speak. We are one resolution away from the next world war."

"Dear God," Charles murmured.

"Who?" Gavriel asked after blowing a gum bubble and popping it.

Boris stuffed the phone in his pocket. "Right now, they're blaming Russia."

# Chapter Four
# The Science Prisoner

SCIENCE PRISONER FORTY-THREE rested her hands on the smooth wooden surface of the desk. She closed her eyes and breathed in. Her palms arched upward, her fingers curled as if gripping a ball. Now.

Her fingertips sprang into action, tapping against the unyielding oak as she began Liszt's *La Campanella*. She pursed her lips and focused on the frenetic rhythm as her fingers darted to the notes. Her awareness slipped inside the melody, lost to the outside world.

They could take away the instruments, but they couldn't take the music. It lived within her, and it would never die while she lived.

The sharp report of a pistol shot broke her concentration.

"Lights out," she said.

The physics laboratory immediately went dark. The prisoner's bare feet sank into plush carpet as she scampered across the laboratory to one of the barred windows that lined the far wall. She peered into the courtyard beyond.

A desolate scene. Spring had given birth to a handful of emaciated weeds that crept through cracks in the courtyard cement only to be choked to death by a ubiquitous haze. The cadets had chained one of their dogs near the laboratory window, a feral, half-starved German Shepherd that strained at its leash and retched as its throat dug too deep into its spiked collar. Bloodlust animated every fiber of the creature's being. The prisoner shivered despite the warmth of the laboratory.

"The window bars are thick," she whispered. "The glass is bullet-proof. It could never break through."

A dozen black-uniformed Youth Corps cadets were busy chaining a group of prisoners to a row of iron loops that hung along a bloodstained concrete wall. Over the shouts of the cadets and the barking of the dogs could be heard the endless clanging and roaring of the prison factory.

Time for the Morning Death.

Eight victims, five men and three women. University students, innocent and reckless. Their free spirits and heartfelt convictions had brought them to the darkest prison imaginable. In a just society, they would become lights among the people, the voices of the future.

Khatizan was not just.

The students wore cotton overalls and slippers that had once been white but had turned a dingy yellowish-brown after months amid the filth and muck of Prison Factory Six.

Once their captives were immobilized, the cadets stepped back, formed a parallel line a dozen yards away, and readied their rifles. Commander Vladimir Firlenko in his dark gray uniform stepped out from the firing line, his trim body taut as a drawn bow. He slid a curved saber from the scabbard on his belt and lifted it skyward.

The litany came next. The Commander pronounced the crimes of the prisoners in his gruff, stentorian voice. She'd heard it countless times over the dormitory loudspeakers. The litany never varied. The alleged crimes of the illiterate farmer were identical to those of the university professor. Rebellion, insurrection, and above all, a treacher-ous affection for democracy.

Once it was over, the Commander would hold the saber upright for two agonizing minutes while the prisoners on the brink of the infinite shivered or screamed or begged for mercy. At last, he would lower his saber, the rifles would burst into fire, and the corpses of the prisoners would sag against their chains.

The science prisoner hurried from the window the moment Firlenko ended his litany. She crouched in an empty corner of the laboratory with her head between her knees and her hands pressed over her ears.

At least bullets were swift. Truth be told, it might be better to be chained to the wall herself one of these days. The Morning Death was the only escape from Prison Factory Six.

Her lips moved quickly in a whispered prayer she had memorized years ago.

"God of spirits and all flesh, you have trampled down death, overthrown the evil one and given life to your world. Give rest to the souls of your servants in a place of brightness, a place of refreshment, a place of rest, where all sickness, sighing, and sorrow have fled away. Pardon every transgression which they have committed, whether by word or deed or thought. For you are a good God who loves—"

Her voice faltered when she heard the gunshots. The Commander was in a hurry today. She forced out the images that leapt into her mind and continued the prayer. A whisper in a hurricane, but it was all she could do for them.

When she finished, she leaned back and waited. It would take several minutes for another batch of prisoners to load the youthful bodies into carts and drag them off to the furnace room for incineration. But their suffering had ended, their sorrows were over.

God grant them peace.

The door handle turned. A shaft of fluorescent light spilled into the laboratory from the hallway outside. Marina Polanska poked her head through the opening.

"Is that you, Elena? Is it over?"

"It just happened."

Marina crossed herself three times, up down left right, a habit from her Catholic upbringing in Poland. She let out a sigh. "How many?"

"Eight. Politicals, university students. They looked like children. So did their executioners."

"We're all someone's children." Marina slipped through the door and closed it softly behind her. "Lights on. Seventy percent."

The room was instantly bathed in the warm glow of an elegant chandelier with dozens of dimmable electric lights. The furnishings in the science laboratory were plush and needlessly expensive, a show-piece for Central Party propaganda on Khatizan's glorious scientific accomplishments.

"You don't have to keep it so dark, you know. Those poor souls couldn't see you in here."

"But what if they did?" Elena shivered and hugged her arms over her chest. "What if the last thing they saw was me in this cozy room with its drapes and carpet and chandelier? How they would despise me."

"At least they would have something pleasant to look at instead of that monster Firlenko. They know the truth. We prisoners all sleep in the same dormitories. We eat rock-hard bread in the same cafeteria, shower in the same freezing water. They know this room is smoke and mirrors, just like the rest of Khatizan."

Elena sat in her desk chair and rested her head in her hands. "We'll never get out, will we? Not until it's our turn."

"I hear there's going to be another inspection." Marina crossed over to the window and closed the drapes. "The factory is behind in production."

"But the superintendent said we were over quota last week."

Marina shrugged. "I'm just telling you what I heard." She moved closer and lowered her voice. "Do you know what I think? I bet something happened."

Elena wiped her eyes. "The Chairman?"

"One can hope."

"If only—"

Her words were drowned out by a loudspeaker that hung over a standing lamp in a corner of the room. The weekly Party Report broadcasted directly after the Morning Death on Tuesday mornings. It aired simultaneously over all media—radios, televisions, cell phones, and the government-owned loudspeakers mounted in every neighborhood.

"Faithful citizens of the Republic, I have important news from Central Command! The Chairman is pleased to announce that we have won a decisive battle on the southwestern front. The terrorists have been driven back to their own borders after suffering heavy casualties. Their spineless leaders begged the Chairman for a ceasefire, but we will not give in. We will fight them to the last man, woman, and child until we rid the earth of the stench of their colonialism. We will…"

Elena closed her eyes and tried to replay the rest of *La Campanella* in her mind to no avail. The voice of the official Party broadcaster shrieked like an electric saw, shrill and abrasive, destroying any possibility of independent thought. With an effort, she calmed her breathing and waited for it to end.

"Weekly production at nearly every factory far surpasses expectations. Trade levels with our allies increase by the day. We are on the brink of an era of unprecedented abundance and growth. The suffering you have undergone will soon bear fruit. Your children and loved ones will give thanks for your faithful service to the Chairman, for you are creating a prosperous future for all Khatizan."

The broadcaster paused. His voice became stern, like a father scolding wayward children.

"But there are still traitors among us. Khatiz terrorists, following orders from their imperialist masters, have hindered production at Factory Three, Factory Six, and Agricultural Facility One. Because of these incidents, the Chairman has ordered that production be increased at all facilities to compensate for the losses we have sustained.

"Remember, a traitor looks like any other citizen. They pose as faithful Party members. They fake allegiance to our glorious Chairman. Do not be deceived. If you notice suspicious behavior from one of your coworkers, report it directly to your local Party representative. Failure to report means that you have become a traitor yourself.

"Above all, beware the Worm, the Ghoul, the Demon…beware of Grigory Vikhrov! The Fiend slinks about in the dark of night, whispering lies to the innocent, turning them away from the path of truth and honor. If anyone repeats Vikhrov's lies, turn them in! If anyone says his name without cursing it, turn them in! If anyone looks like him, sounds like him, speaks like him, turn them in! With your help, we will soon bring our nation's greatest foe to justice.

"Faithful citizens, let us now build the Khatizan of our dreams. The final victory is at hand. Your efforts today are the foundation of our collective future."

Elena and Marina rose as a military band played the Song of the Republic. It was illegal not to stand, but their gesture was more from habit than coercion. When she'd first arrived, the Party had kept strict surveillance in the prison factories, but the cameras and microphones had long since fallen into disrepair. They were never replaced, for they had become unnecessary. A full third of Khatizan's populace willingly offered themselves as human surveillance cameras for the Party. The Chairman's eyes and ears numbered in the millions.

The anthem died off and the speaker fell silent. Marina sat at her desk, pushed her tortoise shell glasses up to the bridge of her nose, and started clicking away at her keyboard. "Well, then," she said, "let's see what adventures await us today."

Marina somehow managed to bring blessed normalcy to the prison factory. She would sit at her desk every morning and set to work with bustling industry, as if she and Elena belonged to an upscale research department instead of the Science Wing of a state-run prison factory. The Morning Death, the Party Report, the feral dogs and shouting soldiers—none of it seemed to faze the woman's equilibrium.

She was a godsend.

"I've been thinking about something," Marina added. "If we speed up the timing of the energy transfer, we could use even larger power sources."

Elena crinkled her nose, the usual response whenever Marina had a terrible idea. "We went over that, remember? If we change the timing, we create instability. The power sources could literally blow up in our faces."

The fusion-based power source was Elena's brainchild, an idea she had formulated twelve years ago when she lived another life in the United States. Memories of those days haunted her dreams like ghosts. Peace and warmth and contentment, the laughter of her two children, the strong embrace of her husband.

The theory had revealed itself to her step by step during a feverish burst of creativity that had kept her locked away in her home office for over a month. An outlandish idea, trapping the tremendous energy released by nuclear fusion within power sources the size of consumer batteries.

The end result? Enough power to keep Chicago running for weeks in handheld power cells.

When she'd presented a paper on the theory at a research conference, it was met with stunned silence that turned to smirks and muted laughter. Aneutronic fusion instead of the usual nuclear fission, a power source made from microscopic layers of synthetic diamonds, a distribution system that could charge thousands of power cells from mere seconds of stable fusion—her ideas proved too radical for her peers.

She'd gone home devastated.

Two days later, men dressed as city employees showed up on her doorstep while her husband and children were away. They kidnapped her and hauled her off to a private jet. She'd ended up in Prison Factory Six in Khatizan, where she'd been clothed in the uniform of a science prisoner and ordered to continue her research into the power source. When her spirits sank, bringing her research to a grinding halt, they'd offered her the greatest of gifts, her one and only friend in the darkness.

Marina Polanska.

"Okay," Marina continued, "what about this? First, we add more boron to the fusion reaction, then we speed up the transfer."

Marina had proven herself a brilliant physicist, but there were moments—and this was one of them—when her closest friend sounded like she'd lost her mind.

"Marina," she replied in a tone as calm as she could manage, "if you add more boron *and* change the timing, you'd lose control of the reaction entirely. You could destroy a whole city, a whole country, and that's not a joke. Fusion powers the stars, remember? At a large enough scale, you could wipe out the entire planet in one failed reaction. We can't change the timing, end of story."

"How far is too far?" Marina asked innocently.

Elena gritted her teeth. "When you're dealing with catastrophic nuclear detonations? Why are you asking me this?"

"Don't bite my head off!" Marina sniffed. "It was just an idea."

Elena sighed and hunkered down over her journal. Marina loved computers and screens and keyboards. Not Elena. She worked out problems by hand, sketching diagrams and formulae with copious notes and scribblings around the boundaries. The world had lost something when it got rid of paper, when people only read snippets on screens instead of real pages in books.

"I'm sorry," she said after a pause. "We're fighting over nothing. It's all just theories and nonsense. None of our plans will ever happen in the real world."

"Maybe you're right," Marina replied, "but I love our theories and nonsense."

Elena grinned. "So do I."

Suddenly, the door to the laboratory flew open. A young woman in a black uniform with three red lightning bolts on the sleeve marched into the room and slid her jackboots together with a sharp snap. Her reddish-brown hair was pinned into a thick, severe bun, her gaze fixed ahead, her arms pressed firmly against her sides.

Elena recognized her at once.

Darya Alexandrovna Kozlova. Dasha, they'd called her, one of the many children who grew up laboring alongside their parents in Prison Factory Six. An only child, little Dasha had disappeared just before her thirteenth birthday, leaving her mother, Stefanya, alone and heartbroken.

That was the way of it. On the cusp of their teenage years, prison youths were secreted away to the Party's Youth Camps. What happened there was unspeakable. If they survived, they became part of the Youth Corps. If they thrived, they became Youth Corps officers and wore three red lightning bolts on their sleeves. One for God, one for the State, and one for Chairman Markhov.

How long since Dasha had been taken from them? Seven years? And now she was here, back in this place, but no longer a prisoner.

Little Dasha had become one of the oppressors.

"I am here under the direct orders of the Central Party," Darya Alexandrovna shouted at the wall. "Science Prisoner Number Forty-Three, Science Prisoner Number Sixty-Two! You are to be transferred to a civilian assignment outside Chozul, effective immediately. I have been commanded to supervise your transfer. You will pack your belongings and be ready to leave within ten minutes. I will wait for you at this location."

Darya Alexandrovna flung her gloved fist into the air in the Central Party salute. From the moment she had entered the room, she hadn't so much as glanced at the prisoners.

Elena crossed the room with swift steps and rested her hand against the girl's sleeve, covering up the crimson lightning bolts. This was Stefanya's little girl, no matter what the uniform said.

"Dasha." Her voice was soft, coaxing. "Your mother passed away last year. Did they tell you? I was at her side. She spoke only of you. She loved you, Dasha. We all love you."

She felt a tremble beneath her fingertips. Dasha's eyes met hers for the space of a breath, a glance that revealed a maelstrom—recognition, rage, sorrow, hope. Elena braced herself for the worst.

Little Dasha, a ray of sunlight in the sullen gloom of the prison factory, would have thrown her arms around her old auntie and planted a kiss on her cheek. A trained Youth Corps officer would bury a bullet in a prisoner's skull for such an act of presumption.

Dasha did neither. The eyes shifted forward again. The emotions vanished. The little girl who used to giggle at Auntie Elena's shadow puppets disappeared.

"You now have nine minutes, science prisoner," the Youth Corps officer snapped.

Marina tugged on the corner of Elena's uniform. Elena pulled on her work boots and followed her friend out of the room. Her mind raced as she hustled down the frigid hallway to the women's dormitory.

Another beautiful child lost to the Party.

A civilian assignment near Chozul.

Were they being released?

A civilian job would mean an apartment, a tiny microcosm where she could be alone. A place to lock the door, turn on a symphony, and slip away into her own world. A place for remembering, dreaming, imagination.

If Dasha wasn't lying to them.

"Are they going to kill us?" she asked Marina as they threw on their tattered but warm prisoner coats. Early April in Khatizan could still bring brutal cold, and it was an even bet that a Central Party cargo truck would have a broken heater. "It's a lie, isn't it? They always lie so you don't resist."

"Don't be foolish." Marina's voice sounded gentler than her words. "You're the most gifted scientist in the country, even if they don't give you any recognition. They would murder the Chairman himself before they laid a finger on you."

"Hush!" Elena pressed her forefinger against her lips. "Don't throw away your life for idle words. We both know nothing has come of my work."

"Nothing they've told us about. You're too naïve."

They packed their few belongings into burlap sacks and hustled back to the laboratory. Darya Alexandrovna awaited them in the same inflexible stance with the exception of her right arm, which she had lowered from its salute.

"Follow me," Darya shouted. She spun on her heels and marched out of the room with stiff, jerky movements, like a marionette with invisible strings. The science prisoners exchanged an anxious glance and hurried after her.

⋘

The cargo truck carrying the science prisoners rumbled down a narrow road that had been torn to pieces in the war. The Central Party was always announcing another wave of infrastructure projects. State news boasted about how Khatizan's roads were the finest in the world, the envy of the nations, about how the Germans were rebuilding the Autobahn in a futile attempt to follow suit.

Elena's fingers gripped the wooden bench beneath her as the cargo truck slammed into another pothole. The engine whined and chuffed, then the truck lurched forward and swerved from side to side.

"What's wrong with the road?" Marina asked. "I thought the war ended years ago."

"Maybe that was propaganda," Elena replied. "NATO could be bombing us right now."

"Couldn't they at least fix the road to Chozul? I'll get sick if this keeps up."

Elena took her friend's hand. "Think of something else. Dasha said we'll be living near the capital. Can you imagine? We could go to a grocery store, a concert hall, even a movie theater! We'll have a normal job, so we can leave when we've finished our shift. We'll have our own apartments, our own bedrooms, our own space."

Marina stared at her. "Have you gone mad?"

"What do you mean?" Elena shot back. "We're getting a civilian assignment. You said you believed Dasha, didn't you?"

"I said they wouldn't kill you. I never said they would set us free. Who knows where we're going."

Maybe Marina was right, but Elena was determined to be positive. She'd waited so long for hope. "Do you remember that little old man, Mr. Prezny, who used to talk about his wife all the time? He worked in a suburb of Chozul before he came to the prison factory."

Marina sniffed. "I remember they chained him to the wall and shot him, God rest his poor innocent soul. And for what? Taking an extra piece of bread after hauling bricks for sixteen hours."

Elena looked away. "I used to wonder what Mr. Prezny's house looked like, what his life was like before the prison factory. Dasha did say we'd be getting civilian assignments."

"Dasha said?" Marina chortled. "Dear little Dasha says something, and you believe her? She isn't Dasha anymore. She's a Youth Corps officer. You know what that means? There's blood on her hands or she would have never earned those lightning bolts. It's the only way."

"Be quiet, Marina. Don't speak of such things."

Marina flung up her hands. "Why should I be quiet? It's the truth. Besides, she can't hear me over that engine. I can barely hear you, and you're sitting right next to me."

The two fell silent for a moment, then yelped as the truck dove into the deepest pothole yet and then roared out of it.

"You're right." Elena lowered her head. "It was only a dream. We're not going to Chozul."

"How do you know?"

"The road was smoother when we first left the prison factory. They say the best roads are near Chozul and the worst are in the countryside. They're taking us somewhere else."

It was impossible to be certain. The back of the truck had been sealed off with a black tarp so the prisoners couldn't see outside, though thin shafts of light snuck in from small holes in the truck bed and the canvas roof. All they could do was listen to the whining of the truck engine, feel the turns as it weaved around the mottled road, and bounce when it bounced.

Marina sighed. "I'm sorry, Elena." She patted Elena's hand. "I complain too much."

"Your eyes are open, that's all. Whatever happens to us, I'm glad we get to face it together."

"There is that." Marina smiled. "I never thought I'd meet my best friend in Prison Factory Six. Ah, I wish I could bring you to Poland and show you around my little town. I know you're Eastern Orthodox, but you'd love our priest. A godly man, and he's been at St. Mary's for decades. And now that I'm thinking of St. Mary's, will you say one of the psalms for me? A nice one, without all the smiting and bloodshed."

Elena folded her hands and thought for a moment. She had memorized most of the psalms when she was a teenager. It was something the Orthodox nuns did in their monastery near her home in Beecher, chanting psalms day after day until they sank deep into the mind and heart. When she showed interest in their practice, they had taken her under their wing and helped her with the herculean task. It wasn't until she set foot inside the steel gates of Prison Factory Six that she realized what a treasure the godly old women had given her.

She began to recite, her voice quavering with every jerking movement of the truck.

*How long, Lord?*
*Will you forget me forever?*
*How long will you hide your face from me?*

The loss and yearning of the words resonated within her. She continued to recite, her spirits rising as despair yielded to hope.

*But I have trusted in your mercy.*
*My heart will rejoice in your salvation.*

*I will sing to the Lord, because he has been good to me.*

"Which one is that?" Marina asked.

"The twelfth psalm in our Bible, the thirteenth in yours."

"And you believe it?" Marina folded her arms over her chest. "That God has been good to us?"

"I know that I have felt lost and alone in the darkness," Elena replied. "For the rest, I try to believe."

Marina fell silent. When she spoke, her voice was so quiet that she had to repeat herself so Elena could understand. "And do you still believe in God?"

Elena heard the longing in her friend's voice. She wished she could say that her faith never wavered, that she never lost hope in essential truth and goodness and beauty. The scars of Khatizan and the doubts they roused within her ran deep. "When I don't, I pray."

The truck came to a halt, then turned to the right. The prisoners braced themselves for the next pothole, but it never came. The new road was smooth as glass.

Elena rubbed her sore neck and remembered her home in America, where all the highways were smooth and the houses had central heating and none of the children were turned into Youth Corps killing machines.

"Maybe we're going to Chozul after all." Marina blew on her glasses and wiped them on the sleeve of her uniform. "It will be everything you said. Quiet bedrooms, grocery stores, concert halls. If there's a bathtub, I'm going to run five hot baths in a row, one after another, until my skin crinkles like a raisin."

Marina leaned against Elena's shoulder and, perhaps in token of her thankfulness for the improved condition of the road, fell asleep and began snoring softly. Elena rested her head against one of the truck bed's metal support frames and closed her eyes.

She imagined Boris and her two children. She had sketched them in her mind a thousand different ways over the years, especially the children. So much of their lives had now passed by without her.

Boris would not have changed too much. And he would still be looking for her. She'd always known that. Even if he remarried, he would look for her. He would never give up.

As she allowed herself to dream, a familiar voice began whispering from the darkest corner of her psyche.

They could be dead, it hinted. There could have been an accident, an illness. Even if they lived and she escaped from this place and flew across the ocean and found them, they would want nothing to do with her. They would hate her, they would have forgotten she existed. None of them had thought of her in years.

As for *him*, he would have a new wife. He was so strong, so confident, so talented. How could it not be true? The new wife would be young and beautiful, a woman who could make him forget all his troubles.

That voice had overpowered her in the early days of her captivity, when the only realities had been Firlenko's harsh litany in the courtyard, the hoisting of the Youth Corps rifles, and the sudden obliteration of human life.

But today was a day of possibilities. She felt the nothingness within her, calling her toward despair, but she released it with a calm breath.

It had taken years, but she had finally forgiven herself for the crime committed against her. They had robbed her children of their mother, her husband of his wife. Her family would forgive her. If not, nothing could keep her from loving them anyway.

The truck came to a gentle stop. She shook Marina's shoulder.

"Wake up. We're here, wherever here is."

If this was Chozul, the city must be under a strict noise ordinance. There was perfect silence until she heard shrill squeaking when the driver and Darya Alexandrovna opened the rusty front doors of the truck and slammed them shut. A few moments later, the tarp over the tailgate was removed. Elena blinked as daylight flooded her vision.

"Out!" Darya snapped. "Hurry."

Elena helped her groggy friend to her feet. They climbed out of the back of the truck. Darya Alexandrovna offered them her hand for support, then quickly backed away from them as if they were diseased animals.

"Look at that, Elena," Marina whispered in her ear.

An ancient stone fortress loomed over them, grim and imposing, sunlight glimmering over its massive battlements. Tendrils of deep green ivy had snuck out of the surrounding forest and waged a lengthy siege, scaling the walls inch by inch, plunging over the ramparts, and finally claiming a final victory among the dizzying heights of the towers beyond.

"This doesn't look like a civilian assignment outside Chozul," Elena said to Darya, her voice low and solemn. "You didn't tell us the truth."

"Silence, prisoner!" Darya shouted, then turned and faced the gate in a rigid stance.

The truck driver, himself a civilian in a dingy shirt and pants that bore witness to the sustaining power of a sewing needle and a good supply of rags, lit up a cigarette and tromped off among the manicured gardens in front of the fortress.

Marina shuffled back and forth on her feet and rubbed her hands together to keep warm while they waited. Darya looked stiff as a statue with her arms clasped firmly at her sides, though her nostrils flared with every breath. Elena closed her eyes and breathed in clean, frigid air laden with the scent of evergreens. She listened to the cry of a hawk and opened her eyes to watch it circling high above them.

A beautiful place to die if death had brought them here. Strange that the Party would go to all this trouble instead of chaining them to the courtyard wall for the Morning Death.

She heard a loud clanking, the sound of heavy chains sliding over gears. The fortress's massive, latticed portcullis rose slowly until the pathway within became clear. A stoop-shouldered man in a light gray business suit shuffled out of the opening and approached them. A deep crimson rose was tucked into the front pocket of his suit coat. Behind him stood a small contingent of Youth Corps cadets who, like Darya, waited in motionless attention.

"You're early, Lieutenant Alexandrovna." The man gave a shrill, nervous laugh. "You must have put wings on that jalopy to get it over the roads in time. My name is Rius Ludovic. I'll take you to your appointment."

Darya's stance grew even stiffer. She appeared to waver on a reply and ended up offering the man a Party salute.

"Spare the nonsense," Rius muttered. "At ease, or whatever they say to make you stop acting like a wind-up toy."

"Yes…" Darya apparently decided to drop the *sir* and instead clapped her hand against her side again.

Rius grinned at Elena. "Our Youth Corps are remarkable creatures when their training is complete, are they not? All that pent-up energy and passion. Like grenades with loose pins." His shoulders trembled as he shivered. "Come, she's ready for you."

They followed him as he walked beneath the spikes of the portcullis and into a covered courtyard where shafts of daylight slipped through narrow murder holes in the roof. The armed Youth Corps cadets stared at them—or, as it seemed, through them—when they passed.

"She finds that a fortress suits her needs," Rius said as they ascended a broad, flagstone stairway leading to the fortress's entrance, an imposing set of arched iron doors, one of which was half-open. "The quietness, the stillness, the sense of power and grandeur. A perfect environment for charting the course of Khatizan. She does not take her responsibility lightly."

Another pair of Youth Corps cadets stood at attention on either side of the doors, their rifles held stiffly across their chests in the port arms position.

"Who is this woman you speak of?" Marina asked. "A Party official?"

Rius gave a derisive snort. "Party official?" he cried in his shrill voice. "No, science prisoner. She *is* the Party."

## Chapter Five

# Darya

DARYA ALEXANDROVNA FOCUSED on her footsteps as she followed the stoop-shouldered Rius Ludovic. She felt her toes tingling within the rigid confines of her jackboots, felt the palms of her hands brush against the sides of her fatigues as she marched at the rear of the group. Constant attentiveness, absolute control of the mind's processes, proprioception—these were her keys to survival, first in Youth Camp, and now years later as a lieutenant of the Youth Corps. The lessons of Youth Camp never left you.

Break formation during marching drills—five strikes with a rod in the presence of your squadron.

Second infraction—ten strikes with a rod in the presence of your platoon.

Third infraction—twenty strikes in full view of the battalion followed by recycling to week one of Youth Camp training.

Right foot. Left foot. Toes warming up from the movement. Hair pinned too tightly.

The stoop-shouldered man used a fingerprint scanner to open a door, then led them into a torchlit stone hallway with a gradual downward slope. It was her first time at the fortress, though she'd heard rumors of the place. The Chairman's secret lair, an impenetrable refuge nestled in the depths of the Karpali mountains southeast of Chozul. Strange that the rest of the fortress had been furnished like a modern-day palace while this hallway lacked even electric lighting. Stranger still that Rius spoke of a woman rather than Chairman Markhov as the heart and soul of the Central Party.

Ahead of her, the two science prisoners leaned their heads together and whispered. She could almost feel their anxiety. They stirred something deep within the walled enclosure of her soul. Something lost, something forgotten.

Right foot. Left foot.

Your mother died last year.

Forward march.

That woman isn't just a prisoner. She's your Auntie Elena. She was your mother's closest friend. Remember her shadow puppets in the women's dormitory at the prison factory? The dog and the bat and the rabbit. Remember all the wonderful stories she made up, night after night, just for you?

Right foot. She felt the unyielding pressure of the stone beneath the soles of her jackboot.

Your mother loved you. You were all she could talk about.

Left—

The toe of her left boot snagged on a pavestone as she brought it forward. She stumbled, stretched out a hand to the wall to steady herself, and froze.

A mistake. The man named Rius had caught it. He'd turned his head, not much, but just enough that she could see the corner of his eye. She'd known from the moment she met him that he was a high-ranking Party official, if not a direct relative of the Chairman. Party elites had a way about them, a snakelike ease of manner that couldn't exist anywhere else in the carefully regimented fabric of Khatizan society.

This was nothing like Youth Camp. There, the discipline was brutal, but at least you knew what to expect. Here in the real world, the boundaries kept shifting. The hammer was poised over your head, but you never knew when it would hurtle down and crush you.

Forward march. Left foot, right foot. Heart beating too quickly, breath coming too rapidly. Shift focus, find a distraction. The shadows of torchlight flickering on the walls, a mad dance of chaotic effervescence. The warmth of the flames against the side of her face. The rich scent of smoke as the thin, slate-gray tendrils drifted upward and disappeared.

Absorbed into nothingness. Only nothingness brings peace.

On average, three thirteen-year-olds out of every hundred died during the first week of Youth Camp. One unbreakable rebel disappeared into the Torture Room and never came back. There was always exactly one. One or two more succumbed to the extreme physical rigors of Youth Corps training. And every now and then, some poor soul died under the rods of the drill sergeants.

They'd never laid a finger on her. She'd learned the lessons fast and kept them with unwavering discipline.

The hall terminated in an arched doorway. Both doors were painted a deep crimson, one with the figure of a black eagle clutching an arrow, the other with a golden lion. Rius shoved the doors open to reveal a spacious throne room eerily lit by the combined glow of a dozen standing torch lamps and a host of candles in a wrought-iron chandelier suspended over the center of the room.

Rius rushed forward, threw himself face down before a black metallic throne, and pressed his forehead to the stone floor. A deep, throbbing pulse emanated from the throne, as if waves of energy coursed through it.

Darya followed the others into the throne room, her skin prickling, her nerves taut as a bowstring. The walls were divided into dozens of mirrored sections that reflected ghostly flickers of light from the massive chandelier and the standing lamps. A woman in a flowing black dress sat on the throne. The regal contours of her face were faintly revealed through her translucent veil. She acknowledged Rius's obeisance with a stiff, almost mechanical lowering of her head.

Two others stood before the throne. The first was a thin Youth Corps officer standing at attention. The other, the one turning to face the newcomers—

Feet together, snap to attention. Salute your Chairman!

"All hail our glorious Republic!" Darya hurled the words from her chest as if they were projectiles. "All hail Chairman Markhov!"

The Chairman turned to her, raised a hand in a dismissive wave, and shifted his attention back toward the throne.

Was *that* the all-powerful dictator of Khatizan? The hand he'd raised trembled as if from palsy. His back was hunched, his body shrunken in on itself. The whiskers over the pale lips were not the deep, virile sable that every citizen of Khatizan knew from the millions of portraits that hung on every street corner, in every office, over every fireplace. The Chairman's famous mustache had turned snowy white.

"Come closer." The command came from the figure on the throne. The sound of that voice—soft, coaxing, seductive—twisted something deep in Darya's psyche.

She'd heard the voice before. Where?

In her sleep. In her dreams.

It was *the* Voice, the one from the recordings every Youth Camp cadet listened to at night in their bunks. The voice that spoke of wonderful things, promises of hope and freedom and glory, visions of a new Khatizan, a land where the men and women became gods and goddesses through the strength of their collective labor.

She obeyed at once. How could she refuse the Voice?

Right foot. Hands sweating. Left foot. Breathe.

The head of the figure on the throne turned to face her. Another stiff, slow movement, as if the woman's head were mounted on a pedestal.

"Do you know what I am, child?" the Voice asked.

Failure to immediately respond to a commanding officer—two strokes with a rod in front of your squadron.

Second infraction—five strokes with a rod in front of your platoon.

Third infraction—five minutes in the Torture Room.

"I don't..." Darya's voice trailed off. What level of respect, what honorific should she use? It was impossible to know. Was the woman on the throne a commanding officer? A Party elite? The stoop-shouldered Rius had scoffed at the suggestion.

"Let me show you," the Voice replied. "Chairman Markhov?"

"Yes, my lady?"

"Bow down before me."

The Chairman's posture stiffened. "I'm getting too old for that."

A deathly silence fell over the room, broken only by the whisper of torch flames and the pulsing sound from the throne. The woman reached out a black-gloved hand, her fingers splayed like a claw.

"You will obey," the Voice commanded, its tone now cold as winter snow and sharper than a scalpel. "Do you need a reminder? Perhaps it has been too long."

Darya's hand strayed toward the pistol holstered at her waist.

The Voice spoke blasphemy! God, the State, the Chairman—those three were sacrosanct, inviolable. The Chairman bowed to no one.

And yet...

"Of course, my lady," the Chairman stammered. "Forgive me."

Then the unthinkable happened.

With visible effort, the aging Chairman of Khatizan went to his knees before the throne. The woman edged a black-shod foot toward him. He kissed the top of her shoe with reverence.

"Now do you understand, Lieutenant Darya Alexandrovna?"

As Darya gazed into the darkness of the woman's veil, she squeezed her fingers into fists so tight that her nails nearly pierced her skin. She had worshipped Chairman Markhov ever since joining the Youth Corps. He was the father of the nation, the savior of the people, the soul of the Central Party.

Until now.

"You are…" She paused as understanding dawned on her. This was why they'd made her listen to the Voice. To prepare her for this moment, for the truth she might one day discover. "You are the true Chairman of Khatizan," she yelled at the top of her lungs. "You are the Supreme General. You are the State. You are the Master of our people."

"Commander Firlenko has done well," the Voice said. "His Youth Camps have surpassed even my expectations. My name is Aryana Voss. Your comrade, Paul Veliu"—the black-gloved hand motioned toward the other Youth Corps officer—"reached the same conclusion you have. He has just returned from a dangerous mission where he secured a great victory over our enemies. Now that you know me, I have a challenge for you. For both of you."

"Yes, Chairman!" Darya and Paul shouted in unison.

"Place your sidearms on the ground."

She and the other Youth Corps officer obeyed instantly. There was a metallic clatter as their twin Berettas made contact with the stone floor.

"Do you see that table on the far side of the room, the one with the candelabra on it?"

"Yes, Chairman!"

"On the table is a revolver. Six chambers, one bullet. Today, the State demands sacrifice. I want to know which of you will show the greatest devotion to Khatizan. When I give the command, run to that table, pick up the revolver, aim it at your head, and pull the trigger until the gun fires. You will not allow the other Youth Corps officer to stop you. You will not let them rob you of your one and only chance to obey Khatizan's true Chairman. Succeed, and your name will be listed among the heroes of our nation. Do you understand your orders?"

"Yes, Chairman!" Darya shouted. Paul Veliu echoed the words a moment later, but his voice faltered.

Darya trembled as a wild, deep-rooted energy coursed through her veins. This was the moment. It had finally come. How many times had she dangled her toes over the infinite abyss? How many dreary nights had she wanted to jump in, only to realize that she couldn't?

The system worked. Once they'd finished with her, she could never deviate from orders. Her ability to make decisions for herself had been meticulously dismantled, broken and impotent like a bone snapped in two. She couldn't even take her own life without permission.

The woman on the throne was showing mercy, offering them the only possible means of escape from a life of unending torment. Darya had to follow orders. She wanted to die. They wouldn't let her die.

Until now.

Every muscle in her body tensed as she prepared herself. She eyed her opponent, sizing him up. A few years older than her, early or even mid-twenties. A thinner frame, but that was deceptive. The silver eagle pin on his chest, a replica of the one she wore, marked him as a decorated officer. Those slender muscles of his would be like bands of steel cable that never yielded an inch.

He met her gaze, and his eyes were those of a cornered animal. He didn't want to die. He wanted to live!

What was wrong with him?

"Now," the Voice said.

Darya sprang into motion. The table was on the far side of the throne room, perhaps forty feet away. She and Paul sprinted from their different starting points and met halfway toward the goal.

Her assessment was spot on. He wasn't trying. He wanted an out, so she gave it to him.

She swept his feet.

Child's play. He let her hook his ankle and went sprawling like a first-weeker at Youth Camp. She heard him grunt as he hit the flagstone floor. The impact made that loud smacking sound that tells you something won't be working right when you get up again.

If nothing else, he was a good actor.

She bolted to the table and snatched the silver revolver. It felt lighter than she'd expected. She cast a final look at her tormentors, the black-veiled monster on the throne, the feeble ghost of the Chairman, and the frog-faced bootlicker Rius. Paul Veliu was back on his feet, rooted in place and staring at her with a childish mixture of disbelief and awe. Blood poured from his nostrils.

She kept her gaze away from the prisoners. Auntie Elena would never understand, never realize that this was the only chance to escape. This world held nothing but darkness. Perhaps she would find light in another.

"For God, for the State, for the Chairman!" Darya shouted. She felt warm tears on her face.

She clamped her teeth over the tip of the barrel.

She heard Auntie Elena scream her name.

She pulled the trigger.

Chapter Six

# Shadow Ruler

*C*LICK.

The revolver's chamber was empty. Darya pulled the trigger four more times in quick succession, her teeth biting down hard on the cold steel barrel. No chance of misfire. No waking up with half her face missing.

*Click. Click. Click. Click.*

One bullet. Six chambers. Of course. They would put the bullet in the last one. The Party always had a flair for the dramatic.

One last pull.

*Click.*

It took her a moment to realize that the gun hadn't fired. She was still alive, standing there with the barrel of an unloaded revolver shoved into her mouth. She removed the gun and examined it. Something was wrong. Something about the weight and the way it felt in her hand.

The truth crashed down on her like an avalanche. The gun was fake, a metal replica of a classic American revolver. A child's plaything.

Was it a joke?

Impossible.

Another mind game from the Central Party, another tool to break the will.

She carefully placed the fake revolver back on the table. She wiped her eyes, but the tears kept coming. She stumbled away, forgetting to march, forgetting to control her breath, forgetting everything.

She made her way to a corner of the room where the dancing lights of the standing torches and the shimmering chandelier yielded to deepest shadow. As the darkness swallowed her, she dropped to her knees, covered her face with her hands, and broke into sobs.

Displays of emotion—two strokes with the rod in front of your squadron.

Second infraction—five strokes in front of your platoon.

Third infraction—three minutes in the Torture Room, then recycled to week one of Youth Camp.

"Stop her!" Rius shrieked suddenly. "Somebody help me!"

Darya looked up.

Eyes bulging, Rius Ludovic struggled to restrain Auntie Elena as she charged toward the throne. Elena's face was pale with fury.

"You devil!" she screamed, prying Rius's arms from around her waist. "Haven't you done enough to her already? Can't you see she needs help?"

The words made Darya tremble.

Auntie Elena still cared about her? Why? Didn't she know that a bloodstained failure like Darya Alexandrovna wasn't worth the effort?

The Youth Corps guards who had stood outside the entry doors rushed into the room, pulled Auntie Elena away from Rius, and shoved her to the ground. Then they hauled her up by her elbows, forcing her to kneel before the throne.

❧

Elena closed her eyes and waited for the ringing in her ear to stop. One of the young soldiers had struck the side of her head and sent her reeling. Her breath came in ragged gasps. Her heart beat a frantic rhythm.

"How could you?" she growled. "Why are you torturing her?"

She glanced toward the corner where Dasha had disappeared. Lost to sight in dark shadows, Dasha's heaving sobs rose above the strange, pulsing noise emanating from the throne.

"You care for her, don't you, science prisoner?" Aryana Voss said.

Elena felt the anger pouring through her own voice. "Don't you have a soul? Aren't you ashamed of what you've done to her?"

"The girl will be safe with me," Aryana replied. "She is no longer your concern." She rose from her throne. The pulsing stopped in the same moment. "You've worked miracles for our cause, science prisoner. I've often thought of you over the years while you labored in our prison factory. I'm the one who sent you there. I gave the command to kidnap you, to bring you from your home in America. I took you from your husband, your children, your nation…everything you loved."

Elena couldn't breathe. A storm of feelings—repressed, denied, forced down—threatened to overwhelm her. "Why?"

"I offered you as a sacrifice to my lord," Aryana replied. "I told him you would transform his Foundation's technology. You've exceeded my expectations."

"Madness!" Elena shouted back. "My work has come to nothing. It's only ideas, dreams. None of it is real."

Aryana stepped down from the dais, extended a gloved fist, and held in front of Elena.

"Your theory has become our reality. We followed your instructions precisely, to the very letter. Or letters, I should say. See? We let you take some of the credit."

The gloved fist opened. A round, silver object clinked to the ground in front of Elena. She picked it up and examined it.

"It can't be." But there it was, the miniature inscription Marina had insisted on adding to that blueprint two years ago. The tiny letters E and P, for Elena Petrova. "I would have known," she said. "Even in the prison factory, we would have heard of this. If the power cells were working, they'd be using them everywhere, all over the world."

She looked to Marina for confirmation. Her friend's eyes were fixed on the ground, her face a living portrait of guilt.

So Marina had known, which meant she had been working for the Party all along, for this monstrous Aryana Voss.

"The world would know nothing if we concealed the technology," Aryana said. "My late master knew that the outside world was not ready for your fusion power source. Within the Foundation, however, we have adapted it to a wide range of uses."

Elena peered into the black veil. A faint profile lay behind it. High cheekbones, a thin nose, a delicate chin. The ghostly contours of a noble face.

Then a sudden, awful terror seized her. There was something unearthly about this woman, something unnatural. When Aryana spoke again, her face didn't move. Not even a quiver of motion in those slightly parted lips. Was she wearing a mask?

"You have earned your reward," she said in her honey-smooth voice. "For our part, we have ensured that your husband and children remain alive. They are well. If you want them to remain so, you will obey my final command to you."

"My husband? My children?" Elena's voice cracked as she spoke the words. "What if you're lying? Prove to me that they're alive."

Aryana nodded stiffly towards Rius. "She may keep them."

Rius knelt beside Elena and placed three photographs on the ground. "You have a beautiful family, science prisoner." He spoke with surprising gentleness.

When she saw the faces in the photographs, her tears nearly blinded her. She picked the images up with reverence, clutching them to her chest with trembling hands.

Her husband, her daughter, her son. How they had grown, how they had changed without her! Sweet Nadia's face, now so much more like Elena's own. Peter's infectious smile and cherub-like countenance.

She gazed at Boris. The man her soul adored, the man whose memory gave her the strength to go on, to hope, to persevere. He, too, had aged. The hair, once a brown so deep it verged on black, now shone with silver. More handsome than ever, regal and strong.

Her brilliant, crazy, unpredictable husband.

"Thank you." In that moment, she understood what Marina had done and why she had done it. This wasn't betrayal, it was survival. Still, there were lines she could not cross, not even for them. "What do you want me to do?"

"One of our researchers requires assistance," Aryana replied. "A small project. Do not take advantage of my generosity. If you betray me, I will destroy everything you love. A great shift is taking place outside Khatizan. When it is complete, you shall be released."

"Released?" Marina exclaimed. "Does that mean—"

"You will both be repaid fully for what you have done," Aryana replied. "You have my word."

"What about Dasha?" Elena asked suddenly.

"As I told you, science prisoner, that girl is no longer your concern."

Elena squeezed her hands into fists. A wrong step now could cost her everything. Boris, Nadia, Peter—she might never see them again.

But she couldn't back down. She couldn't abandon the daughter of Stefanya Kozlova to these devils.

She scrambled to her feet, her heart pounding in her chest.

"No." She kept her voice quiet but firm. "Either Dasha comes with me, or I'll do nothing more for you."

The room fell silent. Elena glanced at the Chairman. A faint smile hovered on the corners of his lips.

Suddenly Aryana came so close that her face was only inches away. Elena heard a peculiar sound from within the woman's black veil, a slight, mechanical whirring, like the moving gears of a wind-up toy.

"You are stronger than I thought, science prisoner." Aryana reached out and rested her gloved hand on Elena's cheek. Elena trembled, too terrified to breathe. "Do what I ask, and the girl will be yours. *After* you finish your final task."

Aryana patted her lightly on the cheek, then signaled to the soldiers. They led Marina and Elena away from the throne room and back to the fortress's entrance.

Outside the fortress walls, their truck driver leaned against the fender of his vehicle, a fresh cigarette perched between his lips. He doffed his cap to Elena as the Youth Corps cadets took them toward the back of the truck. For some reason, he seemed to ignore Marina altogether.

"Where's the officer?" he asked. "The silent girl?"

"Lieutenant Alexandrovna remains here," one of the cadets replied. "My friend and I will follow behind you to make sure there are no complications."

"What about food?" the driver asked. "Can't we stop for lunch?"

"Stuff your face after you've completed the job, citizen," the cadet snapped. "You old RA veterans are soft as jellyfish. You'll need discipline if you want more contracts with the Youth Corps. You have a problem with that, take it up with your section supervisor. I'm sure he'd find a solution."

"No problem." The driver waved a hand at the cadets and walked to the other side of the truck.

Elena's gaze swept over the garden as she climbed into the truck bed. It was a jarring juxtaposition, the untainted beauty of nature alongside the evil lurking in the heart of the fortress. She reached down to help Marina. Once they were both inside, one of the Youth Corps cadets fastened the tarp across the back, plunging them into near darkness.

"A civilian job," Marina cried as soon as the truck engine roared to life. "We'll have our own apartments. Baths, Elena. Can you believe it? Baths, in a real bathtub! And when it's done, we'll leave this terrible country once and for all."

Elena didn't reply. God help her, she couldn't. Marina, her only friend, the only person in this entire country that she could trust—Marina was working for the Party. How long had it gone on? How deep was their agreement?

More importantly, what had Marina done for them?

⚘

Paul Veliu glanced toward the prostrate figure of Darya Alexandrovna. The guards had dragged her from her hiding place and laid her on the ground beside the throne. The only sign that she was alive was an occasional tremble that wracked her body, aftershocks of the storm of emotions that had assailed her.

Poor girl.

The Youth Corps could be a heartless machine, albeit an efficient one. Year after year, Youth Camps swallowed up thousands of Khatiz teenagers from all backgrounds and persuasions. Within ten weeks, the camps transformed them into fervid, nationalistic drones who lacked any power of independent thought.

Such extreme soul-shaping required overwhelming psychological pressure. The weak were broken, the strong survived, and the cruelest found perverse pleasure in their new environment.

Some, like Darya, concealed their humanity beneath the scars. They suffered the most, tormented and twisted into mental knots so tight they could snap under the rigors of Khatizan life. They hadn't learned to keep their distance, to separate themselves emotionally from what was happening around them.

Darya looked to be nineteen or twenty, which meant she had survived the Youth Corps for at least six years. Most like her would have broken down far sooner.

And what of his own soul? He suddenly remembered the German receptionist with her cornflower blue eyes and rose-scented perfume.

The Party must pay for its crimes. They had turned him into a terrorist. They had betrayed him, and he would soon return the favor.

Aryana returned to her throne. The deep, pulsing sound resumed as she sat. Some type of power source, perhaps? What *was* she?

"Chairman Markhov?" Aryana said.

"Yes, my lady?" The Chairman rocked on his heels as he nervously clasped and unclasped his hands behind his back. Paul wondered what would happen if the people of Khatizan could see their fearless leader trembling in raw terror before a woman.

"We near the completion of our goal. As agreed, control of Khatizan shall return to you when the Foundation's work is complete. We will have no further use for your country."

The Chairman bowed. "Yes, my lady."

"You may leave us."

As he turned and ambled from the chamber, the Chairman's eyes shifted to meet Paul's gaze. The look contained a sudden flash of cunning, as if he and Paul shared a secret.

"Approach, Lieutenant Paul Veliu," Aryana commanded as soon as the doors closed behind the Chairman.

Paul's stomach churned as he drew near to the pulsing black throne. He could feel the gaze of the veiled woman resting on him. The specter of Aryana Voss outweighed any terrors of the Youth Corps. Worse than Commander Firlenko, worse than the savage, half-feral snarls of the drill instructors, worse even than the Torture Room at Youth Camp.

Was she even human?

"You did not wish to destroy yourself, Paul Veliu?" she asked him.

Her question concealed a trap. The Youth Corps trained recruits to abandon all thoughts of self-preservation. The self must be sacrificed for the All, the citizen for the State, the child for the Motherland. To deny this was treason.

He had to control his fear. Stay calm, pay attention, form a plan. There had to be a way to survive this.

"It would be the greatest honor to die for my country," he said, "but not by my own hand."

"Fool!" The sudden ferocity in Aryana's voice took his breath away.

"There is no honor in death. The entire meaning of life is to survive, to exist, to crush everyone who threatens your well-being. You know this. I'm told you are a strategist who never loses games of chess or games of war. Is that true?"

He swallowed. "I can't remember ever losing."

"You sense the flowing of the tide intuitively," she went on, her voice now smooth as silk. "You feel the current beneath your fingertips. With a touch you direct its course. A skilled player has a plan for every piece on the board. They control their opponent's pieces as if they were their own. One must remember every piece, no matter how small. I never forget the state of the board. That is true power, is it not, Paul Veliu?"

She went on before he could answer.

"But you have a weakness. You feel compassion for your opponents, even on the battlefield. It nearly caused you to fail in Berlin. I will give you one more chance. This time, you will show no mercy to our enemies. I have great plans for you, but I must be certain that I can trust you. Are you worthy of my trust, Paul Veliu?"

He took a deep breath. His match against the Central Party had begun, and these were the opening moves. He had to follow her lead for now. In time, an opportunity would present itself.

He lowered his head. "I am your servant."

"Then bow before me."

He dropped to his knees and pressed his forehead against the ground.

"You shall lead a team of our most elite soldiers deep into enemy territory. You will strike our greatest foes and bring back a treasure beyond compare. Fulfill your mission, and you will become Vice Commander Veliu, second only to Commander Firlenko himself."

Paul felt a rush of adrenaline flow through him. *Vice Commander.* Even now, after all that he'd learned of the Party's vileness and hypocrisy, the words held the potency of a spell. To rise above his peers, to triumph over all opponents, to rule through power—those were the deepest dreams of the Youth Corps.

He'd been with the Corps for a decade now. He was only twenty-three.

"Where will I go?" His mind was at full alert, ready to examine the pieces on the board as she presented them.

"To the great empire of the West, the United States. Your life is now tethered to my will. Succeed and you survive. Fail and I will destroy you with my own hands."

He rose and squared his shoulders. "I won't fail you."

"For your sake, Lieutenant, I hope you're right."

## Chapter Seven

# The Pact

Paul Veliu hurried through the fortress courtyard and past the raised portcullis, not stopping until he reached the garden beyond, where he paused by a cluster of fragrant rhododendrons, Siberian irises, and willow gentians. He took a few deep breaths, and his heartbeat slowed as the heady mingling of scents took him back to his childhood. Yearning struck him, a longing to be near his parents again, to be home, to be at peace and away from the terrors of the Central Party. He wandered farther along the path.

The garden had been tended with evident devotion. The balance of darker and lighter shades of green, the subtle layering of ornamental trees and grasses, the miniature retreats where stone benches and statuary beckoned to the wandering guest, the bursts of vivid blossoms yielding to subdued verdure—every detail revealed the mind of an artist.

When the Revolution began, his parents had been humble florists with a small shop in the town of Khalensk. They weathered the early years, surviving the Central Party's perpetual wars against the West, the sporadic purges, even the sudden military drafts that scooped up entire villages.

Things changed around his eighth birthday. By some mysterious stratagem of the Party, Khatizan transformed itself from a weak satellite of the old Soviet empire to a strong and independent nuclear power. Within months of the first nuclear weapons test, the prison factories were constructed. Foreigners showed up by the trainload, and the greatest purge in Khatizan's history began. Friends and neighbors and loved ones disappeared into the dark corridors of prison factories and communal farms, never to be seen again.

The day he turned thirteen, a pair of Revolutionary Army guards showed up at the door of his home with an official Party document. Five minutes later, a terrified young Paul Veliu was packed into a waiting military bus with camouflaged paint. The Khatizan Youth Corps had been officially launched. Paul joined the first wave of recruits.

"Your parents are gone," the Youth Corps sergeants told him when he stepped off the bus at Youth Camp. "You will never see them again. The Chairman is your father now. Khatizan is your mother. You need nothing else."

Had it really been ten years since that day? Paul lifted his face toward the cobalt sky and breathed in the pure mountain air. A breeze caressed a row of hardy rosebushes nearby, causing their newformed buds to shudder.

He finally knew the secret behind Khatizan's success. Not the Party, not the Chairman, not the Revolution.

Foreigners. The Magnus Foundation.

Why had Aryana Voss chosen him? What did she want with that other lieutenant, Darya Alexandrovna? He would never forget that image of her, fierce as an Amazon, eyes ablaze with mad ecstasy as she shoved the barrel of a pistol into her own mouth and pulled the trigger.

His fingers brushed a rhododendron with blossoms red as ripe apples.

And what about that science prisoner, Elena Petrova? She had risked her slender hope of freedom to rescue a suicidal Youth Corps officer. Why?

He strolled along the path until he came to a small gazebo with a stone chessboard in the center and wooden benches on either side of the board. There was an active game in play. He sat on one of the benches and reconstructed what must have been the opening moves. White had seized early control of the center with a classic opening. Black had responded with a series of moves that verged on chaotic, though he began to see an underlying plan as he examined the position more carefully.

He heard footsteps behind him.

"I hope I'm not disturbing you, Lieutenant."

Rius Ludovic approached, his shoulders slanting downward, his hands tucked into the fur-lined pockets of his overcoat. His jet-black hair had been tousled by the mountain breeze. His wideset eyes shifted about as if taking in the garden before they settled on Paul. A disturbing gaze. His left pupil was lazy and shifted off to one side from time to time.

"Do you like the garden?" Rius's voice now seemed hesitant, almost anxious.

Paul rose and stepped out of the gazebo. "It's beautiful."

"Thank you." Rius trembled, then gave Paul an odd, cringing bow. He waved toward the chessboard. "You've discovered my favorite part of it. An old friend and I enjoy leisurely matches here, but I'm more of a gardener than a chess player. I once built another meagre garden of sorts inside Magnus Headquarters. All of it underground and indoors. Lord Magnus used to wander among the red oaks by the stream, humming Wagner and plotting humanity's future." He paused. "Had you heard of the Magnus Foundation before today?"

Paul glanced back at the chessboard.

Outwardly, Rius Ludovic seemed no more than a sycophant, common enough in the Central Party. Commander Firlenko kept a swarm of them, aides and junior officers who boosted the Commander's vast ego with their simpering praises, scurrying off to fulfill every whim and fancy that possessed the great leader. No doubt Aryana Voss, whose power eclipsed the Commander's, would attract followers of the same variety.

The theory fit, but Rius seemed more complex. In the throne room, Paul had noticed a shrewdness that sometimes crept into the man's expression when he talked, only to vanish again like the morning mist.

"I'd never heard of the Foundation," he replied. "What is it?"

"The most powerful group of people in the world." Rius rubbed his hands together and cast a quick glance both ways, as if afraid of being overhead. "Too powerful, some say. They direct governments, they start wars and end them, they run the largest corporations, they bury their enemies by the thousands. They'll take over everything someday. They almost pulled it off last winter, but Lord Magnus was betrayed to his death, Magnus Headquarters destroyed, and my paltry garden consumed by flames."

Rius lowered his voice. "We are standing in an extraordinary place, Lieutenant. One of the few spots in Khatizan where you can speak your mind without fear of being overheard."

"What do you mean?" Paul asked.

Rius gave a nervous cough. "Only that you and I are having a truly private conversation. Do you know how seldom that happens in this country? Aryana Voss expanded Khatizan's surveillance system when the Foundation first arrived and we turned the tide in the war with NATO. She's let me in on a few of her secrets."

Rius tucked his hands into his coat pockets and leaned closer. "I'm just an errand boy with a knack for gardening. I can make the big folks feel good about themselves, which is how I got myself close to Lord Magnus. But now I'm terrified, Lieutenant. Aryana is nothing like Lord Magnus. He wanted to heal the world, even if we had to go through hell to get there. But Aryana will kill us all. You look surprised? I'll prove it to you. What I'm about to tell you could cost me my life."

Paul smiled and shook his head. Did the man take him for a fool?

Even a first-year private knew the tricks Youth Corps Intelligence played when they wanted to catch a traitor. First the nonsense about secrets and conspiracies. Mild slander against a politician, clever comments about the flaws of the Central Party, a hint about the Chairman's age. They were lures Intelligence set out for gullible civilians. Swallow the bait, and you'd find yourself scrubbing toilets in a prison factory.

"You drive me to it," Rius went on. "Listen to what I say, then decide for yourself. We need each other, Lieutenant, though our goals are at cross-purposes. I'm trusting you with my life."

Paul pursed his lips. "And what are my goals, Mr. Ludovic?"

Rius leaned so close their faces nearly touched. "Bringing down the Central Party, for starters."

The words were barely spoken above a whisper, but Paul felt as if Rius had shouted them. If there was a microphone anywhere in range, if a surveillance drone silently soared in the clouds above them, then he could be a dead man. This was a trap. Rius was with Intelligence, which meant Paul needed to move fast to prove his loyalty.

"I would never—"

Rius cut him off with a wave of his hand. "I already told you that Aryana Voss set up Khatizan's surveillance system. Cameras and microphones are only the beginning. She's a master at gauging human behavior, understanding the internal levers that guide and govern the machine that lesser minds call free will. Your mission in Berlin was illuminating. What would a thoughtful, idealistic young soldier like yourself do after being forced into such a role by the very Party he was trained to worship?"

Paul stared at him. How much did Rius already suspect? How could the man know inward thoughts that had never been voiced?

"You had never so much as pointed a gun at a civilian," Rius went on. "I wonder why *she*"—he motioned with his head toward the fortress—"chose you? You must be more than you seem. Come, walk with me."

They meandered towards a dense thicket of rosebushes bristling with vibrant pink and red blossoms. The scent lay heavy in the air, reawakening a deep-burned memory in Paul's mind. The rose perfume. Berlin. Those cyan pools in which lingered the question that now tormented his every waking moment.

Why?

"I wish there'd never been a Revolution." The words escaped his lips before he could hold them back, as if they had a will of their own and had demanded release.

Fool! He cast a furtive glance toward Rius.

"It would have been much better for Khatizan," Rius agreed with a vigorous nod, "but not for the world. Khatizan now plays a crucial role in something far greater than itself. The blood, sweat, and tears of your people are building a glorious future, to paraphrase the stale propaganda. But not for Khatizan alone. Your country has been a tool in the hands of the Magnus Foundation. Your prison factories, your agricultural facilities, your nuclear technology, even the Youth Corps— everything feeds into our great work. Soon the next stage will begin, and Khatizan's dreary toil will end. Project Twilight is almost upon us."

Paul frowned. "Project Twilight?"

"Lord Magnus believed our species must endure catastrophic change to survive." Rius's voice trembled with fervor. "The old order with its self-serving, divided nations must burn to the ground. We need a new and united humanity, a people made immortal by their own efforts, attaining the gifts of the gods by sheer force of will. Now Aryana tries her hand at the game, but she lacks the capacity. To be blunt, Lieutenant, she is insane with bloodlust. You saw how she tormented Darya Alexandrovna. Aryana feeds on suffering and agony. She believes it's her destiny to destroy us all."

A new humanity? The gifts of the gods? If the Foundation hadn't already performed the miracle of turning Khatizan into a global power, he would be doubting Rius's sanity instead of Aryana's.

"What is she, Rius?"

Rius shrugged. "Some in the Foundation believe she's humanity's future, others the hell we must escape. She talks as if she desires Project Twilight, but will she stay true to Lord Magnus's vision? Darya Alexandrovna must be protected at all costs. I've only just learned who she really is. We can't let Aryana…"

His words trailed off, then suddenly he grabbed Paul's shoulder. His voice turned fierce, and in his eyes burned the fervid gleam of a fanatic. "I will not betray my master! Lord Magnus entrusted his dying wish to me! Weak as I am, I will either fulfill it or die trying. It can never happen while Aryana lives. She trusts you. I don't know why, but it makes you more powerful than you realize. Help me destroy her and her damnable Central Party, and I'll give you anything you want, even if you ask me for a kingdom."

"Let go of me, Mr. Ludovic."

"Forgive me." Rius took a step back and hugged his arms around his chest. "I lose control of myself sometimes. We stand on a razor's edge. Careful, careful."

Paul plucked a rose blossom and breathed in its scent. What would it take to silence the guilt, the shame? Was this meeting with Rius an unexpected path to his goal, or was it sheer suicide?

"What if the kingdom I want is Khatizan?" he asked at last.

Rius nodded his head. "Yes, Lieutenant, yes! Help me destroy the Party, and Khatizan will be yours."

# Chapter Eight
# Last Rites

ELENA IGNORED THE hollow rumbling in her stomach. She hadn't eaten since Darya had marched into the science lab that morning. She found herself craving the thick nutrient soup and rock-hard bread from the prison factory cafeteria. Tasteless or not, it was better than nothing.

Marina sniffed. "So *that* was the great Chairman Markhov? You remember that nightmare I had where he sentenced me to death in the Citizen's Court and handed me over to Firlenko? He seemed like a giant in my dream. Who would have imagined that the Chairman is nothing but a scarecrow?"

"That woman on the throne is no scarecrow," Elena replied. "What she did to Dasha…"

"Terrible, yes," Marina said, "but the Youth Corps often do such things in their camps, you know. Mind games to break those poor children. Still, who does she think she is, dressing all in black, turning her head so stiffly you'd think it was screwed onto her neck? Like Baba Yaga on her way to a funeral! If it wasn't for the Chairman bowing down to her, I would have thought it was a joke."

Elena shuddered. "The people in that fortress run Khatizan, but I get the feeling that's only the tip of the iceberg. Who are they?"

Marina shrugged. "Maybe she really is Baba Yaga."

"Do you realize that they've never asked us to make weapons?" Elena tried to sound as innocent as she could manage, and she avoided Marina's suspicious glance. "How is that possible? We're physicists working on the cutting edge of energy manipulation. You'd think the Central Party or this Aryana Voss woman would have us building fusion bombs or high-energy lasers. Why haven't they?"

Marina blew her nose on her handkerchief. "All I know is I can't wait to go grocery shopping. Do you think there's any chocolate left in Chozul?"

An obvious deflection. "One can hope," Elena said quietly.

Had Marina already weaponized the technology?

Suddenly the military truck dove into a pothole. Marina shrieked and clutched Elena's arm. A moment later, the truck slammed into another one.

"What?" Elena asked. "What's wrong?" Even in the dim light she could see the terror in her friend's eyes.

"The road!" Marina cried. "It means…no, never mind. What's done is done."

"What is it, Marina?" she asked. "I don't understand!"

Marina clasped her hand. "I've done something terrible, something unforgivable. Lord, how their blood weighs on my soul! But I've also done something brave. Not that one act could ever cancel out the other, that's impossible. But they know, they must know. Oh, Elena, I've been so tormented. I couldn't stay here forever. I couldn't die in a place like this, a place without chocolate." Her laughter was wild and frantic. "All that we've done, all that suffering, for nothing, nothing!"

Instead of replying, Elena lifted Marina's trembling hand and pressed it to her lips. "This wasn't your first trip to the fortress, was it?"

Marina grew quiet. "Last winter," she said at last, "when they sent me to the hospital for the flu, Rius Ludovic visited me. He said his mistress had a plan for me, a great work I must do for Khatizan. He offered me freedom, but I refused until he promised you would go free, too. You know I was gone for weeks, Elena, but I was only in the hospital for two days."

Elena's heart became a dead weight in her chest, as if her very soul had turned to stone.

Freedom. What would she have done for freedom? Had she not just made a bargain with the same people? Those photographs of Boris, Nadia, and Peter were safely tucked in her shirt pocket. She couldn't judge Marina, but she felt no end of judgment against herself.

"What was this great work?"

Marina's voice faltered. "It was a…bomb. An energy bomb. They needed help modifying your power source. Elena, that's what happened in Germany. Thousands of innocent people murdered in the blink of an eye by a weapon I built for the Central Party."

"You must forgive yourself," Elena replied at once. She paused for a moment as the truck rammed into another pothole. "You can't carry that weight. It's not fair, not after all they've done to you. Einstein himself once begged America's president to build a nuclear bomb. Does that make Einstein a monster? And you said you also did something brave. What was it?"

Marina leaned close and whispered in her ear. "I met someone from the Resistance at the fortress. Someone you've seen this very day. I told him everything, all that I knew. I gave him the schematics for the energy bomb. I thought the Party would catch us, but days passed, then weeks, and nothing happened. I thought they didn't know, but I was wrong. They always know."

"Are you certain?" Elena asked breathlessly.

"The road tells me." Marina groaned. "No, you still don't understand. It's better this way. Do you ever dream of chocolate?"

Elena laughed. "Chocolate? Why the sudden fixation?"

"Just thinking," Marina said. "If we had some chocolates right now—really good ones, maybe even from Switzerland—then I wouldn't mind it so much. I'd like to have the taste of chocolate on my lips one more time, wouldn't you?" A tear coursed down her cheek. "Elena, I can't ask for your forgiveness. Thousands of people were murdered because of me, all because I wanted my box of chocolates, my taste of freedom, my chance at a better life. Whatever happens next, remember me the way I was before. Just your friend, your Marina."

"I'll always forgive you, Marina." She pulled her friend close, wrapping her arms around her. "I only wish you'd told me sooner. I could have helped you carry the burden."

What other choice could Marina have made? If she had said no, they simply would have tortured her until she said yes. But to work with the Resistance, to give them the same weapon so that they might bring down the Central Party with it—what bravery Marina had shown!

"I tell you what," she went on, trying to lift her friend's spirits. "The first thing we'll do after we settle in our new apartments is hunt for chocolate. Wherever there's a town, there's bound to be chocolate."

Marina squeezed her hand. "Will you tell me another psalm?"

Elena recited the 22$^{nd}$ psalm in the Orthodox Bible, which was the 23$^{rd}$ for Marina and the Western church. Elena had learned it when she was seven, and from its famous lines her childhood love of the psalms had been born. She felt a strange solemnity as she recited it now, as if she had begun some mysterious and sacred liturgy. Marina held her hand tightly. She could feel her friend trembling and hear her quiet weeping.

When it was over, they basked in a silence that transcended the rattling and squeaking of the truck, the groaning of its engine, and the occasional crash as it bounced through a pothole.

The truck slowed. They heard loud clanking and roaring noises. Even as her mind registered what those sounds meant, the covering on the back of the truck was pulled aside and sunlight flooded into the dark truck bed, momentarily blinding her.

"Get them out!" shouted the voice she knew too well, the voice she feared above all others.

Commander Vladimir Firlenko. The truck had stopped in the courtyard of Prison Factory Six.

A pair of Youth Corps guards, boys who looked no more than fourteen and had never seen their first shave, grabbed the science prisoners and hauled them out of the truck bed.

Elena's mind dully registered what was happening around her. The soldiers all but dragged her and Marina toward the bloodstained wall. Guard dogs barked savagely as the prisoners passed by, one of them straining so hard against its spiked collar that its teeth tore the leg of Elena's uniform. The guard beside Elena laughed and pushed her lightly, just enough that she could have fallen off balance and into the dog's vicious teeth.

She looked beyond the line of Youth Corps infantry with their rifles and saw the window of the science laboratory where she had toiled for the last twelve years. The same window from which she had looked out, morning after morning, at prisoners awaiting their execution.

Her time had come. This was it.

*Lord have mercy. Christ have mercy. Lord have mercy.*

"Elena, I'm terrified!" Marina shrieked as soldiers chained their hands and feet to the wall. "I don't want to die."

Commander Firlenko raised his saber skyward and began his litany. It was exactly as she remembered. Every word, every nuance, every inflection. The soldiers aimed their rifles. She watched their youthful faces, their eyes. Flat, empty stares. Those weren't the eyes of human beings looking at their own kind. It was as if she and Marina were diseased animals, insects who needed to be crushed.

"Don't be afraid, Marina," she murmured. "God forgives us. Now forgive them. Forgive those children. Forgive Firlenko. Forgive everything, Marina. Let us die as human beings."

The litany neared its end. She began reciting the Lord's Prayer. Marina followed her lead.

*"And forgive us our sins, as we forgive those who sin against us. And lead us not—"*

Commander Firlenko lowered his saber. Elena closed her eyes as a dozen Youth Corps rifles burst to life.

❧

The sound of gunfire fell silent. Elena's breath came in ragged, heaving gasps.

She was alive. She was unharmed. How was that possible?

She opened her eyes. The Youth Corps soldiers lowered their rifles and began chatting amongst themselves. Firlenko walked away to talk on his cell phone.

"Marina," she said. "They spared us! They must have fired blanks. A warning, do you think?"

Silence.

"Marina?"

An icy foreboding crept over her as she turned to her friend. One look at Marina's lifeless, bloodstained body sagging against the chains brought a scream to her lips.

"Marina!" she shrieked, as if calling her friend's name could undo the irreversible. One of the Youth Corps soldiers approached with a heavy set of keys. A teenager. Fifteen, perhaps, with wavy, dark brown hair and a somber, regal expression.

She looked him in the eye. "How could you?" She blinked away her tears. "She did nothing wrong, nothing to deserve this! She was my only friend, the only one you people haven't murdered. She could have been your own mother. How *could* you?"

The young man stopped and stared at her. It was easy to forget that they were little more than children. Youth Camps churned out trained killing machines, yes, but underneath all that imposed darkness the divine image remained. The face of God, however distorted.

She kept her gaze locked on him as a whirlwind of fury and despair and grief ripped through her soul. "When this nightmare is over and Khatizan is free," she rasped as he unlocked the chains holding Marina's lifeless body, "then remember this. I forgive you for what you've done today. I forgive you, and so would she."

Suddenly the youth turned on her, his eyes ablaze. "No!" he snarled. "You can't do that. I won't let you! You can't forgive any of us, not for what we do here. If my mother saw me right now, she would curse me. My father would disown me. I'm already dead. Do you understand? You and me, we're both dead. Just like your friend."

"Soldier!" Commander Firlenko's voice cracked across the courtyard like a whip. "Silence!"

"Yes, sir!" the soldier cried as he saluted Firlenko. But when he turned to unfasten the chains holding Elena, he spoke softly so she alone could hear. "Some nightmares never end, science prisoner."

Then he was gone, and she was free of the chains. She glanced past the soldiers at the window of the science laboratory. Soon she would be on the other side of that window again.

Maybe the young man was right. Maybe the nightmare of the Central Party would go on forever.

Firlenko pocketed his phone, then strolled up to her and seized her by the hand. She recoiled and tried to pull away, but his grip was iron.

"Doctor Petrova?" He spoke in a jarringly cheerful voice. "I am Vladimir Firlenko, Commander of the Khatizan Youth Corps. You'll be returning to the fortress now. The Central Party is honored to have you assist us with our research."

Then he smiled at her. *Smiled*, as if he were an old acquaintance instead of the man who had just murdered her closest friend.

The message was clear. Marina had talked to the Resistance, which meant Marina was a traitor. The Party would pretend she had never existed, denying her even the meager reward of being remembered, acknowledged. They would cremate her body, annihilating every trace of her existence, and her ashes would be trod underfoot in this very courtyard.

Another fact registered in her awareness.

*Doctor Petrova.*

In the twelve years she had been a science prisoner, no one from the Party had ever called her by her real name.

"I'm honored to be the first to welcome you to your new life as a free woman," Firlenko went on. "You've done incredible work for the Party, Doctor Petrova. You make us proud. One of my sergeants will show you to your new apartment. Tomorrow, Rius Ludovic will brief you on your next assignment. For God, for the State, for the Chairman!"

He stepped back and saluted her. Instantly, the line of Youth Corps behind him followed suit.

She was being saluted by the Youth Corps. It felt surreal, terrifying. And nauseating.

She knelt and cradled Marina's body, clasping what remained of her friend to her chest.

"You won't be forgotten, my dear one." She kissed the still-warm forehead and gently closed Marina's eyes. "Go in peace. Wake in a world where evil has no power."

A soldier gently pulled her away. The young man with the keys.

"Come," he said. "It's time for you to leave."

He led her back to the military truck and opened the passenger door for her. Before she climbed in, she grasped his hand briefly. "Your parents *would* forgive you. They still love you. They know that you're a prisoner, too."

As he closed the door behind her, she suddenly realized that Commander Firlenko had called her a free woman.

❧

Boards covered the shattered windows of the Vysoti apartment complex in Orlinnye, a small, mountainous town in the shadow of Aryana Voss's fortress. The apartments boasted tiny balconies, some of which displayed a tattered chair or chipped flowerpot.

In stark contrast to the general squalor, gleaming satellite dishes were mounted to the brick walls of every balcony. Gifts from the Chairman. The Party encouraged Khatiz citizens to saturate themselves with official propaganda in all its forms—official news reports, patriotic sitcoms, government-sponsored movies where the heroes and heroines sacrificed themselves for the Central Party.

"It could always be worse," mused the driver with the patchwork clothes as he flung open his door and lit another cigarette.

Vasily Grushanin. The man had driven Elena in silence for the first ten minutes of the trip while she wept, then talked almost incessantly until now. Surprisingly, he had commiserated with her over Marina's death, though barely giving Elena time to get in a word edgewise. Was he trying to help her with his banter? Pulling her attention away from the horror she had just experienced?

She shivered. Her heart felt so empty, so hollow.

Marina was gone.

She would never hear her laughter again, never see that sparkle in her eyes, never sigh with relief when her friend magically brushed aside the nightmares around them and went to work as if their lives were somehow normal. She needed Marina. How could she face Khatizan's darkness by herself?

She was almost startled when the driver crossed over to her side of the truck and opened her door for her. He even held out his hand to help her down.

"Don't give up, Doctor Petrova," he said quietly. "Your friend wouldn't have wanted that. She was a very brave woman, you know."

Elena stared at him. How could he have known Marina? And why was he being so kind?

"I'll take over from here," said a firm, masculine voice. It was the other Youth Corps lieutenant from the throne room, the young man who had lost that cruel race against Dasha.

What had they called him? Paul, that was it. Paul Veliu.

"Thank you, driver," he added.

Vasily saluted Paul, nodded to Elena, then climbed back into his truck and drove off toward the fortress.

"He's a kind man," she said, and immediately wished she hadn't. Kindness was no virtue here. She hoped her words wouldn't get the poor driver in trouble.

"Is he?" Paul replied, his thoughts clearly elsewhere. "Tell me, did you see the garden outside the fortress?"

She nodded and looked away. Her friend had just been murdered by young men wearing uniforms like his. He was another part of their system, that mindless, brutal machine that wiped out so much goodness and beauty and life.

"After we drop off your belongings at your apartment," he said, "I'll take you to the garden. It's a good place to clear the mind and give the heart free reign. You can go there whenever you get a break from your work at the fortress."

She finally glanced up and met his gaze. There was something in his voice, some deeper meaning she couldn't grasp. Whatever it was, it would be foolish to reject his offer. His tone, like that of Vasily Grushanin, was unexpectedly friendly, but his eyes seemed to conceal some great sorrow.

"I'd like that, Lieutenant."

She followed him into the apartment complex. The inside of the building looked every bit as dingy as the outside. Paint peeled off cracked concrete walls, the running carpet was a case study in entropy, and a musty, mildewy scent permeated the air.

"Your unit is on the top floor," he said. "But they told me the elevator's broken."

She followed him up flights of concrete stairs, many of which were chipped or crumbling, occasionally exposing steel reinforcement bars underneath. At least she would get plenty of exercise here if she could keep from twisting her ankle.

On the fifth floor, he led her down a long corridor lined by apartments. Hers was the last one on the right. He took a key from his pocket and unlocked the door.

"After you." Paul stepped aside to let her enter.

The first thing she saw when she stepped through the doorway was the grand piano. A world-renowned brand, and it looked like it was in pristine condition.

That piano alone was worth more than most Khatiz workers could earn in a year.

The rest of the apartment had been furnished on the same scale. The carpets, the chairs, the sofa and dressers, the artwork on the walls— everything was luxurious.

"Why?" she gasped. "Why would they spend so much on my apartment?"

Paul shrugged. He seemed like the sort who kept his emotions on a tight leash. "You'd have to ask Rius. He told me he personally oversaw the furnishings. The piano came from Chozul. He hoped it would bring you some comfort."

He set her suitcase in front of a sleek leather sofa by a fireplace where a warm blaze crackled invitingly.

"Oh, Marina," she murmured. "If only you could have seen this."

"Rius told me what happened to your friend," Paul said. "I'm sorry, Doctor Petrova. You might feel weary, but I think that a walk in the garden is just what you need right now."

Their eyes met.

Her apartment would be under surveillance. If the Party had spent a fortune on the furniture, they would have doled out the additional funds for cameras and microphones. Whatever Paul wanted to tell her, he couldn't do it here.

"I'd like that," she said after a pause. "Let me freshen up a bit first."

"Take your time." He sat in a wingback recliner and crossed one leg over the other. "Rius purchased some new clothes for you. They should be in your bedroom closet."

Her bedroom.

For twelve years, she'd slept in a women's dormitory with dozens of metal beds and not even a hint of privacy. Now she had her own bedroom, a large one, with a queen bed. She sat on a corner of the mattress. Memory foam. The perfect resistance, not too soft, not too firm.

She opened the door to the walk-in closet and stared mutely at the organized array of dresses, blouses, pants, skirts, coats, and jackets. More clothes than she had ever owned in her life. Designer brands, the kind that would have emptied her bank account back in America.

Why was the Central Party doing this? What could it mean?

She changed into a satin blouse and the most comfortable pair of pants she could find, then wrapped herself in a fur-lined coat that was more than a match for Khatizan's frigid spring air.

A few minutes later, she found herself in the passenger seat of a sleek black Mercedes, the kind usually reserved for Party officials. Paul drove along the winding, switchback road up to Aryana Voss's fortress. They hadn't spoken a word, but his tension was almost palpable. Whatever message he had for her must be important.

And dangerous.

He parked the car in front of the fortress gates. She followed him silently along the gravel walkway into the lush garden. She breathed in the fragrant mingling of roses and hyacinths and rhododendrons.

The garden looked like the work of a master, a living canvas of beauty that pierced her soul and brought tears to her eyes. She had almost forgotten that the world could be so lovely, that renewal and life and hope still lay at the heart of reality.

She wept for beauty, and she wept for Marina. Her friend had loved gardening. How often had she talked about the flowers she used to grow back home in Poland?

"Are you all right?" Paul rested a hand on her shoulder, then withdrew it so quickly she almost wondered if she had imagined the gesture.

"No." She wiped her eyes. "I don't know if I'll ever be all right again."

"I know that feeling," he replied quietly. "Have you ever seen roses like these?" He led her deeper into the garden. As they neared a manicured rosebush brimming with yellow blossoms, he leaned close.

"They're sending me off tomorrow on a mission to America. This is our only chance. If you want to see your family again, you're going to have to trust me. We're going to take down Aryana Voss. If she falls, the Central Party will fall with her. Rius is on our side. We have a plan, but we can't pull it off without you. We need you to write a letter for us…"

He then spoke so quickly that his words nearly tumbled on top of each other. He never paused, never gave her a moment to reply, never bothered to even ask her if she was willing to join the plot he laid out before her. They already knew what she had suffered. Truth be told, they didn't have to ask. If she could do anything to stop the devils running Khatizan, she would do it.

"Are you with us, Doctor Petrova?" he said at last.

She nodded, overwhelmed by the things he had revealed. A plan bold enough to take down a regime, yet fragile enough to fall beneath any stray breeze of fate.

If it worked, the nightmare would end. She would go home.

An hour later, Paul drove her back to the apartment complex. She climbed up the grimy stairwell, unlocked the door to her opulent apartment, and headed straight for the piano. Thick books of sheet music had been neatly stacked beside the pedals.

She rested her fingertips on the keys and closed her eyes.

Silence. After twelve long years, silence.

No barking of Youth Corps hounds, no shouts and screams of tormented prisoners, no clanging of gears, no roaring of furnaces.

Nothing now but eagerness, the breathless anticipation of the music pent up within her soul. She pressed a key and held it down. One note, sustained. She let the sound wash over her, over the room and the town and the prison factory and the Central Party and the Morning Death.

She pulled her hand back.

"Marina," she whispered.

After a long reverie, she unlocked the balcony door and stepped out into the pale bluish light of a full moon surrounded by ghostlike tendrils of cloud. On the ridgeline above the town, the sprawling contours of the fortress splayed out like a spiked insect.

The night air felt thick and heavy with the promise of coming storms. She wiped her eyes and went back into the apartment. She sat at the piano and played Rachmaninoff and Chopin, Mendelssohn and Tchaikovsky, Beethoven and Mozart and Lysenko. Played until her fingers ached, until her soul was satisfied, until the fire within her abated and her mind grew weary. Then she showered, put on a warm, maroon bathrobe, brushed her teeth and hair, and felt cleaner than she had in twelve years.

She stood beside her bed and murmured what she could remember of the evening prayers. Then she prayed for Darya Alexandrovna, asking God to let her become a second mother to the broken orphan girl. She wept for Marina, at home with her Creator. She prayed for Paul Veliu, the courageous young man with eyes haunted by some terrible pain.

Finally, she pulled out the photographs of Boris, Nadia, and Peter. She kissed their images, pressed them to her heart, and lost herself in a silent mingling of prayer and longing.

When her spirit grew calm, she slipped under silken white sheets and dreamed of the world Paul Veliu had promised, a Khatizan where the Central Party had vanished like a mist.

She brewed a pot of coffee the next morning. Real, black, Colombian coffee. She savored every sip, cradling the cup near her to soak in the aroma. The gray and watery caffeinated drinks at the prison factory had been a favorite of the other prisoners, but they were a feeble shadow of the real thing.

Someone knocked on the door. Her coffee mug froze midway to her mouth.

It could end now, all of it. The apartment, the piano, the hope of freedom, the chance of ever seeing Boris and Nadia and Peter again. It could be taken away in a single moment.

She had trusted Paul Veliu with her life. Why had she taken that risk? He had seemed so authentic in his desire to destroy Aryana Voss and the Central Party, but what if it had been a test of her loyalty? Was he working with Youth Corps Intelligence?

She set down her coffee mug.

"No," she told herself, speaking the words aloud. "You're going to face whatever this is with courage. Marina was brave. You will be brave, too."

She went to the door, unlocked it, and pulled it open.

Rius Ludovic stood outside, shivering and hugging himself despite his heavy coat and scarf. The morning air felt warmer than usual for Khatizan, though the night had dipped well below freezing.

"Good morning, Elena." He spoke in a low, furtive voice. "Just a social call." He stepped past her. "Can I come in?"

"You already have."

He bumped against an end table, nearly pitching over a lamp. He apologized, called himself a fool, and began pacing back in forth across the living room. She waited for him to speak, but he seemed content with his introspections.

"Do you want some breakfast?" she asked finally.

"What?" He stopped and stared at her. "Oh, food. No, I'm not hungry." He started pacing again. "Do you like chocolate?" he asked suddenly. "I heard you liked it. There's a confectionary by the riverfront that sells gourmet chocolate every Tuesday morning, but you have to get there early, and you have to be on the list. Not many people on that list. Those who are would never tell an outsider, but still…"

As his voice trailed off, he dug his hands into his hair and began feverishly tugging it in both directions.

Was the man insane?

"I want to see Darya," she said. "Can I meet with her today?"

"Not yet!" he snapped. "Forgive me, Doctor Petrova. It's not your fault. Darya isn't well. We have the best doctors looking after her, but she must have her rest. But now that I think of it, maybe you should see her. The problem is the pieces, too many pieces..."

She eyed him uneasily as he paced and muttered to himself. Then he began punching the air and growling at some invisible foe.

Her pulse quickened. This man, like Paul Veliu, now held her fate in his hands. Was he a lunatic? What if everything he had told Paul Veliu was a lie, the delusions of a madman?

Suddenly Rius stopped and stared at her as if he'd just realized what he'd been doing. "What? Oh, yes, the confectionary. Soon, soon. Your research partner at the fortress is a young woman named Sierra Morgan. An exquisite mind, unmatched in her field. She's been with the Magnus Foundation since she was a child.

"I warn you now, Sierra isn't friendly. She isn't sane, and she can be quite dangerous. A blessing and a curse." His eyes gleamed as he rubbed his hands together. His whole torso underwent a bizarre, serpentine writhe that made her shudder. "Now, then, shall we see about those chocolates?"

# Chapter Nine
# Reunion

CHARLES FERGUSON TAPPED his foot on the brake. The Beauty obligingly slipped back below the speed limit. The ultra-luxury sedan Boris had given him had a remarkable habit of zipping from fifty-five miles an hour to a hundred every time he touched the accelerator. With twelve monstrous cylinders and who knows how many hundreds of horsepower, his new car was iambic pentameter for gearheads, a majestic paean to automotive engineering.

It also guzzled more gasoline than the Keystone Pipeline, which was a problem if you happened to be an environmentally conscious biology professor.

Blast it! Why hadn't Boris just bought him another boring, dung-colored grandma car?

They cruised along US-23 north of Johnson City. They were headed for the Home Office of the Anti-Trafficking Alliance in Bethesda, Maryland, the headquarters of Boris's agency.

Across the highway to his left lay a sea of rolling hills blanketed by forest. On the passenger side, a band of newly constructed homes clung together with postage stamp yards and streamlined architecture.

A tentative, lonely outpost of suburban sprawl, clawing away another patch of North Carolina wilderness.

"Don't you think I should drive?" Boris muttered from the back seat. He'd asked the same question four times now since they'd left Asheville.

"I appreciate the offer, Boris," he replied, "but you can't zip along at a hundred and twenty miles per hour when there's a four-year-old in the back seat."

"You could at least drive the speed limit," Boris muttered. "I buy you a dream car and you drive fifty in a seventy. It's criminal negligence!"

"You bought this car with *my* money, remember? And the speed limit's fifty-five."

"Those penpushers changed it?" Boris flung up his hands. "It should be a federal crime to lower speed limits. Well, if I can't drive, at least let me pick the music. That's only fair, don't you think, Nadia, my hyperborean angel?"

Nadia groaned. "Dad, we already listened to your favorite band for four hours straight on the way down."

"Don't worry, my celestial primrose," Boris replied. "I've moved on to new pastures. Tell me what you think of this."

Charles watched in the rearview mirror as Boris tapped on his phone to pair it with the car's Bluetooth system. A few seconds later, a gruff voice began howling lyrics through state-of-the-art speakers while a guitar twanged random chords and a drum pounded out a rhythm completely detached from the other instruments. It felt physically painful, an assault of willful dissonance, like a Jackson Pollock painting converted to music.

"Turn it off!" Nadia covered her ears with her hands. "It's terrible."

"Terrible?" Boris thundered. "This is legendary art, my darling! The Trout Mask Replica."

A saxophone joined the fray, wailing manic tones with the feral desperation of a wounded animal.

Charles was just about to shut off the volume when he noticed

Safiya grinning like the Cheshire Cat in the back seat and bobbing her head to the chaos. "Silly," she proclaimed with the authority of a four-year-old pontiff. *Silly* had been one of her first English words, but she was breaking out new ones every day.

Boris tousled her hair. "You like Papa Boris's music, don't you, my little dimpled seraph?"

Charles sighed. If the kid was happy, there was nothing for it. They were stuck with the screeching fish music for the long haul.

Seventy-five minutes and twenty-nine seconds after it began—not that he was counting—the music ended. Strangely, he was almost enjoying the lyrical chaos by the end, though he couldn't say why. Ten minutes later, Safiya and Nadia both drifted off to sleep. In the rearview mirror, Gavriel's SUV hovered behind them at the same distance it had kept since they left the campground.

"Mr. Charles?" Boris rumbled from the back seat.

"Yeah?"

"This business in Germany is bad news."

"Terrible."

"No…I mean, yes, of course it's tragic. But no one's ever seen a bomb like that. Only the Foundation could have that kind of technology. I'm going to send Raj over there to investigate."

Charles shivered. He'd had the same thought when he heard the news, but he didn't want to believe it. He wanted to block it all out—the Foundation, Magnus, especially Aryana Voss.

She haunted his thoughts, hovering on the fringe like some high-circling bird of prey. That funereal black dress and faintly translucent veil. That soft, silky voice. When he thought of her, he could hear the whine of the surgical drill as it eased its way toward his forehead.

"Do you know how the Foundation began, Mr. Charles?" Boris asked.

"Beats me. Research?"

Boris grunted. "In the old days, when Magnus's grandfather began his empire, they dealt in a single product. They bought and sold it around the world, and with that one product, they built the largest business empire on the planet. Can you not guess?"

Charles tapped the brakes again and veered left as a squirrel bolted across the road. The Beauty swerved as gracefully as an Olympic figure skater. "I don't know, diamonds?"

"People, Mr. Charles. The Foundation's first commodity was human beings, and they never gave up the business. After decades of failed attempts to stop them, the world's governments decided to fight fire with fire. They created my agency, the ATA. Our primary mission was to expose and destroy the Foundation. We knew they accounted for most of the trafficking industry, but we couldn't prove it."

"I'd say you got the job done," Charles said. "We freed all the slaves in Headquarters, didn't we? Magnus destroyed his own technology with his final orders. You took care of those Harvesters. Wherever Aryana Voss is, she's been keeping a low profile. You think they're behind the bombing in Germany, but we can't be certain, can we?"

"There's still a math problem," Boris replied. "Magnus moved hundreds of thousands of human trafficking victims every year. Many went to Headquarters, yes, but there was a second destination. We now believe the amount of human trafficking to that endpoint has multiplied since we destroyed Headquarters."

"Khatizan?"

Boris nodded. "They're smuggling them in on trains and diesels and cargo jets and hauling them to their prison factories. Younger kids work with their parents in the factories. Older ones get shipped off to military training camps."

Charles's stomach tightened. John Flying Hawk's mysterious emails were also going to Khatizan. Taken together, it meant the Magnus Foundation was still in business.

"I'm heading to New York soon," Boris went on, "and I'm not coming back without answers."

Charles sighed. Farewell to the quiet life, the mountain trails, and any hope of avoiding homicidal maniacs bent on global domination.

"When do we leave?" he asked. "We're going to Khatizan, right?"

Boris reached forward and squeezed his shoulder. "I sometimes forget how brave you are, Mr. Charles. One minute, you whine like a babushka. The next, you show the courage of a Navy Seal. But you're too valuable for a mission like this. This time, you'll stay here where it's safe. There's just one minor problem."

"What's that?"

"Safiya's birthday party. Could you move it up a few days so I won't miss it?"

Charles drummed his fingertips against the steering wheel. "What do you have in mind? Burger joint with a play zone?"

"Holy Mother Anastasia!" Boris's Russian accent flipped on like a switch. "A burger joint for my one and only beloved granddaughter? No, no, we're pulling out all the stops. Leave it to Papa Boris!"

∾

Two days later, Charles found himself sipping sugary iced tea—*cha yen*, the menu called it—from a cavernous maroon plastic cup. The Thai Paradise wasn't Wilford's, but if he had to spend the foreseeable future stuck at the ATA Home Office, it would have to do. Apparently, this was what Boris meant by pulling out all the stops.

He glanced across the room at a mural of golden elephants on the march, their trunks raised heavenward. Nadia slipped her hand into his. Thompson was perusing the menu. Across the table, Boris and Gavriel were whispering conspiratorially and casting the occasional glance in Safiya's direction. The rest of the old Project Aeternum team would arrive any minute.

"How was Florida?" he asked Thompson.

Thompson glared at him. "Worst vacation ever."

"Too much rain?"

"Didn't rain at all." Thompson threw the menu on the table. "I take that back. It rained the entire time, but only on me. A metaphorical

100

raincloud followed me around and poured misery on me the entire time. No surprises there. That same cloud has been spitting on me my whole life."

"I see." Charles cleared his throat. "Cherokee was nice. Mostly. We had a little run-in with some cockroaches, but other than that—"

"It's not fair!" Thompson blurted out. "Seriously, can't one woman, one decent, not insane, fair-to-moderate-looking woman, be remotely interested in me? Is that such an absurd request to make of the universe?"

"Asking the universe, are you?"

Thompson stirred the tapioca balls in his boba tea. "You know what I mean."

"I take it things didn't go well with Anna?"

"Oh, things went fantastic with Anna. At least, if your name happens to be Raj Bhandari."

Charles nearly spat out a mouthful of *cha yen*. "Raj? You're kidding."

"Turns out the two of them have been madly in love with each other for months now."

"But they hated each other in Headquarters. They were like a pair of feral cats."

Thompson groaned and covered his face with hands. "Don't say that. By the gods! You should have seen them pawing each other on that beach. Kissing so much it's a wonder they didn't both suffocate. Disgusting." He folded his arms and slouched in his chair. "On the plane ride here, Raj was talking about taking her on some trip to Germany. Doesn't that just give you happy little butterflies all over your intestinal tract?"

Charles shrugged. "At least you still had the beach."

"I barely looked at the ocean." Thompson brightened a little. "In fact, I got caught up on my digital life. That business with Magnus Headquarters set me back a virtual decade in *The Arnor Saga*. The guild kin were ready to toss me to the curb, but I showed up just in time to save myself. I was thirty-two character levels from the max. Thirty-two levels, Charles! So I put in some hard labor at the beach, and now I'm back on top of the virtual world."

"Um, you're talking about a video game, right?"

"No, I'm talking about *the* video game. The only one worthy of every waking hour that isn't devoted to superficial nonsense like sleep and comestibles. I ran raids like a madman to get back on top, and when I did, I reaped my reward. The apex of binary bliss, the delicate crème atop the digital cake. Vindolwynd."

Charles found most video games incredibly boring, a viewpoint that seemed to be shared by exactly no one from his generation. "Is Vindolwynd a what, a who, or a where?"

"Oh, he's a sniveling, snickering toadstool who thinks he's king of the universe. He's been jealous of me since the day we met on the Fjords of Fellhammer. We've dueled forty-three times, and do you know how many of those he's won?"

"How many?"

"None. Zip. Nada. He's a quintessential loser, the paragon of mediocrity, the patron saint of underachievement. One of the greatest joys of my life is pummeling the fragile half-dwarf Vindolwynd into a digital pulp. He'd puffed himself up in my absence and somehow got promoted to Guildmaster. I couldn't steal his title, but I made it abundantly clear to the entire guild that I'm back in the saddle. At least *that* world treats me gives the respect I deserve."

The doors to the restaurant swung open. Zhang Meiying, known among her ATA colleagues as the Chemist because of the potent tranquilizing agents she had invented, strolled in with her easy, catlike confidence. She turned and held the door open for Fazal in his wheelchair. Next came Raj, Anna, and Miguel. For the first time in weeks, the whole Aeternum team was back in one place.

Raj and Anna were holding hands.

"Oh my gosh," Nadia said in a loud whisper. "You weren't kidding, Thompson."

"It gets worse," Thompson muttered. "Much worse."

"Now that we're all here," Boris said, his voice unusually somber and free from even a hint of its usual Russian accent, "let's take a moment of silence to remember the victims in Berlin. We're thankful that Anna's family is safe, but many cannot say the same."

Charles closed his eyes and silently recited a prayer for the dead from the Orthodox prayer book. When he opened his eyes, Safiya was staring at him with wide-eyed curiosity. Apparently coming to some conclusion of her own as to what had just transpired among the grown-ups, she grabbed a blue crayon and dove back into her coloring book. She never stayed in the lines, and her color choices were as predictable as a hurricane. But from what he'd seen of modern art in museums, her whimsical creations rivalled those of far more enlightened masters.

"Now then," Boris went on, "business before pleasure. A few minutes before the bomb detonated in Berlin, a cloud surveillance camera sent footage of an undercover Russian FSB agent, Semyon Federov, leaving the Bann Commercial Building, the epicenter of the blast. Federov disappeared and is believed to be back in Russia."

Boris folded his arms over his chest. "Today's Russian regime commits many crimes, but they didn't do this. We believe it was the Foundation. Mr. Thompson, you told us weeks ago that Aryana Voss wasn't at Headquarters when it was destroyed. If you have anything else you'd like to share, we need to hear it now. I have the feeling you've been hiding something."

Thompson gave a nervous cough and slurped some boba tea through a thick green straw.

"Mr. Thompson?" Boris's eyes narrowed.

Thompson stopped slurping and cast a sheepish glance around the table. "You have to understand, Boris. I really wanted to go on that vacation. We all did. If I'd told you everything at first, you would have kept us caged up in that infernal ATA Home Office forever. It wasn't fair, not after what we'd been through."

"Go on, Mr. Thompson." Boris had switched over to his CIA

assassin voice. Calm and distinct with a razor-sharp edge beneath the surface.

Thompson cleared his throat. "Magnus had Aryana running an operation in Eastern Europe. Khatizan."

Charles felt an icy dread creep over him.

"What kind of operation?" Boris asked.

"Knowing her, I wouldn't be surprised if she's running the whole country. I mean, she used to be in charge of Control, you know."

"Actually, I *didn't* know," Boris growled. "And since you're in such a talkative mood, are there any other details you failed to mention when we debriefed you weeks ago and you swore you'd told us absolutely everything?"

Thompson ran a hand through his hair. "Jeez, I didn't think it mattered. Okay, here's the full scoop. One of the higher-ups in Control told me Aryana worked for over twenty years with Magnus's grandfather, but that must be nonsense. Magnus's grandfather died decades ago, which means Aryana would be in her eighties at least. Magnus had her running Alpha Financial behind the scenes. Rius is her righthand man, and Edwin Trapper's the lawyer for all her operations. Oh, and she fell in love with Alexander Magnus years ago when he was in college. Then she started showing her age, and he ditched her for some young foreigner. That's when Aryana just…disappeared. Everyone thought she was dead, that maybe Magnus had her killed or something. Then she suddenly showed up again, but she had changed. Frankenstein stuff, unnatural. Killing people with her bare hands, smashing walls with her fist—it's probably all nonsense."

Boris pressed his palms against the table and leaned across it so that he loomed over Thompson. "Mr. Thompson?" he said, his voice soft and cold as the snow on a Siberian tundra. The Russian accent was back in full force.

"Yeah?" Thompson squeaked.

Safiya looked up from her coloring book at Nadia with an inquiring glance. Nadia kissed her on the forehead and said something in Arabic. Safiya nodded and dove back into the coloring book.

"Perhaps you have Aryana Voss's phone number?" Boris murmured darkly. "Or do the two of you swap recipes in your spare time?"

Thompson had somehow turned even paler than usual. "That's all I know, I swear."

"If I find out that you're lying to me right now," Boris said, "I'll take you to Siberia and personally feed you to a pack of wolves."

"That's…that's funny, Boris."

"You think so, Mr. Thompson? You know, that's exactly what the brave terrorist Ivan Medorov kept saying, right up until the moment the wolves starting chewing on his—"

"Father!" Nadia cried. "You're at a five-year-old girl's birthday party, remember? No traumatizing five-year-olds on their birthdays!"

Boris threw his hands in the air. "She doesn't even speak English! How can I traumatize her if I'm speaking English? Now, if I were speaking Arabic…"

He rattled something off in Arabic, his voice changing in a flash. He sounded like he'd spent a lifetime in the blazing sun and blinding sands of some far-off desert. Fazal al-Najjar stared at him in evident disbelief. Whatever Boris said, it must have been funny. Safiya giggled, and even Fazal's usually somber face was lit with a smile before he sipped his tea.

Boris crossed to the other side of the table and clapped Thompson so hard on the back that his eyes bulged in their sockets. "Good news, Mr. Thompson! I'm forgiving you in honor of my one and only beloved granddaughter's birthday. Now bring on the vittles!"

The waiters appeared as if on cue, and the birthday meal sailed along with blessed smoothness. Charles relished the opportunity to catch up with his old teammates. Even Anna, understandably out of spirits after what had happened in her home country of Germany, cracked a smile as Raj talked about their vacation in Florida.

The moment the waiters hauled away the pad thai and pineapple rice, Boris and Gavriel vanished to the parking lot, returning a few minutes later with a monolithic, ten-pound cheesecake smothered in blueberry pie filling and strewn with plastic clowns, sugar sprinkles, and rainbows. Safiya's eyes grew wide as quarters when the two men plopped the massive dessert on the table in front of her.

Anna whispered something to Raj, who broke out into peals of goofball laughter. Love had mysteriously transformed the former James Bond of New Delhi into yet another monosyllabic caveman who couldn't take his eyes off his chosen female.

Probably for the best. The old Raj Bhandari would have already flirted with the waitress, the college-aged greeter by the front desk, and, for good measure, the whistling, earbud-wearing busgirl.

Boris reached over and tousled Safiya's hair. "Dig in, my darling. Gavriel and I have business to attend to."

Gavriel whisked out his tactical knife from its sheath under his jacket and stabbed the cheesecake with the stoic complacency of a serial dessert killer. Then he and Boris traipsed out of the restaurant with a mischievous air, like a pair of oversized Russian pixies.

Five minutes and several thousand calories worth of blueberry cheesecake later, the door to the restaurant swung open. Charles's jaw dropped as he beheld the sort of thing that could only happen in lurid nightmares or hikes in the woods with Boris Petrov.

A massive clown loomed in the doorway with its hands on its hips and its face smeared with garish makeup. An unlit Cuban cigar dangled from the corner of its blood-red mouth. It looked like the sort of clown the mafia would hire if it needed to kill all the other clowns and burn down the circus.

"Zeus above!" Thompson leapt behind his chair and held it out in front of him protectively. "If it's taking hostages, I nominate Charles."

The restaurant staff were nowhere to be seen. Either they had been warned in advance of the impending clown attack, or they were back in the kitchen dialing in a SWAT team.

"You think I'm taking hostages?" the clown roared in a thick Russian accent. "Not today, Mr. Pasty Face. I'm here for the birthday party!"

The clown bounded into the room. As it did so, it squeezed an enormous horn that hung suspended from a chain clipped to the pocket of its multihued coat. Instead of squeaking, the horn let out an ear-rattling sound that was somewhere between a Bronx cheer and outright flatulence.

The clown waved its hand in front of its nose. "Was that you, Pasty Face? We might have to check your diaper. Isn't that right, Safiya?"

"Oh gods." Thompson sat in his chair again. He ran his hand over his face. "It's just Boris."

Safiya squealed with delight as killer clown Boris inflated a long, narrow balloon and deftly twisted it into a butterfly. Safiya grabbed the butterfly and flew it around in little circles.

"I didn't know your dad did balloon animals," Charles said.

Nadia shrugged. "Neither did I."

Gavriel marched into the restaurant with an enormous red bag of the Santa Claus variety slung over his shoulder. He wore a matching red clown nose, but other than that, he looked the same as always, which meant he looked like a man who kept an assault rifle in the trunk of his car and knew how to use it.

"Happy birthday, Safiya," Gavriel said in his grim, monotone voice. "We're all so happy for you."

"That's right," Boris chimed in. "And we brought presents for everyone."

Thompson pulled the straw out of his boba tea and guzzled the rest of the drink down as if it were a mug of beer. "You calling the asylum, Charles, or should I?"

Boris snatched the Santa bag from Gavriel and tossed it onto an empty chair. He yanked it open and started pulling out presents bundled up in crinkly wrapping paper.

"One for Anna, one for Nadia, one for Safiya, one for Fazal, another for Safiya…"

Safiya's diminutive fingers fumbled with the golden ribbon wrapped around the first present Boris had handed her. Nadia helped her remove the ribbon and unwrap the paper with its images of balloons and confetti. Inside was a plain cardboard box. Safiya pulled off the lid. Nadia peeked in, gasped, and cupped her hands over her mouth.

"Father," she shrieked, "how could you?"

"What?" Boris raised his arms in exasperation. "She's a little girl. It's a doll, isn't it?"

"Yes, it's a doll. A doll with bullet holes in its face."

There was a time when Little Boris had been a stunning two-foot replica of Nadia's father, but that was before Franz Heimler had shot it twice in the head with his Tessara handgun. Now it looked like the pint-sized villain in a B-grade Halloween movie. On the bright side, Boris the Clown was no longer the most terrifying thing to be found in the Thai Paradise restaurant on that particular Tuesday afternoon.

Safiya pulled the Frankendoll out of the box, hugged it to her chest, then turned it around and sat it on the table.

Bullet Hole Boris stared at Charles with one good eye whose counterpart had jagged, z-shaped stitches running through it. The doll's white T-shirt had the words *I Brake For Hippies* emblazoned on the front in bold letters.

From the look of things, the other presents were as bizarre as Safiya's. Raj Bhandari got a miniature sailboat inside a glass vodka bottle. Anna was given a three-inch-tall cello with a hot pink disposable dental flosser for the bow. Fazal al-Najjar was holding what looked suspiciously like an Arabian princess doll at arm's length, while Thompson was spinning the wheels of a shiny red toy car. A Maserati, of course.

Then Charles noticed Miguel Velasquez. The balding Colombian held a picture frame in his hands. Charles couldn't see the photo from where he was sitting, but whatever it depicted had brought tears to Miguel's eyes.

"Is this..." Miguel's voice faltered. "Was this before the attack? It's nice to have another picture of my brother before he died. It's just—"

"Sweet Saint Hermogenes!" Boris cried. "What do you take me for, Mr. Velasquez? I may not get invited to the cotillion club, but I'm no masochist, especially when I'm wearing a clown suit. Your kid brother's alive and well. A friend of mine in Colombia took that picture last week."

Miguel looked like he was about to faint. "But…he was at my sister's farm when those Harvesters destroyed it. It was his birthday. He always went to the farm for his birthday."

"Look at the picture, Miguel. That glamourous siren draped around your brother is his next-door neighbor in Bogotá. It's true he dropped off the face of the earth right before the Harvester attack hit your sister's village, but that's only because he had fallen into the silky-smooth embrace of the divine Daniella Rodriguez."

"Daniella Rodriguez." Miguel repeated the name with reverence. He broke into a grin and wiped his eyes. "I can't believe it. Thank you, Boris."

"Don't thank me. Thank Daniella!"

"Can I see him?"

Boris shook his head. "Not yet, Mr. Velasquez. My friends in Colombia will send you updates, but after Mr. Thompson's tragically delayed revelation, friends and family are off limits. As far as we know, Aryana Voss believes you are all dead. Imagine what she might do if she knew you were alive and could use your loved ones to get to you."

Charles needed no warnings. When he'd first met Aryana Voss, he was a seven-year-old boy chained to a hospital bed while a screaming drill inched toward his skull. The less she knew about any of them, the better.

"Now," Boris went on, "some of you might be wondering why Mr. Velasquez here gets a real present while you get toy cars and dental flossers. Allow me to explain.

"Mr. al-Najjar, that doll you're holding represents your real-life Syrian princess. She's alive, well, and, according to her new invisible guardians, blissfully single. She mourns for you every day, Mr. al-Najjar.

She pines, she wails, she withers…but not too much. Your parents are also doing well. We assigned a team to watch over them shortly after the bombing of Flight 109. I was worried there could be retaliation given the amount of coverage the bombing received. Your name has been posthumously cleared of all that, but we'll keep the team in place for now."

Fazal's lowered his eyes. "Thank you, Boris." The twenty-year-old math genius blushed crimson. He almost never mentioned the Syrian girl he was in love with, but clearly the poor guy was smitten.

"Now for you, Doctor Mueller." Boris turned to Anna. "When we cleared out Headquarters, we found a charred but otherwise intact cello case. Inside was your grandmother's Leonhardt cello, alive but wounded. We sent it off to a luthier who has done a masterful restoration. You'll find it in your room back at the Home Office."

A teary-eyed Anna rose from her chair and wrapped Boris in an embrace. He patted her back, then blew his nose vociferously on a polka-dotted handkerchief tied to a whole string of handkerchiefs that he kept pulling out of his pocket until Safiya howled with laughter.

"And I can't forget my old agency buddy, the debonair Raj Bhandari." Boris walked behind Raj and curled his broad fingers around Raj's shoulders. "As you know, I'm shipping you off to Germany. I'm afraid you won't find any bronze-skinned sirens lounging about in decadent dishabille like the ones you and Thompson enjoyed in Florida. I also have the feeling you won't mind that deprivation as long as Anna goes along for the journey. And when you get back, you'll find your old sailboat waiting for you."

Raj patted Boris's hand. "Thanks, old man."

"Next is Mr. Thompson," Boris said. "Any man who loves Maseratis is a man after my own heart."

"Wait," Thompson's eyes widened. "You can't mean…"

"Cherry red," Boris replied. "Custom order. It'll be ready in a few weeks. But don't thank me. I spent your own money on it, just like I spent Mr. Charles's on the Beauty. Those OneScan devices of yours are still selling like hotcakes. And now, for my own dear children."

He plopped a crimson envelope in front of Charles and a green one in front of Nadia. "Go ahead, open them."

Charles slid the flap open with a butter knife. Inside was a postcard-sized coupon with a picture of Boris's face on each of the four corners. Written in a whimsical font in the middle of the coupon were the following words:

*ONE HUNDRED BORIS BUCKS*
*Need a break from Boris? These will do the trick!*
*(1 Boris Buck = 100 minutes)*

"I'm a man of my word," Boris said. "Nadia told me I needed to back off a little. A very little, mind you."

Charles did some quick calculating and realized that he held, in his hands, an entire week of Boris-free living. A hundred and sixty-six hours and some change. Seven whole days.

It was a miracle, a windfall, an act of divine mercy.

Seven days!

He could fly, he could dance across the table, he could kiss Gavriel right on his clown nose. Heck, he could whisk Nadia off to Vegas and get married.

"Thanks, Boris," he said in a tremulous voice, struggling to contain his excitement. "This is the best present I've ever been given."

He handed the Boris Bucks back to their namesake.

"What, you don't like them?" Boris asked.

"I love them," Charles said, "which is why I'm using them. All of them. Right now."

Boris put his hands on his hips. "I knew how it would be," he huffed. "Very well, I'll leave at once. Immediately. This very moment."

Charles blinked. "Wait...you don't have to leave *that* fast."

"Oh, but I do! I'm off to New York for a week. And now, my dear ones, laugh like children, eat like pigs, live like angels. Farewell!"

Boris planted a kiss on Nadia's cheek. Then he pulled out a whole menagerie of stuffed animals from the capacious pockets of his clown suit and piled them in a heap in front of Safiya. Backup gifts, apparently, in case the Frankendoll wasn't a hit.

"Goodbye, my little princess." He leaned down and kissed her forehead.

Then he turned to Charles and puckered his lips.

"Oh, no," Charles said. "No way."

Way.

Boris the Clown hauled him out of his chair, lifted him up in a bone-crushing embrace, and kissed him on both cheeks.

"Goodbye, Mr. Prunes and Prisms. You aren't a married man yet. You're not even an engaged man yet, so be a good little boy and don't do anything I would have done in the same circumstances when I was your age! And always remember, Little Boris is watching you. Every word, every moment, every movement. Watching…and listening!"

Boris patted the mangled head of his miniature replica doll, waved farewell to the rest of the party, and capered out of the room.

"Aren't you going with him?" Charles asked Gavriel.

Gavriel blew a gum bubble the size of an orange. It popped and flew back onto his face, which led to a squeal of laughter from Safiya along with the premature demise of Gavriel's clown nose.

Without even a hint of a smile at his own bit of comedy, Gavriel meticulously scraped the gum off his face with his tactical knife. It looked painful, but Charles had the feeling nothing short of dynamite could hurt the stoic Gavriel Abramovich.

"This time," he said, "the boss goes without me."

Chapter Ten

# Infiltrators

Alpha Financial's container ship, vast as a veritable sea monster, plowed through the open waters of the Pacific. Measuring in at fourteen hundred feet, the vessel had twenty thousand containers aboard. Its weight cleared two hundred thousand tons.

A half hour past midnight on the thirteenth of April, the ship drew near to America's Port, a massive, eternally bustling complex along the Los Angeles coastline. Every container but one carried the expected trade cargo. The exception, a green steel rectangle with Chinese characters painted on the sides, had been empty during the long days while the vessel navigated the waters of the Pacific on its journey from Shanghai.

It wasn't empty now.

The ship had received a visitor in the middle of the Pacific. Beneath the serene visage of a waxing crescent moon, a sleek, modern destroyer had pulled up alongside the container ship. Both vessels slowed, and a transport helicopter flew up from the flight deck of the destroyer and hovered over its neighbor at sea. A ladder was lowered from the helicopter, and in the ghostly light of moon and stars, a dozen tiny figures crawled down the ladder until they vanished on the deck of the container ship.

These twelve now sat in pitch darkness inside the dull green container. The air in their steel prison was close and heavy, the only circulation seeping in through an array of quarter-inch holes, invisible from a distance, that had been drilled into the container's four walls.

The twelve wore street clothes. They carried matching pea green backpacks and had wallets with U.S. passports and driver's licenses inside. They'd learned differing dialects of American English as children and spoke them with native fluency.

But they weren't Americans. They were Youth Corps Special Forces.

Paul Veliu was the eldest of the group. Aryana Voss had given him full command of the operation, answering directly to Commander Firlenko. The whole unit knew their initial missions, but Paul alone carried the orders that would follow.

He tapped his watch. An eerie green glow illuminated his strained features and those of the commandos near him. "Three more minutes."

"Yes, sir," eleven voices murmured in reply.

He glanced at the circle of solemn faces. Red Ops One, the highest-ranked strike force in the Youth Corps. They'd carried out dozens of flawless wartime attacks within the borders of Khatizan and clandestine operations in neighboring countries. Skilled, disciplined, and fearless, they were the finest the Youth Corps could offer. Despite their youthful faces, each one was a finely tuned killing machine.

Like all Khatizan's special forces units, Red Ops One was divided into triads, groups of three team members who always worked together on missions. The First Triad in Red Ops One had lost their team leader in their last mission, so Paul was taking his place. He would lead three triads to the target location to prepare for their operation. The fourth triad would fly to New York first to meet a double agent who had infiltrated American intelligence and carry out a mission with him. Afterward, they would rejoin Paul and the others on the following morning.

The shrill call of a Coast Guard siren broke the silence. The mammoth container ship slowed to a crawl and then stopped altogether. They heard footsteps running along the deck and shouts from the crew.

"This is it," Paul said in Khatiz. "Stay calm."

The siren drew closer and then ceased. Five minutes later, the door to their container was unlatched and flung open. Blazing sunlight temporarily blinded the twelve commandos. Two figures stepped into the container's doorway, their silhouettes framed against the light.

"This is the United States Coast Guard. Anyone in there?" one of them announced in a stentorian voice.

"Yes, sir," Paul shouted back with a convincing Texan accent. "We're Americans. College students, sir. We were out backpacking in Moldova. Next thing we knew, we got ourselves shanghaied by a bunch of thugs and ended up in Khatizan. We paid a guy to smuggle us out of there."

There was a long pause. Paul could feel the tension rising among his team. Had the rendezvous gone wrong? Was their contact a traitor?

If so, the contact would die. So would everyone else on that Coast Guard ship. They were still outside the port, barely within U.S. territory. It wasn't too late to escape.

"Is this true?" the man shouted back in fluent Khatiz. "A dozen American college students get kidnapped, and it's not even on their evening news? What's happened to the legendary Western press?"

A few of Paul's team members laughed nervously.

"Lighten up, comrades," the man went on, walking deeper into the container. "It's an honor to serve the Fatherland. I'll take you to the airstrip. You'll be armed and ready for your mission within hours. Death to the foreign imperialists. Death to America!"

"Death to America!" a dozen Youth Corps commandos shouted in reply, though Paul couldn't fake the enthusiasm of his comrades.

As he rode in the cabin of a convincing but fake Coast Guard patrol ship, Paul flipped through the images of their first target on his phone. A three-story building secured with a twelve-foot perimeter wall. Cameras mounted everywhere, of course, and no end of heavily armed personnel to defend every avenue of attack.

Those defenses wouldn't matter when the time came. Once their agents had blown things apart from the inside, the rest would be child's play.

The final image was a mission summary in two lines of text.
*Unit: Youth Corps Red Ops One*
*Initial Target: ATA Home Office*

## Chapter Eleven

# Double Agent

Boris Petrov's footsteps resounded through the concrete stairwell in measured, rapid succession as he jogged up the flights of stairs. He had a dull ache in the muscles of his arms and legs, the result of an aggressive predawn weightlifting routine at a local gym.

Gavriel and the others back at the Home Office called him the *old man* now. Not to his face, but behind his back when they didn't think he was listening. But this old man had good hearing, and he wasn't about to let life slow him down yet.

"On your right," his baritone voice announced by way of warning as he overtook Jon Dasher, the mild-mannered pinstripe suit and tie from the legal office on the third floor. "Morning, Jon." As a security measure, Boris had memorized the identities of most of the employees in the building. He only came to this New York location a few times a year, but it was good practice. Another way to keep the mind sharp, to hold off the dulling grindstone of Father Time.

Jon raised his right hand, which clasped a Styrofoam coffee cup, to return the greeting. His eyes were fastened on his smartphone, which blasted out the tinny roar of a sitcom laugh track as Boris passed him. "Good morning, um…what was your name again?"

"Sergei."

Sergei Ivanov. One of several cover identities Boris had worn over the years, though facial recognition software was rendering that species of deception impractical.

By the time he'd reached the fifth floor, Boris had worked up a sweat. The flat of his hand slammed into a stainless-steel push bar, shoving open the exit door. He entered the hallway and took a detour at the men's room, where he wet a few paper towels and wiped the perspiration off his face and neck.

He examined his reflection in the mirror. The family curse from his mom's side had made its presence known over the past year in the cowardly retreat of his hairline. He now kept his hair clipped within a quarter inch, which made the balding less noticeable and had the pleasant side effect of making him appear more youthful.

No, he hadn't let himself go. Quite the opposite. Elena would have liked that. She had always respected his strength of will, his self-discipline.

What would she look like now? How many times had he tried to imagine the changes that the passing years would have worked into her features?

He ran a hand along his manufactured facial hair. When he transformed into Sergei, he wore a thick, salt-and-pepper beard that hung down almost to his chest. It was incredibly lifelike thanks to Kenjiro Nakamura, his team's operations manager, who had gone out of his way to make Sergei's persona authentic. No matter what needed to be done, no matter how obscure the request, Kenjiro always found a way.

He threw the paper towels in the trash and went back into the hallway. He swung right at the first intersection, scanned a name badge on the scanner next to the doorway, and entered a bustling office. He wound his way through a sea of cubicles until he came to an isolated desk in the back corner, where he sat in a burgundy-cushioned office chair and turned on a desktop computer.

The warranty servicing operation was in full swing, the phones ringing constantly and seventy-three voices talking into headsets while a handful of supervisors meandered about on patrol to smooth over the difficult cases. In most of the office, every inch of available space had been commandeered for corporate use. The exception was the ten-foot perimeter around Sergei Ivanov's island of a desk.

A part of him missed the old days, before facial recognition and military drones and basement-dwelling hackers. The modern techniques were too impersonal. You hid behind a screen and went to war with people on the other side of the world who were also hiding behind their screens. Where was the courage in that?

Bravery was irrelevant now. Adapt to the times or be crushed by the tidal wave of history. That's why he came to this office. When he needed to access the most sensitive information from other intelligence agencies, he gathered it from a neutral location. Another one of Kenjiro's ideas, and Kenjiro was always right about such things. If any flags were raised, the blame would fall squarely on the shoulders of Sergei Ivanov, a reclusive Russian who usually worked remotely but made an occasional live appearance at his dead-end customer service job.

But he wasn't the only agent in the office. Lenny Phillips, a CIA programmer, ran the cover business, and Lenny made sure the security cameras were off when his old buddy Sergei came to visit.

Boris mumbled to himself while he typed, a steady monologue that mingled with the tapping of his fingertips on the keyboard and the clicking of the mouse.

As the hours ticked by, a few braver souls from the sales department wandered past Sergei's island cubicle, presumably on their way to the storage closet in search of paper clips or staples for the copy machine. The boldest of these wandering spies delicately hinted to the office manager, the plump, sweaty, curly-haired Lenny, that the huge weirdo in the corner wasn't doing his job.

Lenny straightened his coke-bottle glasses and responded in a voice that brooked no reply. "I've got Sergei on a special task from corporate. Now get back to work."

Shortly after noon, Boris rose and stretched, pulled an insulated lunch bag out of his backpack, and proceeded to consume two sandwiches stuffed with tuna along with a boiled egg, an apple, a banana, and a single piece of dark chocolate. He then left the office and went down the hallway to the stairwell, raced down the steps, and charged back up them at his usual jogging pace. He returned to the bathroom, wet the paper towels, wiped off the sweat, and went back to work.

"The emails are our only path," he muttered at three thirty-seven after a long period of silence in which nothing had been heard from his cubicle, not even the clicking of the mouse or the tapping of the keys.

A series of random numbers filled the leftmost monitor and continued across two additional screens to the border of the rightmost. He had stared at the numbers for the last twenty minutes. He had been hoping the code might be related to the mysterious pattern of letters and numbers John Flying Hawk had given Mr. Charles, but he couldn't find any obvious connection.

He forwarded the file, clicked on the mouse, and watched as the email vanished into the cybernetic expanse of the Internet. Time to talk to Lenny.

A few moments later, Lenny Phillips stepped out of his office, nodded in the general direction of the island cubicle, then went back into his office and shut the door.

Lenny would help, then.

At twenty minutes to five, Boris stood up, threw his backpack over his shoulders, and made his way toward the door. Lenny scrambled out of his windowed office to intercept him.

"You busy tonight?" Lenny asked, wiping donut glazing from the corner of his mouth. One screen of the double monitors on Lenny's desk had a spreadsheet and an email program tiled side-by-side. The other screen was occupied by *The Arnor Saga*, an online video game

Lenny played forty hours per week at the minimum. Inside the CIA, *The Arnor Saga* was known as Crowdbreak. Given enough time, the code Lenny ran through that game could take down any encryption in the world.

"The usual place." Boris patted Lenny's shoulder and walked out of the office without another word.

∽

That evening, Boris perched on the edge of a secondhand, cobalt-blue sofa in an apartment rented under Sergei Ivanov's name. On the wall beside an ancient CRT television and an even older VCR hung a paper photocopy of one of Hokusai's *Thirty-six Views of Mt. Fuji*. The decor embodied the persona of his alter ego, Sergei Ivanov, a recluse whom time had passed by, a man who read Graham Greene novels and believed ancient voices like Epictetus still had something to say to the world.

The doorbell buzzed at exactly eight thirty. Boris peered through the peephole and saw Lenny Phillips huffing and wiping the perpetual sheen of sweat from his wide brow.

He opened the door.

"Mind if I have an energy drink?" Lenny barged in. "Elevator's broken again."

"Be my guest."

Boris didn't do energy drinks, and neither would Sergei. That nonsense was for the kids.

Lenny plopped down on the sofa, which made the dated wooden frame creak and the stained cushions sag in the middle. Boris went into the kitchen, pulled out two of the red and black canned drinks that he kept stocked in the ancient Frigidaire, and set them both on the coffee table in front of Lenny.

"Thanks, Sergei. Or is it Boris tonight?"

Lenny popped open the lid of the first energy drink, downed it in a series of vociferous guzzles, and crunched the can together between his thick fingers. He always made a weird, grunting roar when he crushed cans, like a four-year-old kid trying to be a lion. A few seconds later, Lenny let out a moist, hair-raising belch.

Boris made no comment. Lenny was the kind of guy who needed a lot of psychological escape vents.

"I've decided to become Assyrian," Lenny announced.

Boris blinked. "To become what?"

"Assyrian."

Boris arched an eyebrow. "You can't *become* Assyrian, Mr. Phillips. It's not like going vegan or grounding yourself or any of that other self-improvement hogwash."

"I know," Lenny said. "Assyrians live in the Middle East. Well, most of them. I've been reading up."

Boris shook his head. "Your hair's bright ginger and curlier than a bedspring. You're two hundred and fifty pounds after a fad diet, and your skin looks like you just took a bath in marshmallow fluff. You can't be Assyrian, I can't be Chinese. Life is cruel."

"Hey, this is the 21$^{st}$ century, pal. I'm going full Assyrian. She's worth it."

"Ah. Who's *she*?"

"Bookstore beauty. I'm telling you, Boris, if the scale goes to ten, this girl's an eleven."

"You went to a bookstore? Didn't you tell me you hadn't read a novel since high school?"

Lenny shrugged. "They've got comic books. Women read, so that's my angle. I like bookstore women. They're not ashamed of their gray matter, you know? You should have seen her, Boris. She was just standing there by the comic book rack like some Mediterranean fertility goddess. Transcendentally hot in every conceivable way."

Boris scratched his fake beard. They both knew Lenny wouldn't have a snowball's chance with a woman like that.

At least, he hoped they both knew.

"Did you talk to her?" he asked.

"Heck yes, I talked to her. She'd just picked up a Captain Fuzzbucket. I kid you not. It was that one where he gets eaten by a transgalactic tapeworm and has to use his proton disphaser to warp himself into the Underverse."

"So what happened?"

"Uh, let's see…Captain Fuzzbucket disphases himself into a Beastbot Fortress in the Ninth Sector—"

"I meant the woman. What'd you say to her?"

"I told her Captain Fuzzbucket was my all-time favorite. She smiled at me, Boris. I think she was into me."

"Did she say anything?"

Lenny nodded. "Sure. She apologized and said she was Assyrian."

"She apologized?"

"Yeah, I told her it was no big deal. She's Assyrian, I'm fat. Who cares?"

"You said that?"

"Of course I said that. What? It's not like she didn't notice I'm fat. Everybody knows I'm fat."

Boris took a sip of iced tea. Sweet as maple syrup, just the way Julia Pearson liked to make it. "What did she say after that?"

"She apologized again and said she was Assyrian."

"That's all she said?"

"Yeah, and that's when it hit me. That's all she *could* say. She doesn't speak English. Well, unless you count saying, *Sorry, I'm Assyrian.*"

"Good on you for trying. anyway."

"Hey, I wasn't done. I improvised. Wrote down my name and phone number and told her that if she called me in two weeks, I'd talk to her in Assyrian. So that means I've got to get myself Assyrianized real fast. Or is it Assyrianated?" Lenny took a swig from the second can of energy drink and then chuckled, which caused green fluid to seep out from the corners of his mouth. "Check it out."

He pulled some books out of a cloth shopping bag.

*My Life Among the Assyrians by Azulhami Rashgar*
*Middle Eastern Marriage Customs*
*A Complete Assyrian-English Dictionary*

Boris peered into the depths of Lenny's soulful eyes.

"That's one heck of a plan, Mr. Phillips."

"Thanks, pal."

Boris brought out a bag of tortilla chips and poured the contents into a mixing bowl. He and Lenny downed them with salsa while they watched a high-octane detective show. The show was Lenny's favorite and a part of their ritual whenever Boris came to town. First nonsense and energy drinks, then TV, and finally business. You had to know how to work with people like Lenny Phillips. The rewards were worth the effort.

"Now what about the emails?" Boris asked after the show ended on an absurdly improbable cliffhanger.

"I've got the guild working on it," Lenny replied. "We'll get them figured out. Speaking of which, I'd better run. We're doing a raid at ten. That encryption's a beast, so the guild and I are going to need all our wits about us. It's good seeing you, Boris. I'll let you know the moment we've cracked it."

"Catch you next time, Lenny. Wait, I forgot to ask you something."

Lenny stopped with his hand on the door. "What's up?"

"Your handler doesn't suspect anything, right?"

"Don't worry, they're not keeping close tabs on me. I mean seriously, I spend five hours a day programming a video game and eight hours a day playing it. I'm giving them all the intel they ask for, so nobody's going to notice if I run a few extra algorithms through the blender."

"You're a hero, you know that?" Boris said. "You've saved a lot of lives since you started helping the ATA on the side."

"Hey, thanks, Boris. I appreciate that." Lenny puffed out his chest a bit, which made his stomach look even more expansive. "Wish me luck with the bookstore girl. I think she might be the one."

"You don't need luck, Mr. Phillips. You need a miracle."

Lenny flashed his lopsided grin. "If the Cubs can win the World Series, I can get a phone call."

"I hope he's wrong about that goddess business," Boris murmured after the door closed. He'd once seen a statue of a Mediterranean fertility goddess in an art museum. The statue was six inches tall. Its thighs were six inches wide.

Not a pretty sight.

He turned off the television and grabbed his 9mm from its holster, which he'd slung onto a weathered coat rack by the door. He slid the handgun under one of the sofa's throw pillows and leaned back on the couch.

Strange that the only man in the world who might be able to break the encryption on John Flying Hawk's emails to Khatizan was an overweight, thirty-something nerd who hauled in eye-popping checks from the CIA for playing a video game. Or, to be accurate, playing, modifying, and manipulating the most advanced video game on the planet, harvesting the collective brainpower of millions of gamers worldwide to break through advanced encryption algorithms.

Day after day, week after week, year after year—Lenny didn't take vacations from his digital life.

Boris, on the other hand, needed a real vacation. That trip in the woods should have done the trick, but he'd been so worked up about Mr. Charles that he'd hardly slept. A tragedy. The one man who deserved his daughter had a modified brain that was a ticking time bomb. Sooner or later, the detonator would trip, and Mr. Charles would be reduced either to lunacy or a vegetative state.

The file he'd found in Magnus Headquarters had been explicit. There had been other child research subjects in the Paragon Project. Most had not survived. Only John Flying Hawk, Sierra Morgan, and another mystery patient had managed to keep some thread of sanity.

Judging from their personnel files, those threads were precariously slender.

That Mr. Charles had made it so long had been considered miraculous by the Foundation researchers. But it was a miracle with an expiration date, and the writing was on the wall. On the neurons, rather.

He closed his eyes and pictured little Safiya as he had last seen her, clutching Little Boris like the doll was her best friend in the world. He drifted off to sleep and was awoken by the sound of footsteps outside the front door to the apartment.

He checked his watch.

A few minutes past midnight.

He reached for his handgun. In the same moment, the door to his room flew open under the force of a terrific blow. Before he had time to draw his weapon, three officers in full tactical gear stormed into his apartment. He found himself on the business end of an equal number of assault rifles.

"Merciful Saint Prisca," he muttered.

Ground Branch officers, the special forces of the CIA. They ranked among the deadliest military outfits in the world.

He would know. He used to be one of them.

But what were they doing in Sergei Ivanov's humble apartment?

"Drop the gun," one of the soldiers barked. He had a faint accent beneath his believable American English, like traces of an older engraving on a palimpsest. "Slow and easy."

A short, bullish man with a dark navy trench coat and matching fedora stalked into the room. He looked to be in his late thirties, hair thinning in front but lacking even a hint of gray.

"Kids these days," Boris muttered as he placed his handgun onto the coffee table. "I take it you're Lenny's handler?"

"That Russian brain of yours works quick," the man replied in a voice so deep it could have originated in the depths of his polished loafers. He signaled to the Ground Branch officers, and they lowered their rifles. "Scan the place," he ordered. "Not that I think you'll find anything. This one's old school."

One of the Ground Branch officers pulled out some kind of handheld scanner, a device Boris had never seen, and began roaming around the room, holding it up toward the walls and floorboards, pointing it at the ceiling. Looking for bugs, of course—hidden cameras, microphones, anything that might be phoning home.

There was nothing to find. Boris crossed his arms over his chest and examined Lenny's handler. The man looked like a bean counter out enjoying a field trip with the boys instead of answering phones and kowtowing to bureaucrats. His outfit belonged in a budget spy movie. Why not just wear a sign that said *G-man* in fluorescent letters?

"You want me to call you Sergei or Boris?" Lenny's handler asked.

"Boris is fine. And you are?"

"Special Agent Rod Walker." Rod walked up to him and shot out a pudgy hand attached to an arm that was stiff as a ramrod. "Central Intelligence Agency."

"How subtle." Boris shook hands. "Next time, come alone and knock on the door instead of breaking it down. If you give me a heads-up, I'll even make popcorn."

"Warn you so you can blow my brains out?" Rod replied with a throaty chuckle. "No thanks. Hand over your phone. Unlocked."

"Over my dead body."

The left corner of Rod's lip curled upward. "If you'd like."

One of the Ground Branch officers raised his rifle again. Boris slowly withdrew his phone from his pocket, scanned his fingerprint to unlock it, and handed it to Rod.

Rod tapped around for a few seconds and handed it back. "This app right here…unlock it, too."

Boris took the phone and looked at the app Rod had opened.

Sweet Saint Iakovos.

Rod had opened the ATA's tier one messaging program, which was encrypted and disguised as a popular weather app. Only a dozen of the highest-ranking ATA personnel knew of the app's true purpose, and they used it solely for exclusive communications with each other.

None of those people worked for the CIA.

"I can't open it," he lied. "Forgot the code."

"Oh, I think you'll find a way," Rod replied coolly.

Boris set the phone on the table. "Your confidence is inspiring. We both know I *can* open it. But I won't."

"Always the Boy Scout, aren't you? Well, we've got other ways in, so I'll settle for the easy stuff tonight." Rod snatched the phone back, tapped on it for a few minutes, then handed it back.

"Who's this Leon Bates you've been texting?" he asked.

Boris carefully masked any sign of his own shock at the question.

Leon Bates was Lenny Phillips's CIA codename, a codename that would have been readily known not only to his handler, but also to anyone remotely involved with the Crowdbreak operation.

Which meant, of course, that Rod Walker wasn't in the CIA's Science and Technology division at all. This op was almost certainly unsanctioned, which meant those Ground Branch officers closing in around Boris could be anything from rogue operatives to outright terrorists.

They were here to kill him. There was no other explanation for that amount of firepower. His time had come, but if he played along with their game, perhaps he could lead them away from their true target.

Mr. Charles, no doubt.

"Leon's an old friend of mine," he replied, keeping his voice relaxed. He'd been in these situations more times than he could remember. Rod would know he was lying, but it was a lie he'd expect from a fellow intelligence agent under the circumstances. It kept the game moving.

"You've got a checkered past with the agency, Mr. Petrov," Rod said, "so when we learn you're holding out on us, we get worried real quick."

Boris grunted. "They must not let you out of Langley very often, do they, Special Agent Rod Walker? When you get back to your office, you should read up on how to conduct an interrogation. For starters, your Ground Branch friends aren't helpful."

Rod's thick lips parted into a grin. "I'll do that, Boris. And to answer your question, I only leave the office when I'm taking the ladies to Aruba."

"Your wife and daughters?"

Rod peeled off his trench coat and sat in a muddy brown recliner with duct tape on the cushions. He hoisted his polished loafers onto the coffee table. "Never married. Take my girlfriends down there. Not all of them at once, you understand." He punctuated his words with a mechanical laugh as if it were part of a script. "Keeps me busy, let me tell you. Women all go crazy for that place."

Whatever Rod Walker was, one thing was plain as day. The man almost certainly didn't have a girlfriend. Between the bizarre voice, the glaring lack of any physical attractiveness, the desperate boasting, and the fact that he likely worked for terrorists, he was probably worse off than Lenny Phillips with the ladies.

"So, Mr. Walker," Boris said as he tucked his phone back into his pocket, "what brings you to my apartment?"

Rod shrugged. "The usual. Information." He dug in the inner pocket of his trench coat, pulled out an envelope, and tossed it on the table. "You ATA boys are getting a little sloppy, dragging live corpses out in public. Care to explain?"

Boris snatched the envelope off the table and tore it open. He stifled a gasp.

Inside were photos of Anna Mueller, Raj Bhandari, and Eugene Thompson. They'd taken their approved vacation at a private beach on Florida's east coast, but Raj and Anna had begged their ATA security detail to give them one afternoon at a public beach. Boris had balked at the request but eventually caved in. What harm could it cause? It wasn't like anyone was actively looking for them.

Or so he had thought.

"Now Langley doesn't go for zombies and aliens and all that," Rod went on, "but when the mortal remains of three deceased, top-level researchers go frolicking on a Florida beach during offseason, well, that gets our attention."

"Thanks for the warning." Boris tucked the pictures back into the envelope and slid it across the table to Rod. "They deserved a break. Life is challenging when you're officially dead."

Rod leaned forward. "I wouldn't know about that. Care to fill me in?"

"You'll have to talk to my director."

"We thought you'd say that." Rod swung his loafers off the table and stood. "Even loose cannons like you hit the target every now and then. You blew a ten-inch hole through the bullseye when you got rid of Alexander Magnus, didn't you? Quite the hero."

Rod's voice had taken on an ice-cold edge. His eyes gleamed with fury. Any lingering doubts in Boris's mind vanished. Rod worked for the Magnus Foundation, which meant the Foundation knew that Raj, Anna, and Thompson were alive.

He hoped Miguel and Fazal were safe from exposure. At least they would be lower priority targets.

Mr. Charles, on the other hand, would be on top of the Foundation's wanted list.

He let out a sigh. "Kill me and be done with it, Mr. Walker. You're not getting any information."

Rod's eyes widened. He reached into his mouth and pulled out a thin electronic device that had rested behind his front teeth. When he spoke again, his voice was at least an octave higher. It had also switched from an American accent to one that sounded almost Russian with just enough of a difference to distinguish it. Khatiz, perhaps? "Well, it was a fun game, Petrov. Where did I make a mistake? Let me see…oh, yes, it must have been Leon Bates. A foolish question, was it? But who could he be? You're close to Thompson and the other two, so no need for codenames with them. And you don't come up here often, do you? I'm guessing Leon is that fat man you visited today, the one you called

Lenny. And since I should have known about him already, he must be CIA. I've wormed my way into all kinds of secrets, but they must have kept him from me. Very good. We'll check in on him as well once our next mission is finished."

Boris lowered his head. Lenny Phillips's fate was sealed. The Foundation would torture everything they wanted out of the poor video game addict right before they put a bullet through his skull.

"Lenny's nobody," he muttered. It didn't matter what he said. They already knew. "He's just a civilian I've hired to keep an eye on someone else."

"And you would never lie to me, I'm sure," Rod said with a fiendish grin. "We'll talk to him just in case. Aryana Voss never forgives, Boris. She wants revenge. She wants everyone to pay, and they will. We're going to tear you apart, one piece at a time. You went camping with Charles Ferguson, didn't you? You and Charles and Nadia and… what's his name, Gavriel? And that little foreign slave girl you're dragging around with you. Dug her out of Headquarters, right? You want my advice? Don't get too attached to her. That kid is a Reap, Boris. The Foundation will finish what it started. The Reaps still have an expiration date, and it won't be long."

Rod tossed a photograph on the table.

"We're always a step ahead."

Boris looked at the picture.

Lord have mercy.

An overhead image of him, Gavriel, and Mr. Charles near John Flying Hawk's cabin moments before it was destroyed by a military drone. Likely the same drone that captured the surveillance photo.

"You're going to watch them suffer, Boris. Your world will crash down around you, and you'll be powerless to stop it." Rod snatched the photo from Boris's hand. "You should have stayed in the CIA with your overweight friend."

It felt like the room was spinning. This was it. These were his last moments. He glanced at Rod, then lunged for his pistol on the table. At least he wouldn't go down without a fight.

Rod snatched the gun away before he could reach it. Two of the fake Ground Branch officers grabbed him from behind, yanked him back onto the couch, and pinned him down.

"So predictable," Rod said. "After what you did to Lord Magnus, I'd love to kill you myself. I begged her to let me, but that's not how this is going to work. She wants you alive, wants you to feel what it's like to lose the things you love the most." He slipped back into his trench coat. "We've got some more social calls to make. Sorry you won't be able to join us." He signaled to the others. "Tie him up. No, wait. A goodbye present first."

Rod pulled some brass knuckles out of his coat pocket and slipped them over the fingers of his right hand. "She said I couldn't kill you. She never said I couldn't damage you."

One of the fake Ground Branch officers wrapped his arm around Boris's neck and pulled him backward, lifting him off the sofa. Rod Walker lunged forward and slammed the brass knuckles into the right side of Boris's chest.

There was a sickening crunch as the metal connected with his rib-cage. Boris cried out in pain, then clenched his jaw firmly shut. He'd heard his own rib bone crack, but he wouldn't give them the pleasure of seeing his spirit broken. He bit his lip to keep from screaming.

The fake Ground Branch officer dropped him back onto the sofa. The other two tied him up with rope, none too gently. Rod reached into Boris's coat, took his phone, and tossed it on the floor. "Don't want you calling the cavalry too early."

Sweet Saint Nectarios, the pain was astonishing. He hadn't felt anything like it in years, not since he'd been kidnapped and tortured by that human trafficking gang in Guangzhou.

He blinked through watery eyes, trying to stay conscious.

"Gag him and stuff him in the closet," Rod said. "We'll call your pal Lenny tomorrow and tell him where to find you. Do us a favor and try not to die in the meantime. She wouldn't like her game to end early." Rod slipped the device back in his mouth. When he spoke, his voice had deepened again, and the accent was that of a New Yorker. He leaned down and patted Boris on the cheek. "See you soon, Petrov."

They dragged Boris into the bedroom closet, shut the door, and turned out the apartment's lights. He sat alone in pitch darkness, groaning and struggling against the ropes. The pain mounted until it became unbearable.

"Christ have mercy," he whispered just before he lost consciousness.

# Chapter Twelve
# Healer's Path

M IGUEL VELASQUEZ WATCHED the pair of double helix structures as they slowly rotated on the computer screen. A mystery lay buried in these genes. The DNA belonged to two presumably unrelated people, which should have meant distinct sets of genetic information. That wasn't the case. The two sequences deeply resembled each other, approaching a complete match with subtle differences.

The first DNA strand was from the blood of Alexander Magnus, gathered by an ATA autopsy after the fall of Magnus Headquarters. The other strand belonged to a mysterious old man from Headquarters who had been rescued from death by means of an implanted Phoenix, cellular technology with mind-bending regenerative properties.

The old man was nearing death once more, this time in a stateside hospital, and there were no Phoenixes left to save him. He hadn't spoken a word since they'd resuscitated him. In fact, Miguel wasn't sure that he could speak at all or understand anything they'd said to him.

The old man's DNA contained unnatural mutations, almost as if it had been intentionally altered. But why were the two strands so similar?

A closer match than even a parent and child. Magnus and the old man could have been twins if not for their age gap.

Their age…was it possible? Could the Foundation have unlocked even that mystery? Artificial acceleration might explain some of the abnormalities in the DNA. Perhaps the old man had been a sort of prototype. What if the connection between him and Magnus went beyond the boundaries of known science?

Miguel closed the analysis program. The riddle remained, but right now he had a more pressing task. A file box had arrived a half hour ago, delivered by a clean-shaven officer who looked like a college freshman.

"It's your new assignment," the courier had said cryptically. "From Boris. Top priority."

The box had remained on the corner of Miguel's desk while he took one last stab at the DNA mystery. The lid was sealed with packing tape.

"Okay, let's see what we've got."

He cut the tape and removed the lid from the box, revealing a row of bulging file folders. He took the first one out, opened it, and began to read.

Detailed notes of a brain procedure a seven-year-old Charles Ferguson had undergone as part of the Foundation's Paragon Project. That Magnus would carry out potentially lethal brain enhancements on children was no surprise at all. The shock was that he had succeeded. Miguel had worked with brilliant scientists at Magnus Headquarters, but when he'd met Charles Ferguson, he'd encountered genius on a different order of magnitude. Charles was an Einstein of biotechnology.

The next folders contained reports on other so-called Paragons. Along with Charles, three more, two boys and a girl, had survived the procedure, though the effects had damaged their sanity. One boy's name was listed as John Flying Hawk. The girl was Sierra Morgan. The other boy was cryptically referred to as Patient Three. The other Paragon test subjects, twenty-three in all, had apparently died within days or weeks of their operation.

He read through the files slowly, meticulously, absorbing the information as well as he could. As always, he envied Charles and his perfect memory.

Three hours later, he returned the fifth folder to the box. Twelve more to go. He'd barely skimmed the surface, but he'd learned enough to realize what Boris wanted. Either Miguel had to perform what amounted to a miracle or else Charles would slowly descend into madness.

From what the files said, the critical factor was dreams, or at least the memory of them. Charles had once told him that he never remembered his dreams. According to the reports in the files, the Foundation believed that was the key to Charles's sanity, an ongoing mental suppression that had protected him. The other surviving subjects were tormented by nightmares so horrific that they very well could be the root of their mental illness.

The problem was that Charles had started remembering his dreams at Magnus Headquarters. Vivid ones about Father Anatoly or prisoners in a concentration camp. What if the stress of Headquarters had weakened the protections set in place by his own mind?

Whether he realized it or not, Charles needed help. But how could they create a new medical treatment based on a box of files and reports? Granted, there were some blood test results from the other child subjects that might prove helpful, but what Miguel really needed was Charles himself. But if they brought Charles here and started poking him with needles, the stress could speed up his mental decline.

Miguel sat quietly in the chair, absently watching the second hand of a wall clock as it charted its patient, relentless revolutions.

If he couldn't have Charles nearby for testing, perhaps Boris could find one of the other survivors, John Flying Hawk or Sierra Morgan? But even if one of them could miraculously be found, the project was too much for Miguel to accomplish alone. He hated what he had to do next, but the sands of time were falling fast. Every grain brought one of his best friends closer to insanity. He pulled his cell phone from his pocket and found Raj's number. The international call took a few moments to connect.

"Miguel! How's it going, old man?" Raj Bhandari's crisp Indian British accent was music to Miguel's ears after a day of solitary research.

"I've been better. How's Anna?"

"She's still working through her grief," Raj replied. "Germany's in a very dark place right now. Half the country is demanding retribution against Russia, and the voices are getting louder by the day. It's hitting Anna hard. So many lives lost in the blink of an eye. She wants to see her family while we're here, but we both know it's too risky."

"Look, Raj, I'll be blunt," Miguel said. "How soon can you two come back?"

"Come back?" Raj chuckled. "We just got here a few days ago! Boris missing me already?"

Miguel glanced at the box on his desk. "Charles needs our help. It's serious."

"How serious?"

"The Foundation did something to his brain when he was a child. He was stable for years, probably thanks to his low-stress life at the university. After all that happened at Headquarters, we think he's become a sort of ticking time bomb. He could permanently lose his sanity if we don't figure it out fast."

He heard Raj's slow exhalation on the other end of the line. "We'll be on a plane tomorrow morning. Are you at the Home Office?"

"No, I'm at Julia Pearson's house in Beecher, Illinois. She and Peter are on their way to the Home Office, so I've got the place to myself. Oh, and Julia has cats. Lots of them."

Raj laughed. "Thanks for the warning. I'll tank up on antihistamines. And just out of curiosity, what made you want to go to Beecher of all places?"

∽

The setting sun glimmered through a celestial field of striated, lavender-gray clouds as Miguel turned onto the newly paved road leading to the hermitage. Soon starlight would blanket the night sky, and the pale, ethereal glow of a full moon would illuminate the monastery and its contemplative inhabitants.

He pulled the compact pickup truck the ATA had loaned him onto the driveway to Father Anatoly's hermitage, a rustic wooden cottage with two bedrooms and an open area that served as both a dining room and a place for the monk to meet with the numerous pilgrims who sought his spiritual guidance.

Miguel had become one of those pilgrims. Every evening after dinner, he would make the ten-minute drive from Julia Pearson's house to Father Anatoly's hermitage. The old monk always had a steaming cup of tea ready for him. They would sit on the porch and talk over the day's events, then head to the evening prayers at the monastery. The tranquility, the prayers, the tight-knit community—with each passing day, Miguel felt himself being drawn back to the faith he'd once held despite all the obstacles in the way.

The largest of those hurdles remained. Charles had told him the old monk would understand, but after years of negative experiences, he had his doubts.

"Welcome back, child!" Anatoly glanced up from pruning a vibrant and aggressive rosebush. The old monk seemed to possess boundless reserves of energy. In addition to the numerous services at the monastery, his own rigorous rule of prayer, and the constant visits from pilgrims, Anatoly also oversaw the massive communal garden he had brought to life, a place where schoolchildren from downtown Chicago showed up by the hundreds for field trips. The children tasted a world of silence and peace, calmness and stability, beauty and wonder and life. A world without the noxious cloud of gangs and drugs that enveloped so many of their neighborhoods.

Anatoly's latest project was on a more modest scale. He had planted a flower garden behind the hermitage. Two rectangular beds, each bursting with all the colors of spring.

The old monk would inspect every stalk and stem, sniff the blossoms, and whisper to the beetles and pillbugs and bees that ambled and flitted about.

"Look at this moth, Miguel." Anatoly waved Miguel over as soon as he stepped out of the truck. "Look at those spots on its wings! A living miracle, isn't it?"

Miguel grinned despite the burdens of the day. Anatoly had discovered a large polyphemus moth with vivid eyespots as it perched delicately on a pale violet blossom of an anemone.

A living miracle indeed.

For a silent moment that held, like a raindrop, the self-complete wonder of eternity, Miguel and the monk watched the moth gingerly crawl among petals that were huddled together like curious children. The moth broke into flight, flitting away into the growing darkness of the forest.

It was time.

He had enjoyed these evenings, and he would hate to lose them, but he couldn't keep his secret from the old monk any longer. Either Charles had been right or else Miguel had no business coming to this monastery in the first place. They wouldn't want him here.

"I need to tell you something," he said. "About myself."

He could hear Anatoly's quiet exhalation. "Go on, child."

Miguel pressed his lips together. It was hard to hope.

"I'm not what you think I am."

He hated this part. The confession, the exposure, the vulnerability. It was worse with religious people. Their faith rested on laws that condemned people like him. There could be no heaven without a hell, no paradise without torment, no sacred community without the excluded, the outsiders. For them to be saved, he must be damned. He was destined to be their scapegoat for all eternity, one of the numberless masses they would forget in their state of endless bliss. One they would never mourn, who would never move their hearts to the slightest pity through the ages. For if the hearts of the saints could be touched by the sorrows of the damned, wouldn't heaven itself become a hell to them? Wouldn't they abandon even heaven to help those in torment?

That was the crux of the matter. Not even the grandest divine love the world had ever known could save him. Such thoughts had tortured him since his childhood.

He cleared his throat.

"Father, I'm gay."

There. The truth was out. Now for the judgment.

But Father Anatoly just patted his shoulder. "Of course you are."

Miguel was too stunned to reply. He was trembling. He could hardly breathe. He'd been so careful to hide it since arriving at the monastery. There had been no outward sign, nothing that could have revealed it.

Nothing.

"How did you know?"

Father Anatoly's smile was tinged with sorrow. "When we pray for others, we begin to understand them. We start to carry their burdens. This is a mystery. This thing you have confessed, it causes you fear?"

"Yes." This was not the conversation he'd imagined. A glimmer of hope rose within him, but it was too early to know where the monk was heading. "I've always been like this. I can't remember a time when I wasn't. My mom said it was this way even when I was two years old. It never changed, though my dad tried his hardest."

"Sometimes that's the way of it." Anatoly's voice was calm, unperturbed. "Some find themselves at a crossroads and can choose which way they want to go, others feel no freedom, as if their path has been chosen for them. That's how it was for Father Arsenios at the monastery."

Father Arsenios?

Miguel had met the portly, middle-aged monk, perhaps in his early fifties, only the day before. He would never have guessed. "He's…like me?"

"He's very open about it," Anatoly replied. "If he had tried to keep it secret, no doubt it would have tormented him, maybe even destroyed him. It isn't all that uncommon in the monasteries. Many feel themselves drawn to this path. You should speak with him sometime."

Miguel ran a hand through his hair. "But my father, the kids at school in the village where I grew up, the priest at our church…" He fell silent. The list from his formative years in Colombia could go on and on. "They treated me like I was broken, defective."

Anatoly pulled out a clump of pigweed that had shot up amongst a cluster of multicolored hyacinths. "We are all broken, dear one. We are all defective. We all need healing."

Confession was over. Now to face the fear.

"Do you think I'll go to hell?"

Anatoly let the stalks of pigweed fall to the ground, then watched them with a curious expression, as if he sought among their sundered remains the answer to Miguel's question. "Tell me, where are you now?"

Miguel blinked. "I'm right here, Father. With you."

The old monk raised his eyebrows in mock surprise. "You mean you're not in hell?"

"Of course not." What could he mean by that? "We don't go to hell until after we die, right? This place, these evenings here…it's the best I've felt in my whole life."

Anatoly nodded. "A refuge for those who need it and a battlefield for those who serve them. Do not fear hell, child. Fear the things that bring it into our lives. Slavery to our own passions and lusts, indifference to the suffering of others. Above all else, fear the greatest evils, pride and hypocrisy.

"The enemy of our hearts is relentless, but Saint Makarios taught us that humility destroys all his schemes. When the love of Jesus takes root in our hearts, we come to life. The song of the sirens loses its grip over our minds. The conscience awakens, the will asserts itself, and we taste the sweetness of life, the reason we exist. The deepest hell cannot withstand the love of God. We were brought here to plunder hell, to empty it of its prisoners.

"To do this, we must sacrifice everything to save others. Material peace demands a high price, but this salvation costs us everything. We must lay down our lives. The war rages around us. Though we fear for the very survival of our species, we will not fail. The path ahead leads us into great darkness, but the love of God shall triumph."

Miguel felt as if his heart were burning. For the first time since he could remember, he dared to hope. He had no idea what would come next, but he knew, whatever it was, he would at least attempt it.

"What do I need to do?" he asked. "I can't change what I am."

"We are always changing." Anatoly ambled up the wooden porch steps toward the back door of the hermitage. "If we wake at all in this life, we wake to find ourselves slaves yearning for freedom. That freedom only comes when the image of God is restored within us. This is the work of Christ. We become like God in his actions, his energies. By grace, the chains around the will are broken, and we receive power to choose what is truly good. Now come, dear one, drink some tea."

Miguel remained a moment longer after the monk disappeared into the hermitage. He closed his eyes and soaked up the quiet murmuring of a spring breeze through forest branches. He had only comprehended part of what Anatoly had told him, but that part left a glimmering brightness, a spark already flickering into flame.

All those years wandering in fear, in darkness.

For now, he only understood one thing, but he knew it from the depths of his soul. It had been revealed to him day after day by the monk's actions toward him. A constant, unwavering reality, like the rising of the sun.

It didn't matter what secrets he revealed to Anatoly. It didn't matter what he had done or failed to do. He was running out of things to confess. Anatoly was a revered monk, a man who had dedicated his life to the pursuit of spiritual truth.

And yet, despite all Miguel had done, that same Anatoly loved him as if he were his own child.

The implication was obvious. The very thought of it brought tears to his eyes. It seemed too good to be true.

If Anatoly could love him, then God could love him, too.

He had no idea what the future would look like, what his path forward would be. Apparently, Father Anatoly was trusting God to handle that part.

He let out a deep breath, went into the cottage, and joined the old monk for tea.

# Chapter Thirteen
# The Attack

T HE HOME OFFICE of the Anti-Trafficking Alliance in Bethesda, Maryland lay exposed before the watchful eyes of Red Ops One like a prone gazelle before a pride of lions.

Paul Veliu led the First Triad—himself, Senan Bebaj, and Andrei Idrisov. They'd positioned themselves on the rooftop of a six-story hotel across the street from the Home Office. The other three triads were in position, the Second and Third Triads targeting different sides of the office while the Fourth Triad was prepared to infiltrate the holding facilities on the lowest floor of the building.

Paul peered through the scope of his bolt-action sniper rifle and aimed at one of the Home Office's rows of windows. He focused on an ATA guard who was positioned beside a doorway. He levelled the crosshairs over the guard's head, adjusting his aim as the target turned and walked down the hallway. He was a decent shot from a distance but little more than a novice compared to his silent teammate, Andrei Idrisov. Andrei's sniper skills were legendary among the Youth Corps.

Paul would have to pull the trigger when the time came, but he would take no lives today. He already had too much innocent blood on his hands.

"What kind of place is this?" Senan asked. "CIA? Military?"

"Neither." Paul leaned back from the scope. "They call themselves the Anti-Trafficking Alliance. They're posing as an international task force, but they're really nothing more than anti-Khatiz terrorists." Another Central Party lie, but he had to repeat it. For all he knew, his teammate could be secretly reporting to Commander Firlenko. Senan would do almost anything to get himself promoted, so the odds were decent. "This is their international headquarters. Our work today will cripple their operation for years, maybe permanently."

Senan pulled a black ski cap from his pack and donned it. "This won't be easy. They've got as many guards as the Chairman's Palace."

"Those guards will have other things to do after the detonation," Paul replied. "Here's the part I haven't told you. We've been given direct orders from Chairman Markhov to capture one of their most important assets and bring him back to Khatizan. Our contact on the inside will deliver him to the Fourth Triad after the attack begins."

"Where will our contact be during the attack?" Senan asked. "And the asset? What if we kill them by mistake?"

"Don't worry," Paul replied. "Our contact knows our plan. He'll secure the asset before the detonation and take him straight to the Fourth Triad. Begin firing the moment that perimeter wall goes down. We'll pull back exactly three minutes afterward no matter what. Detonation in…" He paused as he waited for the second hand on his watch to move into position. "Twelve minutes."

The mood among the triad changed to sober professionalism. Andrei, silent as death, took his position by the fire escape ladder. A half minute later, Paul and Senan were in place.

Paul took a deep breath and released it slowly. The rush of blood, nerves set on edge, his adrenaline-fueled mind lucid as a clear pane of glass, his whole being poised and ready—before Berlin, these had been the moments he lived for. To be the greatest of warriors, the hero who brings the storm.

Now he wanted nothing more than to throw down his rifle and leave. It wasn't a storm they were bringing to the ATA Home Office.

This would be a hurricane.

❦

Charles Ferguson stared into a full-length mirror nailed to the closet door of his quarters in the ATA Home Office. "You're an idiot," he informed his bedraggled reflection. "You've had plenty of time, and you just won't do it. What's wrong with you? Why are you dragging your feet?"

He reached into the inner pocket of his jacket and felt the jewelry box that held his mother's old engagement ring. He'd taken it to a jeweler before the Appalachian trip to have the stone polished and reset.

Boris, true to his word, had disappeared without a trace after Safiya's birthday dinner. The Boris Bucks had said it all. His future father-in-law had given his consent to their engagement and gracefully left the scene. Charles now had all the time with Nadia he wanted, even if that time included a five-year-old who was showing increasing independence and occasional outright rebellion as she became comfortable with her new guardians.

But he still couldn't bring himself to pop the question. Maybe it was the environment. The Home Office felt too sterile with its square tiles floors and its ceilings lined with fluorescent tube lighting. The hallways held a faint, perpetual aroma of bleach. You'd find more romance in the canned goods aisle of a crowded supermarket.

There was also Safiya. They'd find out in a month whether Nadia would become her adopted mother. If that immigration judge said no, what would happen next? He knew without asking that Nadia would follow Safiya to the ends of the earth, even if it meant moving to the Middle East and trying to adopt her there.

Could he move to the other side of the world for a five-year-old, giving up his country and his career?

He glared at his reflection. "What are you saying, you idiot? Of course you could. And you will, too, if that's what it takes. You don't deserve Nadia Petrova, and don't you forget it." He squared his shoulders and pointed at himself. "No more delays. Even if you have to kneel in the blasted lobby with the secretaries and ATA agents staring at you, you're putting a ring on her finger today."

He shoved the door shut, banishing the mirror and its mute reflection into the dark confines of the closet. He left his room, walked down the hallway past a half-dozen doors, and knocked quietly on the one leading to Nadia's room.

She opened the door and pressed her forefinger to her lips. "Safiya is still asleep."

He eased past her and took a seat at her breakfast table, where a thick green smoothie awaited him with the grim inevitability of fate. His stomach churned as he stared at the brimming cup of frothy, unpalatable ooze. These smoothies felt like drinking yard clippings, but Nadia had jumped on a six-week health kick scientifically proven by a lone, single-blind study to promote—of all things—telomere resilience. And resilient telomeres, as any fool knew, were the keys to a long and happy life.

She had begged him to join her, strengthening the argument with a kiss that had made his inner caveman leap and grunt for joy.

What could a mere male do against such heavy artillery?

On the second day of the shakes, he'd offered a feeble objection that an existence filled with indigestible green beverages wasn't worth living, much less extending. She'd informed him that it would taste better after a few days. Then she'd kissed him again, tousled his hair, and told him how thrilled she was that he was supporting her.

Thus died the feeble flames of resistance.

"I have a surprise for you." She raised her captivating gaze from her own cup of liquefied landscaping. He glanced at the far side of her room, where Safiya slept soundly on her four-inch foam mattress.

"Safiya drew another butterfly last night?"

Nadia shook her head. "She's moved on to rainbows. Dad told me a secret during the ride home, and I've kept my lips sealed for five whole days. Aren't you proud of me?"

A secret from Boris? Trouble brewing, and no two ways about it.

"It's nothing bad," she added. "Come on, guess."

"He's joining a commune?"

She burst out laughing, then clapped a hand over her mouth and looked at Safiya to make sure she was still asleep. "Guess again."

"I give up."

She clapped her hands together softly. "Peter and Julia are coming! They're already in town."

He grinned despite the stubborn presence of the lawn juice. By one of those strange mysteries of human interaction, Nadia's brother, Peter, and his caretaker, Julia, had twined themselves around his heart the moment he'd met them, instantly becoming an essential part of that mysterious, sacred space called Home.

"Does that mean Julia knows your dad's real secret now?" he asked. "The ATA and all?"

"Not exactly." She slurped the last bit of her shake. She could down the stuff like it was chocolate milk.

His turn now, blast it. He took a long swig. It tasted just like it looked. Lawnmower clippings after a trip through a blender.

"Dad told Julia we're alive," she went on, "so she knows more than most people. She thinks we're being kept here secretly as part of an FBI investigation involving your scanner."

"Not too far from reality." He forced down another thick gulp of green ooze. Pinching his nostrils shut did seem to help, even if it made him look more idiotic than usual. "What's the plan? Jello and green beans in the cafeteria?"

"Heck no!" She scrunched up her nose in disgust. Somehow, the same woman who could chug twelve ounces of powdered flora couldn't stomach a humble can of vegetables. "As soon as Safiya wakes up, we'll meet them at that coffee shop downtown."

"Just the four of us?"

She sighed. "I wish. Our dear friends in the suits and sunglasses will be keeping an eye on us. We're with Meiying again. And I saw a Brit chatting with her downstairs. Come to think of it, he looked a lot like that guy who used to work at Wilford's."

Charles had just taken in a third swig of viscous vegetation, which he immediately choked on. He cleared his throat. "You don't mean Sanderson?"

"I don't remember his name. The dinner theater butler."

"That's Sanderson, all right. Good grief, were all the restaurant staff around the university working for your dad?"

Nadia shrugged. "Guess he wanted to keep an eye on me when I got hired there. You and Thompson, too. Funny, isn't it?"

"Funny's not the right word." He cast a glance at the terrifying spectacle of Little Boris, who was currently nestled in Safiya's arms as she slept.

Boris was gone, but Boris was never *really* gone. The man had a small army of British waiters and Chinese waitresses and Russian commandos and who knows what else to keep a constant watch on his good friend Mr. Charles.

Not to mention Little Boris. The Frankendoll was probably equipped with state-of-the-art microphones and cameras. The shirt still said *I Brake For Hippies,* but it could just as easily have read *Boris is watching you.*

He shivered. "You know something? I want a refund on those Boris Bucks. We should make them count, use them when we get our lives back and can go anywhere we want."

"Can't come soon enough," Nadia murmured. "There are so many things you can't do when you're officially dead. Like baptisms or renewing a driver's license." She gave him a very pointed look. "Or changing your last name."

Safiya was squirming in bed, a sure sign that her sleep was coming to an end.

Suddenly she started screaming.

Another nightmare.

The poor girl had endured the hellish Level Nine deep below Magnus Headquarters, where human slaves had been kept in cages until they were hauled off by machines to be experimented on by Control scientists. They didn't know how long Safiya had been there or what those monsters had done to her, but the emotional scars ran deep.

Nadia hurried over to her and wrapped her in a hug. "It's okay, darling. You're safe. It was just a dream."

The weeping slowly receded like a thunderstorm yielding to gentle sunlight. He was always surprised at the girl's wakeful serenity, even if her dreams were often troubled.

"I'm hungry," Safiya announced with her faint, adorable accent.

"Good." Nadia kissed her soon-to-be daughter's forehead with visible relief. "How about an apple strudel from that coffee shop you like so much?"

The child's knowledge of English was limited, but it was apparent from the sudden glow that suffused her face that she had full comprehension of the magical phrase *apple strudel*.

◦§◦

"Seven minutes," Paul Veliu informed his teammates.

Senan had taken out his lucky coin, a silver Khatiz quarter with an image of Chairman Markhov on one side and Central Party Headquarters on the other. He rolled it across the knuckles of his right hand.

Andrei had his sniper rifle hoisted and was choosing potential targets as they wandered along the corridors, oblivious to the grim but blessedly swift fate that soon awaited them. Those glass windows were bulletproof, but even they would be dismantled by the force of what was coming.

∽

"Blast," Charles muttered as they stepped off the elevator into the main lobby of the ATA Home Office. "I left my coat in your room. Go on to the coffee shop. I'll meet you there."

Nadia arched an eyebrow. "It's not that cold outside. You really need a coat?"

"I get cold easily."

"Since when?"

Good grief. Couldn't he pull anything past her?

"I'm just chilled, that's all."

She rested the back of her hand against his forehead. "Doesn't feel like a fever. All right, see you down there."

He'd look like an idiot lugging a coat around when it was seventy degrees outside, but he needed the ring. If he didn't act fast, Boris would show up again and he'd never hear the end of it.

He'd get down on his knees in the parking lot of that urban coffee shop right in front of Peter and Julia and Safiya and the ATA body-guards and the whole wide world, and he wouldn't get up again until Nadia Petrova was his bride-to-be. His fate now rested in her hands.

"I'll drive him," said Sanderson, the quondam waiter at Wilford's British pub. He and Zhang Meiying, the Chemist, awaited them in the lobby along with an ATA security detail. "We'll meet up with you at the coffee shop."

"Text me when you leave," Meiying replied. She, Nadia, Safiya, and one of the guards strolled out into a brisk and cloudy April morning.

"Fetch your jacket, Doctor Ferguson," Sanderson said. "I'll wait here."

Charles rode the elevator to the third floor and hustled down the hallway to his room. He went in and grabbed his jacket, patting the inside pocket to make sure the jewelry box was still there.

He was halfway back to the elevator when he heard an unfamiliar voice.

"Charles Ferguson?"

Charles turned to find a stocky, square-shouldered man in a navy suit and tie jogging down the hallway toward him.

"Thank goodness," the man huffed as he came closer. His voice was deeper than a double bass. "I thought you weren't in the building. Jeez, that would have been a nightmare."

Charles frowned. "Have we met?"

The man extended a moist, meaty hand. "Rod Walker. I'm with the Agency. The *real* agency. CIA." He flashed a badge. Did CIA agents really carry ID badges? Didn't that defeat the whole purpose? "I'm a good friend of Boris's."

"Ah."

"I've been looking everywhere for you." Rod Walker checked his watch. "Can we talk for a minute?"

"Sorry, I've got a meeting downtown. This might be the most important morning of my life."

"No problem. I'll walk with you."

Charles tried to think of a clever reason to refuse but came up emptyhanded. "Fine."

He needed to work on saying no. He was too soft, a pushover. Granted, he'd stood up to Alexander Magnus, but that was a matter of life or death. These little, everyday things, that's where he needed to lay down the law.

Boris was fantastic at saying no.

"Mind if we take the stairs?" Rod checked his watch again. "My doc said I got to work on my cardio."

Charles couldn't put a finger on it, but something about this self-important, perspiring CIA agent made his skin crawl. The man already felt like human fly paper, sticky and clammy and hard to shake off. And why was he checking his watch every ten seconds?

"You go first." Rod held open the door to the stairwell. They were on the second landing on their way down to the ground floor when Charles heard a distinct click behind him.

He turned to find himself staring down the barrel of Rod Walker's handgun.

"Sorry, professor." Rod wiped his sweaty forehead with his free hand. "We're going to take a little detour. Go through the door there and turn right. There's another stairwell at the end of that hallway. We'll head to a back exit where my friends are waiting."

"Back exit?"

Rod chuckled. "You're going to miss that meeting of yours. No games, and I mean it. You so much as blink at anybody in the next hallway and I'll kill them on the spot. Then my friends will kill your girlfriend, and that would be a real shame, you know? Your Nadia's a real beauty, professor. You're a lucky man, so don't screw it up. And don't bother looking around for Boris to save you. We've got him locked up in a closet in New York. Oh, you don't believe me? See for yourself."

Rod pulled out a cell phone and held it in front of Charles.

Terror crept over him as he beheld the image of a bruised and defeated Boris Petrov trussed up like a pig ready for slaughter.

Boris was invincible. Boris never lost a fight.

If these people could do *that* to Boris, what chance did he have?

"Me and you are just two friends going for a stroll, that's all," Rod went on. "Got it?"

Charles swallowed. This guy had Magnus Foundation written all over him. "Just don't hurt them."

"Do what I say, and everybody lives. Now move."

᪥

Three minutes later, a series of thunderous blasts levelled the perimeter wall between the hotel and the ATA Home Office. Seconds afterward, the northwest corner of the Home Office erupted into a fiery inferno. All that remained of that entire section of the building was a heap of broken glass, scorched debris, and twisted metal.

And corpses.

The force of the explosions ruptured and dislodged most of the building's bulletproof windows. Little remained between the warm bodies in the Home Office hallways and the cold bullets of the First Triad's sniper rifles.

It felt too easy.

The target, which only moments ago had looked impenetrable, now sat exposed and weak, a stumbling deer with a pack of wolves on its heels. The panicked agents within who scurried about like ants began to drop one by one under a merciless barrage of bullets.

Paul fired his sniper rifle. Another intentional miss. He lowered his weapon and glanced at the legendary Andrei Idrisov in action. The young man's face was a portrait of stoic concentration. His rifle swung from one position to the next as if it were being controlled by a computer program. It moved, stayed in place for the space of a breath, fired, and moved again.

And every time it fired, another human ant in the ATA Home Office died.

Then, suddenly, Andrei froze. His sniper rifle hovered in the same position for the space of five seconds. He didn't fire. Instead, he moved on to another position and quickly resumed his usual rhythm.

Curious, Paul hefted his own rifle and peered through the scope, trying to find the source of the anomaly.

❦

A disoriented Fazal al-Najjar pulled a daggerlike shard of steel framing from the back of his hand. He held it up to the light, examining the vivid crimson smear on the sharp end with childlike curiosity.

Bodies littered the ground around him. Some were moving. A few groaned, though he could barely hear them over the shrill ringing in his ears.

Most of the bodies were silent, motionless.

He peered through the space where a bulletproof window had been seconds ago. Sunlight now streamed through the opening. Clear, life-giving rays of warmth.

A breeze wafted across his face.

"Oh, God," someone screamed from the far end of the hallway. "Somebody help me!"

He looked toward the voice. A man was leaning against the wall, his blood-drenched hand pressed against his insides to keep them from spilling out of his shirt. The man's head suddenly jerked backward as a bullet shattered his skull.

How peculiar.

The ringing in Fazal's ears diminished.

"Fazal, get out of there!"

A familiar voice. Thompson, that's who it was. Charles's curmudgeonly friend. He sounded worried for some reason. Why?

Fazal rested his hands against the wheels of his chair. He tried to push back with both hands, but he discovered that the left hand, the one from which he had pulled the broken shard of metal, would not cooperate. It rested limply on top of the wheel and refused to do anything else.

So many strange things were happening today. He'd have to talk to someone about this, but who? Maybe Thompson would understand. What was it that was happening all around him? Why couldn't he think clearly?

He moved the rebellious hand to his lap and tried to use his obedient hand to work the right wheel, but it still wouldn't move. Something was jamming it. He glanced behind his chair.

Ah, yes. Another body.

One of the corpses rose, almost in front of him.

Gavriel Abramovich. Boris's youthful friend and protégé, the dark-haired Russian Jewish angel of God. And Gavriel really was an angel, wasn't he? One of the most famous of God's messengers.

Gavriel staggered forward. It looked like something was wrong with his leg. He reached down and lifted Fazal out of the wheelchair.

"Thank you, angel of God," Fazal said. "My chair wouldn't move. Do you know what's happening? It all seems very unusual. I don't think it's on today's schedule."

Gavriel didn't reply. He clenched his teeth and stumbled onward toward the end of the hallway, toward a solid place where the walls had not yet caved in.

"Angels must be very strong," Fazal continued. "You carry me as if I weighed nothing. Perhaps I do weigh nothing. Maybe my body is still in the chair, and you're only carrying my spirit. Angels do that, don't they? I'm glad my spirit is so light."

He looked into Gavriel's eyes. So much sorrow, so much pain. Could angels really suffer like that?

Suddenly, Gavriel hurled him forward, tossing him several feet through the air and into the waiting arms of another. A second angel, no doubt. Funny that they would play such peculiar games with mortals. But then everything was bizarre at the moment. Fazal felt himself being pulled into cool, dark, unlit recesses. The borders of Heaven?

He looked back. The angel Gavriel took a heavy step toward him. Something was still wrong with the angel's left leg. It dragged along heavily behind him.

A small speck flew through the shattered window with a sharp whistling sound. In another blink of an eye, the same speck flew out the side of Gavriel's shirt and buried itself in the wall. It was good that Gavriel was an angel and not a human being. If he were mortal, that speck would have flown dangerously close to his heart on its journey through his body.

Then the impossible happened.

The angel of God collapsed to the ground and became perfectly motionless.

The angel of God was dead.

⌁

"Fazal? Can you hear me? Fazal!"

Fazal shivered violently and looked around. It felt like a thick, warm blanket was sliding off his mind, suddenly exposing him to harsh and vivid reality.

He sat in a windowless office lit by a battery-powered lantern. Besides Thompson, there were two strangers, a man and woman in military fatigues huddled in muted conversation in one corner of the room.

"Fazal, look at me. Are you okay?"

Fazal held up his left hand and examined it. It was wrapped in a white cloth bandage stained with blood. He felt a throbbing pain, and with it, the realization that he couldn't move the fingers of his hand.

He looked at Thompson. The man's pale face was covered in ashes and dust, like a Hindu priest or a Karo tribesman. There were streaks in the dust where Thompson's tears and sweat had riven paths.

"Why is my hand not working?" Fazal asked. "And who put ashes on your face? Why are you weeping?"

"You don't remember?"

"No. Wait, yes, I had a dream. We were in a hallway, only it wasn't a hallway anymore. It was a…morgue. There were bodies everywhere, and everything was breaking into pieces, and I couldn't move, and then an angel came, and…"

The truth of what had happened broke upon Fazal's clouded mind with the suddenness of a thunderclap. A groan escaped his lips. "Thompson, they killed Gavriel."

"I know." Thompson said. "I went after him and pulled him away from the windows, but it was too late."

"You did that?" Fazal's eyes widened. He'd always considered Thompson self-absorbed, childish even. "You must be very brave, Thompson."

Thompson hung his head. "I'm no hero. Gods, what a nightmare."

Chapter Fourteen

# The Traitor

"Get me out of here!" Boris Petrov yanked the IV out of his arm and pulled the taped-on heartbeat sensor from his chest. "It's just a few fractured ribs."

Lenny Phillips stared at him, open-mouthed. "Are you insane? When I found you in that closet, I thought you were dead."

Boris swung his legs off the hospital bed. He grunted as a sharp pain exploded in his chest. He took a few moments to brace himself, then stood.

"I've been through worse," he muttered through gritted teeth. "Did you get a hold of Gavriel?"

Lenny shook his head. "Still going to voicemail."

"What about Sanderson?"

"Nope. Heck, I even tried the Home Office's front desk. Nobody answering that, either."

Boris frowned. "They're not answering the front desk?"

He glanced up at the muted television in the corner of his hospital room. The news had just switched from the latest saber rattling between

NATO and Russia to a breaking report. A thick line of black-boxed captions ran across the bottom of the screen.

*…a large explosion this morning at a government facility near downtown Bethesda, Maryland. Reports now estimate that there are at least sixty casualties and over two hundred wounded.*

Boris caught his breath as an aerial video clip filled the screen. That burning, broken shell of a building was the ATA Home Office, its windows shattered, its parking lot filled with debris and smashed vehicles. The northwest corner of the building looked like a crater.

He wiped away sudden tears. His chest felt like it could explode.

Rod Walker had promised vengeance, but Boris had no idea it would be this swift. Or this brutal.

"Nadia," he gasped. "And…merciful God! Peter and Julia were coming to the Home Office this morning."

He grabbed the remote off an end table and unmuted the newscast.

"Guests at a nearby hotel reported hearing gunfire shortly after the explosions," the reporter said in a measured voice. "Investigators have not yet discovered the cause of the blasts. Because of the sensitive nature of the facility, federal agents have closed off the area from journalists. We'll let you know as soon as—"

Boris muted the TV.

"You're coming with me," he announced.

"Wait, what?" Lenny stumbled backward a few steps. "You mean… there?"

"The people who did this were monitoring you yesterday, Mr. Phillips. If you stay here, they could come for you next."

"Can't I just go to Langley and hide out?"

Boris shook his head. "If the Magnus Foundation wants you, not even Langley is safe. Can you help me with my shirt?"

He'd managed to get into his pants without too much pain, but stretching his arms to put on a T-shirt was out of the question. On the plus side, fractured ribs usually healed on their own with time.

"Yeah, of course." Lenny helped him into the shirt and then into his faithful old bomber jacket. "You really think the Foundation could get into Langley?"

"I have no doubt," Boris replied. "Magnus had turncoats in every one of our agencies."

"But you killed him, right? I thought that was all over."

Boris exhaled. "So did I."

A male nurse knocked twice and swept into the room. He looked at them in blinking astonishment, then ordered Boris to get back into bed.

"My daughter was in that building." Boris pointed at the television. "We're leaving, now."

⤙

Boris's ATA SUV flew down the interstate at a hundred and twenty miles per hour, weaving through traffic like a professional racecar, its sirens blaring. Lenny Phillips was pinned to the passenger seat, his face pale as a sheet. He looked like he was trying to decide whether to shriek or vomit.

Just like Mr. Charles had been on his first real car ride.

A maelstrom of emotions tore through Boris's heart. Terror, guilt, anger. Revenge would have to wait. Unless they'd been killed by the ATA's return fire, Rod Walker and his terrorist friends were long gone by now.

His phone rang. He pushed a button on the steering wheel to answer it.

"Boris?"

Jimmy MacPherson. Jimmy had been his supervisor in the CIA, then became the ATA's first director, bringing his protégé Boris Petrov with him into the newly formed agency. Jimmy had retired a few weeks after Magnus Headquarters had fallen, but he was still on an advisory board and had security clearance.

"I'm here, Jimmy."

"Thank God you're alive. How bad is it?"

"I don't know yet. The terrorists got to me first last night. Tied me up and stuffed me in a closet. They knew about Sergei Ivanov. They know everything, Jimmy. I'm on my way to the Home Office now."

Jimmy muttered a curse. "We both know what this means. I won't keep you, but when you get a chance, come on out and see me."

"Will do, Jimmy."

Boris ended the call as they crossed into Bethesda's city limits. When he turned right at the corner of Pinewood Avenue and Third Street, he saw for himself the enormity of the destruction.

It took his breath away.

"Zendivar's lightsword," Lenny murmured. "It looks like the Terrelian home planet after the third Deathbot invasion."

"Stay in the car," Boris said firmly. "Whatever you do, don't talk to anyone."

Lenny reached down and pulled out a comic book from his backpack. "Take your time," he said. "I picked up a new Fuzzbucket this morning at that bookstore by the hospital."

Boris had spent more time within the walls of the ATA Home Office than anywhere else since Elena vanished. The memories, the friendships, the things his team had accomplished together over the years—it was unfathomable that it could all be destroyed so quickly. He stared through the windshield at the burnt-out, smoldering ruins. His heart felt like it had been wrenched out of his chest.

Any of his colleagues in the ATA could be dead. So could Nadia, Safiya, Mr. Charles, Fazal, Peter, Julia, and yes, even Mr. Thompson. At least Raj and Anna were in Germany, and Miguel was safe in Illinois.

He stepped out of the SUV. The air teemed with smoke and dust. He flashed his ID to the federal officers enforcing the perimeter. He saw rescue dogs with their handlers sniffing around in the rubble, looking for survivors…or human remains. He whispered a prayer and crossed himself.

Nadia could be buried under one of those piles of debris.

"Boris?" a familiar voice shouted over the din of firemen, FBI agents, police officers, and EMTs.

Eugene Thompson was sitting on the concrete front steps of the Newgate Hotel across from the Home Office. His arm had been wrapped in a sling, his clothes were torn and covered with debris, and his head looked like it had been submerged in a river of dirt and ash.

"Where are they?" Boris ran across the street. "Nadia? Safiya? Peter?"

Thompson waved a hand toward the hotel lobby behind him. "They're okay. I heard that Zhang Meiying had taken Nadia and Safiya to meet Julia and Peter at a coffee shop downtown, so they weren't here when it happened. The survivors are gathered in the hotel." He lowered his eyes. "You're going to hear it sooner or later, so it might as well be now."

Boris clenched his teeth. He knew what was coming. He'd been given this kind of news before.

"Who is it?" he asked.

"Gavriel." Thompson ran a shaking hand through his hair. "He got hit by one of the snipers. He'd just saved Fazal's life, pulled him out of a hallway that was taking heavy fire. He was standing a few feet away from me, and then he…" His voice quavered. "I went in after him. Pulled him away from the windows, but it was too late."

Boris turned and took a few steps toward the mutilated building. For some reason, he'd never doubted that Gavriel would survive this. So young and strong, so full of life and courage.

"You're certain?" he asked.

Thompson nodded. "Someone said the bullet went through his heart. I'm sorry, Boris."

He sat on the steps next to Thompson.

What would he tell Abram? He and Gavriel's father had chatted on the phone just last week. Abram called twice a month, punctual as clockwork, to check up on his one and only son. Their last talk had been the usual news and gossip along with a wager about whether Gavriel would ever work up the courage to ask Meiying out on a date.

"Who else?" he asked, his voice thick. "Tell me everything."

Thompson wrapped the ambulance blanket more tightly around himself. "Some medics took Fazal to the hospital, but it's nothing serious. Some shrapnel in his hand, so they're doing an outpatient procedure. Sanderson got shot in the shoulder, but they said he'll come through." He paused. "Charles is missing. Someone said he was kidnapped. There are a lot of others, a lot of deaths, but no one else I knew."

Boris nodded. A small blessing that some from his own team had already left the Home Office. Mr. Charles's kidnapping was tragic but expected. The Foundation needed Charles's talents, which hopefully meant they'd keep him safe from harm.

"A lady I talked to saw Charles going into a stairwell with a visitor just before the attack," Thompson went on. "Some CIA guy, can't remember the name."

"Rod Walker," Boris replied.

"Yeah, that's it." Thompson frowned. "But how did you know that?"

"Rod and I met last night." Boris rested a hand on the bandage over his chest. "He broke a couple of my ribs and stuffed me in a closet so he and his friends could do this without me getting in the way. Any idea where he went?"

"Gone without a trace," Thompson replied.

"What about the snipers?"

Thompson shook his head. "Your people fired back, but they were long gone by the time the cavalry showed up. In and out like ghosts."

Boris noticed the sling on Thompson's arm. Then he looked at Thompson's face, pale and strained, as if it cost him a great effort just to hold a conversation. "And what about you, Mr. Thompson?"

"It doesn't matter." Thompson lowered his head. "Look, we both know who did this. You think Aryana's in Khatizan, right? Then that's where they're taking Charles. When you go, I'm going with you."

"If that's what you want."

Boris heard someone calling his name. He glanced up and saw Kenjiro Nakamura hurrying toward him through the crowd of rescue workers and survivors. Even in the middle of a disaster zone, Kenjiro somehow managed to exude his usual air of calm, collected professionalism. He was carrying a cloth bag.

"Thank God you're alive," Boris said as Kenjiro came to a halt in front of them.

Kenjiro gave a curt nod to Thompson and handed Boris the bag. "We found them in the hallway near detainment. That's where the attackers infiltrated the Home Office before the explosions. I'm sorry, boss."

Boris looked in the bag and saw a familiar pair of well-worn leather loafers.

Charles Ferguson's favorite shoes.

The trackers they'd hidden in those shoes were supposed to be undetectable. The kidnappers had known, just like they'd known about Sergei Ivanov.

There could only be one explanation.

The ATA had a mole, and it was someone near the top.

# Chapter Fifteen
# Remembrance

THE RABBI'S VOICE rose in a mournful, haunting dirge that reverberated among the high rafters of Beth Sholom Synagogue.

Boris Petrov watched as flames danced and flickered atop the twin candlesticks perched on either side of Gavriel Abramovich's casket. Safiya leaned over and rested her head against his arm. He held her close. She didn't understand what had happened to Uncle Gavriel. All she knew was that one of her friends was missing. The quiet one, the strong one, the one who flashed her secret smiles and made funny faces for her when he thought no one else was looking.

Gavriel's father, Abram Pasovsky, buried his face in his hands as the rabbi chanted *El Malei Rachamim*, a final prayer promising that Gavriel would find shelter in the wings of God's presence. Officially, all travel between Russia and the U.S. had been closed after the Berlin attack. Boris had pulled a lot of strings to get Abram a red-eye flight on a private jet from St. Petersburg.

God alone knew what the poor man felt as he looked upon the casket of his only child. Gavriel had been too young, too noble, too vigorous to be snatched away like this. Death was always an injustice, a crime against life and beauty.

After the service, Boris and the other pallbearers, friends of Gavriel's from the synagogue, carried the casket to the hearse that would bear it to the gravesite. Once the mourners were all gathered at the graveyard, the pallbearers then carried the casket from the hearse to the grave itself, stopping seven times along the way in accordance with an old tradition.

The rabbi prayed as the casket was lowered, then Abram and some of Gavriel's relatives recited the *kaddish*. Finally, the mourners covered the casket with earth. Abram had brought with him a handful of dirt from Israel that he sprinkled on his son's coffin.

As the crowd began to disperse, Abram came to Boris and wrapped him in a hug. "You were also a father to my Gavriel," he said in a quavering voice. "*Adonai natan, v'Adonai lakach, y'hi shem Adonai m'vorach.*"

Boris's Hebrew had grown rusty from disuse, but he remembered that one from an old friend who worked with Mossad.

The Lord has given. The Lord has taken away. Let the name of the Lord be blessed.

He met Abram's gaze and felt that mysterious kinship reserved for those who share a deep love for the departed. Then Abram handed him a folded note. "General Borokhov of the Free Russia Movement. I know you won't let this crime against my son go unanswered. If you need anything, Borokhov will help. Goodbye, Boris." He patted Boris's shoulder, then turned to embrace one of his relatives.

Boris unfolded the note. An international phone number.

Fyodor Borokhov was the leader of a resistance movement whose Western-trained soldiers had joined the Ukrainians when the Russians invaded them. The general was Abram's brother-in-law and Gavriel's uncle. Surely a few of Gavriel's old friends in the movement would be willing to help. They were used to danger, and nothing could be more perilous than a mission to Khatizan.

⁓

Nadia Petrova watched as beads of rain streaked across the window of her father's SUV. Currents of air grabbed some of the drops and blew them off into the darkness, while others escaped to crawl tentatively across the windowpane toward the same destination. An illusion of free choice, not unlike life itself.

She felt that darkness growing within her. A deep sorrow. A room with no lights, no windows, no doorway. A dank, black cave. A sunless gloaming.

Depression.

Her world had crumbled around her again. The attack on the Home Office, the destruction and chaos, the stark reality of death at Gavriel's funeral. And if that weren't enough, they had taken Charles away from her. They had swept down like a bitter north wind and carried him off, just like they'd done with her mother all those years ago.

Part of her wanted to hope. Another part wanted to sink into the darkness, to give up all the effort and struggle and drown herself in the pain.

Safiya slept blissfully beside her. The child's beautiful, almond-shaped eyes were sheltered beneath their lids, her eyelashes moving in rapid jolts as she dreamed.

Maybe it wasn't a nightmare this time.

If anything could keep Nadia from her own inner darkness, it was Safiya. The girl depended on her. Would that be enough?

She glanced up and caught her father's gaze in the rearview mirror. He looked haggard, worn, and older, as if the past few days had spanned a dozen years. But he still had that same madman's hope in his eyes. It's what made him so good at his job.

They were headed to New York. Her father wouldn't say why, but she imagined it had something to do with the stranger riding in the identical SUV that kept pace twenty yards behind them. She'd seen the man from a distance as he talked with her father. Stocky and baby-faced, the stranger wore thick-lensed glasses and a T-shirt with superheroes all over it.

Was he an ATA agent? If so, she'd never seen him around the Home Office.

Her father and Julia were talking in quiet tones. The image triggered a memory from years before when she was a junior in high school. They'd taken a road trip from her home in Beecher, Illinois all the way to the Grand Canyon. She and Peter had slept in the back of their old Suburban while her father and Julia rode up front. She remembered the two of them talking just like they were now, with somber faces and muted voices.

She reached over and rested her hand on Safiya's knee.

It would have to be enough. Love for this child would shelter her from the shadows within. Even as the thought came, another followed it, cold as ice and sharp as a penknife.

They could take Safiya from her, too.

Not the Foundation. Her own government. The ATA, given the nature of their work, had been granted custody of Safiya until her immigration trial. Nadia tried not to worry about it. After all, who would take such an innocent girl from the people who loved her most only to ship her off to a refugee camp or worse?

Julia Pearson reached into her purse, pulled out two sticks of spearmint gum, and handed one to her father. Nicotine-free gum. Gavriel would have been proud. When Julia spoke again, her words were loud enough to be heard over the soulful strains of an old jazz diva crooning through the stereo system.

"You know what Jack would say?" she asked, Jack being Julia's nickname for Father Anatoly. She had known the old monk before he took his vows. "He'd say it's time to forgive yourself. Do whatever you've got to do first. Admit it, face it, deal with it, and when you're done, forgive yourself and let it go. You couldn't have known what was going to happen, but you can do something about what happens next."

Boris grunted. "Time will tell."

Nadia eyed a mileage sign as it zipped past. Ninety miles to New York City, which meant they'd get there around two in the morning.

"I have a meeting in the city," her father went on. "If I can get my supervisor to approve, we'll be in Khatizan this time next week. If I fail, we're on our own. I'm going either way."

The words kindled a tiny ray of hope in Nadia's soul. If anyone could sneak past Khatizan's infamous border and rescue Charles, it was her father.

The rest would work itself out. Even if the immigration judge proved merciless, she would follow Safiya to the ends of the earth. No hardnosed laws would tear their fledgling family apart.

She felt fingertips gingerly brushing against her hand. She looked over and saw Peter gazing at her with an unusually serious expression. "It's okay, sister," he said gently. He had been so quiet since the ATA attack. She wondered how much he understood. "Everything's going to be okay."

"Thanks, Peter." She forced a smile, and he grinned back with unfeigned pleasure.

Peter's innocent, childlike joy verged on the miraculous. Even here, even with all the dark clouds around her, his spirit lightened her heart. She took a deep breath, let it out, and came to a decision.

Her father would go to Khatizan. She could never take Safiya to that place, and she could never abandon her, not after everything the girl had already suffered. She wouldn't go to Khatizan herself, but that didn't mean she was powerless. A global mesh of network cables tied the whole human race together. A small set of coding languages underpinned every piece of modern technology, including the technology protecting Khatizan and its leaders.

Whoever writes the code rules the world.

And thanks be to God, she knew how to code.

✺

"Nadia, Lenny Phillips. Lenny, Nadia."

Nadia shook the warm, outstretched hand of the mysterious

stranger with the superhero T-shirt and thick-lensed glasses. Boris had driven them to a three-bedroom corner apartment on the third floor of an old building in Queens. The apartment, along with a few others on the same floor, had been purchased by her father's team for top-level witness protection. The walls, floors, and ceilings of the units, her father cheerfully informed them, had reinforced steel plates strong enough to withstand an armed siege.

Nadia, Safiya, Julia, and Peter had spent the night in the larger apartment, which would be the team's base of operations. Lenny Phillips and Eugene Thompson had been given one-bedroom efficiencies in the same hallway.

"Nice to meet you, Lenny," she said.

"This is so frigging awesome." Lenny took a step back and clutched his pudgy fists together in excitement. "I mean, I just shook hands with the brain behind Crowdbreak, the great mother hacker herself, the queen of the white hats! You single-handedly dreamed up the magnum opus of online gaming. The *real* game, with real physics, chemistry, biology…the whole shebang. Did you know we have in-game research guilds that create new technology for the rest of the players? Chemistry guilds that wander Northrim Forest studying virtual flora and fauna so they can create new medicines and poisons for the Free Lands? And all that was—how did you put it, Boris?—*just another stray thought in your mind.* Frigging amazing!"

Nadia blinked. "Dad, what on earth is he talking about?"

"She doesn't know?" Lenny's eyes, with the added amplification of his glasses, grew to alarming proportions. "You seriously didn't tell her?"

One look at her father's face spoke volumes. Her private notebook, again. He had promised her no one would see it, that no would have access to her ideas.

"What did you do, Dad?"

Boris flashed a sheepish smile. "Don't get angry, darling! I might have given the former director of the CIA a few pages from your journal.

You remember that part, right? Using an online game to break high-level encryption? You said the virtual world would have to be realistic, and then you solved your own problem with that game physics engine you worked on during your junior year.

"The CIA *might* have turned it into an official operation, and Mr. Lenny here *might* be the technical lead on that operation. And there might be half a billion people playing your game every day now, and Mr. Lenny might need your help adapting the game to break a new type of encryption."

"Wow." Nadia plopped down on the apartment's navy-blue sofa, which looked like it had wandered off from a budget hotel, and cradled her head between her hands. She'd written those journals in her undergrad years during bursts of feverish creativity. She would be halfway through a Rachmaninoff prelude or a Mozart sonata when a bolt from the blue would descend, as if her brain, once released into more creative channels, turned into a lightning rod for technological invention.

One of those ideas, Chameleon, had given the Aeternum team a way to communicate secretly within the heavily monitored confines of Magnus Headquarters.

Now, without her knowledge, another idea had taken shape and come to life.

She wondered if any of her other journal pages had slipped off into the shadowy corridors of intelligence communities.

A terrifying proposition.

"You promised me you wouldn't show those to anyone."

"What was I supposed to do?" Boris held up his hands. "The idea was brilliant, and we could put it to work right away. I knew it would save lives, and I was right. You wouldn't believe how many."

"Dang straight," Lenny piped in. "Check it out. This is just last year."

He pulled out his phone, tapped on it for a minute, then held up a two-column chart for her examination. One column was a list of crimes. Money laundering, drug smuggling, prostitution rings, online fraud—all the major players in the war against crime were on the list. In the second column next to each crime was a number.

"See?" Lenny said. "Last year, Crowdbreak exposed twenty-six high-profile money launderers. It led to the capture of over two hundred drug smugglers. We cracked the biggest child prostitution ring on the East Coast. Nabbed every one of those scumbags. They thought they were safe behind their encrypted apps until Crowdbreak showed up and laid the smack down like a level 95 Gnomic Archmage. You know what they call you on the dark web?"

Nadia arched an eyebrow. The dark web involved shadowy online forums and sites where hackers plied their illegal wares. "They gave me a name?"

"You bet they did." Lenny's head bobbed like a cork in the water. He flung his arms wide for dramatic effect. "Doomhammer! Whatcha think of that? You deserve it, Mrs. Petrova."

"She's not married, Lenny," Boris chimed in.

"Seriously?" Lenny's broad face crinkled in disbelief. "What's wrong with the males in your corner of the multiverse? If I'd met you a few weeks ago, I would have proposed myself. Anyway, your program, Crowdbreak, is flipping amazing. Criminals see you coming and they scatter like roaches under a floodlight."

"Sweet Saint Gratus of Aosta!" Boris groaned. "Don't talk about roaches, Mr. Phillips."

Lenny raised his hands over his head as if he were carrying an axe. Or an extremely large Doomhammer. "Boom, crash, Doomhammer strikes again!" He sat down and wiped his forehead. "It's frigging awesome is what it is. And now I get to work with you! It's like my own comic book brought to life."

"You'll also get someone else on your team," Boris said. "One of Nadia's old friends, a math whiz named Fazal al-Najjar. He'll be here in a few days."

"I don't even know what we're doing yet," Nadia replied.

Boris pulled a piece of paper from his coat pocket. On it were written the peculiar string of letters and numbers that John Flying Hawk had recited to Charles at the remote cabin in North Carolina. Charles had told her about it in passing, but she hadn't looked at it yet.

"I need you to figure out what this code means," Boris said. "John Flying Hawk might be insane, but I think he gave us this for a reason. Who knows? Perhaps it's the key to breaking into the Central Party's systems."

Lenny took the paper. "I bet it'll be child's play for Doomhammer. Here, see what you think."

Nadia looked over the string of characters, then glanced at the corner of the room, where Safiya was playing with a whole pile of Lenny's comic book action figures. "You're overestimating my superpowers, Mr. Phillips, but if this can help us get Charles out of Khatizan, I'll give it everything I've got. I'll still need to take care of Safiya somehow."

Lenny frowned. "She's your daughter, right?"

Nadia longed to say *yes*. She wished Safiya, at least, could be safe and secure without any chance of being taken away. "I'm trying to adopt her. I'm all she has right now."

"Oh, I can help you with childcare." Lenny's proud grin was quickly followed by a florid blush. "I mean, not me, personally, but I met this fantastic babysitter the other day. She's not an official babysitter, but I'd bet a signed first edition that she's great with kids. Not that she has any kids…yet." Lenny's face turned a deep red that verged on purple. He wiped a layer of sweat from his forehead.

Nadia tried not to imagine what kind of babysitter the sun-deprived, socially awkward man standing in front of her would dig up. She telegraphed her father a definitive no.

"Is that right, Mr. Phillips?" Boris replied with a secretive wink in her direction. "Now remember, this babysitter needs to be a living, breathing female, preferably one with no criminal record. Video game acquaintances and AI apps don't count."

Lenny pushed his glasses up with a thick forefinger. "Breathing female? Heck yes, she is."

"I'll leave you to it." Boris kissed Nadia's forehead, then gave Lenny a resounding clap on his back that made Lenny's eyes bulge. "Duty calls."

⁓

Boris wished the flask in the inside pocket of his bomber jacket really was filled with vodka instead of vodka-tinged water. Or that the chewing gum in the pocket of his jeans had nicotine in it.

On the way to the meeting with the ATA's director, Angela Obasanjo, he heard a breaking news report that chilled him to the bone. A fleet of drones had just firebombed the Russian city of Novorossiysk. The damage was unknown but expected to be catastrophic, with civilian casualties in the thousands. The drones were reportedly Tessara M39s.

Exclusive American technology, or so the world thought.

A world war was now a foregone conclusion. First a Russian FSB agent tied to the Berlin bombing, now an American drone fleet striking Russian territory in seeming retaliation. Both attacks could be pulled off with Magnus Foundation technology, which meant Khatizan. China had already condemned the attack on Russia. Russia had just threatened NATO with nuclear war.

Now Boris sat on a park bench by the Hudson River, trying to convince the ATA's new director to approve a Khatizan mission.

He watched as a peregrine falcon swooped down over the river in pursuit of a terrified pigeon. Newcomers to the area, it had taken the falcons a few years to settle in. Now they were ruling the New York skies.

"You have to let us try, Director." His fingers curled around the arm of the park bench. "If the Russians can be convinced that Khatizan was behind the attack, they'll back off. Same goes for NATO with Article Five. We can have World War Three, or we can have a unified response against the real perpetrators in Khatizan. Send my team across the Khatizan border. Let me get the evidence they need."

"I said no." Angela Obasanjo took a sip of her usual stiff black coffee from a dark green disposable cup. "How are your ribs holding up?"

"I'm a fast healer."

He glanced at her steel-blue eyes as she watched the river's endless flow. He could almost see the wheels turning in her mind, but where was the current of her thoughts leading her?

After two months as head of the ATA, Director Obasanjo remained a perfect enigma to him. She had been appointed by the agency's international oversight committee, though why they chose her was anyone's guess. His old mentor, Jimmy MacPherson, had stepped down as director after the fall of Magnus Headquarters. Jimmy's greatest aim had been achieved, and the wise always quit while the cards are good.

The only thing Boris liked about the new director was her Nigerian accent. True, she also possessed a refined, stoic beauty with more than a touch of the regal. She certainly seemed cold enough to be one of those tyrannical monarchs from the pages of history.

"I don't understand why the Americans are reaching out to Chairman Markhov," she added after another sip of coffee. "The Central Party is a Darwinian jungle. Any show of weakness leads to death. Markhov would never help us, but I know someone who can."

Boris blinked. "You have contacts in Khatizan?"

"Does that surprise you?" She turned her diamond-hard gaze on him. He met it for one moment and looked away. The woman unnerved him. She almost made him feel like a bumbling teenager.

"You see me as an outsider," she went on, "but in my old life, I had to make connections to survive. Yes, Boris, I have contacts inside Khatizan. I'm waiting for a message. Until it comes, you aren't going anywhere. Don't test me on this. Cross that border without authorization, you're gone for good. Wait until we can do the job right."

He crossed his arms. "If we wait, Charles Ferguson could die."

"And if we rush in unprepared, you could all die." She shook her head dismissively. "Your team is too valuable. I won't have it."

The pigeon escaped. A minor miracle given the tenacity of the hunter.

"Understood," he said at last. It wasn't the truth, but it's what she wanted to hear. Why couldn't she see that they had no time to waste, that every delay plunged the world closer to war?

"There's one more thing," she added.

"Yes?"

She crumpled her coffee cup and tossed it into a trash bin. "If you're hiding anything from me, I'll find it. MacPherson may have let you get away with your lone ranger nonsense, but it won't fly with me. If I ever choose to send you to Khatizan, you will do exactly as I say. Is that clear?"

He grunted. "Fine."

She rose and signaled to her security detail. "Then we're done here. Keep up the good work, Agent Petrov."

As Boris walked back to his SUV, one question burned in his mind.

Given her inexplicable reluctance to pursue the Magnus Foundation, was Angela Obasanjo the ATA's mole? Had the agency's own director betrayed them all?

# Chapter Sixteen
# Relapse

Paul Veliu and Andrei Idrisov sat at a breakfast table on the balcony of their hotel room. From their vantage point on the thirty-second floor, they had a panoramic view of Manhattan as it pulsed and hummed and honked and roared in defiance of the night, obliterating the stars above with its own dizzying universe of artificial light.

"This place makes Chozul look like a backwater village," Andrei muttered. "The Party told us that New York City was a dung heap filled with beggars. How did blind capitalism create something like this?"

Paul spread a pat of soft butter across the smooth, flaky surface of a golden croissant, then bit off one of the ends, holding it in his mouth to let the moist flavor wash over his tongue. He could almost taste the individual layers of dough.

Perfection.

"Was it capitalism or colonialism?" he mused.

"What's the difference?" Andrei hugged his arms over his chest as if to ward away the cold though the night air was mild. "I never imagined the Americans would be this powerful. The entire Youth Corps couldn't capture this city, not even if we brought in the old army vets to help us."

Paul's pulse quickened as he heard the disillusionment in Andrei's voice. They were alone on the balcony, and their phones were both in the room. No mics, no cameras, no way for the Party to know what they were saying.

The Fourth Triad had already left the country, escorting Charles Ferguson to Khatizan by private jet. That left only nine soldiers to complete the New York mission. The other Red Ops One team members were in rooms scattered around the hotel. They would not leave those rooms until the following morning. Paul's orders had been clear on that point.

So far, everything had gone according to plan. The first part of the official mission was complete. The second part could be averted if he found a way that left his credibility with Aryana Voss intact. For that to work, he needed an ally, someone on the team who was ready to turn on the Central Party. Rius had suggested Andrei Idrisov.

Time to roll the dice.

"Why didn't you shoot that man in the wheelchair?" He added a hint of accusation to his voice. Rius had a theory about the renowned sniper. If the theory proved true, Paul would soon place his own life and the fate of Khatizan on the young man's shoulders. "I saw you target him at the ATA base, but then you moved on without firing. Why?"

"You saw that?" Andrei's eyes widened. The atmosphere between them changed in the blink of an eye. The sniper turned tense and defensive, like a tiger suddenly brought to bay. A single mistake could land anyone on the wrong side of a Youth Corps firing squad, even the legendary Andrei Idrisov.

Andrei's hand slipped towards the holster at his side. Another confirmation of Rius's theory. A trained, submissive Youth Corps soldier would never turn on his own commanding officer, even if it cost him his life.

Which meant, of course, that Andrei Idrisov was now thinking for himself.

"Kill me if you want," Paul said coolly. "I won't report you for failing to take the shot. I just want to know why you showed mercy instead of following orders."

Andrei's hand remained on the handle of his Beretta. Paul was at his mercy now. With an act of willpower, he shifted his gaze to the Manhattan skyline. Seconds ticked by. He could hear Andrei's ragged breath and feel the intense gaze of those dark gray eyes.

"I don't kill civilians." Andrei spoke the words in a low, trembling voice, as if he were confessing some unspeakable crime. "My father was a colonel in the Revolutionary Army. Did you know that?"

Paul looked him in the eye. "I know nothing of your past."

"The day before my thirteenth birthday," Andrei went on, "he took me for a walk. He'd never said much about the army until that day. He told me soldiers should be modern-day knights, heroes whose valor is matched with humanity."

Andrei spoke with feverish desperation, as if challenging Paul to disagree with him.

"What about you, Andrei?" he asked. "Are you a knight, a protector of the weak?"

Andrei looked away. "I know what you're thinking. I'm the legendary sniper, the great Andrei Idrisov. I've taken so many lives, but they were enemies. They were terrorists, murderers, oppressors of the weak. I kill a few to save many, but I will never forget my father's words."

Now to toss the dice.

"Did you see that large suitcase Rod Walker gave me before he left?" Paul asked.

Andrei nodded.

"It contains nine briefcases. Each briefcase holds an energy bomb keyed to our various fingerprints. They're similar to the bomb we used in Berlin. The latest version, exponentially more powerful."

"Berlin?" Andrei frowned. "But that was the Russians!"

Paul shook his head. "That was us."

Disbelief was written on every line of Andrei's face. "How could you know that?"

"Because I was the bomber."

"You!" Andrei leapt out of his chair and began pacing back and forth on the balcony. "No, I don't believe you. It's impossible. The Party would never do such a thing. Never."

Paul exhaled. "Not long ago, I would have agreed with you. Commander Firlenko told me it would be a pinpoint strike on a terrorist cell. Their offices were on the thirty-fifth floor of the Bann Commercial Building. I killed a man named Jorgen Handelssohn who was supposedly a terrorist. Then I armed the bomb and left it in his office. That bomb claimed tens of thousands of civilian lives."

His voice turned harsh as a fresh wave of guilt swept over him. "Now I'm a murderer, a terrorist. Can you imagine what that feels like? You'd better think about it, because if you follow the Party's orders, you'll become a terrorist, too. As horrible as Berlin was, this was always the real target. Our orders are to place these bombs in nine different locations throughout New York City."

He waved his hand toward the skyline. "Everything you see here will be wiped away as if it never existed. If you and I don't do something, the blood of eighteen million civilians will be on our hands."

Andrei stopped pacing. He lowered his head and clutched the hair over his temples as if he would tear it out. "But how can we stop it? We can't go back to Khatizan without finishing our mission."

"We can't *both* go back," Paul agreed. "One of us must stay here."

Andrei met his gaze. "What do you mean?"

"One of us must defect."

"Defect?" Andrei looked stunned. "Betray Khatizan? My father… what would he think of me if I betrayed my own country?"

"The Khatizan we know will soon collapse," Paul said quickly. "The Party's days are numbered. The truth about Berlin will come to light, and when it does, there will be hell to pay. Do the right thing now, and your father will be proud that his son saved so many innocent lives."

Andrei gripped the railing and gazed at the city. Paul could almost feel the conflict raging in the young man's heart.

Finally, Andrei turned to face him. "Show me Commander Firlenko's orders. I believe you, but I want to see them first. If it's true, then I'm with you, even if it means assassinating the Chairman himself."

❧

The only thing Charles knew was that he was on an airplane. After they'd hauled him out of the ATA Home Office, his kidnappers had placed a helmet over his head, plunging him into utter darkness and silence. The only sounds were his own breathing and the swift rhythm of his heartbeat.

They'd let him take off the helmet briefly during a pit stop on the way to the airstrip. Their leader, a young man named Paul Veliu, had accompanied him to the gas station's bathroom. Paul had seemed to know all kinds of things about him and even about Boris. They'd had a brief, peculiar conversation, then Paul had marched him back to the black van and plunked the helmet on his head. How long ago was that? Five hours? An entire day? He'd slept since then, but beyond that he had lost any sense of time. He felt exhausted.

"Hello?" His voice sounded muffled, as if he were talking into a pillow.

No reply. Maybe they couldn't hear him. More likely, they didn't care.

At least he could still pray.

*Lord Jesus Christ, have mercy on me.*

That ancient prayer had become his steadfast companion since he'd learned it from Father Anatoly.

Nadia had been through this, too, hadn't she? When the Foundation had kidnapped her and Fazal at that airport, she'd had no warning, no idea of what was coming. She had woken as a prisoner in Magnus Headquarters.

Where would he be when the helmet came off again and the world flooded back into his senses? He leaned back against the headrest and closed his eyes, which, in the darkness of the helmet, wasn't much different than leaving them open. He forced down the rapid rhythm of his breathing.

In and out. In and out.

*Lord Jesus Christ, have mercy on me.*

He let the words seep into his fear. Whatever happened, however this ended, God was with him on this plane. Nearer than his own breath, closer than his own thoughts.

The deep hum of the plane's engines reverberated through his body. He let go of the tension and embraced his own exhaustion. No reason to resist the demands of his weary mind. He fell asleep with the words of the prayer on his lips.

⁓

Waves lapped against a sandy beach. He opened his eyes.

A strange, shifting substance covered the sky above him. A vast canopy of rippling movement, stretching out like a gargantuan cloud, swallowing the sun with its darkness.

What was causing the movement? Something small. Thousands… no, millions of tiny objects.

The truth struck him like a blow.

Harvesters.

They blanketed the sky. Millions upon millions of tiny, murderous drones. Alexander Magnus had almost wiped out two-thirds of all human life with them.

He turned from the terror overhead. Before him, the white-sanded beach curved around a bend. On his left, the ocean spread out as far as the eye could see. To his right lay a dense jungle of palm trees and other tropical flora.

Where was he? What had happened to his kidnappers?

A sudden sound, brief but unmistakable, drifted over the soft, endless shushing of the sea.

Children's laughter, followed by a familiar voice.

"It's my turn now. Let me play, too!"

He'd been listening to that voice for months now. It had grown almost as dear to him as Nadia's.

Safiya.

He ran along the beach toward the sound of her voice. He must have escaped his kidnappers! Any minute now he would find Safiya. And wherever she was, Nadia would be close by.

He rounded the bend. A dozen children scampered about on the glistening sand, laughing as the waves washed up around their ankles. And there was Safiya with her shining, jet black hair and her deep, dark eyes that could hold all the wonder of the cosmos in their gaze.

She saw him and ran toward him. Some of the other children stopped their playing to watch.

Why were the children alone on the beach? Where was Nadia? Where were the other parents?

"Safiya!"

He stretched out his arms as she came near. Then, suddenly, he pulled back from her.

Something was wrong.

Safiya stopped a few feet from him.

"Hello, Charles Ferguson." She smiled and took a step closer. "Don't you recognize me?"

She looked just like Safiya, but it wasn't her. Safiya didn't speak in whole, unbroken sentences of flawless English. This child had no accent. Her voice almost sounded artificial.

He knelt in front of her, his face level with hers.

"Are you really Safiya?"

Her laughter mimicked Safiya's, but the tone rang hollow as if it were a recording, an electronic speaker instead of a human throat.

"Who else could I be, silly?" the girl's voice chided. "Come, I'll take you to Mother."

"You mean Nadia?"

She looked at him curiously, head perched to one side with her brow furrowed. Even her eyes seemed wrong. They lacked Safiya's animation, her vibrancy and liveliness.

As the girl blinked, he heard a faint clicking sound, like a camera shutter closing and opening.

His heart leapt in terror.

"I mean Mother." She pointed toward the jungle. He followed with his gaze and spotted, deep within the foliage, the glimmering contours of a sprawling, dome-shaped structure. It rose at least thirty feet high.

"Nadia is in that building?"

Again, the girl blinked. Again, that clicking sound.

"Mother is there."

He reached out and placed his hand on her arm. The moment his fingers touched her skin, he knew the answer.

The girl was cold as the sea. Cold as death.

She wasn't alive. She wasn't Safiya. She was a machine.

He screamed, and the sound of his own voice shattered the fabric of his nightmare.

⤙

*Stavetz! Stavetz!*

*Dizen modelzar. Malden durunetz!*

Warm hands shook his head from side to side. The voices switched to English. "Wake up! Doctor Ferguson. Are you all right?"

Charles opened his eyes. Someone had removed the helmet.

The teenaged face of the soldier in front of him held a haunted expression, as if in its brief years it had already accumulated the sorrows of old age.

"He's fine," the soldier announced to his companions, who stood in watchful silence nearby.

"He'd better be," one of the others replied. "Chairman Markhov would have our heads if anything happened to him. Here, American. Drink. Then the helmet goes back on."

Charles leaned forward and guzzled greedily from the water bottle the soldier held up to him. "I don't need the helmet. Please. I hate the darkness…and the dreams. How long has it been?"

The soldier picked the helmet up from an empty seat. "No more talking, American."

Charles tried to move his head away as the helmet came down, but there was no escape. They pressed it over him, trapping him once more in darkness and silence.

But he had learned something. The soldiers were Khatiz, just as he'd suspected. The name of the Central Party's leader, Chairman Markhov, was one of the few things the rest of the world knew about the isolative country.

If anyone could cross Khatizan's ironclad border and rescue him, it was Boris Petrov. God only knew how, but the crazy old Russian patriarch would find a way.

Boris shoved open the door of the liquor store and walked out into the New York twilight. He had parked his SUV around the corner. He climbed in and drove to the parking lot of the apartment complex, then found a secluded spot, away from prying streetlights. He left the engine running, opened the brown paper bag from the liquor store, and withdrew an unopened bottle of vodka.

"A demon lives in every shot," he muttered.

His grandfather used to say that. He'd probably heard it in the old country, some Soviet slogan to ward off alcoholism in the glorious new republic they were building. But Russians were made for alcohol. Incurable, really. A man could abstain, but only for so long. Eventually, the demon's voice could be ignored no longer. The thirst became necessity.

After years of freedom, it had waited for this moment of weakness. The tide had turned against him once more. He was adrift, defenseless. The siren song lured him toward a sea of oblivion.

It happened all the time in the old days, before Elena came into his life and straightened him out. It happened again briefly when Elena disappeared. Eleven years since his last plunge. Eleven years since his vow to Nadia.

He glanced at the apartment building where she and the others were working on decrypting John Flying Hawk's emails and waiting to hear the news from his meeting with the ATA Director.

The lights were on in their apartments. Working their tails off for nothing.

The door to Khatizan was shut. Director Obasanjo was going to stand on the sidelines and watch the world burn, and he couldn't do anything about it.

"Devil take the woman."

If only Jimmy MacPherson had stayed on a little longer. He would have found a way into Khatizan. When Jimmy ran the ATA, things worked the way they were supposed to. He'd let teams do their jobs. Always there in the background, making connections, building bridges with politicians, coaxing them until they saw the light.

Only Jimmy was out of the game. In his place was a cold micromanager, a hard-edged woman who knew nothing about the ATA family. Angela Obasanjo had already failed the agency. Barely two months on the job, and she'd lost the Home Office and countless agents with it.

She was an outsider, a stranger. She could care less that Charles Ferguson had been carted off to Khatizan on her watch to suffer God knows what fate. She wanted everyone to wait, but Boris knew what that meant. The time would never be right for her, the orders would never come. Charles would die, and she wouldn't care.

Where had Angela Obasanjo been when the Home Office was attacked? Why hadn't she been there on the ground hours later?

An overseas assignment, her personal secretary had said.

He unscrewed the cork on the vodka bottle. The air teemed with expectancy, the demanding presence of alcohol. His heart pounded against his chest like a jackhammer. Sweat beads trickled down his brow. His soul was on fire.

Why resist?

"She's the mole." The words provided the justification, the needed excuse for what he was about to do. "You picked a convenient time for that trip overseas, Director Obasanjo. Almost as if you knew what was coming. You betrayed us, didn't you? Sold us out. Magnus, he planned all of this. You still get the last laugh, you old devil! Even from the grave you destroy us."

The liquor burned his throat as he gulped greedily. He lowered the bottle and leaned back against the headrest.

There. Already the sharp edges were softening. Already the numbness worked against the unending pain.

Gavriel was gone. So many others, gone forever.

"Nadia. Forgive me."

Nadia would understand. He had no choice. He needed this, needed a break from the world. Nadia wouldn't blame him. Nadia understood everything.

No, not Nadia.

"Elena!" He shouted his wife's name as if it could summon her from whatever void she had vanished into all those years ago.

Another long, desperate gulp.

Half an hour later, he stumbled from the SUV clutching a near-empty vodka bottle. He held it up against the orange gleam of a streetlamp, swirling the last remnants of liquid fire, watching with a vague and hungry fascination.

"She's the traitor…Kenjiro." His slurred words sounded heavy in his own ears. "Kenjiro, where are you? Where'd you go?"

He blinked several times and looked around. The parking lot was empty.

"Ah, that's right." He held a forefinger in the air and shook it several times. "I sent you home before the liquor, you little angel. Didn't want you to see me fall. You idolize me, Kenjiro, do you know that? You and all the rest. You think I never make mistakes. Well, look at me now. I've made a mistake!"

He smashed the bottle against the base of the streetlamp and broke into wild laughter.

"She betrayed us, Kenjiro, do you hear me?" he roared. "Our own director in her gray little pantsuit. Isn't it delightful? Mr. Charles will die in a hellhole prison factory because of an ice-hearted woman."

Not that it mattered. Nothing mattered now. No one mattered. Elena was gone, gone forever. They'd taken her, and she would never come back. Just like Gavriel. Just like Mr. Charles.

Now he could disappear, too. A vodka bottle was a doorway. He could step through it and be gone forever.

"Elena!"

He ran to the entrance of the apartment building and fumbled in his pocket until his unruly fingers wrapped themselves around his keychain. He carefully, slowly tried each key against the lock. Why would none of them work?

Oh, yes, the gold one.

He lumbered inside and found the stairwell. "Up, up the winding stairs." He clutched the handrail, half walking, half pulling himself onward. "One two three, look at me!"

Where was he going? Nadia.

And what was the apartment number?

"Three forty-three, look at me!"

Magnus had probably found them anyway, found them in their apartments and killed them. That's why the light in the apartment was still on. He was already too late. The Chemist would be dead. Her security team would be dead. Fazal would be dead. Lenny would be dead. Nadia would be dead. And then, last and least, Boris Petrov would die.

"Nadia!"

He stumbled down the hallway, turned the corner, and came face to face with Zhang Meiying, the Chemist. She barred his path.

"Let me in!" he shouted at her. "I'm still in charge of my own team, aren't I? That cold-eyed hag can't keep us out of Khatizan. We're going, do you hear me? But let me see my daughter first."

Why was the Chemist looking at him like that? Was she angry? Was that pity?

Ah, no, it was good old disgust.

Yes, he remembered that look. Elena had looked at him like that once upon a time. Long ago, in the first year of their marriage, when he had buried the troubles of work in a glass bottle.

He broke into song, an old Russian chorus about snow falling on rooftops in an endless winter.

The Chemist still wouldn't let him pass. What was wrong with her?

"I'll do what I want!" he roared. "You women can't stop me, do you hear? You can't!"

He didn't remember hitting her, but there she was on the ground, looking up at him with her hand on her cheek and fury in her eyes.

Others had arrived, the rest of her security team. Good little soldiers, doing what they're told while good people died because bureaucrats with plastic smiles needed to make money. They can't be bothered with Mr. Charles. They don't even care that Khatizan bombed the Germans. Truth is inconvenient, so please shut up, Mr. Boris, and leave us to our delusions.

"We're going!" He shouted as his own agents pinned him against the wall. The Chemist stood a few feet away, watching him like a shrewd little fox. "We're going to Khatizan. No one can stop us. Do you hear me? No one!"

The door to the apartment opened. A slender, beautiful woman with a horrified expression emerged from within.

That face…it was Elena! He'd failed her all over again. He'd failed them all.

No, not Elena. Nadia.

"Oh, God." He knelt and buried his face in his hands. "Oh, dear God."

﹏

At nine o'clock the following morning, Julia Pearson stuffed Little Boris into his arms.

"You're going to put an alcohol sensor in that mangy doll of yours."

Boris closed his eyes. Last night's vodka was getting its revenge.

Headache? Headaches were for novices. Russians didn't get headaches when they binged. This was an ice pick planted right in the back of his skull.

He stared dully at the mangled countenance of Little Boris. "You want me to put an alcohol sensor in Safiya's toy?"

Julia snorted. The plastic beads in her braids clinked together as she shook her head. "That's no toy, and we both know it. I wasn't born yesterday, Mr. Boris, so get that in your thick skull right now. I explained to her that Papa Boris needed it for a while, so she's loaning it to you. I know that doll's got cameras and microphones and all kinds of spy junk inside."

"Spy…*junk*?"

"You heard me." She folded her arms over her chest. "That's why you gave it to Safiya, isn't it? So you could keep an eye on her, make sure she's safe twenty-four seven?"

Why did God make women so blasted clever? More to the point, since they already knew everything, why did they still ask so many questions?

"Put an alcohol sensor in it," Julia went on. "I know you can do that. You spy people are always blowing our money, aren't you? Uncle Sam's out there spending a hundred billion on this, a hundred billion on that. All those top-secret programs sucking up taxpayer dollars while the good people of America can't pay their hospital bills."

She put her hands on her hips. The woman had more power poses than a Wall Street CEO. "Now I won't complain about stuff I can't change, but I can change you. No more vodka. Not around Peter, not around Nadia, not around Safiya, and definitely not around me. You've got a head full of gray hair, Mr. Boris. Your crazy days are done with. Do you hear me?"

Up until that moment, he'd believed that the new ATA Director was the only woman he feared.

He was wrong.

Julia Pearson's face was now mere inches from his, and it wasn't merely a no-nonsense kind of face. It was a *do what I say or you will die in your sleep* kind of face.

He swallowed. "I hear you, Mrs. Pearson."

She leaned back and gave him a firm nod. "Once your people get the sensor in that doll, you're gonna take it with you everywhere you go. And that means Khatizan, because I know you and you're gonna find a way. Your friends say they can track you with this doll of yours, so I'm going to track you, too. You will use that alcohol sensor every waking hour on the hour or else."

He couldn't help it. He had to know. "Or else what?"

She pressed her lips together and shook her head slightly. Those beads in her hair rattled like bones. "You aren't too old for a whipping, Mr. Boris. If I catch you drinking that devil's brew again, I'll teach you what my momma taught my daddy when he tried to pull that nonsense around her. You do *not* want to go there. That man had to take a pillow to work for a whole week just so he could sit in his desk chair." She sniffed. "And I'll tell you what else, if it happens again, you can say goodbye to grandma's double-fudge brownies."

"What?" He flung up his hands. "You're not playing fair!"

"Never," Julia shot back. "Repeat after me. Never. I'm not messing around."

Nobody in the room at that moment would have accused Julia Pearson of messing around. She was right, of course. The brownies may have lightened the mood, but they both knew this was life or death. If he fell off that cliff one more time, he might never get back on his feet again. No pillow would cushion that fall.

He handed Little Boris to Zhang Meiying. "Do what she says. And since it sounds like I'm taking it to Khatizan, give it the works."

Meiying held the doll for a moment, then looked back at him with tears in her eyes.

"If you ever lay a finger on me again," she said quietly, "I will break it. I don't care if you're my boss. I don't care if you're drunk." She turned and disappeared from the room.

She had every right to hate him. They all did. But it wasn't hatred that had brought those tears. It was disillusionment. They had looked up to him, the whole team. He was a living legend in the ATA.

It was a testament to her loyalty that she still followed orders. She could have reported him to the director. She probably *should* have reported him.

Julia gave him one last glare and left. Now he was alone with Nadia. She had been watching silently from a corner of the room. She rose and walked over to him. He lowered his head, his face burning with shame. The worst of betrayals. He'd broken a solemn vow. How she must despise him!

She cupped his face in her hands and raised his head, forcing him to look in her eyes. "I love you. I forgive you. But I want my father back. Do you hear me? When this is over with, you're going to get help." She kissed him lightly on both cheeks. "Safiya has suffered enough. If you're ever drunk again in front of her, we're leaving you."

When she left, he buried his face in his hands and wept. Not the tears of intoxication. Those came far too easily. These were the unwilling tears of a terrified man who faced demons too strong for him, a man who tiptoed through life like a tightrope walker, always a hair's breadth from falling into the abyss.

In other words, they were the tears of an addict.

# Chapter Seventeen

# Surprises

L ENNY PHILLIPS PUSHED his coke-bottle glasses up to the bridge of his nose. Fervid excitement glimmered in his mud-brown eyes.

"Any news?" Boris asked.

"Heck yes, there's news." Lenny downed the rest of his energy drink, crushed the can with his fist, and let out a thunderous belch. "Doomhammer went ballistic on John Flying Hawk's emails last night while you were getting sloshed. I've got to tell you, Boris, watching your daughter mod Crowdbreak is like watching Mozart compose a symphony. Pure frigging ecstasy. Flying Hawk's emails had this weird multilayered encryption. Never seen anything like it before. So Nadia came up with a new problem for the gamers to solve. She created this fifty-headed Gorgon Underlord, and the gamers had to take down all fifty heads simultaneously. A million of them hacked that sucker to bits across a hundred different servers last night. Decrypted everything in twenty minutes."

The grin on Lenny's face verged on beatific, as if he were lost in the depths of romantic bliss.

"What did you find?"

"Love letters," Fazal al-Najjar replied. "The most top-secret, highly protected love letters the world has never seen. Flying Hawk's girlfriend is a woman named Sierra Morgan. She writes him poetry that makes Edgar Allen Poe sound cheerful. But we found something odd in her last message."

Boris leaned forward. "What is it?"

"An IP address," Lenny answered as he clicked open the lid of his next energy drink. "She wrote this psycho poem about jumping off a building, and right before her skull smashes into the concrete, she looks up into the sky and sees clouds forming a string of numbers. An IP address. It's like a mailing address for the Internet, tells you where a specific computer lives. She wrote the letters *AV* next to it. Also had this random port number, 48123."

Boris always felt like he knew technology until he talked to people like Lenny Phillips. "What is port number 48123? Is that supposed to mean something?"

Lenny shrugged. "It's unassigned, which means it's off the official radar, maybe some homebrew program. Given the encryption on those emails, I'd say this IP address is what we need to focus on next."

"Any luck with the message John Flying Hawk gave to Charles?"

"Nothing yet," Nadia replied. She slipped in from her bedroom and curled up on the couch to listen. "But I'm hoping that message and the IP address we've found might be connected."

Boris folded his arms over his chest. "The ATA's new director won't lift a finger to help us. If we go in, we'll have to do it on our own. God knows what we'll be up against. What you're doing here could mean life or death for us when we're inside Khatizan."

Lenny wove his fingers together and popped his knuckles. "Don't worry, boss, we've got the Doomhammer on our team. So, who is this super-evil villain chick we're fighting? Aryana Voss or whatever her name is."

"From what Thompson said, she sounds almost inhuman," Boris replied. "Incredible strength, or so they say."

"I bet she's a cyborg!" Lenny shouted. "That is so frigging awesome." His eyes suddenly widened, and his mouth formed a gaping O. "But what if she's *not* a cyborg? I mean, it could be like when Captain Fuzzbucket got shanghaied by the Dormanzian Pirates and woke up in the Alterverse. There was this supervillain humanoid chick there named Enigma Three. Well, she looked like a humanoid, but actually—"

Boris held up his hand and Lenny immediately clamped his mouth shut. If he didn't put a stop to it, Lenny would be talking about Dormanzian Pirates until Mr. Charles died of old age. "Lenny, I know you believe that comic books are Delphic oracles unlocking the mysteries of the universe, but right now we have a job to do. Germany is about to trigger NATO's Article Five against Russia. Russia is preparing for nuclear war after the attack on Novorossiysk. If this mission to Khatizan fails, they'll be launching ICBMs at each other by the end of the month."

Lenny nodded vigorously. "Oh, yeah, totally. But no joke, you should read that one when you get a chance. It's the original series, number two fifty-three. And now that I'm thinking about it, I have this crazy idea…"

Boris's phone buzzed. Kenjiro. He mouthed an apology to Lenny for interrupting and answered the call.

"Have a minute, boss?" An unusual tremor tinged the stoic voice of his operations manager.

"What's up, Kenjiro?"

"An old friend dropped by and was looking for you. Can you come to the Newark meeting place?"

"I'll come when I get a chance." He kept his tone noncommittal, but his heart nearly skipped a beat. Kenjiro was using codewords. *Newark* meant a safe house in Queens, the one with an interrogation room. "Might be a while."

He hung up the phone. "Lenny, could you send John Flying Hawk an email for me?"

Lenny shrugged. "Sure, if you want me to."

"Tell him this." He took out a piece of paper and handed it to Lenny. "And do it right away." He gave Nadia a quick kiss on the cheek. "Goodbye, my darling Doomhammer. You're a saint to forgive an old wretch like me." He clapped Lenny on the shoulder. "Let me know as soon as you figure out what's behind that IP address."

⚜

An hour later, Boris peered through the one-way glass looking into the safe house's interrogation room. A youthful Khatiz terrorist had appeared, seemingly out of thin air, and surrendered himself to Kenjiro outside the ATA's temporary headquarters. "And he claims he was part of the attack?"

Kenjiro nodded. "Yes, sir. He knew all the details. That"—Kenjiro pointed at the sniper rifle on the table behind them—"was the weapon he used in the Home Office attack. The ballistics report is a match for several of the victims. He said there were nine shooters total, three groups of three firing from three positions. It matches intelligence reports on Youth Corps Special Forces tactics."

Boris walked over to the table and picked up one of several briefcases, all of which looked as if they had been severely burned. "What about these?"

"He claims that they had energy bombs inside, the same kind as the one used in Berlin."

Berlin? Boris's heart lurched into his throat. He carefully set the briefcase back on the table. "He claims?"

"They were intact when he turned them over, but they all sort of… melted…a few minutes ago. Probably a timed safety measure so no one could reverse engineer them if the attack didn't go off as planned. The briefcases had some kind of scanner lock, but he claimed he couldn't open them. Only his commanding officer could do that."

"He was lying." Boris took a deep breath, considering. "Nine briefcases for nine soldiers, which means he could have opened one of them, at least. Get rid of them, and don't let anyone know about it, not even in the ATA."

"He said their mission was to destroy New York City with those bombs," Kenjiro added. "His commanding officer, a Youth Corps lieutenant named Paul Veliu, was against the attack. He came up with a plan for Andrei to steal the bombs and find us. Find you, to be precise."

"Me?"

Kenjiro nodded. "He asked for you by name. He seemed to know that I worked with you."

Boris exhaled through pursed lips. Another walk through a minefield. Was this a trap? A Magnus Foundation scheme? It seemed too good to be true. Right when he needed it most, a golden opportunity had fallen into his lap.

"Who else knows about him?"

"No one," Kenjiro replied at once.

"Not even our new director?"

Kenjiro held his gaze for a long moment. "No one, sir."

"Keep it that way."

"Yes, sir."

Boris grunted. "Now let's see what this young rascal can tell us."

He stepped into the hallway and prepared himself. Be professional. Get the intel, give the suspect a deal, but don't let anger take over the conversation.

Tough advice when the kid could be Gavriel's murderer. No doubt he'd been brainwashed from childhood by Khatizan's Central Party. He would have been following orders like any good soldier, but that didn't change the fact that he'd gunned down some of the best and most courageous people in the world.

Boris took an unlit cigar, stuffed it in his mouth, and paced in the hallway.

One false move could ruin everything. He'd seen it happen in interrogations. Things got personal, the agent blew their plan of attack, and suddenly the asset locked up like a bank vault. There was no going back once you crossed that line.

He rested his hand on the door, took a final breath, and walked into the room.

"Good evening." He took a chair across from the sniper. "I'm Boris Petrov. I hear you've been looking for me."

Pale-faced, haunted eyes ringed with purple, the Youth Corps soldier looked like an elderly man who'd survived a holocaust and suddenly woke up in a teenaged body. Sweet Saint Eustathius, what was wrong with Khatizan? How could they do this to their own children? If rumors were true, those Youth Camps of theirs were hellholes where the strong preyed on the weak. A state-sanctioned, real-life *Lord of the Flies*.

The youth met his gaze with disarming openness. No trace of fear, no sign of weakness. Only sorrow and, perhaps, regret.

"Are you really Boris Petrov?"

The youth's American accent sounded flawless. He could have walked into any high school in America and no one would know he was a Khatiz soldier instead of the new kid from out of town. That was the point. Khatizan had created an army of multilingual, brainwashed terrorists.

"Yes, I'm Boris Petrov. What's your name, soldier?"

The youth rested his cuffed hands on the table. "He said you'd know what kind of car he drove when you met him."

"Who said?"

"The guy we kidnapped. Charles Ferguson."

Boris made sure he had control of his voice before he replied. "You talked to Charles Ferguson?"

"No, sir. My superior officer, Lieutenant Paul Veliu, spoke with Doctor Ferguson on the way to the airstrip. We could all tell he was an innocent man. We shouldn't have kidnapped him, sir, but those were our orders." He paused. "And I shouldn't have said that, not yet. I'm not supposed to talk to anybody but Boris Petrov. You need to prove that you're him. What kind of car did Charles Ferguson drive when you met him?"

Boris stood and walked to the opaque window at the back of the room. Kenjiro was right. Either the kid was honest, or he was an incredible liar.

He turned around. "Charles Ferguson used to drive an old tan sedan. I bought him the automotive equivalent of the Sistine Chapel, and he still pines for that dung-colored hunk of junk. It's his obsession. Some people love shoes, he loves grandma cars."

The youth nodded. Not even a hint of a smile. "Before I talk, can you promise me something?"

So he wasn't as guileless as he seemed. The kid had leverage, and he was clever enough to cash it in before it went away. What was his angle? Money? Power? Access?

Boris took a seat and folded his hands on the table, his fingertips only inches from the cuffed hands of the sniper.

"First tell me your name, soldier."

The youth didn't hesitate. "Special Forces Sublieutenant Andrei Idrisov, Member of Chairman Markhov's Order of the Saber, Sniper First Class, assigned to Red Ops One's First Triad."

So many titles for a teenage sharpshooter. "And what do you want, Andrei Idrisov?"

"To earn your trust, sir. My great-grandfather fought the Soviets. My grandfather died in battle on our eastern border, and my father fought in the Revolutionary Army. I know what you must think of my country. I didn't mind fighting enemy soldiers, but now they want me to kill civilians. You saw what happened in Berlin. We did that."

Boris caught his breath. This was it. This was the evidence he needed. "You, personally?"

"No, sir. But Khatizan did it. I know the truth now. They can't lie to me anymore."

"I need more proof. How do you know that Khatizan was behind the Berlin attack?"

Andrei replied at once. "Lieutenant Veliu planted the bomb on the thirty-fifth floor of the Bann Commercial Building. Commander Vladimir Firlenko personally directed the mission at the Chairman's orders. Lieutenant Veliu was assured that it would be a pinpoint strike against a known terrorist cell who allegedly kept a block of offices in that building for their operation. He said those devices we were given for the New York mission are like the one he used in Berlin, only much more powerful. Does anyone else have a weapon like that?"

Boris weighed the sniper's words. Who was this Paul Veliu? What was his motive in all of this?

"Why would your lieutenant tell you that?"

"He wanted me to know the truth. He told me I should defect, that I should find you and—"

He cut Andrei off. "Paul Veliu told you to defect?"

Andrei looked at him with astonishment. "Yes, sir. I would never have done this on my own. He opened my eyes to the truth. They turned him into a terrorist, and he's going to make them pay. He has a plan to take down the entire Central Party. That's why I'm talking to you. But you don't believe me, and he knew you wouldn't. There's something else, a letter you're supposed to read. It's sewn into the inside of my coat. If you have a knife, you can get it out."

Boris flicked open his pocketknife and grabbed Andrei's jacket, which was resting on the back of the sniper's chair.

"It's beneath the front pocket," Andrei told him.

A small pouch had been sewn on the inside of the jacket. He carefully slit it open with the knife and withdrew a sealed envelope.

"I haven't read it myself," Andrei said. "Paul knew you wouldn't trust us. He said this would help."

Boris cut open the top of the envelope and withdrew a single piece of folded notebook paper.

*My love, my heart, my Boris…*

Elena's handwriting!

His eyes devoured the rest of the letter while his heart hammered against his chest. He read it three more times, then turned, facing the opaque, one-way glass window. He blinked away the tears that had come unbidden, then slid his finger across his own throat.

Kill the audio tape, Kenjiro. That was the signal. Turn off the microphone and delete the recording. Sometimes intel was too dangerous for anyone else to hear, even in the ATA.

"I'm sorry to cut this short," Andrei said suddenly.

"What?" He turned, and Andrei was standing with his cuffed hands held out in front of him. Boris reached for his sidearm, then realized that Andrei wasn't moving any closer.

"We need you to trust me. That letter is one step toward earning that trust. Now let me do something else for you, then decide what you want to do with me. Lock me up, get rid of me, it makes no difference as long as you believe me."

Was the kid crazy? "You have no idea what this letter says?"

"None," Andrei replied.

"Let's say I trust you. What are you asking of us, Andrei?"

"First, we're going to save your daughter's life," the sniper replied. "They're coming for her. If you want to keep her alive, we need to leave now."

Zhang Meiying answered her cell phone.

"Meiying?" It was Boris. His voice was tense.

She swallowed down her anger. He had been drunk, but that did not excuse him. If she had reported him, Director Obasanjo would have dragged him over a bed of hot coals. Suspended him for months, maybe for life.

That was the problem. Wounded as it was right now, the ATA needed Boris Petrov.

Still, if he didn't keep his promise to stay sober, she'd drag him through those burning coals with her own two hands.

"Zhang Meiying, are you there? It's urgent."

"Yes." She forced out the next word. "Sir."

"Your position has been compromised. There's a hit team heading your way. Their leader is the man I told you about, Rod Walker. He's got three Youth Corps commandos with him. They'll look like Ground Branch. They'll fight like them, too. They're after Nadia. Prepare your team. And make sure you open the kitchen window. That last part's important."

"How much time do I—"

Gunfire erupted in the hallway. Automatic weapons, assault rifles.

"They're here," she said. "I hope you're already on your way."

◆

"Let me get this straight, sir." Kenjiro's voice quivered with exasperation. They were racing across New York City to the safe house. "We're about to give a Youth Corps sniper his rifle and a dozen rounds of ammunition. Then we're going to put him on a roof across from the apartment building where our most valuable assets are staying. I hate to ask you this, sir, but"—Kenjiro flung his hands in the air—"have you lost your freaking mind?"

Boris barked a laugh. "Good for you, Kenjiro! You've shown more emotion in the last twenty seconds than I've seen in the last twenty years. But life is an adventure, and sometimes even sane people need to jump out of airplanes. Madcaps like me always jump long before the sane people."

An apt analogy for Kenjiro, who happened to be a masterful skydiver.

"I trust the kid," Boris went on. "Call it instinct. If this works out, we'll put him on our team."

Kenjiro's eyes widened. "Our team?" he cried. "You couldn't possibly—"

"You told me that no one else knew about him, correct?"

"Well, yes, but—"

"There's a traitor in our ranks, Kenjiro. Rod Walker knows the location of our safe houses. He also knew about our communication app. Only twelve people in the ATA know about that app, and you and I are two of them. We need all the friends we can get, and I believe Andrei Idrisov is a friend. What about you?"

Kenjiro exhaled. "I think you're insane. But I've always thought you're insane, and somehow, you're usually right anyway."

"So you're with me?"

"Do you have to ask?" Kenjiro looked into the rearview mirror, no doubt examining Andrei Idrisov in the backseat. "What do I tell the others?"

"Say he's one of Gavriel's cousins. He's joining us to avenge his relative."

"He might have been the one who shot Gavriel, you know."

Kenjiro could be right, but it was better not to know. "If so, he's going to need the rest of his life to redeem himself. Today's a good day to start."

⁜

Zhang Meiying hung up the phone.

"Get in the safe room!" she shouted to the bewildered researchers in the living room. "Now!"

"But...Safiya!" Nadia shrieked.

"She and Julia went out for a walk with Peter, right? That means they're a lot safer than we are at the moment. These attackers are coming for you, not her. Now move! Just like we practiced. With their firepower, that security door may not hold them for long."

Lenny Phillips leapt to his feet and helped Fazal al-Najjar to the hidden safe room behind Nadia's bedroom. Nadia hurried after them. The fourth asset, Eugene Thompson, didn't move. He just looked at Mei with a strange expression.

"Did you hear me, Doctor Thompson? You need to move, now."

The gunfire in the hallway fell silent. She clicked on her two-way radio.

"James? Perry? Report. Are you there?"

Silence. As if in confirmation of her fears, there was a series of dull thuds as the security door was hit with the blasts of an assault rifle.

"You're alone, aren't you?" Thompson said. "Your teammates were in the hallway."

She pulled out her briefcase, set it on the table, and flipped it open.

"Yes, Doctor Thompson, I'm alone. But not for long. In a few minutes, I'll have more company than I can handle. My sacrifice—a swift one, no doubt—will be in vain if you don't get into that safe room. If we're lucky, it will take their strike team time to get in here and more time to get past me. Maybe even long enough for Boris to show up."

"I'm not going," he replied stubbornly. "I want to help you."

She pulled six darts filled with bluish-green fluid from her briefcase kit and loaded them into a pair of pistol-sized tranquilizer guns that had enough force to pierce through the thickest clothing. She carefully tucked three more darts into her belt. If she found a place to conceal herself, she might get one or two of the attackers before the others unloaded on her with those assault rifles.

"This is a job for professionals." She was surprised by her own calmness. A gift from her uncle, part of the peculiar training he had given her before she joined the ATA. "There's no point in killing yourself for nothing, Doctor Thompson."

"I'll distract them," he replied without hesitation. "Listen, I have a plan. You know I was an assistant director of Control, right? No one from the Foundation survived the attack on Magnus Headquarters. For all they know, I'm still on their side."

Mei suddenly remembered that this same scrawny-looking professor had waded into a hail of sniper fire in an attempt to rescue Gavriel only days before. It was the sort of thing Gavriel himself would have done. Maybe there was more to him than she had realized. That was certainly the case with Charles Ferguson, and the two were close friends.

"What do you propose?"

"Tie me to a chair. I'll start talking as soon as they come in. Whatever you're going to do, at least you'll have a chance."

"You're either incredibly brave or incredibly stupid," she replied.

He snickered. "That's a false dichotomy. It's entirely possible that I'm both at the same time."

There were more dings as the attackers turned their gunfire on the outer wall. Good luck with that. The wall was reinforced with thick sheets of solid steel.

She glanced back at Thompson. He was brave, no doubt about it. And in his strange, nutty professor kind of way, he was borderline cute. Not that she would ever tell him that. And not that it would matter if she did. If those attackers had the right explosives, she and Thompson would both be dead within the next five minutes.

"Fine," she said at last. "Open that window, then grab a kitchen knife or whatever weapon you can find. Probably won't help, but it'll be better than nothing."

She ran to one of the bedrooms, snatched a faux leather belt from the closet, and rushed back to the kitchen.

The gunfire fell silent.

Did they have explosives?

Thompson was dutifully sitting in one of the dining chairs with his hands clasped behind him.

"Not too tight," he grumbled as she cinched the belt around his wrists.

"When you're ready to be free," she said, "just twist your hands like this." She rolled his wrists forward and the belt slipped free. "Got it?"

"Yep. Nothing to it," he said between quick, frantic breaths.

She rested her hands on his shoulders and leaned close to him. "Look at me, Doctor Thompson. You're going to be okay. Do you understand?" A lie, but he did seem to start breathing a little easier. "They're not here to kill you. They're here to kidnap you."

Another lie. This time he cracked a nervous smile.

"Now I'm going to disappear," she added.

His eyes widened. "You're…what?"

She turned, took three steps, and leapt onto the kitchen counter-top. She pulled herself up into the small, shadowy niche between the tops of the cabinets and the ceiling. A few feet of clearance draped in shadows made a perfect hiding place. With any luck, she'd get a few shots off before the attackers realized what was happening.

The blast came a half minute later. It took down the front door and a huge chunk of the steel wall. Bits of shrapnel flew outward, but thankfully none made it to the kitchen.

What had she been thinking? That blast alone could have killed Eugene Thompson. He was still a high-priority asset even though he kept putting himself in harm's way.

Three attackers stormed into the room. Two looked like CIA Ground Branch officers, just as Boris had predicted. The third—Rod Walker, no doubt—was dressed in a dark gray suit.

"Don't shoot!" Thompson squealed. The man was good at squealing, apparently. A minor virtue under the circumstances. "I'm Eugene Thompson. I'm with the Foundation."

One of the two in combat gear hoisted his rifle and pointed it at Thompson. It was too early to spring her trap, but what else could she do? She aimed one of the tranquilizer pistols at the gap of exposed flesh between the attacker's helmet and his vest. If her dart touched his neck, he would be incapacitated almost instantly. He'd also be alive, which meant the ATA could pump him for information. Her finger was closing on the trigger when Rod Walker spoke.

"Wait." Rod lifted his hand, and the soldier lowered his assault rifle. "Why are you tied up, Doctor Thompson? Word in the Foundation is that you're working for these folks now. Were we wrong?"

The three attackers were beside Mei now, and they hadn't noticed her. A few more feet and they would be in the perfect position.

Why were there only three? Boris had told her there would be four, Rod Walker and three others.

"On their team?" Thompson shrieked. "Are you insane? They captured me at Headquarters and hauled me away. They keep trying to get me to talk, but I won't."

Rod Walker snorted. "That's not what I've heard."

There was a click, and a switchblade appeared in his hand.

"I heard you betrayed Lord Magnus, that you worked for Ferguson and Petrov. And I trust the people I serve more than some lily-livered scientist. That lying tongue of yours is about to get cut out."

Mei took a deep breath in. No more time. Their position wasn't perfect, but she would have to make it work.

"No," Thompson shouted. "I'll talk! I've got intel on them. I know everything."

Rod gave a husky laugh as he walked toward Thompson with his knife lowered in his right hand. "So do I, Doctor Thompson."

Now.

She fired from both hands with the tranquilizer pistols as she dropped down from her hiding place. Both shots struck home, piercing the necks of the two fake Ground Branch officers.

She landed catlike on her feet as her first two victims hit the floor and raised herself to fire the last shot at Rod Walker.

But he was too fast.

He spun and flung the switchblade in one perfect, fluid motion.

A sharp, blinding pain shot through her arm as the knife pierced her right shoulder.

Thank God she was ambidextrous.

As Rod pulled his handgun from his holster, she got out a final shot from the tranquilizer pistol in her left hand.

Her aim wasn't perfect under the circumstances, but it was good enough. A second later, Rod Walker hit the ground.

❧

Eugene Thompson freed himself and rushed to Mei. That Foundation monster had hurled his knife straight into her shoulder. She was kneeling over with pain, her blood dripping to the floor, her hand gripping the hilt of the knife.

But she had won the fight. She had taken down all three of them in a matter of seconds. He felt like he was seeing her for the first time. He'd been so infatuated with Anna that he'd barely noticed Mei. She never put herself forward, never drew attention to herself, but the woman was incredible, fearless, with a quiet beauty that was all her own. How could he have missed what was right in front of him?

Gods, don't let her die.

"Are you okay?" he asked, then cursed his own stupidity. How could she be okay when she had a knife sticking out of her shoulder?

What was he supposed to do now? If he pulled the knife out, the bleeding would get worse. "Don't worry, I'm sure Boris will be here soon."

"There's…another." Mei had forced out the words through gritted teeth.

"Another what?"

He looked up. *That's* what she meant.

A fourth attacker stood in the gaping hole that used to be a doorway. The man walked into the room casually, his assault rifle raised, a slight smirk playing over his lips.

"Look out!" Thompson cried. He pointed his finger at the attacker as if that futile act could somehow stop an armed assailant.

Thompson firmly believed in science. He had no patience for magic or mysticism, and he was highly skeptical of coincidences. But in that moment, by some twisted possibility that could only exist in the realm of chaos theory, the duel between an index finger and an assault rifle ended as quickly as it had begun.

The index finger won.

The attacker toppled backward to the ground and lay still.

"What did you just do to him?" Mei asked. Hissed, rather, through evident pain. "Did you throw a knife?"

"What?" He stared at her for a moment, uncomprehending. Then he burst out laughing. Wild, hysterical laughter.

"My knife?" he cried. "I forgot all about it."

She'd told him to arm himself, so he had dug frantically through the kitchen cabinets until he found a knife.

A butter knife.

He reached into his back pocket, pulled out the dull, gleaming utensil, and held it up for her inspection.

"Then…how?" she murmured.

Before Thompson could answer, Boris Petrov ran into the room, followed by a swarm of ATA agents and first responders.

"A sniper took him out from across the street," Boris said. "Good thing you remembered to open that window. Now try to relax, Mei. We've got an ambulance outside."

Thompson stepped away as ATA agents surrounded Mei. Moments later, she was hustled out on a stretcher by a medical team. Thompson wanted to go with her and make sure she would be okay, but he felt too weary to move. What could he do for her, anyway? It wasn't like she would want him to be around. Women never wanted him to be around.

He sat down on the kitchen chair and put his hands on his forehead.

Twice now. Twice he'd stared down death in as many weeks. Charles was right. They should give this whole mad business up and go back to the university. College freshmen could be the most annoying creatures in the known universe, but at least they didn't try to kill you with assault rifles on a weekly basis.

"Why weren't you in the safe room, Mr. Thompson?" Boris rested a hand on his shoulder.

"I couldn't let her face them alone. I was a…distraction."

Boris barked a laugh. It was the first time Thompson had heard that rich, deep sound since the attack on the ATA Home Office. Much as he hated to admit it, he had missed Boris's humor.

"You'd better watch out, Mr. Thompson," Boris rumbled, elbowing him in the ribs. "If you don't stop acting like a soldier, I might put you on my team."

Their eyes met, and Boris stopped laughing.

"I wish you would," Thompson said quietly.

⁓

Boris pulled the SUV into the gravel driveway of Jimmy MacPherson's cottage and killed the engine.

Just being here made him feel better about everything. Jimmy was a man's man, a humble hero, a legend in the intelligence community. He hadn't retired in style in some suburban cookie-cutter mansion, not Jimmy. Just a humble log cottage with a pond on one side and miles of national forest on the other. Boris spied a fishing boat moored to a wooden dock. When Jimmy had been the ATA's director, every vacation he'd taken had been a backwoods fishing trip.

Now Boris needed his old director's guidance. He'd always talked to Jimmy one-on-one before every mission, going over every detail, planning out all the possibilities. He couldn't do that with Angela Obasanjo. He didn't trust her, and even if he did, how much did she actually know? What missions had she been on? How many times had she been in the crosshairs while the bullets were flying?

The front door to the cottage creaked as it swung open. Jimmy MacPherson lumbered out. He'd grown a beard and looked heavier around the middle since his retirement, but it was still the same Jimmy. Five feet and ten inches of homegrown Texan toughness.

"Well, look what the cat drug in," Jimmy said with a baritone chuckle. "Glad you dropped by. How are you, Boris?"

"I'm alive," Boris replied, "which is more than I deserve. Gavriel is dead, along with too many of our people. And we barely stopped an attack at a safe house. The enemy knows all our secrets, it seems."

Jimmy swore. "Gavriel's dead? I loved that kid. Reminded me of you at that age. I figured he'd be doing your job one of these days. I'm sorry, Boris. It hurts to lose the good ones. You got any leads on who's behind it all?"

"The attackers came from Khatizan," Boris replied. "I have a plan, but I need to talk it over with you."

Jimmy's eyes narrowed. "You know I'm retired, right?"

"I know you kept your security clearance," Boris said. "You're still on the advisory board, aren't you?"

Jimmy leaned over and spat on the ground. Chewing tobacco, a not-so-subtle reminder of the man's other passion in life, baseball. "Board hasn't met since the attack, but yeah, I've still got my clearance. Look, Boris, I'm not your director anymore. Now I'm just an old fart who likes to fish and watch the Rangers."

"The Foundation took Charles Ferguson," Boris said. "I think that was the real reason for the attack. I'm going to Khatizan now to get him back."

Jimmy sighed, then he cussed, and then he spat dark brown tobacco juice into the dirt beside his boot. "You hear about that F-16 that crashed out in Alaska this morning?"

Boris nodded. "Saw it on the news. Mechanical failure, wasn't it?"

"Mechanical failure my foot!" Jimmy said. "Pair of Russian Su-35s crossed into Alaskan airspace and took it out."

"What?" Boris cried. "Russia attacked us? Have we retaliated?"

"Kremlin's keeping it quiet, but a friend of mine in Moscow told me those two Su-35s went down over the Bering Strait around the same time." Jimmy shook his head. "The sand's running out of the hourglass, Boris, but you know how things work in Washington. Those desk jockeys will still be sitting around jabbering at their conference tables when the nukes start falling. You've got to stop this thing, Boris, and you'd better do it fast. If you think Khatizan is behind all this, then you need to find proof. Now let's grab a case of cold ones, sit out on the dock, and figure this thing out. Aw, heck. I should have remembered, sorry. Forget the beer. How about some iced tea?"

Boris had done his last breath test with Little Boris forty-five minutes ago, which meant he had another one coming up soon. "Thanks, Jimmy."

# Chapter Eighteen

# Broken Minds

Elena Petrova unwrapped the golden foil enclosing one of the gumdrop-shaped pieces of dark chocolate that Rius had bought for her. She reveled in the crinkly sounds of the wrapper, then the softness of the chocolate itself as it rested in the palm of her hand. She lifted it to her face and breathed in its rich aroma. After years of deprivation in the prison factory, it almost felt like a sin.

"Marina." She whispered her departed friend's name into the silence. Then she wrapped the foil back around the chocolate and placed it on the dining table in front of her.

Her soul had been torn in so many directions. She needed help. A priest, a church…anyone. She closed her eyes and said the Lord's Prayer, then began reciting psalms.

A sudden, insistent knocking on her door broke her concentration. Breakfast, no doubt. If it weren't for the meals that arrived by courier every day, she would think the Central Party had forgotten she existed.

It wasn't a courier.

"Good morning, Doctor Petrova," Rius Ludovic said the moment she opened the door. "Feel that glorious sun! My garden will be singing today."

"Yes, it's…wonderful."

The weather outside was just above freezing. Her body ached for the real warmth of an American summer, just as her soul yearned for anything from home. American cars, American newspapers, American radio, even the stupid American sitcoms she'd hardly ever watched.

"Your new assignment begins today," Rius went on. "Are you ready?"

Her pulse quickened. She had begun to hope that Aryana Voss had changed her mind about the mysterious assignment. "Give me a moment. Let me grab a coat first."

As they walked along the sidewalk outside her apartment building, the gloomy fortress battlements glowered at them from the mountains beyond the town.

"You'll meet Sierra Morgan today," Rius said as he clicked a button to unlock his black Mercedes. He opened one of the back doors for her, then climbed into the driver's seat.

"You told me once she could be dangerous," she replied.

Rius started the ignition. "Oh yes, she's clinically insane. For the most part, her mental illness doesn't affect her research, but she's been struggling with her latest project and needs an assistant. We've tried pairing her with others, but no one has been able to manage her. How about a little music for the drive?"

They navigated the winding, switchback road that led up from the town to the fortress. Elena sank back into the sedan's plush leather seat and drank in the captivating strains of Smetana's *The Moldau*. So many creature comforts after years of deprivation.

They reached the fortress, and the music died suddenly as Rius killed the engine. She stepped out into the brisk morning, hugging her arms over her chest to warm herself. "When can I see Darya?"

Rius cast a shrewd glance at her. "Very clever, Elena. A surprisingly mercenary tactic for a humble woman of faith. Lord Magnus thought religion needed to be purged from the human race, but I've always seen it for what it is, a valuable tool to manipulate those around us. You figured out who Darya really is, didn't you? Her mother must have told you before she died. That's why you keep pretending to care about the girl."

"Pretending to care?" Elena snapped. What could the man be talking about? "I know exactly who Darya Alexandrovna is. She's the only child of Stefanya Kozlova, one of the few friends I've had since you people brought me to Khatizan. Stefanya's daughter might as well be my own. I will not stand by and watch you destroy her."

Rius started to speak, then hesitated. "Are you telling the truth? Yes, I think you must be. Perhaps you really are as selfless as the rumors suggest. And that selflessness may be of use. Darya isn't recovering as quickly as we'd hoped. If only we had known sooner, we could have spared her the horrors of the Youth Corps. Very well. Aryana won't like it, but I'll let you meet with Darya after I introduce you to your new coworker."

He led her through the front gate and up the stairway to the entrance of the fortress. She followed him through the imposing antechamber with its vaulted ceilings and its lifelike sculptures of lithe women in flowing robes, stern Roman emperors, and Greek philosophers with scrolls in hand. The polished marble floors sparkled beneath gilded chandeliers bristling with electric lights.

"Before Aryana came here," Rius said, "this fortress was in shambles, a haunt for foxes and wild beasts. We've changed so much in Khatizan. Amazing what a trillion-dollar investment from the Magnus Foundation can do for a backwater country."

She followed him down a series of corridors lined with crimson and gold rugs. Original artwork from some of the world's greatest painters hung on the walls. Lifelike statues of gods and rulers, burnished suits of armor, solid gold urns for exotic plants and flowers—the exorbitant wealth on display would rival that of the greatest monarchs of old. Youth Corps soldiers marched on patrol, hurried about on errands, or stood guard near doorways. She saw civilians, too, mostly in suits or lab coats. They walked with swift steps and kept their heads down.

Rius rested his hand on a door scanner at the end of a lengthy hallway. The door slid open to reveal a lobby with a half-dozen elevators.

"We've already added your fingerprints to the security system," he said. "This particular area has highly restricted access."

"What will I be doing?" Elena asked.

Rius shrugged. "I'm no scientist, so I don't understand it myself. Something about a large-scale power system, I believe, but Sierra dabbles in all sorts of projects. Ah, here we are."

The elevator opened onto a stark, white corridor with recessed lighting and a black tile floor. The design felt strikingly modern, especially after the classical furnishings on the ground level. Instead of statues and Renaissance-style artwork, these walls were lined with framed geometrical patterns in various lurid colors.

"Platonic solids." Rius waved an idle hand at the artwork as he led her down the hallway. "Aryana is fascinated by them. She once told me that Plato's theory *should* have been correct, that the world should have been constructed by such mathematically pure conceptions."

He placed his hand on another scanner to open one of the many stainless steel doors that lined the corridor. Beyond lay a short hallway with three doors, one on each side and one at the end. A man in a dull brown uniform sat on a bench by the door on the right, his weary gaze fixed on his own tattered shoes. She recognized that uniform, the same one the maintenance prisoners wore at Prison Factory Six.

If Rius noticed the prisoner, he showed no sign of it. "Your laboratory is the one on the right. Hopefully your new colleague isn't feeling violent today." He walked ahead of her and opened the door. The prisoner didn't even glance at them even though they were only a few feet away. "After you, Doctor Petrova."

Elena was first struck by the peculiar ambience of the laboratory. The fluorescent light panels were tinted sky blue, altering the color of the lighting so that the entire room felt like the inside of an aquarium.

"The blue lighting helps calm Sierra's nerves," Rius explained. He folded his arms over his chest. "I wonder…where has she gone off to this time?"

Elena walked past a few desks, glancing at the stacks of disheveled papers that covered every inch of available surface. Schematics, mostly. Intricate drawings of mechanical parts and devices. Some were patterned after the same Platonic solids whose forms had lined the hallway. Others looked like mechanized animals, and some even mimicked the human form.

"I don't think anyone's here," she said at last.

"Oh, she's here somewhere." Rius ducked down to look under one of the desks. "She's hiding, which means someone told her you were coming. She always does this with the new assistants. Sierra, where are you? I've brought a friend to play with you."

"What kind of friend?" The shrill, feminine voice emanated from a closet whose door was cracked open a few inches. "I'm tired of all the stupid people you bring me."

"This one is very intelligent," Rius replied soothingly. "Our best scientist."

"That's what you said last time. Did you kill him like I asked?"

Rius held up his hands apologetically. "The Party doesn't like to kill their own scientists, Sierra."

"You call those idiots scientists?" the voice snapped. "They couldn't solve my cloud equations, they couldn't understand the diffusion paradox, they couldn't keep me from having nightmares, and the fat one smelled like fried onions. I won't do anything else for you until they're punished."

"Oh, but we did punish them." Rius shot Elena a knowing wink. "We have them shoveling refuse at a waste processing plant. In fact, they told me only yesterday that they hate their lives now."

There was a rustling noise in the closet, then the door slowly swung open. Sierra Morgan peered out cautiously. She wore an unusual navy-blue outfit that looked like a pilot's flight suit. Her bleach-blonde hair hung down in matted locks that would take hours to detangle. Her roving gaze looked positively feral.

"Shoveling refuse?" she tittered, then laughed wildly. "That's what they deserve, especially the onion girl."

She slipped out from behind the door and leaned back on it to close it. Then she crept forward into the pale bluish light and blinked at them. She was around thirty, perhaps, and stood a little taller than Elena. Her striking jade eyes roamed about constantly, now looking at Rius, now darting a furtive glance at Elena, now shifting to focus on one of the schematics or some inscrutable point of interest on the floors or ceiling.

She suddenly snatched a piece of paper from one of the desks and thrust it at Elena.

"What do you make of it?" she said in a low voice. "No one else understands it, not even the witch."

Elena recognized it at once. It was her own work, after all. "It's the mathematical proof for my power cell."

"Liar!" The woman snatched the paper from Elena. "*Your* power cell? What reaction is involved?"

"Stable nuclear fusion in a microreactor. For most applications, the microreactor would be all that's needed. It's not unlike the fission reactors that power nuclear submarines. For smaller applications, we designed a new type of power cell that can store the released energy."

Sierra's face now hovered mere inches from Elena's. Wildness rippled through her every expression. "And what substance is inside those power cells?"

"Microscopic layers of interlocking synthetic diamonds."

Sierra's gaze shifted to Rius. "You told her?"

"She knows because she invented it," he replied drily. "She's been doing her research for years at one of the prison…I mean, *production* factories. If she helps you, can you finish your project?"

Sierra stared at the ceiling and swayed her head and shoulders hypnotically. "Maybe I can, maybe I can't," she replied in an eerie, singsong voice. She lowered her gaze and fixed it on Rius. "Have you found Mommy yet?"

Rius cleared his throat. "Not yet. We'll keep looking, I promise."

"I need her. I'm having the nightmare again."

"Any better this time? How are the children doing?"

Sierra's eyes widened to a startling degree. Every muscle in her face turned taut as a bowstring. "How are they doing?" she shrieked. "They're dead, all of them!" She stormed across the room, waving her hands about her head spasmodically. "Mechanization always kills them. Rips them into pieces. Burning, melting, choking, gasping, smoke for clouds, ashes for air, skin boiling off bones, screams for help, prayers for death. And they're only children. Murderers, murderers!"

She let out a terrifying scream and flung herself on the ground, writhing back and forth and howling at the top of her lungs.

Lord have mercy. What a tormented mind!

The door to the laboratory burst open. The prisoner in the dull brown uniform ran across the room and knelt beside Sierra.

"Quiet now, it's all right." With a voice gentle as a mother's, he cradled Sierra in his arms and rocked her back and forth. His accent was American, no doubt about it. A touch of a Southern drawl, though nothing too pronounced. How long since she'd heard those homely strains? "It's not your fault, Sierra," he went on. "Think about the stars. Which ones did we look at last night?" As he spoke, the prisoner cast an accusatory glance at Rius.

Sierra stared blankly at the man. "Stars? Yes, we saw stars last night, didn't we? The bear and the maiden. But I want to see the scorpion again. When will the scorpion come back? It's been gone for so long."

"Soon." The man stroked her hair as if she were his child.

Rius stood. "Forgive me, Mr. Ferguson. I should have known better than to press her. I'll leave her to your care. Finish up your project, Sierra, and you can have all the scorpions you want." He winked again at Elena. "Maybe we'll even find Mommy for you."

Then he came close to Elena and lowered his voice. "That man,

Mark Ferguson, is her keeper. He'll stay just outside the door while you work. Yell for him if you ever need help. He's the only one who can pacify her, but you can't talk to him. Aryana strictly forbids contact with him, and he'll be the one to suffer if you try." He raised his voice. "I must be off. Aryana never rests, a habit that tragically draws me into its relentless orbit."

He doffed his hat and left the room.

Sierra had grown docile under the gentle comforting of the maintenance prisoner. Mark Ferguson, Rius had called him. He whispered something else to Sierra, then got up and followed Rius out of the room.

Elena's pulse quickened when she realized that she was now alone with Sierra Morgan. At least there was an anodyne to the woman's madness.

"Are you okay?" She reached a tentative hand toward Sierra. "Is there anything I can do?"

Sierra leapt to her feet, her green eyes blazing. "I'll tell you what you can do, you blabbering fool! Help me give them the energy they want. Enough to power the Island, all of it, everything they're planning. But first, you must learn about the walls I'm building. Walls of skin. Walls of drones. Walls to keep them in, walls to keep us out. Walls around their brains, walls around their bodies."

Sierra scrambled onto one of the desk chairs, wrapping her arms and legs around the back of it like a spider. She reached behind her, snatched another piece of paper off the desk, and squeezed it between her fingers.

"Come here, scientist. I'll teach you the mysteries."

⌘

As Darya Alexandrovna stepped into the kitchen, a summer breeze wafted through the open windows, bearing with it the scent of freshly mown grass as it lifted the blue gingham curtains. A mug of steaming tea awaited her on the countertop. She leaned over and breathed in the sweet, apple-like aroma of chamomile.

The lock to the kitchen's back door clicked open. Her mother walked into the house, dressed in a dark blue prison uniform. It was the only outfit Darya had ever seen her mother wear.

Had Elena lied to her? Was her mother still alive?

Mother offered her calm, long-suffering smile, the one Darya remembered so well from her childhood in Prison Factory Six. "Elena told you the truth," she said, as if reading Darya's thoughts. "I died last year. An illness they refused to treat, but perhaps it was for the best. Come, sit with me."

They went into the living room. Cozy, bright, airy, it was the sort of place where children could laugh without restraint, where memories quietly wove themselves into the tapestry of time. Darya sat next to her mother on a faded burgundy sofa with squeaky cushions. Her mother reached over and patted her hand. "I'm proud of you, Dasha."

She wanted to throw her arms around her mother's neck and kiss her cheek, but something held her back. Instead, she took a sip of tea, but it wasn't chamomile anymore. Black tea. Pungent, almost rancid.

"I'm afraid, Mother," she said, her voice trembling. "Everything is so dark here. Everyone seems so…evil."

"Even Auntie Elena?" her mother replied. "But she's not your auntie anymore. She's your mother now. Remember that."

Darya looked up. Her mother was gone. Gone, too, were the open windows with their spring breezes. She now sat alone on a top bunk in the women's dormitory of Prison Factory Six. She was clutching the revolver from the throne room in her hand, only this one was real and no child's toy.

She heard a familiar voice and peered down from her bed.

Auntie Elena knelt beside the lower bunk, her lips moving, her voice a soft murmur. She wore the uniform of a science prisoner. "And the child, our dear Dasha," she prayed, "deliver her from evil. Let her know that she is loved. Let her know how much I love her, how much—"

Darya felt the tip of the revolver pressing against her temple. Her hand was acting on its own accord, and there was nothing she could do to stop it. Her finger touched the trigger.

*Dasha!*

She opened her eyes. The dream shattered, replaced by bewildered consciousness.

"Dasha!"

Auntie Elena was beside Darya's bed in the fortress, gently shaking her shoulder and calling her name. Was this another dream?

"Dasha?"

Their eyes met. In the next moment, Elena was beside her on the bed, cradling Darya's head against her chest.

"My dear child. My beautiful girl."

Could this be happening? Could it be real? How could Elena still love her despite everything she had done, despite the blood on her hands and the darkness in her heart?

Darya groaned, then broke into violent sobs. She had no idea how long it went on. Elena held her through it all, whispering words of mercy and comfort and love.

The healing words a mother would speak to her own daughter.

And then, when the tide of emotions subsided, Darya told Elena her darkest secret. "It happened a few months ago. My unit is assigned to one of the Youth Camps. We help train the recruits. One day, my superior officer, Lieutenant Dragos, ordered me to handle the security patrol for the camp that night. He told me to do it by myself, which seemed odd since we always do our patrols in pairs.

"While I was making the rounds, I came to a part of the camp where the perimeter fence passed near the edge of a forest. I noticed that the security lights had been disabled beside the fence, and I was about to turn back and report it when Lieutenant Dragos suddenly showed up. He had been hiding behind a tree, waiting for me. He was the one who had turned off the lights."

She shivered as the nightmarish memory returned in full force. "He…grabbed me, pulled me down into the grass. I tried to scream, but he punched me in the face, then snatched my handgun from its holster and flung it away into the grass." She lowered her eyes as a fresh wave of shame swept over her. "He punched me again and started pulling off my jacket. He called me terrible things, said that I belonged to him from now on, that he would murder me if I ever told anyone, and then…"

Darya bit down on her lower lip. Elena held her as she trembled. "It's okay, Dasha. You don't have to say any more if you don't want to."

"No." Darya wiped her eyes. "I *need* you to hear this, Elena. You say you love me, but you don't know what I've done. Dragos was trying to unbutton my pants when I remembered that my boot knife was still in its sheath on my ankle. I didn't think, I just…acted. I don't know how many times I stabbed him. When I realized he wasn't breathing, I shoved him off me, ran straight to the Camp Office, and told them what had happened. I must have looked like a madwoman, my hair disheveled, my shirt torn, my nose and lips bleeding, my hands and uniform covered in Dragos's blood. I expected them to arrest me, maybe even execute me. Dragos was my superior officer, after all. But do you know what they did? They laughed at me. Laughed, as if it were all a joke! They said Dragos had always been a wretch, that it was about time one of his victims fought back. And then they promoted me to his position. That's how it is in the Youth Corps. You don't get promoted until you've shed blood. But I didn't meant to kill him, Elena. You have to believe me! The knife was in my hand, and I just…I was so terrified. Now I'm a murderer, and I hate myself, and…"

She looked up at Elena, fearing that she would find judgment and horror and loathing in her auntie's eyes.

But Elena just leaned over, kissed Darya's forehead, and cupped her face in her hands. "My sweet, beautiful Dasha. You did nothing wrong. Do you hear me? What that man tried to do to you isn't your fault. You survived. You are not a murderer. You did *nothing wrong*." Elena nodded to herself, as if agreeing with some silent, interior argument, then went on in a much firmer voice. "Trust me, my dear one, if I had been there, I would have dealt with him myself and spared you all this guilt."

Darya's eyes widened, but there could be no doubt that Elena was telling the truth. It felt like a terrible weight was sliding off her chest. She broke into half-laughing sobs as Elena embraced her again.

A tranquil silence descended. Elena took her hand. "Do you remember what I taught you in the prison factory? The prayers and the psalms?"

Darya nodded. "I remember some of them." She hadn't said a prayer since the day they'd taken her from her mother. It had felt so pointless, like a child's game.

"I've been praying for you every day since you left us, Dasha," Elena went on. "I know it isn't much, but it was the only thing I could give you. Prayer can be a light in the darkness."

The door opened.

"It's time," Rius Ludovic said, motioning to Elena.

Elena rose from the bed, then leaned down and kissed Darya's forehead again. "I'll be back as soon as they let me. Remember that you are my daughter now. Remember that I love you. Now rest, Dasha."

The door closed. Darya was alone again.

She let out a deep breath. Then, for the first time since she was a little girl in Prison Factory Six, Darya Alexandrovna Magnus smiled.

## Chapter Nineteen
# Nightmare

CHARLES SHIVERED AND hugged his arms around his chest. The dinner hour had arrived at Prison Factory Six. He stood near the back of a line that wrapped itself around the walls of the barebones cafeteria and snaked out into the frigid courtyard beyond.

If the last few evenings in the prison factory were any indication, he would stand in this line for another half hour. He'd shiver and bounce from one foot to another to keep warm and try not to think about the terrifying barking of the German Shepherds or the fact that he had, that very morning, watched six people get chained to a wall and shot to death twenty feet from where he was standing.

The cruelty of this place defied comprehension. He'd only been here a few days, and already his mind and spirit felt numb as ice.

Why had they brought him here? What did they want?

The guards treated him like an animal. As for the inmates, the moment he spoke to them in English, they backed away and glared at him as if he bore a plague.

*"Stranca?"* an unfamiliar voice whispered in his ear.

He turned to find a wizened man with narrowed eyes and a wrinkled face covered in pockmarks and scars.

"*Stranca?* American?"

He nodded. "Yeah, I'm American."

The man tapped himself on the chest with a gnarled forefinger. "Serbian."

"Not Khatiz?"

The man shook his head. "Serbian." He lifted his eyes for a moment, as if deep in thought, then tapped himself on the chest again. "Slave. Serbian slave."

Then the man tapped Charles on the chest.

"You…American slave. Yes?"

So these prisoners were slaves, then. Human trafficking victims.

"Yeah, I guess that's about right. I'm an American slave now."

The man stayed by his side until they finally reached the front of the line. A scowling, grimy cafeteria worker in a prison uniform rewarded Charles for his endurance by dumping a heap of dry rice on his dirty platter. The rice was then soused with an oozing paste that might have been related to beans in some distant past life. To round out the nutrients, a crust of bread so hard it would make a decent baseball clanked onto his platter. He went to the second station in the line, where a gaunt, morose prisoner stuffed a metal tumbler of mysterious, half-frozen gray liquid into his hands.

Not quite water, not quite coffee. Not quite anything that a rational, self-preserving human was supposed to be drinking.

He'd spent the last eleven hours hauling boxes of who knows what from one of the assembly lines to a loading area where another batch of prisoners hoisted the boxes onto the back of military trucks. The calories in the cafeteria meals weren't near enough to sustain that kind of hard labor.

How did these people survive?

He found a seat near the edge of one of the metal tables in the cafeteria. The old Serbian prisoner sat across from him. Charles took a sip of the icy gray liquid and nearly gagged. Maybe the prisoners didn't survive at all. Maybe that was the point.

"Khatizan," the man said. "Here."

Charles nodded. "Right."

"You're American. In Khatizan, American is devil."

"Ah." He was ploughing through his food like a starved animal. Slow down. This is all he'd get, so might as well make it last. "That would explain why everyone's been so friendly."

"Friendly?" The man's eyebrows furrowed in thought. "No friends here. Spies. Slaves and spies. Be careful, American."

The old man crammed a last bite of bean paste in his mouth, tucked his bread into his pocket, and hurried off.

Charles lowered his head into his hands. On the other side of the world, the most beautiful woman he'd ever known was safe and well. The downside was that there was no way for her to find him. That fake CIA agent knew what he was doing. There would be no clues, nothing to trace, no trail to uncover. Boris would guess he was somewhere in Khatizan, but what good would that do? Khatizan had repelled a NATO invasion. No intruders who crossed their border survived.

What could anybody do?

"There you are, Doctor Ferguson."

He recognized the voice. The sound of it made his stomach turn.

He'd met Rius Ludovic the year before at the Tolleson Hotel, where Rius had introduced himself as a manager of an investment company called Alpha Financial. The man hadn't changed. The same pinstripe suit, the timid, anxious smile, the outward display of fawning servility that hinted at an undergrowth of brash self-importance. Aryana Voss had been at that meeting, too, and while she had kept her distance, her presence in the room—the black veil, the funereal dress, the deathly still watchfulness—had made his skin crawl.

It had all been a sham. Alpha Financial turned out to be a shell company belonging to the Magnus Foundation. They gave Charles a real contract and mass-produced his scanner, but he had paid a heavy price for his success.

Rius took the seat vacated by the Serbian. A pair of young soldiers flanked him, resting their hands on the pistols at their sides. Their solid black uniforms, devoid of any insignia or badges, were noticeably different from those of the prison factory guards

"I'm sorry, Doctor Ferguson." Rius looked around anxiously, his voice just loud enough to be heard over the clanking of trays and silverware and the hushed conversations of the other prisoners in the cafeteria. "I tried to get Aryana to show mercy, but she's relentless. After all, you did murder her master."

Charles leaned back in his chair. "So this is her revenge?"

"Dear me, no." Rius snickered. "When I was a child, I always dreamed of being a magician. The sleight of hand, the puff of smoke, *abracadabra*! Life had other plans for me, but I still enjoy a skilled performance as much as anyone. The bombing in Berlin, the drone attack in Russia…what does it all mean? Is she really trying to start a world war? Or is she merely angry over the death of Lord Magnus?" He sighed and lifted his eyes, as if the actions of Aryana Voss defied human knowledge. "Manual labor is far beneath you, Charles. She has a higher task in mind."

"Thanks, but no thanks."

Rius ran a hand through his undignified mass of oily hair. "You once seemed so shy, so humble. Now you've grown bold, haven't you? You'll need every ounce of that courage soon enough. And in case you're clinging to false hopes, I should tell you now that Boris Petrov won't rescue you this time. Did you ever hear about his wife, Elena?"

"Of course."

Rius shook his head mournfully. "The poor woman. Lady Voss has kept her here in Khatizan all this time. Elena spent a dozen years toiling away in this very prison factory. In fact, her laboratory was the room where you are now quartered. Isn't that a remarkable coincidence?"

Dear God. Nadia's mother had been *here* all those years?

"Where is she?" he asked, not bothering to mask the eagerness in his voice. "Can I see her?"

"She is where she can be of the most use. The point is, Elena has been a prisoner in Khatizan for over twelve years now. Don't you think Boris would have set her free if he could have? You're not going anywhere, Charles. Aryana brought you here because she needs the information trapped in that magnificent brain of yours."

Rius drummed his fingertips on the table for a moment. "I've always wondered how you adapted so much better than the rest of us. Your dream suppression was a factor, of course, but perhaps it was also how much you refused to learn."

Charles felt a strange, prickling sensation creep over him. "What are you talking about?"

"Why did you never read philosophy? Why not study the classics? Our minds can replay anything we've seen or heard or read in perfect detail. We connect information at impossible speeds, organizing and arranging it as only an enhanced human brain can. But you intentionally limited the range of your input. You locked yourself into a small intellectual room and refused to leave. I always thought it was immaturity, your fear of new experiences. Aryana thinks it was your subconscious protecting you, just like it did with the dreams. If you learned too much, you could destroy your own psyche like the rest of us."

*Our minds can replay anything we've seen or heard in perfect detail.*

Rius knew exactly what had happened to Charles all those years ago, which left only one logical conclusion. "You were one of the other children in the Paragon Project?"

"The only other sane one," Rius replied drily. "This part of me, at least. Did anything change for you last year? When you met that monk in Illinois, you read some of his religious texts. Was something different afterward? Psychologically, I mean?"

Charles rested his hands on the table. "God happened, I guess. Not just in some abstract sense. Either I found God or God found me. Call me deluded if you want, but it's true. It wasn't all at once. I had these dreams, the first dreams I had remembered since the procedure, and—"

Rius stood abruptly and signaled to the guards with a quick flick of his hand. "That's splendid, Charles! And it saves us a great deal of time. I feared we would have to resort to extreme measures to initiate the process, but the work has already been done. Dreams are exactly why Aryana has brought you here. I need to ask you another question, but not around all these listening ears. Come with me."

Rius turned and left. The guards motioned for Charles to follow suit. Remembering the Serbian prisoner's example, he stuffed his piece of iron-hard bread into the pocket of his prison uniform, took a last swig of half-frozen mystery drink, and hurried after Rius.

The hallway where they stood was empty. Rius signaled to his guards, who stationed themselves a few feet from them in either direction.

"Some people," Rius began, "like Elena Petrova, for instance, can stay in a place like this for years without breaking. For others, a front-row ticket to the Morning Death is enough to shatter their resolve. I think you're one of the latter types, Charles. I really want what's best for you. Answer truthfully, and we'll get you out of here. Just one question. Have you ever dreamed about the Island?"

Charles's pulse was racing. How did Rius know about his nightmare? John Flying Hawk, another survivor of the Paragon Project, had also known. What could it mean?

"I hardly ever remember my dreams."

"Don't play games, Charles," Rius said impatiently. "Your life now depends on your honesty. For the rest of us, our dreams of the Island became all too vivid. They eventually overwhelmed us, invading our waking awareness. If Lord Magnus hadn't offered me a way out, I would be wearing a straitjacket in an asylum. Let's hope your sanity holds out longer than ours did. Now tell me the truth, have any of your dreams involved the Island?"

Charles fidgeted with the sleeve of his uniform. His throat suddenly felt dry as ash. Was he going to lose his mind just because he was dreaming about an island?

He decided to lie. "No, I've never dreamed about an island."

"Is that so?" Rius paused, seemingly lost in thought. "How unexpected…and unfortunate. It's time you learned the truth, Charles. The procedure we underwent wasn't only about enhancing our mental faculties or improving our memory. Those were merely fortunate side effects. Lord Magnus needed a machine that could think at a higher level, analyze the most difficult of problems from a loftier perspective."

"And he chose me?"

Rius's face turned dark as a thundercloud. "Not *just* you!" he yelled. "He chose me…he chose *all* of us!" He turned away and clutched his head between his hands, moaning. When he faced Charles again, his head was lowered as if in shame. "Forgive me, Charles. *That* wasn't me. Not anymore. Every now and then *she* slips across the boundary. I must resist her.

"We were all chosen, but you did the impossible. When the enhancements were complete, they presented our brains with the same problem to solve subconsciously. A task for our minds to work on without our own cognitive awareness. For the rest of us, the problem disrupted our psyche and eventually shattered our sanity. Lord Magnus still found uses for us. Because of my talents, I received a great blessing, an uncharted path to mental stability. Perhaps he also pitied me because of my devotion to him. The other two test subjects never recovered. We all dream about the Island, but our dreams are uniformly nightmares. Our minds can't solve the problem, and if the problem doesn't get solved, the entire world will be destroyed.

"Magnus thought the experiment had failed. He wanted to bring you in when you were still a child. He was already plotting new strategies to achieve his goals, the Reaping and Project Aeternum. Aryana convinced him to wait. She alone believed that the procedure had worked, and she was willing to do anything to keep you sane. She spoke with someone—we'll call him a Foundation employee—right after your procedure. He convinced her that any major disruption to your life would damage your psyche and drive you into the same madness that had taken the rest of us. That's why Magnus left you and your mother alone and allowed you to grow up like a normal child."

Left them alone? Hardly. Charles knew for a fact that Magnus had watched every step he had taken since the day he left that research facility.

"Maybe he left my mother alone," he grated, "but what about my father? What happened to him?"

Rius eyed him closely. "Believe it or not, your father joined the Foundation of his own free will."

Charles caught his breath. His father had abandoned him for the Magnus Foundation? "Where is he now?"

"We found an unexpected task for him," Rius replied. "One that has served us well. I'm surprised you even want to know about him. After all, what kind of father would sell his own son for money? I certainly don't miss *my* father." Rius clenched his fists, his features contorting into a mask of hatred. Then he shivered and grew visibly pale, as if he were about to faint. "You seem to bring out the worst in me. I'm struggling to suppress her. A dangerous tendency, but it's not your fault. Now come, it's time to get you out of here."

Charles felt like his heart had turned to stone. He never imagined his father's betrayal would run so deep. Wasn't selling your own child to a shadowy foundation bad enough? Did the man really have to abandon his family to join that same foundation?

The moment they stepped into the prison factory courtyard, one of the guards grabbed Charles while another one slipped a black sack over his head.

At least they didn't tranquilize him this time.

"You should have told me the truth, Charles," Rius said coldly. "I may have been able to stop Aryana's plan for you, but now you leave me no choice. Soldiers, get him in my car. We're heading to the fortress."

✥

Charles had been riding in the back seat of Rius's Mercedes for what seemed like hours. He couldn't see thanks to the hood the soldiers had pulled over his head, but he could feel the quality of the road changing from bad to atrocious. One pothole after another. Then, after a single turn, it became smooth as polished marble.

"Can I get something to drink?" he asked.

"Better if you don't," Rius replied. "It's not a good idea before these kinds of procedures."

Charles's heart started racing. "As in *medical* procedures?"

Rius didn't answer. An hour later, the car came to a stop. The guards helped Charles out of the back seat, then grabbed him by the elbows and led him forward.

The air felt brisk and fresh. There was a crunching sensation beneath his feet. Pea gravel, perhaps. He heard the eerie cry of a hawk overhead and the whispering of tree branches in the breeze.

"Where are we?" he asked. "Can you take the hood off now that we're here?"

Rius patted him on the shoulder. "Don't worry, Charles. It will all be over soon."

The guards halted after a short distance. There was a loud, clanking sound along with a dull grinding, as if something large and heavy were being raised on chains. Then forward again, up a flight of stone steps, and through a whole rabbit's warren of twists and turns along carpet-lined corridors.

Finally, one of the guards removed the hood.

It took a moment for Charles's eyes to adjust to the light. When they did, his breath froze in his chest.

The room was a near replica of the one he had been taken to as a child at the Magnus Research Facility in backwoods Michigan. The surgery table with the blinding lamp suspended overhead. The mysterious, terrifying machine with its stainless-steel dials and flickering status lights. A surgical drill was attached to the machine. It had a razor-thin beveled tip that was transparent, as if made of glass. Some kind of cable ran from the drill's handle to a computer on a wheeled cart nearby.

He wanted to scream. He wanted to die. Anything but this.

"I'm sorry we have to do this to you, Charles." Rius's eyes revealed genuine grief. "This place terrifies me just as much as you. But Aryana cannot be resisted. Her will is law, and I am but a worm beneath her feet."

Charles tried to run, but the guards grabbed him and slammed him to the ground. "What are you going to do to me?" he gasped.

"I already told you she needed information. I gave you the chance to give it to her willingly, but you refused. You are a terrible liar, Charles."

Rius walked up to the machine, flipped a switch to turn it on, and pulled the trigger on the drill. Charles clamped his hands over his ears as the drill howled to life. The exact same sound from his childhood.

Rius turned the machine off again. "One more chance, Charles. Have you dreamed about the Island?"

"Yes," he cried. "Why does it matter?"

"You should not have lied. It makes it very hard for her to trust you now. How many times have you had the dream?"

"Often." He couldn't pull his eyes from the drill and its narrow glass tip. His heart was pounding so fast he thought he might pass out. He wanted to vomit. "I went into a coma when Headquarters was destroyed. When I woke up, I started having the dream. It felt familiar, somehow, as if I'd been dreaming it my whole life."

"Did you tell anyone else about it?"

"No." Another lie, but he wasn't about to put his friends' lives in danger.

Rius watched him closely. "I hope you're telling the truth. She always finds out, one way or another. In your dream, what do you see on the beach?"

"I always see children. Dozens of them."

"Good!" Rius cried. "And the children...are they happy?"

Charles looked at the stone-faced guards as if they could help him out of this insane interview. What was he supposed to say? What did Rius want to hear? They had only brought him here to scare him into talking. They would never actually use the drill on him, would they?

"The children are happy," he said at last. "They're like any kids playing on a beach. They dart in and out of the tide, chase each other, and build sandcastles. But they aren't really kids. They're machines."

"Then it's true!" Rius shouted. "You have accomplished what we couldn't. Aryana was right all along." He turned to the guards. "Quickly now, there's no time to waste. Strap him to the table. We'll begin the procedure at once."

"What?" Charles shrieked. "I'm telling you the truth!"

"I know you are, Charles." Rius wiped his eyes. The man was weeping for joy, but why? What did the dream have to do with anything?

"But you said that if I cooperated…"

Rius held up his hands apologetically. His face still looked radiant, yet now a hint of sorrow swept over his features. "If it were up to me, you would have been free long ago. I'm afraid Aryana holds all the cards. Who am I to resist her?"

The guards grabbed Charles by his arms and hauled him toward the table. He struggled and tried to squirm out of their grip, but it was no use. Boris could have tossed them to the floor by now and knocked Rius senseless for good measure, but he wasn't Boris.

The door opened behind him. A surgeon and two nurses walked into the room.

"No," Charles cried breathlessly. "Don't do this, Rius! I'll tell you whatever you want. I'll tell you everything that happened in my dream."

"I'm sorry, Charles. There's no going back now."

He made a final, desperate lunge to free himself but was shoved to the ground face-first. The guards pinned him down with their knees on his back. One of the nurses jabbed a syringe into his forearm. He began to feel lightheaded, detached from his own body.

"Easy." Rius's voice sounded strangely distant. "He must remain conscious for the initial connection. You can still apply the local anes-thetic. Be liberal with it. I can't stop what must happen, but at least we can ease his pain."

Rius and the surgeon began speaking in muffled Khatiz while the soldiers heaved Charles onto the operating table and secured his arms and legs. He had no strength left to resist them. A strap of leather slid over his chin and tightened down. The nurses began rubbing a damp cloth against the right side of his skull near the ear. A curious, tingling numbness followed the movements of the cloth. Soon even the tingling dissolved into nothingness.

"Progress is always a child of suffering." Rius's pale, dolorous face loomed over him. "If it's any comfort, we won't be making modifica-tions this time. First, she wants to probe you for the answers we need. Then we'll plant new problems into your psyche and harvest the results as your brain generates them. With luck, we may even be able to estab-lish a remote connection between your brain and our servers. I'm afraid this will be the first of many sessions."

The drill whined as the surgeon held it aloft. Charles felt his own hot tears sliding down the sides of his face.

The surgeon muttered something in Khatiz. The drill became louder and shriller as it neared his head. He could feel it now, feel the small puff of air from the whirling tip, feel the skin prickling as the tip made contact.

Rius motioned for the surgeon to pause and raised his voice to be heard above the drill. "One more thing, Charles. This procedure will almost certainly shatter your sanity, but perhaps we should consider that a blessing. You won't be consciously aware of your own suffering, and I'm afraid you will be suffering a great deal from now on. You murdered Aryana's master, and she will have her vengeance. From this moment onward, the Island will become your only reality. Goodbye, Charles."

Rius leaned down and kissed Charles's forehead, then turned and left the room.

Charles closed his eyes as the doctor and nurses resumed the procedure. An unexpected calmness settled over him. Perhaps it was the anesthesia, or perhaps the realization that nothing could change what would happen next. He had survived this once. He could survive it again. At least he wouldn't feel as much pain this time.

"Lord Jesus Christ, have mercy on me."

The prayer was on his lips as the drill pierced his skull.

# Chapter Twenty
# The Central Ring

"THIS WAY, VICE Commander Veliu." The driver's words were muffled by the cigarette perched in the corner of his lips. "Can't be running late on official Youth Corps business."

After Andrei's defection, Paul had taken most of the Red Ops One team to their extraction point outside New York City, where a Khatiz sympathizer provided them with a private jet. The Third Triad had remained behind in New York for a final kidnapping mission with Rod Walker. He could only hope Andrei had contacted Boris Petrov in time to thwart it.

The rest of the team had flown back to Chozul after the failure of the New York mission. Rius had assured Paul that Aryana's top priority was the ATA Home Office attack and the extraction of the scientist Charles Ferguson. If that succeeded, Aryana would be content. The moment Paul got off the plane in Chozul, he received a message that he had been promoted to Vice Commander of Khatizan's Youth Corps. He was ordered to report to Aryana's fortress to receive his official promotion.

In other words, Rius had told the truth.

At the ripe age of twenty-three, Paul now stood second in rank to Commander Firlenko himself. After the ceremony in Aryana's throne room, he immediately felt the power of his promotion. As he walked through the corridors in his new uniform, the Youth Corps guards at attention showed him the same fervent devotion they showed Firlenko himself.

"Sir?" the driver hinted. "Are you ready?"

Paul brushed his hand over his dark gray uniform, a near replica of Firlenko's. "Let's go."

The driver opened the back door to the Humvee. Paul climbed in and settled himself in the torn fabric seat.

"Chozul?" the driver asked. Despite his narrow frame and threadbare clothing with numerous patches, the man had the look of a former Revolutionary Army soldier. If that were true, he probably despised the novel but deadly efficient Youth Corps.

"That's right." Paul cast a final glance at the somber, rigid contours of the fortress. "I have a meeting with a Party official at seventeen hundred."

He had no idea who he was meeting. An orderly had relayed the request right after the ceremony and given no further explanation. No doubt it had to do with his promotion to Vice Commander.

The driver grunted and turned the ignition. The old Humvee came to life with a gasping roar like an asthmatic lion, then slowly rolled into motion.

"It'll be a few hours, Vice Commander," the driver said. "Not a bad chance for some shuteye if you need it."

Paul nodded. "I might take you up on that."

"Ever visited Pashko, Vice Commander?"

The offer of sleep sounded tempting, but Paul had the feeling he would have to listen to the man's chatter instead. "I've never been to Pashko. What's your name, civilian?"

"Vasily." The sergeant tossed his spent cigarette out of the window. In the same motion, he snatched another from the pocket of his jacket, planted it in a corner of his mouth, and lit it with a silver lighter, all while navigating the winding mountain road that led down from Aryana's fortress. "Vasily Grushanin. Do you believe in God, Vice Commander?"

Paul stared at the driver. Was it a trick question?

Everyone knew that God was woven into the Central Party, a personal—albeit invisible—friend and confidante of the Chairman. The two maintained a symbiotic relationship. God gave the Central Party leadership the moral authority to justify whatever atrocities and social injustices they wanted to commit. In exchange, the Chairman offered ceremonial obeisance to the official God of Khatizan in his speeches.

Khatiz citizens were allowed to attend state-run houses of worship, where Party officials in suits or surplices wove a majestic synthesis of God and State that, through a process verging on the miraculous, merged the two entities into one. No one in Khatizan needed to believe in God. No faith was required. God existed, just like the Chairman existed and the Central Party existed. Belief in any one meant belief in all three.

Belief…and blind, unquestioning obedience.

"Of course, I believe in God," he answered coldly. "Don't we all?"

Vasily Grushanin barked a laugh. "Ah, Vice Commander, that's the real question, isn't it?"

Paul frowned. There was something unusual about Vasily. He couldn't put his finger on it, but the realization quickened his pulse. It was dangerous to stick out in a place like Khatizan. Vasily must have known that, so what was he really trying to say? Could he be involved in the resistance, the Movement? That phantom haunted the periphery of the national consciousness. A band of rebels, murderers, and thieves.

Or so the Central Party claimed.

"Were you always a civilian, Vasily?" he asked.

Vasily cast a dark glance in the rearview mirror. "I used to be a sergeant in the RA."

"Then it's good to meet you, Sergeant Grushanin," Paul replied.

Vasily's features relaxed. The animosity between the Youth Corps and the Revolutionary Army was only natural. The Youth Corps had gradually replaced them, costing most of the RA officers their careers. "When I was a boy, my neighbors in Khalensk were Grushanins," he added.

Vasily blew a small cloud of smoke out of the window, then grinned at him. "Khalensk? Ah, there were some lovely girls there when I was your age. We took a road tour, some friends and me. Those girls danced with us all night. My cousin Denis said we'd found the Garden of Eden. We cancelled our plans and stayed a whole week. Best week of my life, Vice Commander. In those days, you could get in a car and go wherever you wanted. Nobody breathing down your neck and telling you what to do every minute of every day. It was a different world."

"A better world, Sergeant?" Paul asked in a casual voice.

Vasily coughed and straightened his posture. "Not better, Vice Commander. Much, much worse. Khatizan is best under the Chairman."

"Of course, Sergeant."

Vasily lapsed into determined silence. Paul leaned back in his seat and closed his eyes. Not a rebel after all, just a talkative driver.

Sleep had mostly eluded him these past weeks. Every time he laid on his bed, his relentless, unforgiving mind would drag him back to Berlin and present the innocent face of the blue-eyed receptionist. He would hear her soothing, melodic voice. So carefree, so full of life. His nights were consumed with unanswerable questions.

Who was her family? Who were her friends? Had she been single? Could he have rescued her? Would she have despised him when she discovered who he really was?

Other images haunted his insomnia. A drawing of a father, a mother, and three smiling children. Little Johann wondering why his beloved papa never came home. A highway filled with wrecked cars. An entire city block transformed into a crater.

He had obliterated thousands of lives. Each one distinct, each demanding its equal portion of human worth and dignity, each interconnected to innumerable other lives and destinies.

Vice Commander? Hardly.

Murderer. Terrorist. Monster.

Now he could add to his crimes the blood of those who fell in the attack on the ATA Home Office. If he had sabotaged *that* mission, he would have betrayed his true intentions to Aryana Voss and Commander Firlenko. If the greater plan was going to succeed, they had to make sacrifices.

He'd told himself that, but was it true? Was there really no other path he could have taken with the American mission?

The Humvee veered off the fortress road and rattled down one of crumbling highways leading to the agricultural districts. Paul picked up an old army trench coat from the floor beneath his feet, rolled it up, and stuffed it behind his neck for a pillow. He didn't expect any sleep, but at least he could close his eyes and let his mind drift as the vehicle rumbled toward the capital.

❧

Paul woke with a start. He rubbed his eyes and glanced at his watch.

"One o'clock already?" he asked.

Vasily grunted in affirmation.

They'd left the fortress around nine in the morning, which meant he'd slept for nearly four hours. They should have been in Chozul long ago.

"Where are we, Sergeant?"

Vasily tossed the butt of his cigarette out of the window. "Pashko," he muttered. "Middle of nowhere."

"Pashko?" Paul's mind snapped to full attention in an instant. "But I have to be in Chozul by seventeen hundred!"

Vasily stuffed a fresh cigarette in the corner of his mouth. "Don't worry, Vice Commander. It's a planned detour."

Paul rested his hand on the handle of the Beretta holstered at his side. Rius had said nothing about this. Treachery against the Youth

Corps was unheard of in Khatizan, but times could change. "The truth, Vasily Grushanin," he said, forcing his voice to remain calm. Showing fear would only embolden a rebel. "Why are we here?"

Vasily pulled the Humvee to a stop on the side of the road and turned to face him. "It's hard to explain, Vice Commander."

Paul switched off the safety on his Beretta. "Try."

Vasily reached over and turned on the radio, which immediately began blaring one of the state-approved pop bands. He lifted his hands in the air to show he was unarmed, climbed out of the front seat, and opened one of the back doors of the Humvee.

Paul slid his pistol out of its holster and trained it on Vasily. "Not too close, Sergeant Grushanin."

Vasily put his hands behind his head, but he showed no sign of fear. "There could be bugs," he explained, his voice just loud enough to be heard above the radio. "They put them in the dashboard sometimes." He climbed into the back seat next to Paul and closed the door. His next words were so rushed they nearly tumbled on top of each other. "There's an American general in Khatizan. The Party knows nothing about it. He's meeting with some of our people. They say the Americans might be able to help us. Supplies, maybe even weapons. Our people thought you'd want to be there."

"What do you mean, *our* people?"

Vasily's eyebrows furrowed in confusion. "I mean the Movement, of course. I thought you'd already guessed."

Paul's heart nearly leapt out of his chest. "You're kidnapping me? Handing me over to traitors?"

"Not kidnapping," Vasily protested. "You're still in charge, Vice Commander. If you want to meet them, then we'll go. If not, I'll take you to Chozul and you can hand me over to the Central Party. Either way, you're the one holding the gun."

"Party Intelligence would skin you alive. We both know that's not a figure of speech."

Vasily didn't flinch. "I know the risks, Vice Commander. For the record, I believe in God, too, just not in that monstrous idol that the Chairman hoists over the people. My father was a pastor. A real one, you know? I rebelled against God for a while, but you never really forget what you've learned. When the Chairman came to power and the purges began, I had to do something. We can't just pretend it's not happening."

Paul exhaled and leaned back.

This piece hadn't been on the chessboard. He needed to examine it, view its position, determine if it could be utilized or if it was only another trap. Vasily could be lying. This could be Aryana Voss testing the loyalty of her new Vice Commander. A single mistake would mean death.

On the other hand, the Movement would provide invaluable allies in taking down the Central Party from within. Who knows what connections they had, what doors they could open, what opportunities they could provide.

He had to try, even if it cost him everything. But it wouldn't hurt to be cautious.

"Why did you choose me, Sergeant?" he asked.

"It wasn't my decision," Vasily replied at once. "*He* heard about you, something about Berlin. He thought you might want to meet with him. That if you also met the American general and heard the whole plan, maybe you'd give us a chance. It's all his idea."

He had watched Vasily closely as he spoke, looking for any hint of deception, but it was impossible to know. Either the man was an artless liar, or he was exactly as he seemed, a plainspoken, stalwart follower of Khatizan's resistance movement. Could Boris Petrov have sent the American general? It seemed unlikely, but he had to find out for himself. "Whose idea was it, Sergeant?"

Vasily looked him in the eye. "Grigory Vikhrov."

Paul inhaled sharply.

Grigory Vikhrov was the Traitor of Khatizan. The Rat, the Demon. The founder and face of the Movement.

A half hour later, Vasily parked the Humvee next to a military out-post, which was a generous word for the run-down concrete structure that had been slapped up beside the farm road. He killed the engine, hustled out of the driver's seat, and opened Paul's door for him.

"Through that door, Vice Commander." The old soldier offered Paul a firm salute. It was a small gesture, but Paul felt the weight of it. It meant something to earn the respect of a man like Vasily Grushanin. If he was what he appeared, then he represented the old RA at its best. Fearless, courageous, idealistic.

"You're not going in?" Paul asked him.

"It's not allowed," Vasily replied. "I'm just a driver, a little fish in the game. I only found out about the mission this morning."

"Have you ever seen Grigory Vikhrov?"

Vasily shook his head. "I've never met anyone who has. They say that's the only reason he's still alive. Only his inner circle knows the secrets of the Movement, and he's the greatest secret. And you get to meet him! It pays to be a Vice Commander, eh?"

"We'll see." Paul shook Vasily's hand, took a deep breath, and turned to meet his fate.

Two RA veterans stood guard outside the door to the checkpoint. They offered a slight nod in acknowledgement of Paul's rank, but nothing like a salute. Their hands remained glued to their M4 carbines. Excellent guns, those. Far superior to the old Soviet rifles the Youth Corps cadets had inherited from the RA ammunition depots. Maybe these people weren't RA at all, though their uniforms certainly looked the part.

The door was opened inward by a foreign-looking soldier. He was dressed in black and gray camouflage and had a Glock 19 handgun on his belt. Paul knew from his officer training that the model was a favorite of American special forces. So far, Vasily's story about the visitors was lining up.

"This way," the man said in an American accent. Southern, like he'd grown up on a farm in Alabama. "Right through here."

He followed the man through another door into a dark, open room. A circular conference table had been placed in the middle of the room with eight folding chairs around it. All but one chair was occupied. In the center of the table stood a single kerosene lamp with its burner turned so low that only a dim glow illuminated the features of those attending. He scanned the faces around the table but didn't see the well-known profile of Grigory Vikhrov, which meant that the traitor of Khatizan was one of the two men with their backs to him. One of those men had dark hair, the other gray with snowy streaks.

The dark-haired man turned around. Paul's blood turned to ice.

Commander Vladimir Firlenko.

"Good afternoon, *Vice Commander.*" Firlenko placed a mocking emphasis on Paul's new rank. "Sit with us."

"Commander Firlenko?" Paul blurted out before his mind wrapped itself around the reality of his situation. The meeting was a trap, a sting. He'd prided himself on being cautious, but he'd fallen right into it.

He was a dead man.

"You were expecting someone else, perhaps?" Firlenko replied in a bantering tone. His words were met with gruff laughter from around the table. "I already told you to sit down, Veliu. Or maybe now that you're Vice Commander you no longer feel the need to follow orders from a superior officer?"

"Yes, sir," Paul said quickly. "I mean, no sir. I mean…"

An older, heavyset man across the table leaned back in his chair and roared with laughter. "Good, good! Make the little rat squirm."

As Paul's eyes adjusted to the dim lighting, he began to recognize the other faces around the table.

They weren't Americans.

The heavyset man who was wiping tears of laughter from his eyes was Fyodor Malvori, head of the People's Agricultural Commission, which controlled every inch of forest and farmland in Khatizan. Next to him sat the prim, dapper Alfons Denizov of the Social Wellness Commission, which oversaw the Party's herculean efforts to brainwash

Khatiz citizens. There were three more across the table, the highest-ranking generals of the Youth Corps Ground, Air, and Intelligence divisions.

This wasn't the inner circle of the Movement. This was the Chairman's Central Ring.

Paul pressed his lips firmly together, as if that small act of willpower could hold back the trembling that threatened to seize his entire body. He crossed the room with faltering steps and collapsed into the open chair next to Firlenko.

"I'm glad you're entertained, Fyodor," Firlenko replied. "And I apologize in advance for what must happen next. That our new Vice Commander would willingly meet with the Traitor of Khatizan is a cause for great concern, but we have not yet established his guilt. Of the man who brought him here, however, there can be no question. Bring the driver."

A Youth Corps guard standing in a corner of the room saluted the Commander and hurried out. Paul took the opportunity to examine the others around the table more closely, beginning with the gray-haired man who had been facing away from him when he entered the room. He had been so distracted by Commander Firlenko and the Party leaders across the table that he had almost forgotten this last stranger.

The man turned towards him.

Paul could have screamed.

Chairman Markhov himself. His appearance had undergone a radical transformation since Paul had last seen him in the fortress throne room. Gone was the feeble, doddering old relic who had bowed down and kissed the feet of Aryana Voss. The man now looked vigorous as an oak tree. His sharp eyes and jutting chin mirrored the portraits hung all over Khatizan. His visage looked stolid as a mountain, the face of the great and terrible father of the nation. Powerful, ruthless, godlike.

Paul shot to his feet. For some inexplicable reason, Firlenko had presented him with a potential escape from death. He would have to make the most of it. "All hail our glorious Republic!" he shouted, extending his fist straight forward in a salute. "All hail Chairman Markhov!"

The leaders gathered around the table burst into laughter. The Chairman, however, kept his stern gaze on Paul, lowering his head slightly in acknowledgement of the salute. He motioned for Paul to sit. Paul obeyed instantly.

"The driver, Vasily Grushanin," the guard announced as he led Vasily into the room. Vasily had a fresh cigarette perched in the corner of his lips. As he entered the room, he quickly snubbed it out on his belt, stuffing the half-burnt remains into his pocket.

Once again, Commander Firlenko and Chairman Markhov had turned their faces away from the door so that the newcomer couldn't recognize them.

"Mr. Vikhrov?" Vasily called in an eager, almost childlike voice. "Such an honor! Where is he sitting? But that looks like…no, that's not possible!"

Commander Firlenko turned to Vasily. "So you want to meet Vikhrov, traitor? That can be arranged."

Vasily's face turned gray as ash. He tried to escape, but the guards closed in on him. They forced him to his knees in front of Firlenko. The Commander withdrew his pistol from the holster at his waist.

"I executed Grigory Vikhrov eight years ago," Firlenko said coolly. "In the early days of your so-called Movement. I held this very gun to his head, just like so…"

He pressed the tip of the pistol against Vasily's forehead, just above the bridge of his nose.

"—and I ordered him to give me the names of every one of his accomplices. And guess what, traitor? He did it. Vikhrov was a spineless fool. His friends, the benighted politicians and bureaucrats of the old order, wanted a war with the Chairman. Vikhrov, young and charming and well-connected, was chosen to be the star of their rebellion. How could he resist?"

As he spoke, Firlenko's gaze shifted to Paul. "Temptation can seize any of us. Truth be told, I should have let Vikhrov go. The Movement has a real leader now, and you, Vasily Grushanin, are going to tell me who he is. Give me the names of every rebel you know, and I'll let you live. I'm not interested in gutting the little fish, as you call yourself. We captured your handler, which allowed us to set up today's entertainment, but I'm sure you can name others. Who do you know in the Movement?"

"I won't tell you anything," Vasily's voice quavered with defiance. His face was suffused with rage but then grew calm. "I'm not afraid of you, Firlenko. I'm not afraid of any of you. I've made my peace with God. No matter what you do to me, Khatizan will be free."

Firlenko's eyes narrowed. "A pity that such courage should go to waste. The Party could have used a man like you."

The sharp report of the gunshot filled the room. For a moment, Grushanin remained on his knees, his eyes now opened to a startling width. A thick crimson dot above the bridge of his nose revealed the entry point of the bullet that had pierced his skull and buried itself in the floor behind him. He dropped to the ground, lifeless.

"Get rid of the body," Firlenko said. "And wipe up the blood. I don't want us slipping on our way out."

While the guards scrambled to obey him, Firlenko returned to his place at the table.

"These rebels are brave but deluded. If they were all we had to worry about, we could sleep easily at night. The real threat to our nation lies elsewhere."

Paul was too terrified to move. He could feel the Chairman's eyes on him, twin drills boring into his soul.

"You also wanted to meet Grigory Vikhrov, *Vice Commander* Veliu," the Chairman said suddenly. "Isn't that right?"

Paul's tongue turned heavy as lead. He swallowed, licked his dry lips, and tried to think of something to say that wouldn't lead to a bullet in his brain. He would never forget that look on Vasily's face, the calmness as he spoke to Firlenko, the triumph even in death. At least Paul would die in good company.

He had lost the game. He couldn't offer justice to all the victims he had wronged, but at least he had tried.

"The truth is—" he began, but Commander Firlenko interrupted him.

"The truth is," Firlenko said, "you were only doing your duty as a Youth Corps officer. You agreed to meet with Vikhrov so that you could gather intel about the Movement. You planned to hand him over to the Party afterward, didn't you, Vice Commander?"

Paul was too stunned to reply. The Commander had just saved his life. The price for such mercy would be terrible.

"I'll get straight to the point," Firlenko went on. "The Magnus Foundation has overplayed their hand. Aryana Voss ordered us to carry out the attacks on Berlin and Novorossiysk within weeks of each other. She believes NATO and Russia will be thrust into a war neither can win while she watches from the sidelines and waits to pounce.

"We followed her commands. We sent you to Berlin. We deployed the Foundation stealth drones against Russia. When we welcomed the Foundation with open arms years ago, we believed they would help us save Khatizan. Now they are our masters, and even the Chairman is forced to grovel like a slave.

"No longer. Aryana and her followers must be destroyed. Once that happens, we'll tell the world that the Magnus Foundation was behind the attacks. In exchange for their understanding, they will be given access to any Foundation technology within Khatizan's borders. The Central Party will regain its rightful place, and we will emerge from our long isolation with strengthened ties to both East and West. Of course, we will never yield our absolute power over our own people."

Paul's mind raced through the new possibilities as the Commander spoke. A terrible choice lay before him. He had hoped to find allies in the Movement, but it was clear that Khatizan's rebels would never be strong enough to help him. He was pinned between two great evils, the Central Party and Aryana Voss.

Or was there another option? Could Rius's plan still succeed?

"What do you want me to do?" he asked.

"A simple task." Firlenko's steel gray eyes flitted from the Chairman back to Paul. "One of our sources at the fortress has learned that Aryana Voss will leave Khatizan soon to meet with other leaders of the Magnus Foundation."

"Leave Khatizan?" Paul cried. "If that's true—"

Firlenko waved him to silence. "She will return here a week later. At least, she will *attempt* to return. If the Chairman or I were to visit Voss's fortress unannounced, even in her absence, our every movement would be heavily monitored. But she favors you, which means you can come and go as you please without raising suspicions."

Firlenko leaned toward him. Paul felt as if he were trapped in the cold, calculated malice of the Commander's gaze. "We may never have another opportunity like this. We could never defeat Voss on our own. She is beyond human. But that worm of hers, Rius, is flesh and blood."

The Commander signaled to one of the guards, who gave a swift salute and left the room.

"I understand that you and Rius are now on friendly terms. I warn you, he is a very dangerous man. You don't earn a place in the Magnus Foundation by planting gardens and playing the fool. I wish we could still rely on your loyalty to the Central Party, Vice Commander, but after your near failure in Berlin and your actual failure in New York, we have decided that external pressure is in order."

The guard returned, this time leading a blindfolded prisoner. The prisoner's hands were cuffed. Her ears were covered by a thick pair of safety earmuffs.

Paul's breath caught in his throat. He scrambled out of his chair. "Mother!"

She couldn't hear him. The guard moved her a few steps into the room and then pushed on her shoulder, forcing her to her knees.

"I'm afraid, Vice Commander," Firlenko said, punctuating his every word, "that your mother *might* be a rebel, a part of this Movement." He strolled across the room to her and withdrew his handgun. "Youth Corps Intelligence received an anonymous tip two days ago. If the report is true, I will have no choice but to do to her what I did to Vasily Grushanin. But perhaps our informant was wrong. What do you think, Vice Commander? Should your mother be spared?"

Paul's heart was beating so fiercely he could hear the pulsing in his ears.

"If you do not assassinate Rius Ludovic when we give the signal," Firlenko went on, "then your mother will be executed. If you whisper a word of our plans to anyone within the Magnus Foundation, your mother will be executed. If you deviate in any direction from our orders, your mother will be executed. Obey us and she lives. You will be free to visit her and your father when the Foundation has been removed from Khatizan. With Rius gone, we will seize the fortress ourselves and make sure Aryana Voss never sets foot in our country again. What do you say, Vice Commander?"

Paul lowered his head.

Murderer, terrorist, monster.

And soon, assassin.

Such was life in Khatizan. Either he would cower in the dust and survive, or he would have to make the most terrible of sacrifices. What child could do that to his own mother?

"I'm with you." He spat the words through clenched teeth. "What will be the signal?"

"Give him the watch." One of the guards handed Paul a narrow, black smartwatch. "Keep that near you at all times, even when you charge it. If it gets farther than six feet from you, we will assume that you have betrayed us. It has a microphone that transmits everything you say and hear. You will receive a text message on that watch when the time has come. As soon as you get it, assassinate Rius Ludovic, then notify my headquarters near Prison Factory Six. It will be a day of bloodshed. Too many Khatiz are connected to this accursed Foundation. We'll get rid of them all. If we don't hear from you by the end of that day, your mother will die with the rest."

Paul nodded without raising his head. If the past were any guide, this new purge would be terrible beyond calculation.

"What about Darya Alexandrovna?" he asked. "Will she be spared?"

The Chairman suddenly leapt to his feet.

"Spared?" he roared, slamming his fist on the table. His features contorted with hatred. "Spared? By the devil! I'll have Darya Alexandrovna's head on a pike. Oh yes, I remember her. The witch's pretty little apprentice. Tried to blow her brains out for her mistress and failed, but I'll finish the job. And that science prisoner they're keeping near the fortress, do you have any idea what *she's* done? That harmless old hag and her former colleague created the very bomb you carried to Berlin. God knows what other monstrosities she's cooking up for the witch. My list has been growing for years, Vice Commander. I don't forget anything, and I don't forgive anyone. They've been hauling foreign trash into our country by the trainload, polluting our land with their filth and poverty. I'll cull them, the beasts! Khatizan will be purged, cleansed, wiped clean as snow. We won't have a foreigner within a hundred miles of Chozul. We'll get rid of them all!"

The Chairman's voice broke in a gasp. His face had turned purple with wrath. His fingers curled around the papers on the table in front of him. He tore them to pieces and flung them to the ground. Still shaking with the violence of his emotions, he lifted his gaze to Paul.

In that moment, Paul wished he had stayed in America, defected with Andrei Idrisov. But the cost would have been too high. Besides the lives of his own parents, it would have doomed Boris Petrov's hopes of entering the country. He needed to prepare for Andrei's return with Boris's strike force, but how could he do that now?

"You've made the right choice, Vice Commander," Firlenko said in a calm voice, as if the Chairman's outburst were nothing unusual. "You're one of us, after all. When this is all over, you'll be a true Vice

Commander. Your parents will be given high honors from the Central Party. Now get back to the fortress. As you may have guessed, your meeting in Chozul has been cancelled."

Paul saluted the Chairman and Commander Firlenko, then turned and left the room. He climbed into the back of the Humvee, which was now driven by a Youth Corps soldier. He slipped his hands into his coat pockets to warm them. As he did so, his fingers brushed against the cool, metallic contours of a cell phone Rius had given him. Now he had two electronic leashes, one from the Foundation and one from the Central Party.

He'd felt cornered by the Chairman and Commander Firlenko, trapped without any possible escape. But now, with fresh countryside air washing over him through a half-opened window, he found his self-confidence returning.

Watch or no watch, he still held the power to choose. He could throw in his lot with the Chairman and hope for the best, or he could betray the Central Party and side with Rius.

Either way, he had to find a way to keep his parents safe. Could Rius do that?

The Youth Corps soldier turned to him from the driver's seat. "You're heading to the fortress, Vice Commander?"

"That's right." Paul withdrew the phone Rius had given him and wrote a brief text message.

*Heading your way. The usual.*

He hoped the phone's security was as ironclad as Rius had boasted, but one could never be too safe in Khatizan.

Four hours later, the Humvee parked in front of Aryana Voss's fortress. Paul thanked the driver, clambered out of the vehicle, and strolled into the depths of Rius's garden.

Did Rius get the message? Would he come?

He freed his pistol the instant he heard footsteps. Even if the Party had somehow intercepted the text message to Rius, Paul wouldn't go down without a fight.

A young woman in blue jeans and a sea green sweater emerged from around a curve in the path. Her chestnut hair hung in smooth waves around her shoulders. She leaned over to smell the fragrance of a vibrant purple iris.

Darya Alexandrovna, the other lieutenant he'd met in Aryana Voss's throne room.

But could it really be the same girl? Her face, her clothing, even her expression—she looked so different now, so calm and at peace.

He'd since learned that she was much more than a mere Youth Corps lieutenant. If Rius spoke the truth, Darya was the future heiress of the Magnus Foundation, the natural daughter of the late Alexander Magnus. Did she know the secret of her own birth?

She noticed Paul and froze.

"Darya?" he said.

Her expression suddenly cleared. "You're the other lieutenant. Paul, wasn't it? You saw what happened that day. You saw them…break me."

She spoke in a faltering voice. Surprisingly gentle, despite everything she had been through. It somehow reminded him of the receptionist in Berlin, and he felt a sudden anger at everything Darya had suffered. Aryana Voss, the Chairman, Commander Firlenko—they were all responsible for what had happened to her, for what had happened to all of them. He was also responsible, for hadn't he abandoned Darya to her fate in the throne room? What had she done to deserve that kind of cruelty?

As he examined her face, pale and beautiful, his anger gave way to compassion.

Commander Firlenko would be listening through the smartwatch. Let him hear it, then.

He holstered his gun. "I don't know what's worse: the things they do to us, or the things they make us do." He drew closer to her. "They had no right to plunder our childhood, to steal us away from our parents, to imprison us in their Youth Camps. The whole system is criminal." He took her hand. She pulled back for a moment, staring at him with frightened eyes that gradually grew calmer beneath his gaze. Her hand relaxed in his.

"I should have protected you that day in the throne room," he went on. "I should have been the one pulling that trigger, not you. I was a coward, too afraid to die." He felt the heat of shame rising to his cheeks. He had failed the secretary in Berlin. He would not make the same mistake again. In truth, he felt something more stirring within him, but he forced it away. A monster like him didn't deserve the affection of any woman. He was a pariah, a terrorist. "Are they keeping you prisoner here?"

She shook her head. "I've been unwell, that's all. They even let me see Elena. Do you remember her? She was a friend in Prison Factory Six. Now she's like a mother to me."

As Darya spoke, he sensed a new strength in her, a health he would never have expected from the shattered girl in the throne room.

"Elena…she was one of the science prisoners?" he said. "I saw my own mother a few hours ago. Commander Firlenko held a gun to her head and said he would kill her if I don't follow orders." He trembled, his heart churning with anger at the Central Party and fear for his mother's life. "I doubt I'll ever see her again. They have my father, too, so I'm all alone now. I have no one left."

He didn't know why he kept talking, why he was baring his soul to her. He felt powerless to stop it. Perhaps Firlenko would kill his mother for words like these, but what did it matter? The Party would kill her anyway, sooner or later.

Darya looked at him searchingly for a long moment, then suddenly embraced him.

"Don't give up, Paul. Do you understand? You saw me the other day. I wanted to kill myself, but Elena gave me a new reason to live." She pulled back and met his gaze, her hands resting on his shoulders. "And you're not alone. We're really the same, you and me. If Elena can be my mother, then you can be my brother. Would you like that, Paul Veliu?"

He felt unbidden tears in his eyes and quickly wiped them away. He took her hand and pressed it to his lips. "You don't know what I've done. I don't deserve to look you in the face, but if it's what you want, if it will bring you any comfort, then yes, I'll be your brother."

Her smile lit a fire in his soul. Who was this woman? How had she changed so quickly? What did this new horizon mean for his own future, for his plans with Rius or the Chairman?

They gazed into each other's eyes in silence. Suddenly, she seemed almost afraid of him. If her heart was pounding like his, he understood why.

"There you are!" Rius Ludovic's voice broke the spell. Alarm passed over Darya's face as she pulled away from Paul, but then she offered him another brief, radiant smile.

"Goodbye, Paul," she said softly. "Don't forget me."

She turned and walked toward Rius.

Forget her? If he didn't see her again until the day he died, he would never forget her.

"Is that you, Darya?" Rius went on. "I didn't expect to see you here." He gave her a deep bow. "Still a bit feverish? I'll summon Liza Khartoff. She had no business leaving you alone like this."

"There's no need," Darya replied. "I'm going back to my room now."

"Remarkable girl," Rius said as she disappeared around a turn in the garden path. He shot Paul a knowing glance. "Good for her to make some friends, too. I hear that she and her aide, Liza, haven't been getting along. Not that Liza gets along with anyone. Shall we walk, Vice Commander?"

They came to the gazebo with its chessboard and benches. It looked like the same game Paul had seen earlier, only now it had reached a critical point. Both sides had sacrificed pieces to develop their position. The black queen, likely the aggressor in a recent exchange, was hedged in on all sides. Her fate was all but sealed.

Or was it?

As he looked more deeply at the position, he realized that she had a single path of escape, a road that would inevitably lead to victory.

"I'm surprised you play such a slow-paced game out here in the garden." He turned his attention from the board to Rius. "Aren't you afraid one of the guards might wander along and scramble the pieces?"

"It's of no consequence," Rius replied distractedly. "I never forget the state of the board. But we didn't come here to talk about chess, did we?" He suddenly grabbed Paul's arm and leaned close. "What happened, Paul? When I got your message, I nearly fainted. Is it…no, she'd murder us!"

Rius stepped away and bit down on the knuckle of his forefinger, then waved his hands around his head wildly. "Aryana knows, doesn't she? She'll grind our bones with her bare hands! She'll tear our limbs off our bodies. You don't know her, you haven't seen. She's inhuman, a devil! Have you noticed those buses that come here in the dead of night? They're filled with prisoners from the factories. She hides them in cells beneath the fortress and subjects them to terrible experiments. Things no human should have to suffer. Now it will be us in those cells, won't it? Ah, she's so clever. Even if she knows, she won't tell us. She'll wait until we lower our guard, then she'll grind us to bits!"

Rius's nervousness had risen to a feverish state. Spittle flying from his lips, his frantic gaze roving in all directions, his hands flailing around his head—he looked like he could break out screaming or roll around on the ground at any moment.

"She may not know anything." Paul held up the watch Firlenko had given him as if he were checking the time. "Nothing that would endanger us."

Rius froze. "Ah." He leaned forward and examined the watch closely. "Forgive me. Sometimes I let my fears consume me. You're right, of course. I'd better get back before she realizes I'm gone. Goodbye, Vice Commander."

But Rius didn't leave. He met Paul's gaze and motioned for silence. Then he withdrew a narrow, rectangular device with a single red indicator light from his coat pocket. He held it next to the watch. The device beeped three times, and then the light turned green.

"Firlenko?" he asked.

Paul nodded.

"Fools," Rius muttered. "As if such a child's toy could work against the likes of us. You may speak freely, Vice Commander. The watch's surveillance is disabled until you choose to turn it back on, and they'll be none the wiser for it. Here, keep this." He handed the cylindrical device to Paul. "You saw how it works. Use it again to turn the surveillance back on whenever you want them to hear you. The arrogance of those idiots! Did they forget that we created Khatizan's surveillance equipment?

"But we mustn't tell them about our foreign visitors, Boris Petrov and his allies. Make sure you don't slip up about *that*. Now tell me exactly what happened at the meeting. I already know they murdered my accomplice, Vasily. He had communicated with Marina Polanska, one of the science prisoners. When Firlenko executed her, I knew Vasily was in danger."

Accomplice? Vasily had certainly been with the Movement. That could only mean that Rius himself was part of it.

Could he even be the Movement's new leader?

He told Rius about his surprise meeting with Chairman Markhov and his Central Ring, leaving out nothing.

"A catastrophe!" Rius cried as soon as Paul had finished. "They think she's returning in a week? Ah, but no, they must know the truth and were only deceiving you. Aryana already left and will soon be back in Khatizan, which means the Chairman will act this very day." He grabbed Paul's arm. "You must save her! You're the only one who can."

Paul pulled his arm free from Rius's grasp. The man's frantic behavior made his skin crawl. "Who do you want me to save?"

"The list!" Rius shrieked. "The purge! Those two devils will paint Khatizan red with the blood of their enemies before they turn on each other. We must save who we can. Elena Petrova will be one of their targets. Darya as well, but she'll be safe here. Surely Aryana has already seen to that. Or did she?" Rius glanced up at the gloomy fortress walls. "The murderers could be heading to Darya's bedroom this very moment! What do we do?" He pressed his thumbs into his forehead and groaned as if his thoughts brought physical pain.

"Yes, you must rescue Elena Petrova first," Rius went on. "She is important to Darya's well-being and therefore must be protected. They'll send a death squad to her apartment, but you'll have time if you hurry. Take my own car and bring her here. It's the only safe place. I'll warn fortress security about Darya's safety. I'll also make sure your parents are moved to a secure location. I promise you that they'll survive this." Rius lowered his hands, and a cunning grin lit his face. The coldness of it made Paul shiver. "Markhov and Firlenko want you to kill me, do they? Ah, it's a perfect opportunity. When our dear Chairman and the Commander come to claim this fortress, they'll find a nasty surprise waiting for them. Death is almost too kind for those wretches. With them out of the way, Aryana will be our only remaining obstacle. Now hurry, Vice Commander, or Elena will die."

# Chapter Twenty-One
# The Caretaker

Elena Petrova had just finished brushing her teeth when she heard a violent knocking on the front door of her apartment.

A late meal delivery? The courier always arrived around six o'clock with her dinner, but they'd never shown up tonight. Desperate for sane human interaction after several days of working with Sierra Morgan, she ran to the front door. A Youth Corps soldier making a delivery might not be the best conversation partner, but it was better than nothing.

She flung the door open.

"Thank you so much for—"

Her words hung in the air as she faced a grim-looking Paul Veliu. Whatever had brought him here, it wasn't good. She clasped her hand over her heart. Paul now wore the dark gray uniform of a top-ranking Youth Corps officer. It was nearly identical to Commander Firlenko's attire, which might explain why she was struggling to breathe.

"What is it?" she asked. "What happened?"

"Something we didn't expect." He peered past her into the apartment. "Are you alone?"

It took a moment for his words to sink in, but there could only be one possibility. No secret could stay hidden for long in Khatizan. The inmates at the prison factory used to say that when an ant went missing, the Chairman knew where it was.

Only it wasn't the Chairman this time. It was Aryana Voss, Khatizan's true ruler, the woman they were plotting to destroy.

"I'm alone," she said. "Come inside."

He shook his head. "We need to leave, now. Pack up anything you want to keep, but don't take long."

So this was it. Escape within the borders of Khatizan was out of the question, and crossing the border was impossible. Days, maybe only hours—the Youth Corps would find them. At least she would see Marina again in a better place.

"Who are they sending?" she asked, though she already knew the answer.

He looked both ways to make sure the corridor outside her apartment was still empty. "A Youth Corps death squad."

She swallowed. The phrase sounded much more terrifying when it was spoken aloud. "You know we won't get away," she said quietly. "There's nowhere to hide."

Strangely, her words seemed to surprise him. "The fortress will be safe. Now hurry, grab your things."

"The fortress!" she exclaimed. "So it's not—"

His sharp look silenced her. Foolish, running her mouth like that, as if the Party didn't have eyes and ears in every apartment building. No doubt their microphones were tuned to pick up specific phrases and names, and Aryana Voss would certainly be one of them.

If only Boris were here. He was so good at his classified work, never revealing more than he should. She wasn't made for intrigue and subterfuge. Still, if the fortress was to be their hiding place, then Aryana Voss was not the one trying to kill them. Who else could it be?

She rushed to her bedroom and hurriedly flung her belongings into the burlap sack she'd brought from Prison Factory Six. She bid a silent farewell to the apartment that had, albeit briefly, given her a small taste of a more civilized world.

On the way out of the kitchen, she snatched one of the boxes of chocolates Rius had purchased for her. If today was going to be her last day, at least she would die with the taste of chocolate on her lips. Marina would have liked that.

Paul took the sack from her and arched an eyebrow at the chocolates. "Follow me."

She ran to keep up with him as he hustled down the hallway of the apartment building, down four flights of stairs in the grimy stairwell redolent with cigarette smoke, and out into the parking lot, where a black Mercedes with dark-tinted windows awaited them. Paul threw her bag into the back seat. She opened the passenger door, sat down, took a deep breath, and opened the box of chocolates.

The short drive to the fortress was uneventful, though Paul kept checking the rearview mirror as if he expected to see the death squad tailing them at any moment. Elena recited psalms under her breath. They had been a refuge for her all these years, and they didn't fail her now.

Rius awaited them outside the fortress gate, wringing his hands and stalking back and forth in a state of visible panic.

"You're alive!" he cried the moment she opened her door. He ran up to her, grasped her hand, then released it again awkwardly. "Any trouble in the town, Vice Commander?"

"None at all." Paul fetched her bag from the trunk of the car. "You don't think they'll come here when they realize she's gone?"

"Here?" Rius shivered. "No, the villains aren't that bold yet. Firlenko, at least, has learned a few things about the fortress defenses. It will take the rebels a few days to carry out their purge and stabilize the Central Party. When they're ready, they'll send you the order to execute me before coming here themselves. As long as Aryana returns before they attack, we'll be quite safe."

"What about my parents?" Paul asked. "You didn't forget, did you?"

Rius blinked. "Of course not, Vice Commander! Do you think I could…that I would possibly…" He pulled a phone from his pocket. "Both your parents are now tucked away in a safe house where the Chairman will never find them. Why don't you talk to your mother yourself? Here, it's ringing now. I'll show Doctor Petrova to her room."

Elena caught Paul's worried expression as he took the phone from Rius. A moment later, his face showed visible relief. He shot Rius a grateful look and walked away for a private conversation with his mother.

"We'll drop by Darya's room first," Rius said as he led her through the raised portcullis into the fortress grounds. "Then there's someone else you need to meet. An unrivalled genius, but I'm afraid he's in a very bad way. Aryana forced him to undergo a series of experimental treatments that have tragically shattered his sanity. Perhaps you could ease his suffering."

Another broken soul. So many people in Khatizan needed healing. She wondered how much more she could give. "I'll do what I can."

She spent a few hours with Darya and was amazed at the improvement in the girl's psyche. While signs of her lingering illness remained, a vigorous bloom of health was beginning to surface. And there was something else now, something Elena couldn't put her finger on. A brightness, a hopefulness, perhaps some joyful mystery in the girl's heart.

After she left Darya's room, Rius led her up a winding stone staircase to a quiet hallway that was empty except for a few guards on patrol. The running carpet was thick and soft beneath her feet, and the only sound was the ticking of a gilded grandfather clock that looked ancient.

"This is the best we could do for him," Rius said. "The poor fellow has suffered terribly. Back when Khatizan had a royal family, these quarters were reserved for visiting aristocrats. Aryana feared that providing such luxuries to our Youth Corps soldiers would soften their will, so they all sleep in the old servants' quarters. But there's no fear of spoiling Doctor Ferguson."

He knocked twice on the heavy oaken door next to the grandfather clock. "Doctor Ferguson? Are you awake?"

No reply.

"Probably sleeping." Rius pitched his voice just above a whisper as he opened the door. "They dragged him down to the dungeon for another treatment this evening. Happens every day. Aryana's orders until she returns."

Elena entered the room. On a massive four-poster bed with a mahogany frame lay a young man with a pale, troubled face and disheveled, dark brown hair damp from sweat. He groaned feverishly, muttering indecipherable phrases and rolling his head from side to side.

"That," Rius said softly, "is the renowned Doctor Charles Ferguson. He became a household name last year after he and his colleague invented a portable medical scanner, the OneScan device. It can detect hundreds of medical conditions within minutes. I believe they've sold almost a billion of their scanners now. A new commodity no home can do without. Doctor Ferguson was a brilliant man. The world will be a lesser place without him."

Elena pursed her lips. She didn't like it when people spoke of the mentally ill as if they were dead or defective. Some people had talked like that about her son, Peter, as if Down syndrome somehow made him less than human. As for Sierra Morgan, it hadn't taken long to realize that the American prisoner who was her caretaker was also the only person in the fortress who viewed Sierra as a human being. What was her caretaker's name? It seemed important now for some reason.

"The world isn't without Doctor Ferguson yet," she said firmly. "I don't know what that woman has done to him, but where there's life, there's hope."

Rius looked startled. "Of course, Doctor Petrova! I wouldn't dream…but then, he's different, so very different from what he was only a few days ago. He and Sierra are far more similar than they seem, though the story would take time to tell. There's an adjoining suite just through that door where you'll stay. You might keep the door open when you sleep in case he needs your assistance."

Elena suddenly remembered the name of Sierra's caretaker.

Mark Ferguson.

As she looked at the young man lying on the bed, she recognized the uncanny resemblance between them, the one like an older, thinner version of the other. She had seen Mark every day while she worked with Sierra. They hadn't spoken a word to each other, though Elena had tried despite Aryana's prohibition. Mark would look at her in his sad, distant way, but he wouldn't reply.

The similarity was too strong for coincidence. Was Charles his son?

"Sierra told me that you finished the project," Rius added. "I congratulate you, Doctor Petrova. There's no need for you to work with her further, which I'm sure must be a relief to you. You can now devote your full attention to Doctor Ferguson. He needs someone to care for him in his waking hours, as you will soon discover."

She stared at Rius. Sierra thought their project was finished? They were months, if not years, from being close to completion. Aryana Voss had demanded the impossible.

Unless…

"Did Sierra know more than she told me?" she asked. "Did I only see part of the project?"

Rius shrugged. "To tell you the truth, I don't know the details myself."

"Is Sierra still in the fortress? And her caretaker…Mark Ferguson, wasn't it?"

For a moment, Rius's eyes narrowed. The hint of a cruel smile played over his lips, but it quickly vanished. "They're around here somewhere, I'd expect. I'm surprised you remember Mark's name. You didn't break the rules and try to talk to him, did you? It would be unfortunate for him if you did."

A diabolical punishment, cutting Mark off from everyone else, forcing him to communicate only with a woman who was both violent and insane. Elena shivered. Wasn't a similar punishment now being meted out to her?

Suddenly Charles Ferguson sat straight up in the bed, staring at her. His eyes held a look of surprised recognition, though it was impossible that he would have known her or, for that matter, anyone close to her.

Or so she thought. When he opened his mouth, Elena nearly fainted.

"Nadia!" He shouted the name with the wild exultation of a madman, then flung the bedclothes aside and scrambled toward her with open arms. "Nadia, you came for me!"

# Chapter Twenty-Two
# Doomhammer

Nadia Petrova slid open the patio door and stepped onto the balcony of the New Brunswick apartment that served as their new safe house. She collapsed into a plastic patio chair, lowered her head into her hands, and wept.

The mysterious code John Flying Hawk had given Charles had to be the key to everything, but they couldn't break it. The random letters and numbers refused to betray any hint of meaning or connection. Even Lenny was beginning to realize that the Doomhammer wasn't all-knowing. She needed Charles. Anything was possible when he was with her. He was part of her now, inseparable. They'd grown that close. She couldn't move on without him any more than she could move on without her own soul.

Merciful God in heaven, where was he? Slaving away in a prison factory? Screaming in pain in a torture chamber?

She broke into a sob, then shook her head angrily.

No giving up. He's still alive. He must be alive.

She took a deep breath and wiped her eyes.

She'd received an encrypted message from her father an hour ago. A few days after joining up with some of Gavriel's old comrades-in-arms, Boris and his team were now deep within Khatizan, riding an old bus toward Aryana Voss's mountain fortress. One small strike force against an entire army.

They needed a miracle, which meant she had to break into the Foundation's network. If they could get access, she could help her father's mission, maybe even unravel the mystery of Aryana Voss. Lenny had a peculiar theory about Aryana, something he had discussed with her father before he left. Zany comic book fiction or not, her father had made a contingency plan in case Lenny was right.

Not that it would matter if she couldn't break the code.

The IP address and port number from Sierra Morgan's poem had led them to an unexpected discovery, a lifelike virtual reality simulator with staggeringly advanced encryption. They'd purchased some VR equipment, and Lenny had entered the simulation. According to him, the whole thing was a complex security program. To get past it, they needed to provide the name of a specific geometrical shape. They would only get one guess.

The mystery shape and John Flying Hawk's code had to be connected, but how?

"Lord have mercy."

She peered up into the hazy, starless murk of Brooklyn's night sky.

"Glousermorg's up there somewhere, isn't he?" She smiled despite the pain in her soul. Charles always teased her about her made-up constellation, a sprawling dragon who spanned the heavens. She hadn't told him that she knew many of the real constellations. Stargazing was one of the many advantages of a childhood outside the city limits. Life moved slowly around Beecher, Illinois. Crops grew in the fields, cows wandered the pastures, stars lit up the darkness in their glorious multitudes.

She would always hunt for Orion's belt first. Three stars in a diagonal line. What were their names again? Something Arabic.

Alnitaq, that was the one on the left. The common name, anyway.

The real eggheads, the astronomers, called it something else, something like—

She froze. Something like HR1948.

That was it. That was the answer.

She scrambled to her feet, flung the door open, and rushed into the apartment.

Lenny was staring at his laptop screen with bloodshot eyes. Fazal had fallen asleep, his head resting on a textbook filled with advanced geometrical patterns. Julia had long since put Safiya and Peter to bed and then gone to bed herself.

Nadia closed the door behind her. "I've got it! I know the answer."

Fazal's head shot up from the textbook. He rubbed his eyes. "You… what?"

"The message, the one John Flying Hawk gave Charles in North Carolina. I know what it means. We were right, it's the key to the security program. It will give us the geometric shape we need."

Lenny stumbled out of his rolling desk chair, cheese cracker crumbs tumbling off his Captain Fuzzbucket T-shirt. The poor guy needed a vacation.

"Slow down there, Doomhammer." He took off his glasses, rubbed his eyes, and put the glasses back on again. "You're saying all those random letters and numbers make a shape? Is there a cipher or something?"

She grinned. "I don't know how, but John Flying Hawk knew exactly what we needed. And he told it to Charles so that Charles could break through the Foundation's security program."

"What is it?" Fazal was wide awake now. "What's the answer?"

She pointed upward. "Stars."

✺

It took them over an hour to identify all the official star names encoded in John Flying Hawk's message. The tricky part was that he hadn't just used one astral classification system. He'd used them all. Some of the stars were in the Morgan-Keenan system, some in the Yerkes system, others in the Bright Star Catalogue, and still others in the Harvard system. But now they had the key to the cipher.

When the work was done, they had identified thirty-two stars. Charles had perfect memory, which meant there could be no doubt that these were the right ones.

"Your turn, Lenny." She handed him a piece of paper with the list of stars.

"Wait, what?" Lenny mumbled through a mouthful of chocolate snack cake. "What am I supposed to do with them?"

"We have the stars, now we need the shape. There must be a three-dimensional pattern behind the coordinates of all these stars. We have to connect the dots, just like a children's puzzle. Thirty-two dots in three dimensions and lots of ways to connect them. We could use Crowdbreak. Add the star coordinates to the Arnor constellation database, then get the astronomy guild on it. It shouldn't take them long to give us some possibilities. Assume the solution will use all the coordinates but take other answers just in case."

Lenny wolfed down the rest of his snack cake with a long guzzle of energy drink that made his Adam's apple dance. "I'm on it, Doomhammer!"

"He'll need your help, Fazal."

"Why me?" Fazal mumbled. "I haven't contributed anything yet. I feel like I'm wasting everyone's time."

Fazal had been talking like that ever since the attack on the ATA Home Office, the day Gavriel had died rescuing him. He'd even stopped saying the daily prayers, which, for a devout Sufi, was a clear sign of profound inner turmoil.

"You haven't been useless," she coaxed. "You've been studying all kinds of geometrical patterns, right? The encryption key can't be a completely random shape, because no one in the Foundation could remember that. The gamers can come up with possibilities for us, but we'll have to choose the right one, the answer that makes the most sense."

She laid a hand on his shoulder. "We both know Gavriel died doing his job. That's not your fault, Fazal. And it's not your fault you couldn't get out of that hallway on your own. The only people to blame are the ones behind the attack. We have a chance to stop them now, to make sure they never hurt anyone again. If we can get into their network, we just might save Charles."

For a moment, he didn't reply. Then he reached up and clasped her hand. "I'll do my best."

Two hours later, they had an answer.

The guild of pretend astronomers in the imaginary, digital world of Arnor had identified a variety of possible shapes using some or all of the coordinates as vertices. Fazal then narrowed it down to one shape that was the closest match to the star configuration.

Lenny pushed his glasses higher on his nose as he examined the 3-D printed model Fazal had created. "What is it?"

"A polyhedron that spans over a billion light years." Fazal's voice and expression verged on reverence. "Isn't it magnificent? Every Platonic solid has a dual that is also a Platonic solid. Together, they form a polyhedron. Beautiful, mathematical harmony, the real music of the spheres. This one is a dodecahedron combined with an icosahedron. When I realized that there were thirty-two stars—or vertices, rather—I thought the shape would be a rhombic triacontahedron, but I was wrong. I like this one even better."

Lenny burped vociferously. "Um, okay. What about those two drawings? They look like stars themselves, or maybe that one's a star inside a star?"

"Ah." Fazal rubbed his hands together. "So the polyhedron we're looking at is the first stellation of the icosidodecahedron. If you took our polyhedron and expanded the various faces infinitely in all directions, you'd end up with infinite and finite regions. In fact—"

Fazal loved mathematics the way Julia Pearson loved cats, which meant pure, unadulterated obsession. His geometrical monologue could go on forever, just like the expansion of his polyhedron. But time was one resource they didn't have. "Fazal, let's focus here," she interrupted. "Just answer one question."

Fazal blinked. "Sure, what is it?"

"Are you positive this is it? We only get one chance. Are you absolutely certain?"

"Well." He scratched the back of his head for a moment. "It uses every star as a vertex, the coordinates are the closest match, and it creates a mathematical object of sheer beauty. This is it."

She grabbed the VR equipment and handed it to him. "Then do it. Lenny, get us connected to that IP address."

Lenny scrambled over to his laptop. "I'm on it!"

Fazal al-Najjar stood in the nave of a vast medieval cathedral. Dust motes floated among shafts of sunlight slanting downward through the mullioned windows.

Fazal *stood*.

He'd spent most of his life in a wheelchair. Ever since the day that an American bomb destroyed his boyhood home in Lebanon, he'd been forced to look up at everyone else while they hurried about on their own two legs.

The sense of loss would always be a part of him, but his days of envy and grief were long past. His limitations were nothing compared to all the things he could still do. And yet, the novelty of this new experience brought tears to his eyes. He gazed down at the virtual feet the Magnus Foundation program had given to his avatar. The avatar wore dull brown Oxfords, from the look of it. The sort of thing Charles Ferguson would wear.

"Welcome to the Secure Access Portal," intoned the smooth, silken voice of the Foundation's AI Computer. "Do you know the way in?"

"I know the way."

"Then tell me what you want, and I will create it for you. Succeed, and access will be granted. Fail, and you will be banned forever. You only have one chance."

A small lump of clay appeared in his right hand. He held it up in front of him. "Give me the first stellation of the icosidodecahedron."

The clay floated away from his hand and began molding itself in midair, reforming until he saw the polyhedron he had requested.

"Welcome, Magnus Foundation administrator," the Computer said. "External primary access granted. Closing the Access Portal simulation."

The cathedral vanished, leaving Fazal in pitch darkness. He removed the virtual reality helmet.

"Did it work?" he cried.

Lenny gave him a thumbs-up. "We've got access to everything, every program and device in the whole frigging Khatizan government. And something else, too. Jeez, what is this stuff?" He ran his hands through his hair. "Robotics, maybe? This is over my paygrade. It'd take me a month to figure this out, but I don't have to, do I? Your time to shine, Nadia. Bring on the Doomhammer!"

Chapter Twenty-Three

# The Purge

"YOU'VE SURPRISED ME, Andrei. I didn't think your hairbrained plan would work, but here we are." Boris hugged his arms over his chest and tried to stop shivering. The Khatizan wind was cold as ice, and this blasted Civilian Public Bus was missing half its windows.

Andrei Idrisov had snuck them across the Khatizan border the night before. Paul Veliu had told Andrei about a gap in Khatizan's otherwise flawless perimeter defenses, a well-concealed cave system whose entrance lay on the northern border of a neighboring country. How the cave had remained unknown and unguarded by both governments was a mystery Boris didn't want to ponder. The secret path had worked, and that was all that mattered.

Guided by a pair of flashlights, Andrei, Boris, Kenjiro, Thompson, and a dozen Russian commandos trained by Western forces—the latter courtesy of General Borokhov of the Free Russia Movement—had hiked through the winding subterranean tunnels through a bitterly cold night, emerging at dawn into the alpine wilderness of Khatizan's southern border.

Exhausted, hungry, and blinking in the glaring sunlight, they stumbled through an ancient, uninhabited forest until they reached an old lumber mill at a set of coordinates Paul Veliu had given Andrei. As Paul had promised, a dilapidated public bus with a full tank of gas awaited them behind the mill.

It was astounding that Andrei had been willing to return to Khatizan after betraying the Central Party. Who knew what they would do to the poor kid if they got their hands on him?

"How far to the fortress?" Thompson leaned forward in his seat to be heard over the howling wind and the whining of the bus engine. The man hadn't complained once, not when they nearly got lost in the tunnels, not when they marched through the forest for hours without a break, and not even now, when the biting wind had his teeth chattering like a nutcracker.

"Two hours if we're lucky." Andrei pulled the bus onto the entrance ramp to a highway. With his tattered clothes, the standard garb of Khatizan's impoverished peasantry, and his shapeless hat cocked to one side, the young sniper looked like he'd been driving rundown buses for years. "We'll never get there if the Party's set up a checkpoint today."

"Checkpoint?" Kenjiro cried. "You never mentioned checkpoints when we were drawing up our plan."

Andrei flashed a grim smile. "I didn't want to make things sound worse than they already are. The Party sets up random Youth Corps checkpoints on the highways. If you try to escape, they catch you, and you disappear. If you're on a watchlist or you're a foreigner or you forgot your ID that day, they catch you, and you disappear."

Boris grunted. That sounded like the Soviets in his grandfather's day. "We brought our IDs, Andrei, made by the best counterfeiters in the ATA."

"Yes," Andrei replied, "and those IDs will be useless when they run our faces against the Youth Corps Intelligence database. Like I said, I didn't want you to get discouraged. If we make it to the rendezvous with Vice Commander Veliu, we just might get to the fortress alive. Pray there's no checkpoint."

"I'm no saint," Boris muttered, "but on the bright side, we know a guy who's well on his way to the golden nimbus, and the odds are extremely good that Father Anatoly will be praying for us today."

A half hour later, the traffic slowed to a crawl. Boris leaned forward, peering over Andrei's shoulder at the winding rows of red taillights. "Checkpoint?"

"Maybe." Andrei's voice was taut. His hands clutched the broad steering wheel with a white-knuckled grip. "I don't want to fight the Youth Corps. I've turned against the Party, but the Corps was my home."

Boris patted the young soldier on the arm. "We won't fight. If we get caught, we'll have to rely on this Vice Commander of yours to get us out of trouble."

For the next hour, they edged forward at a painful pace. The tension in the frigid old bus became palpable. Thompson sat in shivering, meditative silence, his hands folded, his eyes closed. Kenjiro was reading a detective novel that he must have packed with his gear. The commandos huddled near the back with their assault rifles clutched in their hands. Boris had told Andrei they wouldn't fight the Youth Corps, but it would be hard to hold those freedom fighters back if things got dicey. He kept his gaze locked on the traffic jam. Were those police? Two trucks with red lights flashing. A checkpoint?

"Sweet Saint Christopher," he cried suddenly. "It's a fender bender!"

Andrei cast him a curious glance. "Who's Saint Christopher? And what's a fender bender?"

Boris laughed. "When we get back to America, I'll introduce you to that monk friend of mine. You'll hear all about the multifarious saints and saintesses of our beloved Mother Church. As for fender benders, see for yourself." He pointed forward toward the flashing lights of the emergency vehicles. "There, by the side of the road."

A four-door sedan that would have been going out of style in the nineties had rammed into the back of an eighteen-wheeler whose trailer, halfway off the road and turned sideways, was emblazoned with images of enormous tomatoes.

"Ah, a car accident," Andrei replied. "Fender bender, you called it? I like that. Fender bender."

They made it the rest of the way without incident. Andrei pulled the bus into the parking lot of a warehouse and left the engine running. They huddled together near the front of the bus, grateful for the hot engine air blowing through the vents. They watched the warehouse door, waiting for it to open as the minutes ticked by.

Where was Paul Veliu? He should have been there half an hour ago.

"Don't worry," Andrei said, as if reading his mind. "If he doesn't come, we'll go straight to the fortress. That's the backup plan. I know how to get there."

An hour later, there was still no sign of the Vice Commander.

"What do you think, boss?" Kenjiro asked. "If we turn around now, we could still go home."

Blast it, Kenjiro was right. Paul Veliu was likely dead. Either that, or he had betrayed them. If it was a trap, could Andrei be in on it?

The kid was looking at him right now with those soulful, intense eyes. Waiting for orders. Whatever treachery the Vice Commander might have committed, Andrei was innocent as any lamb. A lot like Gavriel, that one, not that anyone in the world could ever replace Gavriel Abramovich. But Andrei was a true soldier through and through.

"I've waited years to get into Khatizan," Boris said. "I'm not turning back until we've found our friends. Take us to the fortress, Andrei."

Andrei held up a hand. "Wait a minute."

The bus radio had been playing a traditional Khatiz polka, but the blaring accordion died off suddenly, replaced by a shrill voice that sounded increasingly tense.

"What is it?" Boris asked. "What's he saying?"

"A public execution," Andrei said breathlessly. "Party Leader

Troyov. He was the Chairman's closest advisor." His face turned ashen gray. "Yes, it's as I feared."

"What? Tell us."

Andrei swallowed and licked his lips. "There's a purge going on all over the country, a terrible one. Sounds like they're in the third day of it, and the body count is rising fast. What do we do now?"

"Hmph." Boris pulled a thick Havana cigar from his backpack and clenched it between his teeth. This had to be more than a coincidence. Khatizan's first purge in years at the exact same time his team infiltrated the country.

The Foundation was up to something, but what?

More importantly, did they already know that Boris Petrov was on their home turf?

"Mr. Charles is in that fortress," he said finally. "Come what may, we have to find him."

❧

Darya hustled down the empty fortress hallway. She was somewhere on the fourth floor, a place she'd never been allowed to roam. Instead of the opulent and aristocratic furnishings that filled the lower levels, the floors here were bare tile, the lights fluorescent, and the doors plain and unmarked. It looked like a modern office building instead of a medieval fortress. What were these rooms used for? Likely, she would never know since all of them seem to be locked.

Her personal aide, Liza, had never shown up that morning, and the hallway outside Darya's room had been deserted. Not a single Youth Corps soldier in sight. No civilians, either. Where had they all gone? Where was Elena? Where was Rius Ludovic?

A flicker of movement through one of the broad windows facing the front of the fortress caught her attention. She cupped her hands over her eyes to shield them against the glare of the sunlight.

A lone military jeep snaked up the mountain road toward the

castle. Darya watched with a quickened pulse as it pulled to a stop in front of the open portcullis. She breathed a deep sigh of relief when the driver stepped out.

Paul Veliu.

She had been thinking about him constantly since the day she met with him in the garden. Wondering where he was, what he was doing. She raced down three flights of stairs to the ground floor, then paused to catch her breath. Was the entire fortress abandoned?

"Elena!" she shouted. "Liza, Rius?"

Silence.

She ran through the atrium and shoved open one of the fortress's massive front doors. Paul had already crossed the courtyard and was halfway up the broad flight of stone stairs, running at a dead sprint. He froze when he saw her, then pressed a finger to his lips.

She nodded and watched with silent fascination as he pulled out a cylindrical device with a green status light, held it up against the smartwatch on his wrist, then pushed a button on the device. The device's indicator light turned red. Paul moved the watch close to his mouth and spoke in a low voice. "I'm at the fortress. I've captured Rius Ludovic and have him tied up. I'm going to execute him now."

He pulled out his Beretta, turned toward the empty courtyard, and fired three shots.

"It's done," he murmured into the watch. "Rius Ludovic is dead. As requested, I'll send you video confirmation of the kill." He pulled out his cellphone and tapped on it for a moment, then pressed the cylindrical device against the smartwatch again. This time, the device beeped three times, and its status light turned green.

He motioned for Darya to follow him out of the courtyard. They had barely set foot in the garden when he suddenly turned on her.

"Dasha!" he cried. "Why are you still here?"

Was he angry at her? No, that wasn't anger. She could see it in his eyes. It was fear.

"What's going on, Paul?" she said. "Where is everyone?"

He took her hands in his, and she immediately felt the heat rising to her cheeks. Foolish girl! Paul was like a brother, that's all. The rest had to be her own imagination. Still, the sensation of his skin against hers sent a tremble through her body. Those alert, storm gray eyes of his were filled with concern.

"You should have left with the others," he went on. "Didn't Rius warn you?"

"Warn me of what?" she said. "When I woke up this morning, everyone was gone."

Paul looked away for a moment, his brow furrowing. "This doesn't add up," he said at last. "Rius called me on my way here. Aryana Voss has already returned to Khatizan. She could be here any minute. Rius told me he had ordered the evacuation of the fortress and was fleeing Khatizan himself. I was supposed to meet with Andrei Idrisov and an ATA strike team—"

"Andrei Idrisov?" she cut in. "The sniper?"

He nodded. "Andrei's a good guy. He's on our side, working against the Central Party. The plan was for me to meet him today, but then Firlenko sent me the order to kill Rius. I had no choice but to come here. We knew the order was coming soon, and Rius had his own so-called execution planned out. He sent me the video to pass on to Commander Firlenko, a deepfake that supposedly shows me putting three bullets through Rius's skull. Once the Chairman and Firlenko see that, they'll come straight here to seize the fortress." He shook his head. "But now I have more questions than answers. Why would Rius leave you here? He's a careful person, not one to make a mistake. I'm certain he would never put your life in danger, which means he must believe you would be safer here despite the Chairman and Firlenko. But that doesn't make any sense unless..."

He gazed off into the distance for a moment. He still held her hands in his, though he seemed unaware of it.

"I don't know how Rius and Aryana are connected," he went on, "but that must be the way of it. I've suspected the truth for some time now. I have to stop Rius, but there's still Andrei to think about…"

He sighed. "Dasha, I hate to do this, but could you help me?"

She forced down her own fear of the Chairman and Firlenko and Aryana Voss. Elena would be brave in a moment like this, wouldn't she? "What do you need? I'll do it, even if it means fighting Aryana and the Chairman myself."

He blinked. "Fight them? That's the opposite of what I want. With any luck, Aryana and the Chairman will fight each other. You need to stay safe, no matter what happens. I know you're a soldier, and we're not supposed to be afraid of anything, but this time, I want you to be afraid." He pulled a piece of paper and a roll of tape from his pocket and handed them to her. "Put this paper on the window of your bedroom. Andrei Idrisov will recognize the symbol on it. Lock yourself in your room and don't come out until Andrei and his team arrive. If they follow the backup plan, they should be here before long. Can you do this for me, Dasha?"

She turned her eyes from his eager gaze. "I don't want to stay here. Can't I just put the sign on my window and then leave with you?"

She trembled as he gently brushed some wayward strands of hair from her forehead. How her cheeks must be burning! "I wish you could," he said, "but it's too risky. I know it sounds crazy, but if Rius thinks you're safer at the fortress, then that's where you should be. I have a feeling Aryana Voss would be the last person in the world to harm you."

"What do you mean?" she said. "I don't trust Rius."

"Neither do I. There's no time to explain, and I'm not sure I understand it myself. I have to find Rius. I thought I was ahead of the game, but they've been playing us all along. If you and I don't see each other again…"

He looked away, and she thought he was going to leave her without another word. Then, suddenly, he pulled her close and kissed her fiercely on the lips. In that breathless moment, everything she feared—Aryana, the Chairman, the Central Party—ceased to exist. There was only her and Paul, two broken Youth Corps soldiers who had somehow found each other.

"I'm sorry, Dasha." He pulled away from her. "I shouldn't have done that. It was wrong of me. I just…"

She took his hand and pressed it against her lips. "No apology necessary, Vice Commander."

"Really?" He stared at her in disbelief, then broke into a radiant, almost childish grin. It was the first time she'd seen him smile. She prayed it wouldn't be the last. Brief as it was, he looked like a young man for once instead of a war-weary soldier. But time was a luxury they couldn't afford. They ran back to the fortress, stopping in front of the main doors.

"Goodbye, Dasha," Paul said. "Remember, you must stay safe, you must survive." He turned and hustled back down the steps. She watched until he was beyond the portcullis, then hurried back to her bedroom. She locked the door behind her, taped the paper to her window, and sat on the edge of her bed.

What if she never saw him again? What if he were captured?

Foolish girl. No sense borrowing trouble. She rose from the bed, donned her Youth Corps uniform, and tidied up in the attached bathroom. When she was ready, she examined her reflection in the oval-shaped standing mirror beside her nightstand.

Shoulders back, head erect, arms firmly planted at her waist. Ironic that all those years of Youth Corps training now served to prepare her and Paul for rebellion against the Party.

She rested her hand over the three lightning bolts on her sleeve.

*For God. For the State. For the Chairman.*

No longer. Her world had changed, and with it, her purpose.

*For God. For my country. For Elena and Paul.*

A deep sense of calm settled over her. Through Elena's love, her soul had broken out of the hellish prison the Party had forced upon it. Now a new fire burned within her. In life or in death, she was a free woman.

She sat in a silent reverie until she suddenly heard the massive front doors of the fortress slamming open. In the same instant, a voice in the hallway called her name.

It was Liza Khartoff, the aide the Youth Corps had assigned to her.

Her heart began pounding. If Liza was still here, it could only mean one thing. The woman had openly despised her. Now Chairman Markhov, the man Liza worshipped, was on his way to the fortress.

Liza would kill her as a sign of loyalty to the Chairman, proof that Liza's devotion belonged solely to him and not Aryana Voss.

Darya ran to her nightstand to fetch her pistol.

Gone! Someone must have stolen it.

Rius Ludovic? Or maybe Liza. Only those two would have known it was there in the first place.

"You're in there now, aren't you, Darya?" Liza shouted. The door rattled as Liza's thick fist smacked against it. "Open up. Please, Darya! I'm sorry for how I've treated you. I know you won't believe me, but it was all an act. We're out of time. I need to talk to you. Aryana's already in the fortress. You must hurry!"

A part of Darya wanted to obey. Liza sounded terrified, which was not at all like her. Or perhaps that was part of her trap? What if the Chairman had arrived instead of Aryana Voss? That seemed far more likely.

Besides, Paul had told her not to open her door for anyone until Andrei arrived. She could at least do the one thing he had asked of her. She ran into her closet and closed the door behind her. She crawled back into a corner, covering herself as much as possible with the unworn dresses and gowns on hangers.

Gunfire erupted seconds later.

Liza Khartoff was shooting the lock on her bedroom door.

## Chapter Twenty-Four
# Fortress Approach

ELENA PLACED THE back of her hand on Charles Ferguson's burning hot forehead. Just like the old days when one of her kids came down with the flu. Despite his suffering, his features now hinted at a rare serenity, as if the nightmare tormenting him had given way to a vision of paradise.

If only he would wake from his dreamworld. She had so much to ask him, so much she wanted to learn about him. From his fitful murmurings in sleep, it was clear he wasn't actually insane. Wherever they took him, whatever they were doing to him in those dark hours of the night was the cause of his madness.

"Nadia." He called her daughter's name for the hundredth time that day. "Where are you? Tell your father about the Island. Forget about me. Forget about Khatizan. The Island, the Island! Nadia, can you hear me?"

The sound of her daughter's name plucked the pain within Elena's heart like fingertips on harp strings. He clearly loved her daughter. Judging from his ramblings, that love was returned. Through him, broken as he was, she felt closer to Nadia and Boris and Peter than she had in years. But like the torture of Tantalus, she could reach for the life-giving waters but never taste them. His mind was too broken. Whenever he looked at her, he called her Nadia and continued his feverish monologue as if she were only another part of his dreams.

"Tell, me, sleeping one," she murmured, "does my Boris still love me? Does he even think of me?"

The question churned the pain and made her throat tighten like a knot. The old voice from the shadows of her heart whispered again, insistent.

*He doesn't love you anymore. He forgot you years ago. They've all forgotten you.*

She fell to her knees. In the same moment, Charles's eyes shot open, and he sat bolt upright in his bed. His troubled gaze wandered toward the window. A ray of sunlight had pierced the dark clouds, a single shaft of brightness that shone on the floor around her.

"Nadia, the Island is all that matters, all that they care about. Everything else was a distraction. You understand that, don't you?" He leaned back against the headboard. His face grew paler by the hour. Whatever they were doing to him, he couldn't survive it for long. "Did you tell Boris yet?"

She brushed damp strands of hair from his forehead. How his skin burned with fever! Why were they tormenting him?

"I'm not Nadia." How many times had she told him that? How many times had he stared at her in disbelief, only to call her by her daughter's name in the very next breath? "I'm her mother, Elena. You're having another dream. Whatever they're doing to you, they did it again last night. They brought you back hours ago. You've been sleeping."

He pressed his hands against his head. "The pain...I can't think. The children, the waves...the Island. Always the Island. And something else I can't remember. Nadia, it's taking me. I'm becoming like the others. The dream is taking over. I can't keep it out much longer."

Tears came unbidden to Elena's eyes. This was as lucid as he had ever been, yet still his mind was wrapped in illusions. She laid her hand on his cheek. "Rest, Charles. One day you will see her again."

"I'll see her?" His smile was radiant against his sunken features. A moment later, it vanished. "Why haven't you told your father, Nadia? Why isn't he doing something?"

She dipped a washcloth into a bucket of icy cold water and placed it on his forehead. "Rest. You need your strength."

"Pray for us, Nadia," he murmured. "Pray for me."

She clasped his hand in hers and said the Lord's Prayer.

"Yes," he replied softly. "Beautiful, isn't it? On earth as in heaven. Not the Island, no. Something much better. Nadia, look out!"

His eyes widened in sudden fear. He was pointing past her, at something over her shoulder. Another phantom of his mind. It was getting worse. The things he dreamed about were terrible. Children who were actually hideous machines wrapped in human flesh. A writhing sky made of murderous mechanical insects. An enormous building that housed an advanced, artificial Mind, a being that called itself Lilith.

"We meet again, Doctor Petrova."

Her breath froze at the sound of Commander Firlenko's voice.

Charles wasn't hallucinating. She turned, placing herself between Firlenko and Charles, as if, despite her weakness and powerlessness, she could protect him from the Commander.

"Get him up!" Firlenko shouted. His voice seemed unnatural, too loud and almost shrill. He crossed the room and stood at the foot of Charles's bed, his hand resting on the hilt of the curved saber at his waist. Those dark patches on his uniform—were those bloodstains? "Aryana Voss has summoned you both to her throne room. She just executed Chairman Markhov and commanded our troops to return to Chozul. Since I'm the only soldier left here, she ordered me to bring you to her."

Aryana Voss killed Chairman Markhov? Could it be true?

It could explain the blood on Firlenko's clothes. He seemed anxious, agitated, and his eyes kept darting from one of part of the room to another. His fingers opened and closed over the hilt of his saber.

The man was terrified.

But Aryana's request was absurd. Charles needed to rest. "Aryana Voss will have to wait," she said. "Can't you see how weak he is? Those devils have tortured him more than he can bear."

In the blink of an eye, the tip of Firlenko's saber was pressed against her throat. She swallowed and tried not to breathe as he slid its razor edge slowly across the hollow of her neck.

"Resist me again, science prisoner," he said in a deadly calm voice, "and I will carve you limb from limb while he watches, then drag him to the throne room myself. Markhov ran his mouth at the last moment and paid the price, but I'm no fool. I'll beg and grovel before Aryana now and be the next Chairman of Khatizan myself soon enough. She ordered me not to kill him, but she didn't say anything about you. Now help me move him." He slammed the sword back into its scabbard, grabbed Charles's arm, and dragged him from the bed. The moment Firlenko released him, Charles tumbled to the floor.

Elena raised her trembling hand to her throat and saw dark crimson splotches on her fingertips. Another inch and Firlenko's saber would have killed her. She had assumed she would die in the courtyard of Prison Factory Six like Marina.

No matter. Here or there, the result would be the same.

Firlenko crouched down beside Charles. "I don't know what's wrong with you, but if you don't want me to slit this woman's throat, then you will get up and walk. Do you understand?"

"Don't hurt her," Charles groaned. "Nadia is innocent. I'll come with you. We're all trapped on the Island anyway. What does it matter if we walk to one side of it or the other?" He pressed his hands against the ground to raise himself, but he was too weak.

"Here." Elena knelt and wrapped her arm around him. "I'll help him."

Charles wasn't too heavy, thankfully, and she managed to get him to his feet. He stumbled along beside her into the hallway and down the stairway toward the ground floor, one laborious step at a time. He had to stop and catch his breath at the foot of the stairs. The poor man looked like he had aged half a century in the space of days.

Firlenko had told the truth. The Youth Corps soldiers were gone, the hallways were silent. The entire fortress seemed to be abandoned.

"Dear Lord," she murmured under her breath, "let him be saved. I ask nothing for myself, but for Nadia's sake, don't let them destroy him."

Firlenko sniffed impatiently. "Exert yourself, Doctor Ferguson. Let fear be your guide. I've seen children in our Youth Corps march for hours on a broken ankle because they knew we were watching them, knew what we would do to them if they stopped."

"I'm ready," Charles gasped, though he leaned heavily against her. He had no strength left.

So be it. She would be his strength now.

Boris rubbed his hands together to warm them. "There's no one? Are you certain?"

Andrei Idrizov glanced down at him from his perch on the branch of an oak tree. He was at least thirty feet above the ground.

"Not a soul. No patrols, no vehicles, no guards at the entrance. It looks deserted."

Boris now confined his swearing to Russian. Nadia had jumped all over him when he'd accidentally let one fly in plain English in front of Safiya. What was a red-blooded male supposed to say when he smashed his own finger with a hammer instead of the blasted tent peg? So he'd switched to Russian invectives for the rest of their camping trip. Not that it helped. That little pint-sized human sponge of a child was absorbing Russian just as quickly as she was absorbing English. He'd have to start cussing in Chinese soon.

"You know, Andrei," he said. "I'm starting to wonder whether this Paul Veliu of yours is a traitor or just a plain idiot. He magically discovers a secret entrance into Khatizan. He somehow provides us with transport. He doesn't meet us at the rendezvous, which implies treachery, but he never actually betrays us. He sends us to an abandoned fortress in the mountains, but there's no sign of an ambush, and we can just turn around and leave whenever we want. What's his end game? What is he doing right now?"

Andrei clambered down the tree as nimbly as a monkey. He brushed off his pants. "Paul Veliu is no idiot," he retorted. "He's no traitor, either. Show some respect, American. I don't know how things work in your country, but in Khatizan, people disappear every day. He wasn't at the rendezvous point, yes. Most likely, that means the Party suspects him and is torturing him as we speak. But the fact that they aren't here means he hasn't told them where we were going. In other words, the torture didn't work, and he has saved our lives by keeping his mouth shut. I hope I'm wrong, but that's how the game tends to play out here."

Blast it, the kid was right. Maybe Paul Veliu wasn't to blame, but they'd come so far, over a border that no foreign aggressor had crossed in years, and for what? If the fortress was empty, it would all be in vain.

"Forgive me, Andrei," he said at last. "We're here now, so we move forward. Since it's deserted, should we march right up to the front door?"

"Not the front," Andrei replied. "Paul told me what to do if he couldn't meet with us. We'll use the gate in the walls behind the fortress. Once we're past the gate, we'll try to sneak through a window on the second floor of the main keep. Darya Alexandrovna's room, though I doubt she's here anymore."

"Who is Darya Alexandrovna?" Kenjiro asked.

Andrei shrugged. "I've never met her. Paul said she's important to some group called the Magnus Foundation. She's the daughter of one of their old leaders."

"Sweet Saint Theocaris!" Boris cried. "You said Alexandrovna?"

"Yes, why?"

"Then she could be Magnus's daughter." The prospect of Alexander Magnus having a child was terrifying. If the daughter was anything like her father, the world had just become much more dangerous. "Let's hope, for her sake, that isn't the case. Lead on, Andrei."

The sniper guided them through the woods along the eastern shoulder of the mountain, skirting around the fortress at a safe distance. The fluted spirals and turrets of the keep were visible through patches in the forest canopy, but the strike team would remain concealed from any but the most determined observers within the walls. They stopped directly behind the fortress, their position now veiled by a dense line of oaks and aspens.

Boris's watch vibrated against his wrist.

Time for another breath test. The fact that he was in the middle of a covert ambush far behind enemy lines apparently didn't qualify as an excuse in Julia Pearson's book. He pulled Little Boris out of his backpack, tapped the doll's cheek twice to activate the breath sensor, then breathed onto its face.

"Good job, big man," Little Boris announced after a brief pause.

He grunted and stuffed the doll into his backpack. He heard the Russian commandos chuckling softly, just like they did every single time he took the test.

They'd have to break cover for the final approach, but the fortress looked even more desolate and abandoned from this angle than it had from the front.

"That's our entry?" He pointed toward a solid steel gate, perhaps twelve feet tall and half that in width, nestled near the southwest corner of the wall.

"That's it," Andrei replied. "I'm going up for a better look."

With the gear he'd brought, Andrei could climb trees almost as quickly as he descended them. He made it to a branch twenty feet up a sprawling oak, then he raised his sniper rifle and peered through the scope.

"Any sign of Paul Veliu?" Kenjiro called up.

"No," Andrei said glumly. "Wait, I've spotted something."

"What is it?" Boris asked.

"There's a piece of paper with a red circle in the center taped to the window. Black line through the circle."

"From the excitement in your voice, Andrei, I take it that means something to you?"

"It means good news." Andrei lowered his rifle. "It's a signal we used in Red Ops One. Only Paul and the other team members would know it. He's telling us the path is clear. He's still alive."

Boris grunted. There was another possibility, of course. Paul could be a traitor and they could get shot the moment they came within range of the walls. Their lives now rested in the hands of a complete stranger. A terrorist who had set off the bomb in Berlin, who had spent his life serving an enemy state, who had failed to meet them as promised at the rendezvous point.

"Are you ready?" Andrei asked as he clambered down the tree.

This whole thing felt wrong. Aryana Voss's fortress should have had an army of guards even in her absence. Paul Veliu should have met them and used his authority as Vice Commander to get them past those guards. He was supposed to be their ticket into the fortress, a Vice Commander escorting a foreign delegation. This backup plan was insanity. Truth be told, they were flying blind.

In other words, business as usual.

Boris pulled out a stick of gum in honor of Gavriel and popped it into his mouth. "Let's move."

They stayed behind tree cover until they were within a dozen yards of the wall, then crawled on their stomachs through the shin-high grass behind the fortress. Their caution was needless. When they reached the gate, there had been no sign of movement from the fortress.

"The moment of truth," he murmured as Andrei Idrizov rested his hand on the gate. If the way was clear, then surely Paul Veliu would have at least had the foresight to open the gate for them.

It was unlocked. Andrei pushed it open and motioned for them to follow him into the courtyard behind the fortress. They headed straight for Darya Alexandrovna's window. As they approached, the window swung outward silently. An unseen hand lowered a rope to the ground.

Wonderful. Rope climbing. It had been a few years, and his back was already sore from crawling through that grass like a snake. Time was making its demands felt, even for the legendary Boris Petrov. They would put him out to pasture soon, trap him behind some desk so he could sign paperwork and bother all the young folks with stories about the good old days.

But not today.

He watched with envy as one of the young, lithe Russian commandos scrambled up the rope and disappeared into the open window. Kenjiro went next. Despite being only five years younger than Boris, he made the climb at a respectable pace.

Boris folded his arms over his chest. "Can you do me a favor, Andrei?"

"Of course, sir. What is it?"

"The next time you and your buddy come up with a backup plan, make sure that plan doesn't involve gray-haired men scaling castle walls."

Andrei gulped. "Yes, sir. Sorry about that, sir."

"Go on, you're next," Boris told Fyodor, the leader of the freedom fighters. "I'll bring up the rear."

"With respect, sir," Fyodor replied with a hint of a smile, "it might be best if you went first. Then we can help you out if needed. Not that you'll need it, of course, but we do this kind of thing all the time in training."

Blasted kids. If Fyodor hadn't been halfway respectful about it, the two of them could have had an old-fashioned brawl right then and there. They would learn real quick that the old man still had something left in the tank.

"Have it your way." He spat on his hands and rubbed them together.

He grabbed the rope, readied himself, and started the long climb to Darya Alexandrovna's window. Five minutes later, with Fyodor's help from behind, he tumbled through the opening.

The infernal march of time! It wasn't his arms. They remained strong as ever. It wasn't his lungs, though years of cigars hadn't helped in that respect and his fractured ribs still throbbed when he pushed himself too hard. It was his knee, his blasted left knee, the one that got sore every time he went jogging. The thing had locked up on him halfway up the climb, and it had taken Fyodor's strength and some heavy pulling from Andrei to get him the rest of the way.

He leaned back against the wall of Darya's bedroom, panting and massaging his knee. "No one tell Mr. Charles!" he barked. "Poor kid still thinks I'm invincible."

❦

Eugene Thompson peered up the twenty-foot expanse of stone wall leading to the open window. A slender rope hung down from the window to the ground in front of him.

"Great." Thompson stuck out his chest and started talking to himself in his best imitation of Boris Petrov. "All you have to do, Mr. Lab Rat, is grab this rope and haul yourself up to the window using those bulging muscles you develop when you spend your life focusing microscopes and lecturing to neuron-deprived freshmen." He had kept himself at the back of the line, and for good reason. Those commandos had made climbing two stories look like child's play. At least Boris had struggled near the top.

He spat on his hands and rubbed his palms together just like Boris had done. He had no idea how human saliva could get him up to that window, but it was a universally acknowledged magic ritual necessary to any rope-climbing venture.

He wrapped his hands around the smooth tactical rope. What next?

Something about propping his feet on the wall, then yanking himself up. Or maybe he should do both at once?

He leapt upward as high as he could, frantically grabbed at the rope, tried to swing his feet up to the wall, then slipped and landed hard on his backside.

"Gods," he moaned.

He looked up at the window again. Boris was peering down at him, and even from that distance Thompson could see the mirth dancing in the old scoundrel's eyes. Boris mouthed something at him, but he couldn't make it out. Then Boris tugged up a length of rope and pretended to wrap it around his waist.

Right. The old sack-of-flour approach.

Muttering imprecations with indiscriminatory abandon against the pantheon of divinities and other sacred cows strewn across the timeline of human history, Eugene Thompson wrapped the rope around his waist.

"Zeus's boxers," he grumbled as he cinched the rope and tied it off. He suddenly realized that the childishly simple knot he'd made was about to be the only thing holding him in midair at a distance of twenty feet.

Would you die if you fell twenty feet? Would the flickering candle of his existence be snuffed out because of the interesting fact that he didn't know how to tie knots?

Double knot, then. Shoelaces never came apart with a double knot, did they?

He swallowed and raked his hands through his hair.

"If I don't die," he said, "you'll owe me this time, Charles. And if I *do* die, you'll owe my imaginary children, the offspring of that blindingly gorgeous supermodel I would have married if I hadn't come here to rescue you."

He gave Boris a thumbs-up.

Three terrifying minutes later, he was lying on a smooth tile floor, gasping and sputtering and biting off archaic invectives that would have made a street rapper blush, assuming the rapper happened to know ancient mythology.

He looked around the room.

A lavish setup, like the set of one of those Victorian costume dramas Nadia subjected poor Charles to on a regular basis. A cumbrous chandelier suspended from the ceiling illuminated a large four-poster bed with gauzy curtains. At the foot of the bed lay a dense Persian rug, its vibrant pattern of blue and gold woven with dazzling intricacy. A set of carved mahogany dressers and nightstands with claw-and-ball feet rounded out the decor. He was no expert, but it all looked vintage and authentic, which meant this bedroom alone could cost millions.

One piece of furniture was out of place, a wrought-iron table lying on its side near the door. Two of the table's legs were missing. It looked almost as if they had been ripped off by brute force. Given that the table was made from thick, solid iron, that should have been impossible.

Kenjiro, Andrei, Boris, and the Russian commandos were all staring at the wall beyond the poster bed, at some spot hidden from Thompson's vantage point. Whatever it was, it had them rapt in eerie silence. He clambered heavily to his feet and crossed the room to join them.

"Guan Yu's beard!" he muttered.

On the far side of Darya Alexandrovna's bed, a human body hung suspended against the wall. Two narrow iron bars—the missing table legs, no doubt—had been driven through her shoulders, pinning her to the wall as if she were a prized butterfly in an entomologist's display case.

He saw Boris cross himself Orthodox style. The Russian brute squad followed suit.

Thompson swallowed down the bile that was creeping up his throat and moved closer to investigate. He'd seen things like this in Control at Magnus Headquarters. One would think the brain would grow accustomed to such casual and calculated savagery, but he was out of practice. Or maybe he had a soul, like Charles and that monk friend of his kept insisting.

It was a woman's form, her face concealed by a black veil. Aryana Voss wore a black veil. Could this be her?

One of the Russian commandos lifted the veil from the woman's face.

Terrifying. Locked in an expression of primal terror, the wideset eyes forever open, the lips pulled back in a feral rictus.

"So…I take it that's our contact, Darya Alexandrovna?" he asked.

Andrei shivered visibly. "I don't think so. I've never met Darya, but Paul said she was…well, you know…beautiful."

An unlikely adjective for the face before them, even under friendlier circumstances. The woman's features were too expansive for classical beauty, and her face and neck were mottled with pimples and some preponderant warts.

"Then who is it?"

Andrei shook his head. "I have no idea. She's wearing a Youth Corps uniform."

As Andrei spoke, the closet door slowly swung outward as if of its own volition. The rifles of the Russian commandos were instantly levelled on the opening.

"Wait!" cried a woman's voice. "Don't shoot!"

Boris signaled to the commandos to lower their weapons.

"Come out," he called. "We aren't going to hurt you."

A young woman emerged from the darkness of the closet, her face pale as a vernal moon on a clear night. Her eyes shifted nervously from the commandos to Boris and his team. Her symmetrical features and supple form revealed a beauty masked in part by the tight braiding of her hair and the starched angles of her black Youth Corps uniform.

"I'm Darya Alexandrovna." She fixed her wandering gaze on Boris. "You are Elena's husband, are you not?"

"Sweet Saint Anthony!" Boris staggered backward and sat heavily on the bed. "It's true, then. You…you know my Elena?"

A bittersweet smile curved the corners of Darya's lips. "I've known her for as long as I can remember. She was in the women's dormitory with my mom and me in Prison Factory Six. I used to call her auntie, but now she's like my own mother."

Prison Factory Six. The riddle of Boris's wife and her mysterious disappearance was finally solved. Gods, what a nightmare! Elena must have spent all those years trapped in a Khatiz prison factory.

"Where is she?" Boris grabbed Darya by the shoulders, then seemed to realize what he was doing and stepped back. His eyes glistened with tears. "Forgive me. I was afraid to hope. Please, take me to her!"

"If she's still in the fortress," Darya said, "then she's probably with Aryana. Aryana's the one who did that." She pointed toward the corpse affixed to the wall, though her gaze avoided looking at it. "When he left, Paul told me to lock the door and wait for you. A few minutes later, I heard someone rattling the handle. It was Liza, my aide. She's only loyal to the Chairman, so I thought she had come to kill me. I hid in the closet. Then she shot the lock on my door. She entered the room and started calling my name, but I didn't answer. Then *she* came, Aryana. You can hear her when she's nearby. There's a strange whirring sound, like a gear moving.

"I heard gunshots, then Liza started screaming." Darya trembled. "I've never heard anyone make a sound like that. It stopped as suddenly as it began. Seconds went by. I knew *she* was still in the room. Then, I heard two loud, cracking noises, one after another. It must have been the table legs. I heard Liza's body being dragged across the floor, and then…" She lowered her eyes. "When it was over, I could see Aryana's shadow beneath the crack in the closet door. Nothing but that door stood between us. She came closer, and I knew she was going to murder me. I was too terrified to move. But she turned and left. I waited a few minutes, then came out and lowered the rope in case you showed up. Paul told me you would be here sometime today, but I didn't know you were coming so soon. I was afraid Aryana might return, so I hid again. I found this on Liza's body." She handed an envelope to Boris. "It says it's for you."

Boris tore the envelope open and unfolded a piece of paper. Thompson leaned over and could just make out the writing. The note was handwritten, its cursive script ornate and meticulous.

*I have the ones you seek, the woman you love
and the one who betrayed my master.
Judgement awaits you in the throne room.
Vindicta mea est.*

"My Latin's a bit rusty, but that's *vengeance is mine*, right?" Thompson said.

Boris nodded, his grim face like a wall of granite. "We'll deal with Aryana Voss, but it's strange that Liza's gunshots didn't harm her. Maybe she has some type of body armor. Either way, the ammo we've brought could put holes in a tank. Who else is in the fortress?"

Darya lowered her eyes. "Paul said the Chairman and Commander Firlenko were coming. They didn't know Aryana was already here. They're planning to rebel against her."

"There's no one else?" Boris asked. "No other soldiers?"

She shook her head. "You see what happened here. Aryana doesn't need guards."

Boris translated all that Darya had said to the Russian commandos. As he did so, several of them crossed themselves again. Even Kenjiro looked shaken.

"Where did Paul go?" Andrei asked suddenly. "Why did he leave you here?"

"He said he was going to find Rius Ludovic," she replied. "He told me it was too dangerous, that I'd be safer here."

"Any thoughts on all this, professor?" Boris said, turning to Thompson. "You know more about Aryana than any of us."

Thompson scratched the stubble on the bottom of his chin. Thoughts? Honestly, they should tuck their tails and get the blazes out of there. Run away and never look back.

But Aryana had Charles, which meant they had to face her.

"I say we open fire on Aryana the moment we see her. Don't even try to negotiate. If half of what I heard about her in Control was true, the element of surprise may be our only chance. If nothing else, some of us can distract her while the others escape with Charles and Elena. If your guns don't work, we're going to have a rough time of it. For what's it worth, I volunteer for the distraction bit. Apparently, I'm good at it."

Boris folded his arms and gave an appreciative nod. "Once again you surprise me, Mr. Thompson." His Russian accent was suddenly in full swing. "You look like a plant that's been kept in a basement for decades, yet you're brave enough to be special forces. You make me proud."

Thompson let out a startled yelp as Boris grabbed him and wrapped him in a bear hug. "I'm no hero, Boris." He straightened his shirt after Boris dropped him back on the ground. "If I'd kept Charles away from the Foundation in the first place, none of this would have happened. If he had escaped back then, if he had never met Alexander Magnus—"

"If Charles Ferguson had never met Alexander Magnus," Kenjiro cut in, "then Magnus's Reaping would have happened last winter, billions of lives would have been lost, and we would all be slaves of the Foundation. Or corpses."

"Then we might as well go out with a bang, right?" Thompson said. "Speaking of which, could one of you loan me a gun?"

Boris barked a laugh. "A nun would have more luck with a firearm than you, Mr. Thompson. But I have something better than that." He reached into his backpack, pulled out Little Boris, and handed it to Thompson.

"Um…" Thompson looked down at Little Boris. The pint-sized,

militant replica of its much larger namesake now sported a crimson eye patch over its missing eye along with army fatigues and a black t-shirt with the words *Hack Attack!* emblazoned across the front in bold white letters.

"What, Little Boris isn't good enough for you?" Boris cried. "Then here, you can have this, too."

He dug into his backpack a second time and fetched a peculiar-looking silver whistle on a chain. He slung the whistle over Thompson's neck. "Now listen." Boris lowered his voice. "If things go south in that throne room, blow the whistle, then give Little Boris a squeeze. Trust me, he's a lot tougher than he looks." He leaned closer, and his voice descended even further into a very Russian-sounding whisper. "The whistle will draw Aryana's attention, which means there's no going back once you blow it. Make sure it's the right time, because you'll probably die a few seconds later." He patted Thompson on the back. "There, don't you feel safer now?"

## Chapter Twenty-Five

# The Endgame

Paul Veliu's foot shoved the gas pedal down as far as it would go. The military truck's engine whined in protest, but the vehicle rumbled ahead like a galloping elephant, topping off its speed at eighty-five kilometers per hour. He would only get one chance to catch Rius, so he had to make it count.

He swung the truck onto the on-ramp to Highway Three, which headed straight for Chozul. The highway was smooth as silk, repaved every winter so the Chairman's car wouldn't hit any bumps on its way to the fortress.

"Another day of bloodshed," he murmured. "And if Aryana kills Commander Firlenko, I'll be the highest-ranking officer in the Youth Corps."

Which meant *he* could become the next Chairman, young as he was. The military trumped all in Khatizan. Before Markhov had become Chairman, he had been Commander of the Revolutionary Army. If Markhov ever died, the Youth Corps Commander's path to succession was unquestionable, a fact Rius would have known all too well.

"Hurry up, blast you!" he yelled, smacking the dashboard with the

304

palm of his hand. The truck engine kept roaring, but no amount of coercion would speed it up beyond its mechanical limits.

After leaving Dasha at the fortress, he had run to the gazebo in the garden. Just as he'd feared, the chess game had come to an end. The black queen and king stood alone on the board, with the white king lying prostrate before them. Everything else had been captured.

It deepened his suspicion. In their last meeting in the garden, Rius had echoed an unusual phrase, one that Paul had heard before from Aryana's lips. He didn't understand exactly how the two of them were connected, but if he could catch Rius in time, he might finally unravel the mystery of Khatizan's shadow ruler.

Thompson gingerly clutched Little Boris in his hand as if the doll were a grenade with a loose pin. Maybe it was. Turning a child's toy into a squeezable explosive was exactly the sort of thing he'd expect from Boris Petrov. He absently fingered the whistle around his neck. It was thicker than a normal whistle and seemed to have some kind of electronic device on the back of it.

"I feel like an idiot," he announced.

"That's because you *are* an idiot, Mr. Thompson," Boris replied cheerfully. "But at least you're a brave one."

"Quiet," Darya hissed. "She'll hear us."

They crept down the marble stairway single file, with Darya in the lead and the Russian commandos bringing up the rear. The fortress's interior was as opulent as Darya's bedroom. Gilded furniture, hand-woven tapestries and embroideries, medieval suits of armor bearing pikes and spears and broadswords—it felt like they were stepping back into an age of feudal power, bereft of the wonderful complexities of democracy and social justice.

An age of tyrants. Alexander Magnus would have loved this place.

"There's the hallway to her throne room," Darya whispered. "Through that door on the right."

The door was cracked. Boris shoved it open and led them down a stone hallway lit by torches in iron wall sconces. They reached a pair of massive double doors that joined in a pointed arch at least twelve feet high. On the left door was an engraving of a lion rampant, his claws lifted for battle. Alexander Magnus's old insignia. On the right door was a black eagle clutching an arrow between its talons. Aryana Voss's own heraldic symbol, no doubt.

Boris signaled to the commandos. They took positions on either side of the twin doors, ready to storm inside. One of the commandos had given Darya a handgun, and Boris and Kenjiro both had their pistols out and ready. The commandos and Andrei Idrisov had their assault rifles hoisted.

Thompson took a deep breath and rehearsed the plan in his mind. Boris and the commandos would charge Aryana Voss and, if necessary, deal with the Chairman and Commander Firlenko. Darya, Kenjiro, and Andrei would free the prisoners and escape.

What did that leave for the fearless Eugene Thompson?

Blowing a whistle and squeezing a doll.

Paul swerved onto the dirt road and led the truck deep into the alpine forest. The airstrip was a state secret tucked away in secluded woods that were Chairman Markhov's personal property. A perfect place to bring in foreign dignitaries whose presence in Khatizan required discretion. Paul had learned about it only days ago, a part of his intelligence briefing after being appointed Vice Commander. It provided a logical escape route for Rius Ludovic.

The dirt road, if the two worn ruts in the grass deserved such a title, curved sharply to the left. He braked hard to make the turn without crashing into a tree, then edged the truck out of the woods and into a clearing. A private jet was parked at the beginning of the dirt runway. Rius's Mercedes was nearby. Paul hit the accelerator, drove the truck between Rius's car and the jet, and slammed the brakes.

Rius Ludovic stood outside the driver's door of the Mercedes, watching Paul with remarkable calmness.

Almost as if he were waiting for him.

Paul slipped his Beretta from its holster and clambered down out of the truck.

"Get your hands up," he shouted. Rius instantly complied despite the smug, knowing look on his face. "Stay right where you are, Rius."

Rius chuckled. "I was wondering when you'd show up, Vice Commander. You almost had me worried. You noticed my little mistake in the garden, I take it?"

"It's more than a coincidence, isn't it?" Paul edged his way around the back of the car, keeping his pistol trained on Rius. "You and Aryana said the exact same words, that you never forgot the state of a chessboard. What are the odds that two people would have such a rare talent and describe it identically? Then I saw the end of your game. You're the king, she's the queen. What is she? How are you connected to her?"

"We are closer than you could possibly imagine, Vice Commander. She is the first step in my personal evolution. She grants me freedom from my own shadows. The next step awaits me on the Island."

With the darkened windows, Paul couldn't tell if anyone was in Rius's Mercedes. He glanced at the jet, but it looked empty, at least on the outside. Either someone was hiding inside, or Rius could fly that thing by himself.

"Where's your pilot?"

Rius shrugged. "It's a Foundation jet, which means it will fly itself wherever I want. How much do you know? You noticed the apparent mistake I made, but that was, in fact, intentional. I needed you to follow me here, and you did not disappoint. I wanted us to have one last chat before I leave Khatizan forever."

Paul saw a quick flicker of motion and heard a rustling sound. He whirled to his left, aiming his gun toward the sound. Just a startled robin flitting between branches. "Why didn't you bring Darya with you?" he asked. "You told me she's the daughter of Alexander Magnus and the heir of your Foundation. Or was that just another lie?"

"You are truly clever, Paul Veliu." Rius chuckled. "A dangerous virtue in Khatizan. When it comes to authoritarian regimes, blessed are the ignorant! But I'm a clever man, too. Do you know the problem with chess, Vice Commander? Once you've become better than everyone, no one can challenge you but yourself. Germany and Russia, Markhov and Firlenko, Khatizan's resistance movement, you and Darya, your American ATA friends, even Aryana Voss—I've been playing every side of the board, controlling all the hands. Surely you suspected that? I am the king, after all.

"I left Darya because I had no choice. I could have forced her to join me, but she would have resisted. Her health, mentally and physically, remains fragile. She needs to be here now, with you and that Petrova woman. I could never harm the daughter of my late master. When Darya is ready to take what's rightfully hers, the Foundation will welcome her with open arms.

"You've kept your word, Vice Commander, so I will keep mine. Within an hour, the Central Party will declare you the new Commander of Khatizan's armed forces. They'll make you Chairman shortly afterward. Both positions are open, believe it or not. I'm the one who planted all the evidence Markhov used for his purge. I have ensured that leaders of the Movement now hold all the key positions throughout Khatizan's government. They know you are their man. If you want to please them and the West, you can announce Khatizan's first free election in decades." He grinned. "Our poor Khatiz peasants would hardly know what to do with themselves if we gave them even an ounce of political power. But power is a quickly acquired taste, is it not?"

"What about Aryana Voss?" Paul asked. "You'll make her leave the country?"

"You still misunderstand our…relationship," Rius replied with a shiver. "Manipulating Aryana is delicate work. But to answer your question, she will leave today, after we get our revenge on Boris Petrov. She'll take what remains of the Foundation's technology and weaponry with her, though most of it has already been transferred out of Khatizan. The Island is everything to her now, though even she has no idea what awaits her there. I've learned how to keep secrets even from her.

"As for the global conflict, evidence will soon be released showing that Chairman Markhov ordered the attacks on Germany and Russia. Markhov has already received his due punishment. You will be given access to Khatizan's nuclear arsenal, so I doubt the rest of the world will be interested in further consequences beyond the usual sanctions. But we led them on a merry chase, didn't we?

"The future of the nation is in your hands now, Paul. Make peace or start a war. Hold Khatizan's first election in decades or crush the peasants under your feet. Enjoy your power while it lasts. A new day approaches, and every government shall be dissolved in the Twilight of the Gods."

Rius bowed, though every line of his face betrayed mockery. "Now if you'll excuse me, great and powerful Commander, our foreign friends are about to arrive in the fortress's throne room. Aryana requires my full attention."

Paul had been mystified by Rius's words, but when Rius took a step toward the plane, he raised his pistol. "The only place you're going is a prison cell. Get on the ground!"

Rius clapped his hands together and laughed despite having a gun trained on him. "Always the hero! So amusingly predictable. I'm afraid the old weapons won't help you, not anymore. But don't worry, Commander. I will only incapacitate you. Darya still needs you, at least for now." He cleared his throat. "Paul Veliu is the target. Immobilize him."

It happened in the blink of an eye.

One moment, Paul had his gun trained on Rius. A second later, something flew out the airplane's open door as swiftly as a bullet and stung him twice on the neck. Was it some kind of insect? The Beretta slipped from his fingers and clattered on the ground. His arms and legs and chest felt like lead. He dropped to his knees.

The insect flew to Rius and landed in his open palm. It looked like a metallic locust.

"The last surviving Harvester." Rius patted Paul on the head as he walked past him toward the jet. "But I will soon restore their ranks. Take care of yourself, Commander. More to the point, take care of Darya. I'll be in touch." Rius raised his voice. "Come along, prisoner. We're leaving."

The back door of Rius's Mercedes opened. A gray-haired man in a brown prison uniform got out first, followed by a younger woman with blonde hair who wore what looked like a navy-blue flight suit. Rius signaled impatiently, and the man led the woman onto the plane.

Paul's mind grew heavier, heavier. As the jet engines roared to life, he collapsed face-first into the dirt.

⸎

Thompson's heart was doing somersaults in his chest. His whole body trembled with waves of nervous energy.

"On three," Boris whispered to the commandos. "One. Two. Three."

The commandos shoved open the double doors to the throne room and charged inside. A moment later, a man shrieked. The unnatural sound turned Thompson's blood to ice. The strike team's assault rifles blazed to life. Boris followed the commandos, a pistol in each hand. Kenjiro, Darya, and Andrei slipped inside next, staying close to the outer wall.

"You're an idiot, Eugene Thompson," he whispered to himself. He was now alone in the hallway. "Boris was right about that. An idiot who's about to die blowing a whistle and squeezing a plush doll."

But in the final analysis, did it really matter whether he died with a whistle or a machine gun? If Charles escaped and got back to Nadia, it would be worth it. Those two deserved some happiness after all they'd been through.

He cradled Little Boris under one arm, clutched his whistle with his free hand, and stepped into the throne room.

The scene within verged on the surreal.

In the center of a dark room lit by standing lamps and the flickering lights of a massive chandelier, Aryana Voss sat on a throne in her voluminous black robes, her veiled head raised and watching them. She remained perfectly still, a remarkable fact considering that Boris and the team of Russian commandos were unleashing a perfect hailstorm of bullets on her. The impact of the endless barrage tore her dress, shredding it in parts, but it seemed to have no other effect on her. The ripped sections of her clothing revealed only a deeper layer of some black, leathery substance underneath, almost like the skin of a reptile.

On either side of the throne sat two mangled corpses, one at Aryana's left, the other at her right. The body on the right was instantly recognizable as Khatizan's notorious Chairman Markhov. His arms and legs were broken into hideous contortions, and his neck had been twisted sideways at an impossible angle to face Aryana Voss. The body on her left, similarly mangled, had a dark gray uniform. That had to be Commander Firlenko. At least, what was left of him.

Thompson watched, mesmerized, as the ineffectual bullets thudded against Aryana Voss.

"What *is* she?" he murmured.

He spotted Charles sitting beside a blazing lamp on a side wall, thankfully far enough away to be safe from the gunfire. Charles was trussed up like a pig, his arms and legs tied with black cords. Next to him lay a woman, similarly bound, who looked almost like an older Nadia. Must be her mother, Elena Petrova.

Kenjiro, Darya, and Andrei had made it halfway to the two prisoners.

Aryana Voss still hadn't moved, not even the merest fraction of an inch.

Was she already dead? If so, who had killed Markhov and Firlenko? Who had tied up Charles and Elena? And how could a dead body stay motionless while assault rifles blasted it mercilessly? *Rigor mortis* was one thing, but an armored convoy couldn't have held up against that kind of firepower.

Over the deafening clatter of the rifles, he began to hear a deep, pulsing sound that grew in intensity until he felt it reverberating in his own chest. It mounted and rose until the whole room throbbed with unreleased energy.

Boris and the commandos formed a loose semicircle facing Aryana. They kept up their barrage of firepower though it had no visible effect on her. Darya and Kenjiro darted forward suddenly, rushing toward Charles and Elena.

Thompson took another step into the throne room.

In the same moment, Aryana shot to her feet and sprang into motion.

She reached one of the commandos after two blindingly fast strides. He gave a surprised shout as she hoisted him up by the throat with one of her black-gloved hands. He dangled in the air, legs kicking at her while she strangled the life out of him. Two of the other commandos ran to help. The others were yelling at Boris, at each other, but there was nothing they could do.

A second later, the kicking stopped, and the dangling commando became motionless. Aryana hurled the lifeless body into the wall with such inhuman force that the very stones cracked. The commandos nearest her backed away with their rifles hoisted. Aryana turned to face them, her movements stiff and mechanical.

"Pull back!" Boris shouted. He now had a grenade in one hand and a pistol in the other. "Get Elena and Charles out of here. Don't stop firing. Slow her down!"

Thompson took two more steps into the room. No question now.

The rumors he'd heard during his days in Control were true. If anything, the old Magnus Foundation leaders had vastly underestimated Aryana Voss's unearthly power.

Thank Neptune she hadn't been in Headquarters when they betrayed Magnus.

The volley of gunshots resumed, but they might as well have been firing blanks for all the good it did. Aryana's dress was shredded by bullets, but that pitch black barrier beneath it seemed impenetrable.

Kenjiro, Darya, and Andrei freed Charles and Elena from their restraints and were leading them back toward the doors of the throne room. What had happened to Charles? He looked awful, and he kept wandering away from them, his lips moving, his eyes staring vacantly as if he couldn't see or understand what was happening around him.

So far, Aryana hadn't noticed the escaping prisoners. Or was she just toying with them? She now stood alone on one side of the throne room, her silent gaze fixed on her attackers.

As the remaining commandos began edging back toward the door, Boris hurled the grenade at Aryana, A second later, there was an ear-splitting blast and a blinding flash of light followed by a small cloud of smoke.

Did it work? Was she dead?

Through the dissipating haze he could see her. Motionless, standing in the exact same position. Watching them.

Suddenly, she struck again, running so fast it seemed as if she flew across the stone tiles. She snatched two commandos this time, one hoisted aloft in each arm. Thompson nearly emptied his stomach when she smashed the two soldiers into each other, instantly crushing them to death. He turned away from the blood-chilling spectacle.

They were going to die. All of them. Charles, Elena, Boris—no one would survive this. Gods above.

God have mercy.

With a shaking hand he brought the whistle to his lips. In the other hand, he held Little Boris, ready to squeeze the doll when the time came. It wouldn't be long now, not at this rate. He would soon be the only one left to face her. He would survive for mere seconds, but maybe those seconds would be enough time for Charles and the others to flee.

When he steeled himself to face the carnage once more, only Boris and one commando remained. The other soldiers lay prone, scattered about the throne room in horrific silence. Were all of them dead?

Kenjiro and Darya now carried Charles between them. He looked too weak to stand on his own. With Elena and Andrei close behind, they slipped past the door and left the throne room. Had Aryana still not noticed them? If Charles and Elena were so important to her, why had she let them escape?

Suddenly he remembered what Darya had said earlier, that Aryana had come to her bedroom and murdered that girl, Liza, but then left instead of killing Darya as well. Was that why Aryana wasn't attacking Darya and those near her now?

"Retreat!" Boris shouted. He and the last commando were already near the door. They kept firing, the bullets tearing new shreds in the remnants of Aryana's dress. She stood a half-dozen yards from them, her latest victim lying in a broken heap at her feet.

She charged at them. Fyodor, the leader of the commandos, dropped like a stone as her fist smashed into his face, but it had only been a glancing blow. Boris had pulled the man back just in time to save his life.

That was precious time lost. Now Aryana had Boris by the throat, holding him in the air, watching him dangle and twitch with a curious tilt to her head.

Then she spoke.

"You murdered my master." Her voice was so smooth it verged on sultry. "Know that when I am done with you, I will murder your wife with my own hands. Then I will go to America and murder your children. I am Death to you, Petrov, and to all who oppose the will of Lord Magnus."

Boris's frantic movements were weakening. He would be dead within seconds.

The time had come.

"Aryana Voss!" Thompson shouted at the top of his lungs.

He placed the whistle between his lips and blew.

Gods, it was loud! It must have some kind of mechanical amplification. The sound filled the entire throne room with a violent, howling screech.

That got her attention, all right. She dropped Boris to the ground, where he lay gasping and clutching his throat. Her head swiveled toward Thompson with a jerky, mechanical movement. Whatever lay behind that veil, it was watching him now.

Farewell, sweet universe. But he wasn't going down quietly.

"Come on, witch!" he shouted. "Scared to take on a biology professor?"

Aryana's head lowered. Then, as if it were an afterthought, she brought her foot down hard on Boris's leg. A slow, nauseating act of cruelty, like watching a pet dog being slowly crushed by an elephant. There was a stomach-rending crunch as her foot ground down into the floor, crumpling the leg beneath it as if it were made of tin.

Boris screamed in agony.

Then Aryana was running at full speed, heading straight for Thompson.

"Here goes nothing."

He raised Little Boris aloft and squeezed for all he was worth. The lights on the toy guns in Little Boris's hands lit up, blinking red.

*"Pew, pew, pew!"* went the guns.

Thompson could have screamed. *That* was Boris's secret weapon? It was all a game, one last joke from the hilarious Boris Petrov.

But then Thompson felt a strange, trembling sensation, as if some mechanical device inside the doll had suddenly activated.

Aryana was right in front of him. He could see the pale contours of a woman's face behind that torn, translucent black veil. He closed his eyes, waiting for her sable gloves to squeeze the life out of him.

In the same moment, Little Boris made a loud humming sound and flew out of his hand as if by magic. He opened his eyes. The doll had shot straight at Aryana Voss, arms outstretched as if it meant to embrace her. It landed right on her face with a distinctly metallic clank.

A moment later, Thompson's feet left the ground as Aryana Voss hurled him across the throne room.

✧

"Are we connected yet?" Lenny shouted. "The guilds are ready for the contest, but I've lost Little Boris's visuals. Things weren't exactly going well in there. If we can't get connected to her fast, it'll be game over."

"Not yet," Nadia said through clenched teeth. *Game over.* The words flowed like ice through her veins. This was no game. If they failed, both of her parents and the man she loved would be dead. Lenny may have guessed the truth about Aryana Voss, but no one could have known just how powerful she was. Using the camera hidden behind Little Boris's remaining eye, they had watched in horror as the bullets failed to harm her…or *it*, rather. They had continued to watch, helplessly, as Aryana brutally crushed the commandos with her bare hands.

Little Boris was supposed to be the last resort if all else failed. So many contingencies would have to fall into place, so many possibilities would have to become realities. Even if everything lined up, success or failure would depend on an army of online gamers using Crowdbreak to shred the Foundation's code.

"Hang on, Dad," she whispered. "We're coming. What are you waiting for, Thompson?"

And then, suddenly, it happened.

The satellite transmitter in Little Boris sprang to life. They could only intercept the encrypted signals coming to Aryana Voss if the doll got extremely close to her. That's why they'd put a high-tech flight mechanism inside Little Boris before sending the doll to Khatizan with her father.

"We're online!" she shouted.

"We are?" Lenny leapt to his feet, upending a can of bright green energy drink and a massive bowl of cheese puffs. "I knew it! I knew Aryana was like Enigma Three in the Alterverse. Frigging Captain Fuzzbucket saves the day again!"

That flight mechanism was classified Department of Defense technology, something the Chemist, Zhang Meiying, had known about only because of her security clearance. But it wouldn't keep Aryana from ripping the doll to shreds, which meant they would only have seconds before Aryana removed and destroyed Little Boris.

Seconds were all Nadia needed. Or, more accurately, all that the three million gamers who had signed up for the online battle of the century needed. The first guild to take down the great monster Diabolos would receive five million dollars in cold, hard cash.

She'd already found the flaw in the Foundation's programming, and she had written code to let Crowdbreak exploit it. One command from her and the Crowdbreak gamers would crush the imaginary monster Diabolos along with the real-world monster Aryana Voss.

"Bring her down, Doomhammer!" Lenny hollered triumphantly.

And that's exactly what Doomhammer did.

◈

The world was spinning, whirling around Thompson. Then he hit the stone floor of the throne room and everything turned hazy. His breath came in desperate gasps as he clambered onto his hands and knees, struggling to get air back into his lungs. A shrill ringing filled his ears, then slowly subsided.

Every inch of his body hurt, but he was alive, and miraculously, nothing seemed to be broken.

Aryana Voss was ten feet away from him, grabbing at Little Boris with both hands. She had tossed Thompson across the throne room as if he were no heavier than the doll. He watched her, waiting for her to rip Little Boris into pieces, hurl it to the ground, and then do the exact same thing to him.

He waited, but it never happened.

Aryana's hands grasped Little Boris, who, in turn, was wrapped around her face, pressing against the black veil as if locked in a desperate embrace. Yet neither of them moved. They were frozen like ice sculptures.

Aryana's arms dropped to her sides. Her head lowered toward the ground in one swift, jerking motion.

Thompson scrambled to his feet.

Was she still alive?

Then, suddenly, Aryana toppled backward to the ground like a collapsing wall, her body perfectly straight, her knees not bending an inch. She landed with a deafening crash that cracked the stone floor. There was a loud hissing sound, and then smoke began rising from Aryana's prone body.

Thompson stared at her in disbelief.

What had just happened? How had Little Boris flown through the air? What had the doll done to Aryana?

Boris's agonized groaning roused him from his reverie. Wavering between terror and wonder, he edged around the room toward Boris, keeping his eyes locked on the motionless form of Aryana Voss.

A glance at Boris's impossibly crushed lower leg turned Thompson's stomach. It looked like something from a realistic war movie, the kind that involved minefields and shrapnel.

"Thompson?" Boris's voice shook with evident pain. "Is she dead?"

"I don't know. She…fell."

"Not Aryana. My wife, my Elena."

Thompson rested his hand on Boris's shoulder. "She's okay. So is Charles. Kenjiro and the others got them out in time."

"And we stopped the monster," Boris said. "Nadia did that, didn't she? Our darling little Doomhammer." A faint smile flickered over his lips but was quickly replaced with a paroxysm of pain. "I can't move my leg. Does it look bad?"

Thompson swallowed.

*You're a medical biologist. You've watched people's chests get pried open for heart surgery. You can deal with this. Moreover, you can do it without vomiting.*

"It's, uh…not good, Boris."

"Can you do anything?"

Do anything? The bleeding, right. It was the lower leg, which meant the blood was coming from the lower femoral artery. Probably the anterior tibial artery as well.

Tourniquet?

It was the only way. The leg below the kneecap was already a lost cause. No reconstructive surgery could piece that back together. But he needed to add some pressure first, anything to slow the bleeding while he improvised.

"This is going to hurt." Thompson pulled off his shirt. "It might also save your life."

"Do it," Boris said through gritted teeth. "I don't care about the pain, just do it."

Thompson wrapped the shirt around the upper part of Boris's leg, just below the groin, and tied it as tightly as he could.

"Iliac artery, inguinal canal," he whispered. It didn't seem impossible if he talked himself through it. "It's just science. The human body is just another form of science. You can do science."

"What did you say?" Boris's voice was growing thick.

"I said you're doing great. Hang on."

Suddenly Darya Alexandrovna was standing beside him.

"What can I do?" she asked in a remarkably calm voice.

"Keep his wife away, for starters."

"Already done," she replied briskly. "We feared the worst, but I had to come back just in case. Now what can I do?"

He motioned toward Firlenko's corpse. "That dead Commander of yours…is that a sword at his belt?"

"Yes." She looked at Firlenko's mangled body with obvious disgust. "Why?"

"I need the sheath. And his jacket."

Darya sprinted to the Commander, cut the sheath free with her tactical knife, and brought it back to Thompson. Another sprint, and the Commander's sable jacket was at Thompson's feet.

"I need you to cut that into strips. As long as you can get them." He suddenly realized he was barking orders like a general. "Please."

She obeyed at once. That knife of hers had the job done in a flash.

"Now call 9-1-1 or whatever you people do to get an ambulance. He's going to need a real tourniquet. And a surgeon."

She nodded. "I'll be back soon. I've heard there's a surgeon in the village."

Fast as an arrow, she was gone.

A surgeon in the village? Hermes's sandals! These people really were living in the Dark Ages, weren't they? Hopefully the good doctor wouldn't bring leeches to drain out Boris's excess humors.

The shirt wrapped around Boris's upper leg had slowed the bleeding, but he'd have to try the makeshift tourniquet farther down. If that surgeon showed up in time, Boris might just make it.

"You hear that, Boris?" Thompson tried to make his voice sound cheerful, but he couldn't keep it from trembling. A man's life was in his hands. "Help is on the way. I've got one more thing to do. The bad news is it's going to hurt even worse."

Boris clutched his arm in a vice grip. "Inside pocket. My jacket."

"What?" Thompson tried, and failed, to pull his arm free.

"Get it, Mr. Thompson!"

"All right, all right! Let go, will you?"

He fished inside Boris's jacket and pulled out a small silver flask. He hurled it away. "Alcohol? That nonsense only works in the movies.

You've got a bleeding problem, which means a blood thinner isn't your friend right now."

"It was water," Boris rumbled darkly.

Water in a liquor flask? "Oh…um, sorry about that. Here, bite down on this."

Thompson pulled his wallet out of his back pocket. Boris clamped his teeth over it and closed his eyes. Thompson wrapped the longest strips from the Commander's jacket around Boris's upper leg, a few inches above the knee.

The sheath to the Commander's saber for the tourniquet's windlass. Double knot that won't slip. Here goes.

He began rotating the sheath to tighten the tourniquet. He could feel Boris's body tensing as the pressure increased. Boris raised his head and shoulders off the floor to watch.

"It's working!" Thompson cried, then realized that he shouldn't have sounded so surprised. Real doctors were always so blasted confident. "That is, of course it's working, which means you're going to be just fine. Maybe. Probably."

Boris nodded and laid his head back on the ground. "I'm glad I put you on our team, Mr. Thompson. You're the real deal, you know that?"

Thompson wiped the sweat from his brow and exhaled. The tourniquet was as tight as he could get it. He tied down the sheath with another strip of cloth from the jacket so it wouldn't unwind. Then he got up to check on Fyodor, the leader of the Russian commandos. The man still had a pulse, and he was breathing. No bleeding or visible signs of broken bones. Hopefully the glancing blow Aryana had given him had just knocked him out without causing actual brain damage.

A few of the other commandos had started groaning. He was amazed that any of them had survived Aryana's brutality.

"Wonder what happened to her?" he murmured, looking at Aryana's prone body. There was still smoke rising from it. "Is she dead?"

"Good question," Boris replied. "Maybe you should check."

"Gods, no," Thompson groaned. "I'll leave that job to the next reckless idiot. How did that Little Boris trick work, by the way? Did it knock her out somehow?"

Boris's rumbling chuckle ended in a hoarse, wheezing rasp. "Blasted ribs," he muttered. "All I know is that it has something to do with Captain Fuzzbucket and the Alterverse. You'll have to ask Lenny when we get home."

Thompson arched an eyebrow, but Boris didn't elaborate.

Thompson went to check the other survivors, but their broken bones and internal bleeding were beyond his meager equipment and expertise.

Before it seemed possible, the doors to the throne room opened. Darya entered first, followed by medical teams with ambulance stretchers.

Not a leech in sight.

He patted Boris's shoulder. "Well, you old rascal, looks like you're going to make it after all."

"I owe you one, Mr. Thompson," Boris replied. "And I'm good at paying my debts."

Elena Petrova darted into the room and ran straight to Boris. She cradled his head to her chest, weeping, her raven hair falling over his face as the medical team prepared to transfer him to the stretcher.

"I'm here, my love," she said, kissing him on the cheek. "I'm coming home. I mean, if you want me to. If you haven't already…"

Boris let out a pained grunt as the medics hoisted him onto the stretcher. He grabbed Elena's hand. "You're the love of my life, Elena." He brought her hand to his lips. "There could never be another."

# Chapter Twenty-Six
# The Girl from Lagos

NADIA LEANED OVER and kissed Charles's forehead. Thanks to his new treatment, his calm, even breaths as he slept were like waves gently breaking against the shore and then receding.

Fifteen minutes ago, he had been ranting like a madman as he stormed around his hospital room, shouting about an island and the end of the world. He had never frightened her before that moment. She had never seen him so angry, so out of control. Right before the hospital staff charged in, Miguel had shown up with a novel medication that he, Raj, and Anna had been working on.

So far, so good.

"It's only a first step." Miguel rested his hand on Charles's shoulder. "It should settle down the parts of his brain that are overactive, but it's not a cure. We don't know exactly what's happened to him yet, but we'll figure it out. We won't give up."

She nodded, blinking away tears that would come no matter how hard she tried to hold them back. They had won, after all. Aryana Voss was defeated and Rius on the run. Better yet, her own mother had been rescued. Mom still had that same peaceful spirit Nadia remembered from her childhood, which was a miracle considering all Elena had suffered. After twelve years apart, they had so much catching up to do, so many things to learn about each other. She almost felt shy around her own mother.

Dad had survived his injury and was in good spirits despite the loss of his lower leg. He hated hospitals, despised physical therapy, and had sworn that very morning to sneak away and get back to work.

But the victories all rang hollow without Charles. He was here, right in front of her, but his mind was trapped in a world of illusions. What had they done to him?

While everyone else was busy with the Khatizan mission, Miguel, Raj, and Anna had been trying to create a therapy for the madness that had now seized Charles. They had uncovered tantalizing hints in the files her father had found in Magnus Headquarters. Now that Charles was back, Miguel was running him through a gauntlet of bloodwork and scans. They'd figured out how to calm him down, but they needed something more. One of the other Paragons, the children the Magnus Foundation had experimented on years ago.

She'd heard her parents talking about one of them, a young woman named Sierra Morgan. Her mother had worked with Sierra in Aryana's fortress, but Sierra had apparently been taken by Rius Ludovic when he fled Khatizan.

That meant their only option was the elusive John Flying Hawk. She and Lenny had sent him a message from Boris using John's own encryption, but so far nothing had come of it.

"I know you won't give up, Miguel," she said gently. "And there's no one else I'd rather trust with his health."

Miguel tried to return her smile, but he looked as afraid as she was. What if there was no cure? What if Charles was like this for the rest of his life?

There was a knock on the door. Her brother, Peter, walked into the room. Peter always tiptoed around hospital beds, his eyes wide with childlike amazement at all the flashing lights and beeping monitors.

He sidled up close to her, peering curiously at Charles.

"Is he okay?"

Peter had asked the same question a dozen times since he had arrived at the hospital. His Down syndrome made it difficult to understand what Charles was going through. Not that any of them really understood. All Peter knew was that Charles was one of his best friends, the kind who was always up for a board game. He knew something was wrong with Charles now, and it scared him.

"He's okay. Right, sis?" His voice trembled a little.

She took a deep breath. "He will be, Peter."

Peter nodded sagely. Then he edged a little closer to her. He had no problem hugging Boris, but with everyone else, including his own sister, Peter was very careful about physical touch. Sometimes he would stand close to her as his way of showing affection. Peter's invisible hugs, she used to call them when they were kids.

But Peter suddenly did something he'd never done before. He wrapped an arm around her and pulled her close. It took a moment for Nadia to realize what had happened.

Peter had just given her a hug. A real one.

Boris Petrov knocked twice on the door to Director Obasanjo's office. The ATA's temporary headquarters in New York City was a modest affair, an empty office building that had undergone a hasty conversion to serve the agency's staff. It was also the last place on earth he wanted to be.

Well, the *next* to last place on earth. Even here was better than that infernal hospital.

"Come in, Mr. Petrov." Director Angela Obasanjo's voice sounded colder than a Himalayan winter. He took a deep breath, turned the handle, and walked into the room.

"Sit down." Her face looked calm, but her eyes flashed murder. She was flanked by two heavily armed ATA officers. Not a good sign.

He crossed the room with a stiff gait. Someday, he'd get used to his new prosthetic leg, but for now he stumped around like a blasted pirate. He took a chair across from her. "It's good to—"

"Shut up, Mr. Petrov." She slapped a folder onto her desk and flipped open the cover. "You disobeyed a direct order from your own director. You went rogue."

She let the ominous word hang in the air for a moment, then continued her assault.

"You upended our entire Khatizan operation, which has been years in the making and involved a dozen intelligence agencies around the world. Instead of walking the line, you made a secret alliance with freedom fighters and led an unsanctioned assault on foreign soil. You got several of those volunteers killed, and you exposed one of our key operatives, which led directly to her murder. And that isn't even the worst of your crimes."

"Now wait a minute!" He held up his hands in protest. "I'll admit my methods were unorthodox, but we defeated Aryana Voss and ended the Foundation's presence in Khatizan. Chairman Markhov and Commander Firlenko are both dead, and Khatizan is beginning a new chapter. As for your operative, I can assure you that we never blew anyone's cover."

She pulled a picture from the folder and slammed it down in front of him. "Recognize her?"

Sweet Saint Mitrophan. The poor girl from Darya's bedroom, the one they'd found pinned to the wall like an insect. Liza, wasn't it?

He sighed. "She was already dead when we entered the fortress. I never met her, Director. How could I have exposed her identity?"

The director's eyes narrowed. "Liza was a double agent, allegedly a spy working for Chairman Markhov to keep tabs on Voss and Rius. Rius was aware of that role and allowed her to stay in order to give Markhov a false sense of security. She's the one who told Markhov that

Voss was out of the country. But even Rius was blind to Liza's true loyalty to us.

"You *did* expose her, even if you didn't realize it. Liza knew the Foundation's trap was in motion, which meant our own attack was imminent, an attack that shouldn't have happened for another week. She broke her normal routine and sent an urgent message along a different channel. That message reached us, but it was also caught by Rius's surveillance network, which meant that it was intercepted by that creature we called Aryana Voss. It was heavily encrypted, but we both know that our best encryption is child's play for the Magnus Foundation.

"Liza's cover was blown, and you know what happened next. She went to Darya Alexandrovna's room to warn her, but her own fate was already sealed. Would you like to hear the last message Liza sent us?"

Boris pressed his palms against his forehead. Why would that poor woman sacrifice herself? Why didn't she just run away when her cover was blown? "Go ahead."

The director withdrew a piece of paper from the folder, cleared her throat, and began to read. "*The theory is correct. AV is a machine directly controlled by R. The nature of their connection remains a mystery, but R is the mastermind. The prisoner is alive, but his mind is damaged from torture. The lost wife has joined him. The girl is the heiress. I'll find a way to bring them to the border and meet you there. You should NOT have launched the mission early. Whatever you do, keep your team away from the fortress. I'll report again soon through the normal channel.*"

The director set the paper back in the folder. When she spoke again, her voice trembled with anger. "If you could have followed my orders for *one single week*, Liza would have reported through her regular channel, and you could have taken her intel with you on a sanctioned mission to Khatizan. You could have coordinated with her, rescued the prisoners, and never had to deal with that killing machine. As for your freedom fighters, did you know that their identities have now been leaked to the Russian government? The Russian ambassador in Washington wants to know why an American agent of the supposedly neutral ATA joined forces with sworn enemies of his government. We are just now backing down from nuclear war with Russia, which means the optics here are terrible. I am going to take a political bullet for you, Petrov. This could end my career."

She leaned back in her chair. "I should send you home with your tail between your legs and your career in flames, but you might deserve worse. There's a traitor in the ATA. Someone near the top."

Boris desperately wanted a cigar. And a bottle of vodka. No, scratch the vodka. At least he could have a piece of that stupid nicotine gum after this bloodletting was over.

"I break the rules sometimes," he rumbled, "but I'm not the traitor, if that's what you're thinking."

"And neither am I," she replied icily. "I bet that surprises you, doesn't it? They offered me this position so I could find the mole, and while you were off playing cowboy, I did my job. Here is your traitor." She snatched another photo from the folder and slammed it in front of him, right on top of the picture of the late Liza Khartoff.

The grinning portrait of his mentor and former director, James MacPherson, hit Boris like a punch to the gut.

"That's impossible!" Even as the words left his mouth, he felt a flicker of doubt. "Jimmy would never…"

She shoved the folder in front of him. "While you were still backing out of his driveway, Jimmy was already on the phone with his handler in Khatizan."

Boris folded his arms over his chest. No, it couldn't be true. The ATA had been like Jimmy's own child, his life's work. He grunted and thumbed through the paperwork, though he already knew what he would find. Phone records, calls to the Central Party, even direct calls to Aryana's fortress. Emails, contacts with Magnus Foundation members living and dead.

Personal meetings with Alexander Magnus himself.

It had to be a lie.

"Jimmy oversaw the attack on Magnus Headquarters." He clung

desperately to his strongest argument. "He was the director! If he's the traitor, why didn't he warn Magnus that we were coming?"

The director leaned forward. "We believe that Rius is the other Paragon, the one the project files didn't identify. Based on files found at the fortress, we know that the real Aryana Voss died during a Control experiment thirteen years ago. With Magnus's support, Rius, who was seventeen years old at the time, replaced Aryana with his masterpiece, an AI machine that he could control directly through a neural implant. Our best guess is that Rius then split his personality, forcing all his rage and pain and hatred into the persona of the new Aryana Voss.

"Jimmy reported directly to Aryana, which meant it was Aryana—the darkest part of Rius's personality—who knew about the attack on Magnus Headquarters last year. Instead of warning Magnus, she encouraged Jimmy to move forward with the attack. Aryana wanted the Foundation for herself."

The director drummed her fingers on her desk. "But you're right, there is also good news. The new Chairman of Khatizan has already shut down the prison factories and is releasing over half a million human trafficking victims." She took the folder from his hands and closed it. "We are going to be very busy for the next year, and it will be the work we love the most, finding new lives for rescued victims. Truth be told, your plan may have worked better than ours in the end. That doesn't change the fact that you went around your own director, that you disobeyed orders, and that good people died as a result. So, here's my verdict."

She stood, and he immediately did the same, his heart pounding in his chest. This was it. This would be the end of his career, his last moment as an ATA agent.

"First," she said, lifting her index finger, "you will take a one-month vacation. Spend some time with Elena. Your wife is an incredible woman, by the way. I think we really hit it off. She did tell you about our little chat, didn't she?"

He felt his mouth hanging open and slammed it shut. "You spoke with Elena?"

"I went to check on you when you first arrived stateside," she said. "You were asleep, so I met with your wife. You'd better treat her right, Mr. Petrov." She held up a second finger. "Number two, you will step down as a team leader and get off the field."

There it was, the dagger he had feared, the one hanging over his head since the day he'd seen his first gray hairs in the mirror. "Director—"

"We're not arguing about this," she cut in, her voice sharper than a switchblade. "When your vacation is over, you will report to our new Home Office in Virginia where you will take over as the agency's Chief of Operations. Khatizan's new Chairman discovered some horrific secrets in the dungeons of Aryana's fortress. Mysterious biological equipment, human research subjects, a walk-in freezer filled with dismembered bodies—it sounded a lot like Level Nine in Magnus Headquarters. We're not sure what it all means yet, but I have the feeling our battle with the Foundation isn't over yet. In your new role, you will personally oversee every field mission the ATA conducts around the globe."

His protests died on his lips.

Sweet Saint Gleb, was the woman *rewarding* him? Sure, he would miss the field, but if he had to be chained to a desk job, this one above all others would keep him in the game. "I don't know what to say, Director. I'm honored."

"Number three," she went on, "you agree never to go behind my back again. I'm trusting you with every mission we conduct. I need you to trust me, too. I realize that will take time."

"Why are you being kind to me?" he asked.

She glared at him for a moment. Then, suddenly, her lips parted into a smile. The warmth of it stunned him, as if a glacier had suddenly transformed into a sun-dappled field of wildflowers. "A good question, Mr. Petrov. The answer involves a young orphan learning the ropes on the streets of Lagos and finding herself in way over her head. It also involves you. Does that help jog your memory?"

Merciful Saint Onouphrios, was it possible? The Lagos rescue operation happened over thirty years ago. A stranger at a café in Lagos, Nigeria had given him a tip about dozens of children locked in a warehouse. Terrorists had seized them off the city streets. He'd been in the middle of a separate CIA mission, but once his team heard the details, they agreed to help him rescue the victims.

Director Obasanjo must have been one of the girls they'd freed.

"I see that you do remember," the director said. "Enjoy your vacation, Mr. Petrov. You're dismissed."

# Chapter Twenty-Seven
# Love is Blind

"Y ES, THANK YOU. Just give us a few moments first." Paul Veliu hung up the telephone and leaned back against the supple leather of the desk chair. He looked around the imposing office that had once belonged to Chairman Markhov.

It was Paul's office now.

Darya Alexandrovna sat across the desk with her dark eyes fixed on him and her chestnut hair spilling over her shoulders. He wished he could hold her close to him, run his fingers through that hair, and tell her that he loved her. It would be a remarkably selfish act. A dark path now lay before him, one she could never share. False hope would only cause her more pain.

"I still think you should go to America," he said. "I can work it out with their embassy. We'll find you a place near Elena. I know you had some time together before she left, but wouldn't you like more? You could meet her children, get to know Boris. You'll be happier in America. There are too many terrible memories in Khatizan."

"Are you tired of me already, Chairman Veliu?" she teased. "We just went on our first official date last weekend, you know. I was hoping I'd last a month, at least."

He rolled his eyes. "Don't be ridiculous, Dasha. And don't call me Chairman, you know I hate it. We shouldn't have gone on that date. The election is in three weeks, and then I can be done…with everything."

Her cheerfulness vanished. She leaned over the desk, her gaze boring into him. "Is that why you want me to leave you? You're really going through with it?"

"I have no choice." He rose and walked to the row of bulletproof glass windows overlooking Chozul's Central Square. Last night, a mob of citizens had pulled down the thirty-foot-tall statue of Chairman Markhov that had towered over the square for decades. Paul had watched from the window as they gleefully smashed the statue to bits with sledgehammers.

Not a bad start, but it would take more than well-deserved vandalism to heal the brokenness in Khatizan.

"I owe it to the Germans," he said. "They need to hear the truth from my lips."

"No, they don't!" Darya slammed her open palm on the desktop, then let out an exasperated sigh. "I'm sorry, Paul. I know I'm being selfish, but you don't need to tell them it was *you*. They already know Khatizan was behind the attack. Isn't that enough?"

He closed his eyes and pictured the secretary in Berlin. The bearded face of Herr Gorstadt, the innocent businessman he had murdered. The drawing Gorstadt's son had made for his father. "I'm sorry, Dasha, but the victims must be given justice."

"And what if the Germans don't let you pay?" she shot back. "You're the Chairman of Khatizan, and the people might make you our first Prime Minister in three weeks whether you want them to or not. You're the only reason we're opening our borders again. You're the one bringing democracy to our nation, Paul. Without you, this could all fall apart."

He went back to his chair and collapsed in it. "I don't have all the answers. I just know it's the right thing to do, and the sooner the better."

Darya crossed to his side of the desk and knelt beside him. She took his hand in hers. "Then I'm not leaving you," she said quietly. "When you go to Germany, I'm going with you. If they lock you up in prison, I'll visit you every day until they release you. I'm not leaving, so you'd better get used to it."

There was a knock on the door. Darya's eyes widened. "Wait, tell me that isn't—"

He gently kissed her forehead. "I'm sorry, Dasha. I didn't know how to tell you. I just needed you to be here." He raised his voice. "Come in."

A short, plump woman with graying hair and a stern expression walked through the door. Paul extended his hand across the desk. "Frau Schneider?" he said in German. "I'm Chairman Paul Veliu. This is my…assistant, Lieutenant Darya Alexandrovna."

"An honor to meet you, Chairman," Frau Schneider replied in flawless Khatiz. She crossed the room with swift steps and gave him a firm handshake, then nodded briefly to Darya. "Lieutenant." There was a distinct frigidness in her manner. "On behalf of my government, I would like to thank you for the unexpected invitation to meet with you in person."

"Thank you for coming to Khatizan, Frau Schneider, despite the circumstances between our countries. Please, take a seat."

She complied, but instead of following her example, Paul began pacing behind his desk. His chest felt like it was being squeezed by a vice. Darya was watching him with eyes that revealed both fear and more than a hint of anger. He should have warned her about the meeting, but what was the point? She would never understand what it felt like to be a terrorist, to have the blood of tens of thousands on your hands.

"There's no easy way to say this," he began, "but I have a confession to make. Your people have the right to know exactly who was behind the Berlin attack."

"We already know that Chairman Markhov ordered the attack," Frau Schneider replied at once.

"No, that's…not what I meant. I mean the actual bomber. In other words"—he looked her in the eye—"I mean *me*. Yes, Frau Schneider, I'm the one they sent on that mission." He pressed the palms of his hands against his eyes and groaned. "I'm the one who went up that elevator, who met with Viktor Gorstadt on the thirty-fifth floor, who talked to the secretary with the rose perfume, who left the suitcase with the bomb under Gorstadt's desk after I murdered him. I did every vile thing Commander Firlenko whispered into my ear. I'm the monster. I can't surrender myself to your government yet, but in three weeks, after our elections are over, I'll board a plane to Berlin. I wanted to warn you so that you could prepare. Perhaps you could arrange for some policemen to arrest me at the airport?"

Frau Schneider shifted in her chair, drummed her fingers against her pants leg for a few moments, then nodded to herself as if coming to a decision. "I'm afraid you're mistaken, Chairman Veliu. Our intelligence community already identified the culprit after receiving an admission of guilt from your government. The bomber was a young woman who was a member of Youth Corps Intelligence. Surveillance cameras clearly showed her entering the building with a suitcase. Several minutes later, she left the building without that suitcase and drove away from the scene in a black sedan."

"It wasn't her!" Paul nearly shouted the words. "She was just my driver. It was me, do you understand? She can't have been on your surveillance cameras. If she was, then the video has been manipulated. I'm the one who—"

Frau Schneider held up her hand. "Forgive me for interrupting you, Chairman. I know that's not a very diplomatic thing to do, but you are indeed mistaken. As I've already said, the cameras prove that this woman you speak of carried out the attack. If the new Chairman of Khatizan had been on those surveillance feeds, don't you think our intelligence agencies would have noticed?" She let the question hang in the air as she tapped her forefinger against her lips.

So Dasha was right. The Germans already knew he was the bomber, and they wouldn't let him turn himself in.

"No doubt you are feeling the weight of your country's collective guilt," she went on, "and now you want to make amends. An honorable sentiment, Chairman. You show great wisdom despite your relative youth."

"I can't forgive myself, Frau Schneider," he said quietly. "Surely you can understand that. I *want* to face justice. I want you to imprison me, execute me! Anything to pay for what I've done. I know there can never be redemption, but at least the families of the victims would see that I paid for the crime."

"Yes, Chairman!" Frau Scheider replied, her voice almost fierce. "The families do want to see payment for the crime. That's exactly it! But what form of payment will be best? Do they want the blood of a young man who has been brainwashed from the age of thirteen, who knew that his own father and mother would be brutally executed if he didn't carry out every order to the letter, who lived in terror of the depraved tortures his government carried out against its own citizens every single day? Would the senseless death of that young man somehow dignify the senseless murder of their own loved ones? Wouldn't they rather see the deaths of their beloved friends and family members become the seeds of a better future? What if the guilt of those behind the attack led to the deliverance of an entire nation from the nightmare of tyranny and oppression? I can assure you, Chairman, this is the greatest gift Khatizan can give to Germany, because it is the best assurance that a Khatiz terrorist will never again strike on German soil. Continue the path you have begun. Become our friend and our ally. Open your doors to diplomacy, to democracy, to freedom. We cannot raise the dead. We cannot bring them back to their families, but we can bring light to the darkness. Let that be your justice. Let it be your path to redemption."

✍

Boris Petrov stepped out of the elevator on the fifth floor of the Golden Meadows apartment building in Brooklyn. The time had come to repay his debt to Mr. Thompson.

"I can't believe you're friends with Vindolwynd!" Thompson cried. "I know that's just his screen name, but who is he? What's he like?"

Boris grunted. Strange, this modern world. Vindolwynd was the name Lenny Phillips used when he played the Crowdbreak video game. Even though Thompson had spent time with Lenny at the safe house, the mysterious Vindolwynd was a perfect stranger to him.

"Wait, don't tell me," Thompson went on. "He's a total loser, isn't he? You know, the kind of guy who's never been on a date. I bet this is his parent's apartment, right? What is he, forty-five? Fifty-five?"

Boris shrugged. "You'll have to see for yourself."

They walked down the hallway, following the odd numbers until they came to five twenty-three, an ATA safe house that now belonged to Lenny permanently. The CIA and ATA had come to an agreement about Lenny, a partnership that kept both agencies happy and, more importantly, kept Lenny safe. Boris rapped the door twice with the back of his hand.

"He's probably levelling up," Thompson snickered. "He's almost eight levels behind me now. I couldn't believe it when I logged on last night. I mean, we were in Khatizan for a week, so I thought I'd be the one catching up. Poor sucker. Some of us are born for greatness, others are made for participation trophies."

The door opened and they found themselves face-to-face with a black-haired, olive-skinned Mediterranean goddess. Boris had seen Lenny's mysterious bookstore girl from a distance a few days ago. Lenny

337

wasn't kidding about her looks. If beauty were baclava, her piece would be twelve layers deep and oozing with honey.

Not, of course, that Boris was interested in the baclava. Elena Petrova was the only woman he would ever need or want. That's just the way his universe worked.

The goddess wore form-fitting blue jeans and a flowery, foreign-looking blouse that hinted at much while revealing little. "Can I help you?" Her words were deeply flavored with a Mediterranean accent.

Thompson was clearly too stunned to speak. Boris let him squirm.

"You are looking for someone?" she prodded, half-closing the door.

Thompson coughed. His face had turned beet red, a minor improvement over its usual sallow tint. "Sorry," he said, or rather squeaked. "We must have the wrong…no, scratch that. You're *exactly* who I'm looking for. In fact, I've been looking for you my entire life. So if you don't mind, I'll come in, shut the door on my friend here, and you and I will drink gallons of wine and delight in each other for as long as we both shall live."

The woman arched an eyebrow, which somehow made her look even more beautiful. A quizzical goddess. "You are looking for Lenny, yes?"

Thompson's features turned rigid. He mouthed the word *Lenny* and stared at Boris.

"We are," Boris said. "Unfortunately, my friend here suffers from a rare social disorder that only flares up when he's around women. Particularly women like…yourself. His name is Eugene Thompson. He met Lenny a few weeks ago. What he didn't know was that he and Lenny had already forged a bond playing a video game made for children…and people like Mr. Thompson."

Her eyes lit up. "You are Lenny's friend? Wait, you are the one, aren't you? You are Alathar."

"I am." Thompson squared his shoulders. "Vindolwynd and I have fought many duels on the fields of Fellhammer. I win those duels, mind you. Every one of them."

She grinned and clasped her hands together. "Yes, Lenny has told me about you. You poor man! All alone in the world, like a little puppy with no home. He's so kind to let you win all the time, but that's my Lenny. Come in, come in. He will be so happy!"

Thompson's eyes bulged in a distinctly froglike manner. "How exactly do you know Lenny? Are you related to him? His stepsister, maybe?"

"Related?" The woman rested her hand on her chest, where a diamond ring hung beside a golden cross on a thin chain necklace. "Soon we'll be related, yes. Lenny is my fiancé."

Boris barked a laugh. "The man doesn't waste time, does he? And I must say, your English has improved drastically in the past few weeks. When Lenny met you at the bookstore, he said you only knew a single phrase."

She burst out laughing, and her accent all but vanished. "I always do that around American men until I have a chance to learn more about them. Usually, I don't like what I find, but Lenny proved a delightful exception. I'm actually working on my master's degree in psychology at New York University. Won't you come in?"

⤙

"That's it." Thompson took a long guzzle of ale and brought his mug to the table with a resounding clink. "That's the final proof, the last straw, the *fait accompli*. There is no God, Boris. God would never make a universe in which a useless half-dwarf mage like Vindolwynd—I mean Lenny Phillips—ends up with a woman like that."

Boris shrugged. "Interesting theory, but Lenny's not really a half-dwarf, you know. He's a man of many talents. He's honest, he's kind, he helps save the world on a daily basis. Women like that."

"But you *saw* her, didn't you?" Thompson cried. "Do you have any idea how it feels for someone like me, a man who—unlike everyone else, apparently—has never been on a single date with a beautiful woman? It's a cosmic injustice. I'm no James Bond, but gods, I'm not half as hideous as Lenny. If there was a God, don't you think he could make one woman out there who wants to be with me? You do realize there are four billion of them, don't you? I'm only asking for one."

Boris sipped his iced tea. Drinking tea in a sports bar. Nadia and Elena would be proud of him. Gavriel would have been proud, too, for that matter. "Mr. Thompson?"

"Yeah?" Thompson muttered.

"You might work on your pickup lines. And when I say work on them, I mean get rid of them altogether. None of that *gallons of wine* nonsense. Just be yourself."

"Thanks for the advice, but trust me, being myself is the last thing I should do around women."

Boris leaned close. "Do you know how the goddess and Lenny came together? Captain Fuzzbucket. That woman is obsessed with comic books, just like Lenny. Honesty worked for him, and I think it will work for you." He turned and spotted Zhang Meiying, the Chemist, heading their way. She looked absolutely stunning in red. Dressed to kill, and given the desperate state of her target, the odds of success were astronomical. "In fact, honesty may work for you in the next few minutes."

Thompson raised an eyebrow. "What are you talking about?"

"Sorry I'm late! Mind if I sit here?" Without waiting for a reply, Mei took the empty stool between Boris and Thompson. "Have you ordered yet?"

Thompson cast a half-frantic glance at him. Sink or swim, the professor would have to figure this one out on his own.

"We haven't ordered," Boris replied, "but I was just on my way out. Date with Elena." He climbed out of the bar stool and nearly faceplanted in the process. Blasted prosthetic leg. "You two should catch up. Mei was worried sick about you while we were in Khatizan, Mr. Thompson. I had three voicemails from her when I got home, and in each one she asked about you, in particular. I wonder why?"

Mei's eyes shot daggers at him, of course. They were speaking, at least, but could she ever forget what he'd done to her in that hallway? Unlikely, but maybe this would help. She wasn't the sort to start the conversation with a guy she liked, and if she waited on Thompson to make the first move, she would die a confirmed spinster.

By the time he reached the door of the sports bar, the sound of Mei's laughter drifted across the room like the gentle rustling of cherry blossoms. Boris hung his head and sighed. A devil in every bottle. How could he have ever raised his hand to strike such a wonderful creature?

Lord have mercy. Christ have mercy.

A strange world, indeed. Thompson hitting it off with Mei was just as miraculous as Lenny and his Mediterranean goddess.

Come to think of it, Mr. Thompson was a lot like Mr. Charles. Minus the faith, of course, but Father Anatoly wasn't one to give up easily.

Mr. Charles.

As Boris reached into the pocket of his bomber jacket, his fingers brushed against the jewelry box they'd found in the pocket of Charles's jacket in Aryana's fortress. Within was an engagement ring, a ring that would rest on Nadia's finger if Mr. Charles ever woke from his illusions.

Not if. When.

Now for that vacation with the woman his soul worshipped, the woman he had longed for these past twelve years like a parched wanderer in the desert. Speaking of miracles, what had Elena ever seen in him?

"*Amor caecus est,*" he murmured as he pushed open the door of the sports bar.

Love is blind.

He climbed into his SUV, started the engine, and was about to shift into reverse when he suddenly noticed someone in the back seat. A man in a plain gray sweatshirt, blue jeans, and a baseball cap pulled low enough to conceal his eyes, though Boris could make out a light brown face with prominent cheekbones and a narrow, aquiline nose.

"Sweet Saint Zosimus!" he yelled as he yanked his handgun free from its holster.

"Put that away," the man said, his tone breathy and almost melodic. "I don't want to hurt you."

A very odd statement considering that Boris was the one holding the gun.

"How did you get in my car?" As the words escaped his lips, Boris noticed a flicker of movement out of the corner of his eye. Something was crawling across the dashboard of his SUV. He glanced over and saw six roaches in a perfect line, watching him. Before he could react, skittering and clinking sounds erupted all around the interior of the vehicle. Roaches were suddenly everywhere, crawling across the seats, along the windows, upside down on the roof.

Mechanical roaches.

"I got your message," John Flying Hawk said. "I will do something for you, and then you must do something for me."

# Epilogue

RIUS LUDOVIC STEPPED off the jet and set foot on the Island's sandy, shell-strewn beach for the first time in his life. How often had he dreamed of this place? How many hours had he spent overseeing the plans, perfecting every detail? Now, he beheld it with his waking eyes.

He had done it. No one had believed he could, least of all Lord Magnus. But here it was.

The Island that would soon become the cradle of a new civilization.

A Foundation security officer rushed forward to greet him. "Welcome, Lord Rius."

Rius gave a slight nod, the sort he'd often seen Lord Magnus offer to underlings in the Foundation. He needed to remember his new position and abandon those cringing mannerisms he had adopted in Khatizan. He now stood at the forefront of the Foundation. An uncomfortable position. Too vulnerable, but thankfully, it wouldn't be for long. "How is he?"

"Well, he's…" The officer cleared his throat. "You might call it confused, sir. He's resting now."

"His mind will clear with time. There are two others on the jet, Mark Ferguson and Sierra Morgan. They are to be kept under close watch."

"Yes, sir. They'll be staying in the Labyrinth?"

"For the moment. We'll dispose of them soon enough. What's the report on the new power generator?"

The officer grinned. "Just finished the construction this morning, sir. It'll be online by the end of the week. Engineers said those plans were perfect."

Of course they were. Together, Elena Petrova and Sierra Morgan could accomplish miracles when it came to physics. And whatever details they had lacked, Charles Ferguson's mind had already provided. A pity Aryana hadn't survived so she could bring Charles here, but no matter. If Charles ever recovered his sanity, he would have to find his own place in the New World.

*"A pity?"*

The soft, seductive voice spoke within his mind as clearly as if Aryana herself stood next to him.

No. Not again!

*"Worm!"* she hissed. *"Maggot! Why did you run away from me? If you had been there, I would have survived."*

He groaned and clutched his head between his hands. He had known she would return, but he'd hoped it would take longer than this. He needed more time. With a feverish effort of will, he forced the voice down, shoving it back into his subconscious.

That little trick wouldn't work for long, a fact he knew from bitter experience.

"Are you all right, Lord Rius?" the guard asked uneasily.

"Take me to the Labyrinth," he snapped.

"Yes, sir. By the way, I'm very sorry to hear about Lady Voss. She'll be missed."

"Thank you, officer," Rius replied through clenched teeth.

As he followed the security guard to the main compound, he flexed his hands spasmodically, tightening them into fists and then releasing them. He could feel Aryana inside him, feel her pulsing, roaring hatred. She was pure evil. Vile, filthy, murderous. He had to find a way to get her out of his mind again.

While he still had a mind left.

The tunnel into the Labyrinth felt like the throat of some gargantuan, mechanical beast. At the end of the passage, a pair of steel-reinforced double doors slid open as Rius and the guard approached. Alexander Magnus would have approved of the furnishings inside the building. Lush, ornate, and regal, the Labyrinth's interior was fit for a king. Just as it should be, for a king among men now dwelled there.

"Where are the Harvesters?" he asked.

"Some are below, sir, on the laboratory floor. Millions more stored on the eastern side of the Island. Still need to be programmed and all that. The newer models just came in this week, and some are no bigger than ants. Heard our boys in Khatizan had those prison factory slaves working twenty-hour shifts to get them here on time. Would you like to see them now, sir?"

Millions of Harvesters.

Aryana laughed softly.

*"Blood,"* she whispered.

Rius was nearly overwhelmed by her obscene lust for violence.

Those Harvesters meant the end of the world's militaries with their tanks and jets, their squadrons and platoons. The end of every vestige of resistance.

The death of every foe.

Aryana giggled. *"Oceans of blood!"*

Rius could already feel himself changing, shifting, as her words reverberated through his psyche.

The Foundation wouldn't be stopped, not this time.

*"You see, Worm? You and I can work together."*

"I'll look at them later, officer." He shivered and wiped sweat from his brow.

He couldn't let Aryana win again. He had to find a way to force her out. "I want to see *him* first."

"Very well, sir. Right this way."

*"Who is he?"* Aryana asked, her tone suddenly urgent. *"What are you hiding, Worm?"*

Good. At least it was still a secret, even to her.

He followed the officer through the myriad hallways of the Labyrinth. With its honeycombed design, it resembled the name the guards had given it.

They came to a pair of crimson doors engraved with the golden lion rampant, Lord Magnus's sigil.

It had all happened here, in silence, while the world was distracted by terrorist attacks and drone bombings. The seed had sprung to life. The chrysalis of the future, the hope of humanity.

*He* was here.

"Open the door."

The guard cleared his throat. "Sorry, sir. Can't."

Rius bit back a curse. "What do you mean, *can't*? Don't you know who I am?"

*"Murder him,"* Aryana cooed. *"Rip his heart from his chest with your bare hands. It will make the rest of them fear you. Make them worship you."*

"Forgive me, Lord Rius," the guard stammered. "It's that AI system, sir. You told it to protect him. We see him on the monitors, we leave food at his door, but we aren't allowed in. The AI is taking care of him now, what with those robots and all. But if *you* were to ask, I'm sure it would be different."

Rius squared his shoulders. Perhaps he had given the Foundation's AI system too much freedom. An absurd thought. It was purely a matter of calculation. The AI could only do what Rius himself had programmed it to do.

"Computer!" He made his voice as deep and commanding as he could manage.

The Computer remained silent. Aryana broke into mocking laughter.

The guard cleared his throat. "I forgot, sir. It's…well, it's calling itself Lilith now, sir. Started this morning while you were on your way here."

Rius pressed his lips together firmly. Maybe Lord Magnus had been right. Maybe no machine could be trusted. But he'd seen that name before, hadn't he? Yes, in one of the reports gathered from Charles Ferguson's brain. Of course. Since Charles was now directly connected to the AI, the name was to be expected.

Every move, every detail in place.

"Lilith, is it?" he muttered. "Very well, I'll play along. Lilith!"

"Yes, Lord Rius?" came the crisp reply.

"Open this door. Let me see him."

"Confirmed."

The door slid open, revealing an opulent bedroom illuminated by a ring of broad, rectangular skylights forty feet overhead. Rius rushed into the room. A figure slept peacefully on an oaken four-poster bed with kings and queens carved into its boards and pedestals. Monarchs whose visages once shook the earth had slept upon that same bed.

The world's future king slept upon it now.

A grim smile curved Rius's lips as Aryana howled and shrieked in disbelief. She had once loved Lord Magnus, which meant she had hated him all the more when her love was not returned. She had betrayed him at Headquarters, and now she feared what the worm Rius had accomplished without her knowledge.

No mistaking the face of the sleeper. Younger, in the prime of health, but it was *him*. The master's blood in the gift of the vial, the plans to rebuild the Foundation's AI, the digital map of Lord Magnus's brain and detailed recordings of his memories and experiences in the storage device—Aryana had never imagined what the master had left for her in that little box.

The Twilight of the Gods had begun. Lord Magnus had returned.

# Acknowledgements

*"We do not write in order to be understood;*
*we write in order to understand."*

- *C.S. Lewis*

W HEN I BEGAN writing *The Reaping*, I had no intention of committing myself to an entire trilogy. But as the final chapters came into view, I'd grown too attached to the characters to let them off the hook so easily. There was much more to their stories and to the Foundation they struggled against.

*The Endgame* felt ominous from its original opening scene, where Elena Petrova peers into the gloomy courtyard of Prison Factory Six. At the back of the narrative loomed a mysterious figure draped in black, pulling all the strings from the shadows. Like the reader, I myself didn't know exactly who or what she was until the very end.

Writing *The Endgame* proved much more difficult than *The Reaping*. I ended up rewriting it twice, changing the title, and making some severe content cuts to keep the pace moving. Without the unfailing support of my wife, family, and the many friends who support my writing venture, it certainly would have never been published. The imperfections are all mine, while a number of its best ideas arose from the honest critiques and commentary of close friends and beta readers.

With that in mind, I'd like to particularly thank my wife, Carol, who is always eager to read through the latest versions and who always manages to see so many details to which I am curiously blind.

I'd also like to thank Cati Goyer, Dan Long, Trisha Wells, and Chris Long, all of whom provided excellent critiques and feedback of different versions of the story.

Once more I'd like to thank Jim Hart, who believed in this trilogy and provided lasting encouragement in my journey as an author.

Finally, my greatest thanks to you, reader, for going on another adventure with me.

*Soli Deo gloria.*

# About the Author

Matt began writing stories when he was seven and loves reading classics both old and new. He and his wife lived in Southeast Asia for two years, where they worked with a minority language group on a dictionary project and helped develop a multilingual education program. They now live in Texas with their three children, mother-in-law, and an indomitable cat who deigned to move into their garage. Matt's debut novel, *The Reaping*, won the ACFW (American Christian Fiction Writers) Genesis Contest.

Visit Matt online at mattaynes.com

Facebook: *https://www.facebook.com/mattaynesauthor*